LUTHIEL'S SONG
the WAR *of* MISTS

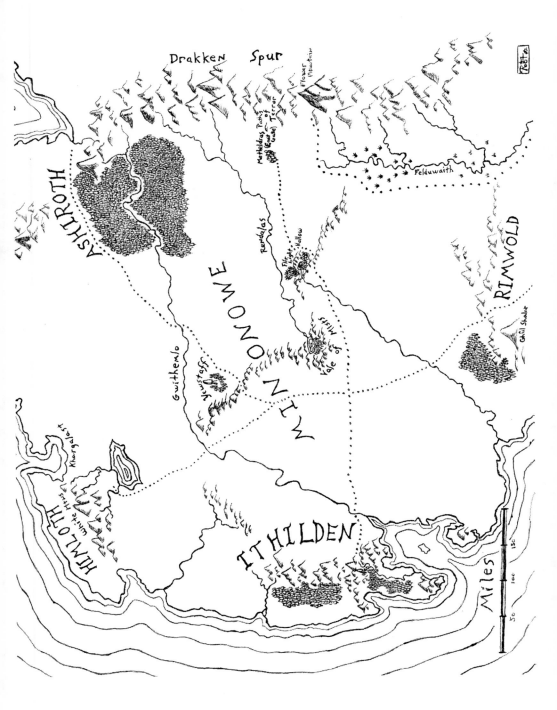

LUTHIEL'S Song

the WAR of MISTS

ROBERT MARSTON FANNÉY

DARK FOREST
PRESS

Edited by Matthew Friedman

www.luthielssong.com

Cover design by Matthew Friedman
Cover art by Marek Okon

Library of Congress Catalogue in Publication Data
Fannéy, Robert
War of Mists/ Robert Fannéy
p. cm. (Luthiel's Song ; bk. 2)

SUMMARY: At the end of Luthiel's journey to save her beloved foster sister, Luthiel
finds herself promised to defend the dread Vyrl of the Vale of Mists against an army of
her kindred sent to destroy them.

ISBN: 978-097642261-7

To my wife, Catherine,
who loves all creatures,
great and small...

Contents

Book V: Queen of the Faelands

Appendices

FOREWORD

When I began writing *Luthiel's Song*, thirteen years ago, I never imagined it would be anything more than another silly tale I made up, harmlessly occupying the pages of one of my many discarded journals. I never imagined it would become a passion that would involve so much of my life and life's work. But, from an innocent seed, it grew first into an exploration of my imagination, next into a challenge of craft, and finally into an honest search for meaning, morality, and the nature of the ancient conflict between darkness and enlightenment, between the freedom of hearts and minds and the forces of domination.

That this conflict would surround the life of a woman, yes a faerie creature too, but at her heart of hearts, a woman, was never a question to me. It was an idea that had grown in my mind, in my teen years, when my father first stood firm against the unjust rules of his father — who called my mother a witch. A witch for nothing more than being an independent and a spiritual lady. A witch for nothing more than raising my sister and I under the ideals of equality and not the old system of patriarchy. It was not in my grandfather's nature to be capable of seeing the true good in my mother. Her works of charity and her honest calling to follow the brighter side of her Episcopal faith, first by serving as an educator at our church, and then as a Social Worker and counselor who has steadily guided hundreds of hearts out of the darkness of their personal struggles. For him it simply hinged on a so-called god-given right to dictate and to be obeyed without question.

The family matter is a personal one and, for years, I have wrestled with the impulse to keep it quiet. This is, after all, a matter of my own life. And so, over the years, I have nurtured this darkness. Unwittingly letting it be by not publicly speaking truth about it.

Perhaps it is a strange coincidence that as I wrestled, the forces of domination and dominion were growing again in the world. Beaten back after a period of unprecedented enlightenment and growth during the 40s, 50s, and 60s, the old, misled, religious guard sought again to blackmail the spirit of humankind with the ancient threat of eternal damnation. The focus of spiritual doctrine shifted from love, forgiveness, acceptance of difference, to judgment, intolerance, and prosecution. This so-called Reconstruction built an awful army of enforcers, fearmongers, and political manipulators. And a clear drive of this new, dark spirituality was to roll back many of the rights women had fought centuries to achieve.

It took me years to finally come to grips with the terrible reality that the darkness that existed in my father's father was firmly entrenched in the dogma, myths, and practices of my religious faith. And though it was not without a clear opposition, even within the faith itself, the visible rise of this force not only in religious power, but in political influence became a clear call to act. To shine a light on the ancient evil and attempt to banish it.

Perhaps it was the incessant push of the religious right to roll back women's rights. To deny ERA. To deny choice. To deny equal pay for equal work. Perhaps it was a Presidency far too cozy with the forces of intolerance and ever so willing to lie to achieve power. Perhaps it was a Vice Presidential nominee who claimed the prayers of her witch hunting pastor were the reason for her having attained such great political recognition. Perhaps it was a priest crying out against 'rebellious women' being widely publicized in local media. The poor ladies' one rebellion? The cardinal sin of being gainfully employed.

"Enough!" shouted a voice of reason. And some heard the voice and added theirs to its call.

I will no longer sit quietly holding back both the truth of my experience, nor the reasons for my convictions. I will no longer suffer the belief of Dominionists, extremists, and those who would invoke the ancient curse of witchcraft — in word or in deed — to spiritually denigrate women everywhere. Nor will I continue to keep private the purpose of writing these fantasies.

That purpose is to through mythic tales reveal that, like my father, I will stand up in defense of women's rights to self determine, to hold power, and to stand beside men and not beneath them. To reveal in metaphor the strength of women's values and character — as I have experienced it through the strong ladies in my life. And to attempt to give hope to all ladies who have wilted against the seemingly impossible odds that history, society, dogma and laws have leveled against them.

Like *Weiryendel* there is a sword for each of your hands. Like *Weiryendel* it is both stronger and more just than the awful weapons used against you. And like *Weiryendel* it is only waiting for your compassion, your love of others, and your value of self to forge it.

In this world, as in the world of *Luthiel's Song*, there is, indeed, magic in dreams. And if you love women, not for their submission but for their unique strengths, then you will stand with me in holding up this dream like a light to the world — there is nothing wrong with a spiritual lady, and the power of a good 'witch' is never to be feared. Perhaps, if we are fortunate, we can make this world a kinder place for ourselves, our mothers, our wives, and our sisters. Until that time, we are all faced with a *War of Mists* in our lives, our religions, and our politics.

The *War of Mists*? I bet you never thought you'd get to it, especially if you were one of those kind souls who have waited three and a half years for its publication. But before I begin, I will need to beg a few more moments to thank so many of you who helped me so much along the way. If the first book was a struggle to produce, then the second was a war hard fought on many battlefields. Often, it was uncertain if the *War of Mists*, in some form or another, would ever reach you. But it finally has, in large part, due to the efforts of others.

Special thanks are, therefore, due to Anne Cummings, Maria Jacobson, Anne Richards, Charlie Fontz, Julie Richardson, Debbie Harris, Joanne Pruett, Suzzanne Miller, Sue Covert and all the other Media Specialists who were so kind to invite me to present at their schools. Of them, Page Weideman is due a special mention for being the first to invite me to visit a school, for showing me the ropes, for being an amazing aunt, and for providing a springboard, without which Luthiel would be little more than a pile of faded pages. It was an honor and a gift to have had the opportunity to inspire your students! I would also like to thank Brandon Mull, author of the fantasy series *Fablehaven*, for his friendship, his kindness, his generosity and his excellent stories. Special thanks are also due to Matthew Friedman. Without Matthew this novel simply would not exist. The same can be said for my wife, Catherine, who has fought at Luthiel's side through every battle, tough spot, or moment of doubt. Seena Grzeskowiak is due both kudos and gratitude for kindly reviewing the book pre-publication and for sending a hundred warm letters of encouragement on MySpace. Also, author Dani Lliteras' wise words and guidance have proven invaluable. Thank you Dani! You are correct, every book is, indeed, a miracle. Thank goodness this one came through. Thanks to agent Simon Lipscar for teaching me, once again, that a strong adversary is often the best teacher. Thanks to Christopher Paolini, author of *The Inheritance Series* for passionately seeking truth in his writing and for sending such a kind letter of encouragement at a very dark hour. Special thanks to author Tee Morris for being so darn cool. And thanks to Robert Friedman for the wisdom, kind words, a writer's haven and for slotting me on CSPAN's book TV. You are good friend, a kind heart, a great spirit and a brilliant intellect. It is an honor you know me as 'one of the guys.' To Kevin McFadden for making the Virginia Festival of the Book the grand, diverse, and exciting venue that it is. In my opinion, all the VAbook authors — past, present, and future — owe a share of gratitude to you for the fantastic house of literacy and community you've so graciously built for them. To Monte Joynes author of *Naked into the Night* — you're awesome and I think that says it all. To my friends on MySpace, many who have been with me now for four years — Gwen, Lucia, Shane Moore (author of the *A Prisoner's Welcome*), Lee Stephen (author of *Dawn of Destiny*) and so many others — thank you! It is unlikely anyone would have heard rumor of Luthiel without you.

Last of all I want to thank you. Yes *you*. It is the most essential thing for an author to have people read his or her stories. Without a reader's imagination, a book would be as dead as the pages it is printed upon. Though I have written this book, your vision is what gives it life. So thank you again!

Without any further delay, I will return you to the world of *Luthiel's Song*. I hope you're prepared. It's quite an adventure coming up and I can't wait to hear your thoughts on the events that are to follow — *if* you and Luthiel make it through. When it's done, please send me a message at www.luthielssong.com, telling me you safely completed the journey. Until then, *May your feet ever walk in the light of two suns. May the moonshadow never fall on you.*

PROLOGUE:
A MEETING IN THE DARK

On a bald hill, ringed by trees, strange and macabre creatures gathered. First came spiders, drifting through the wood like ghosts, black bodies whispering through branches. Clusters of green eyes shone from tapered heads. Horns rose up in place of ears. Away and behind them lay a trail of venom drops and dead grass. They stopped just before the woodline and flexed their legs, pulling shadows overhead like a blanket. Not a sound passed between them as they waited for no one knew what—the owl certainly didn't.

Strange happenings in these parts, he thought. He knew well enough the spiders were dangerous and best left alone. But he stayed, for he was oddly curious and felt confident no one would notice him at his perch high in a nearby tree.

Next came a dragon, slithering upon its belly. Smoke covered it, but the owl's keen eyes spied the oily snake-form. It rose and whirled, taking long switchbacks, jigging and jagging up the hill until, at last, it came to a halt across from the spiders. Dragon eyes shone through the murk. Wary, the owl slipped deeper into the leaves.

There was a long pause in which both dragon and spiders sat still. Moons and clouds slid by and drowsiness fell over the owl. He was about to drift off when a cold voice sang out. Startled, the owl fluttered awake. The howl rose like a winter wind, beginning as a low moan and then building as it was joined by first one and then another. Soon, a chorus of six voices filled the night. Then came six white wolves, each bearing a dark rider. There was something wrong. As the owl watched, he slowly noticed that the wolves didn't breathe and neither did their riders.

Terrified, the owl forced his wings to keep still.

Overlapping plates of gray armor covered them head to foot. Only faces were exposed—wan and sickly, like those of drowned men bobbing in a slate sea. In their hands they held dim swords.

Can't move now, the owl thought after a moment of panic, *that dragon will notice*.

When they came to the hilltop, they stopped. There they stood, still as statues.

The spiders watched them, but made no move; the dragon watched them, but it sat silent in its smog. Moments passed, a breeze rustled the trees, a flutterfler, its slumber disturbed, unfurled its hind wings and let the wind carry it off into the night. Then, for a while, all was still.

Finally, a lonely figure approached. Robed in black, it seemed to glide more than walk as it climbed the hill. Wolves lowered bodies to ground and six riders sheathed swords. The dragon nodded and spiders swayed nervously on creaking legs.

"Are we alone?" the figure asked. His voice was both fair and commanding. The owl recognized it immediately. And though he had never seen them, he knew the six riders from stories.

"There are none here but those we called," the first rider replied.

None but one, the owl thought slyly.

"Then let us begin," the dark figure said.

Slowly, the spiders slipped out of hiding. They were cautious, moving until only their heads and forelimbs were visible. The dragon moved only its head. It rose until it was level with the figure on the hill.

The figure turned, taking them all in. Then he approached one of the riders.

"Tell them what you told me," he ordered.

"Yes, Lord," the rider replied and turned to the monsters. "The Vyrl want peace."

The spiders snapped their forelimbs in astonishment and the dragon snorted smoke.

"Worse," the rider continued, "There's a woman with them. She seems to have an influence over Vyrl. A sorceress, I'd say, and dangerous. We lost Vaelros to her."

The figure motioned with his gloved hand. "Sorceress?" he asked.

The rider looked at him with thin eyes. "If I misspoke, Lord —"

"You did not, " the figure replied. "But humor me and say *witch* instead."

"By your will," the rider said. His lips drew thin lines around the words as they slipped, hollow, from his mouth. "A witch, then."

"Do you know who this witch is?" the dragon hissed. A plume rose from her mouth and her voice sounded like water on hot coals.

"She wouldn't give her name," the rider replied. "Instead she left a riddle."

The spiders scraped their forelimbs together and a clicking, screechy sound rose in the night.

"A riddle?" they asked. "Tell us."

"She said she's a web foiler and a Vyrl saver, the singer in dreams and secret daughter of the Moon Queen, among other things I cannot remember."

"Perhaps you remember enough," the figure in black replied. "There's only one Moon Queen. We know her well."

"Merrin," the dragon hissed.

"Yes," the figure answered. "And there *was* a dream singer."

"The one who was so loud?" the rider asked.

The dark figure nodded.

"Her tracks led toward the Vale," the rider whispered.

For a while, there was silence among the macabre ensemble. The owl rustled his feathers.

Daughter of Merrin? he thought. It slowly dawned on him what it meant and how much it would change things. *What news! What wondrous news! I must get away! I must tell them!* Then, he almost leapt off the branch, almost made a desperate rush to escape the hillside. Just at that moment the dragon lunged as its great jaws clamped shut. There was a puff of feathers and a shrill bird call suddenly cut off. A dimril, nighthawk of the mounds, had flown too close. The owl trembled and decided to stay put.

"There was one who passed through our webs," a spider screeched. The sound, though hushed, was shrill and carried far into the woods.

The figure in black raised a hand.

"Quiet!" he snapped. He turned his head slowly as if listening. "Have a care."

The spider bobbed and then continued, this time quieter. "She seemed only a girl," it said. "But she slipped past our best watchers and entered the Vale."

"Merrin had only one daughter," the rider said. "She's dead."

The dark figure was silent for a moment.

"What if she's not?" he said. "Merrin is shrewd. There are still things she's kept from us."

"I saw to the child myself," a second rider said. "There is no heir to Vlad Valkire left living."

Again the dark figure was silent.

"Then how have the Vyrl returned to sanity?" he said at last. "How was Vaelros turned? *Secret daughter of the moon queen.* The answer to her riddle is plain."

He turned to the second rider.

"You failed."

The rider stumbled back as though struck and, for a moment, the owl could see his face. A dark mist rose from a black and blood-red box at his breast. It encircled his body then covered his head like a hood. Its ends seemed ragged and in those ends, the owl saw tiny hands digging into his skin. His face was white—like a dead man but his eyes seemed very alive. In them, the owl could see terror. The claws drew blood and his mouth opened in a silent scream. He fell to his knees. The claws released. The mist dispersed and he let out a death-rattle cough.

He sat so still the owl thought he was petrified. A breeze waved through the grass. Finally, the rider stood. At first he faltered. Slowly his features seemed to change. He grew paler. More terrible. His face—a little more like the dead.

"*He has paid,*" a harsh, almost feminine voice, said. It seemed to come from somewhere behind the rider. The owl looked around, startled, but couldn't see the speaker.

"A hundred times over," the figure said dispassionately. "But it doesn't fix our problem."

"She restored the Vyrl," the dragon mused.

"Yes," the figure replied.

"What must we do?" the spiders clicked.

"Tonight, strike the elves. Draw the noose tight. No one escapes the Vale."

"And what do I do?" the dragon hissed.

"Watch the Red Gate," the figure whispered.

"If she comes?"

"Do what you want, eat her if you like. I don't care, so long as she dies or is turned back."

The dragon lifted its head and laughed. It was low and barely audible but the branch beneath the owl's feet trembled.

"Could she escape?" the first rider asked.

"It is a possibility," the dark figure replied.

"What then?"

"She's a *witch*, remember? Her own people will see to it."

The spiders clicked their forelimbs in laughter.

The figure turned his head and, for a moment, the owl could see his face. It was both beautiful and sad. "Go now."

Spiders faded into their shadows and dragon slid down the hill. Wolf and rider filed away and the dark figure glided into the night.

When all was quiet, the owl spread his wings and, silent as a feather riding smoke, set out to find the others, to spread word about his new mistress. With each wing flap he could feel his strength returning, his fear falling away. Pride swelled in his feathered breast that she had chosen him to bring the news. As he flew, a dark cloud of mist rose from the land. At first, it only blurred his vision. It gradually grew thicker until he had difficulty finding his way. Disoriented, he settled closer to ground.

There was sudden motion, a snap, and then pain. Long teeth tore him. His last sight was of his feathers—white with red flecks—falling to earth.

BOOK III:

ESCAPE FROM THE VALE

THE DREAMING

I am dying!

Pain in her neck, wrists, and side made her back arch in agony. Breath came in little explosions. Hands balled into fists, she struck the bed, leaving smears of black on the white. Her Wyrd Stone—*Methar Anduel*—gave just enough light for her to see the blood. But darkness pressed in from all around.

There was an owl. She was the owl. Torn. Pain filled her, like the gnash of a hundred teeth.

She felt herself falling. Her eyes grew black and the light of *Methar Anduel* faded.

Far away, she heard voices. But nearer there was a *presence*. If followed her as she dropped away.

No! She is ours! shouted the Vyrl in her thoughts. *Death shall not take her!*

A hand touched her. But it seemed far away. Then, something hot and wet filled her mouth.

There was an explosion of light. It was so beautiful tears fell as she opened her eyes and saw *Methar Anduel* burning, bright as a star, on her belly. Slowly breath returned, but in painful bursts. Her mouth was hot with Vyrl's blood. She could feel its healing energy coursing through her. The strength and a sense of renewed life flooded back so fast it made her stomach sick and heavy.

Methar Anduel's glow showed the three Vyrl—Ahmberen, Ecthellien, and Elshael—standing over her like tall shadows, hands linked, voices lifted in anger. The great rulers of the Vale of Mists looked down on her. Their black eyes swirled with tiny flashes of light and unreadable emotion. *Could they be afraid for me?* she thought. *Can a Vyrl even feel fear?* Through her bond with them she could sense only fury. Their thoughts flashed through her like lightning. She flinched at each violent and strange emotion.

I've lived with them for weeks, but I still don't understand them, she thought as she struggled to push them out of her mind. She felt shaky and wanted some solace from their wild thoughts.

Turning her eyes from the Vyrl's swirling gaze, she saw Mithorden standing at the foot of her bed, a Wyrd Stone ablaze in his fist. Unlike the Vyrl, she could see naked concern in the sorcerer's eyes and though the rulers of the Vale towered over him, his light and the shadow he cast filled the room in a way that made him seem their equal. There was a sense of strength about him and his steady smile reassured her. She gulped air and tried to calm the pounding in her chest.

Her gaze shifted to Vaelros who clutched his sword tightly, seeming ready to strike at an unseen danger. His strained face and stiff stance made her wonder if he would ever fully heal from the curse that had nearly killed him. The shadow of that nightmare still seemed to lay long and dark over him. He caught her gaze and his eyes flashed—warm and worried. She struggled to smile—as much to reassure him as herself.

Melkion perched on an overhang above her, dragon wings spread wide, fanning cool morning air over her. He was small—no larger than a cat—and his brilliant scales threw the light back in a hundred little rainbows. She felt grateful for his comforting wing flaps. Her smile broadened as she faced him and felt his cool puffs of air washing over her. She picked up *Methar Anduel*, sat up, and tried to collect her thoughts.

Her hand touched the Stone and its light grew. The shadows fell back, revealing the werewolf Othalas on her room's far side. Here was the Vyrl's great hunter. The one they sent to gather children and take them to the Vale of Mists. *No more,* she thought as the smile touched her eyes. *Now he is my friend.* He paced by the far wall with worry plain in his massive yellow eyes. His great bulk nearly filled the chamber, making it awkward for him to turn. He seemed nervous as a hen and this sight brought Luthiel fully out of her daze. He looked so silly she laughed aloud.

"Othalas, you look ridiculous!" she croaked hoarsely.

Soft as a flower petal falling, Melkion dropped from his perch and alighted beside her on the bed. "She's alive!" he whispered, as though afraid a loud noise might break her.

The great wolf let out a growl before bursting through the Vyrl to give her one great lick with his paddle tongue. Melkion's eyes narrowed and he looked sidelong at the great wolf.

"You never lick," the dragon said to the werewolf.

Othalas flashed a row of knife teeth at the dragon. Melkion shook his head and snorted smoke.

"Well I'm blessed. You actually care for someone."

The great wolf looked away, pretending the dragon hadn't spoken.

"Othalas wasn't the only one worried," Mithorden said with a kind, if strained, smile. "You gave us all quite a scare."

"What's happened?" she asked between breaths. She felt sore and beat up. As if she'd just run ten miles and at the end fallen off a cliff. Wiping blood from her mouth, she stared as the reopened wounds in her wrists and neck slowly closed.

"You nearly died. It took strong magic and Vyrl's blood to bring you back," Mithorden said. "As for what happened, I think you know quite a bit more than any of us."

All eyes were on her. She sat still a moment, staring out the slit window, doing her best to compose her thoughts.

Outside, the night slowly faded as the edge of Oerin's ellipsis neared the horizon. Spiders were out there—swarming beneath the Vale of Mists' Rim Wall, invading its forests. *Like the spiders in my dream, if it was a dream. The Widdershae who make all things their prey.* She blinked her eyes, slowly remembering. This morning they were to venture out. To try and break through the Widdershae and their thick spun webs of nightmare. To reach the elves and ask them to forgive Vyrl.

She turned her eyes away from the lightening sky and looked at her hands. *It is still only night. But it seems so much time has passed. If this adventure were not enough, now there is my dream. A dream that wounded me.* She shook her head as if that small motion could clear it of all worry and looked back at her companions. They would want to know what happened.

"It is all still very odd to me. And the only thing I can remember plainly is the death. But I will do my best to explain," she said in a soft voice. "I dreamed I saw through an owl's eyes. It was spying on a meeting. Widdershae, a dragon, Zalos' riders, and a man robed all in black. They—I think they were planning to kill me. When the meeting ended, the owl flew away. Then, I think the dragon kill—"

Her voice broke and she couldn't continue. Melkion hissed as Ahmberen and Mithorden leaned closer.

"You saw what it saw?" Ahmberen said. His swirling eyes seemed draw all of her inside them.

Luthiel nodded.

"And this happened to you when it died?" the Vyrl continued, motioning with a long-fingered hand to her hurts.

"I think so." Luthiel looked around in amazement. "How could it happen?"

The Vyrl turned to one another and she could sense thoughts whispering between them. Finally Ecthellien spoke.

"*The Dreaming*," he said.

Mithorden nodded. "Valkire's gift. Now his daughter's."

Luthiel watched them with a growing sense of dread. "What's *The Dreaming*? If *that* was a dream, I've never seen anything like it before!"

"It's not a usual dream," Mithorden said. "*The Dreaming* is deeper. Waking or sleeping, your father could share others' experiences. Sometimes, he could speak to hundreds or even thousands as they slept. The danger is you can share a body. If the body dies—the Dreamer can die too."

Luthiel put a hand to her head. She could still feel her heartbeat pounding there. "So that was real?"

"You're hurt, aren't you?" Mithorden said.

Luthiel stared at the bloodstains, still trying to take everything in. "I feel better now."

"It's the life in our blood," Ahmberen said. "But for Melkion's watch, you would have perished in your sleep."

A Bright Song

Luthiel picked up *Methar Anduel* with a shaking hand, looking deep into the Stone as if trying to see some mystery hidden there. *A dream that could let me walk in the thoughts of others. A dream that could kill.* The Stone's light seemed to come from far off, like the ghost of an oncoming dawn. "So you call it *The Dreaming*? And what part did you play, my little Stone? I wonder." She felt sad and afraid. She knew it had something to do with Father. They were talking about his *Dreaming*. His gift and her inheritance. But it was more. It was a dangerous thing—and not just to her. She suspected *The Dreaming* had snared the owl—snared it and killed it.

For the brief span of her dream she had lived as the owl. Saw through its eyes. It had seemed such a rich and full being. A life as vital as her own—gone in the flash of dragon's teeth and falling feathers.

"You know that owl died trying to help me?" she said to them with shame. She lifted a hand to her face and wiped away tears before they fell. She choked. "To show me something I needed to know. It was just so wrong." They stared back. Othalas cocked his head in puzzlement but Mithorden's eyes narrowed with concern as he nodded knowingly. "I could see what he saw. Feel what he felt," she continued. "This is just as bad as a person dying." She paused but the others were silent, listening to her. The Vyrl's eyes swirled coldly and she could hear an angry rumble rising in Othalas' chest. Even Melkion's tail swished from side to side in agitation. There was still blood on his mouth from his night-time hunting. Mithorden's eyes were the only ones that seemed warm to her then.

"A person?" Othalas growled finally. "It was just an animal. No better than food."

"Animal?" Luthiel said, trying to keep the distress out of her voice. "You're an animal! You just don't understand. If you saw what I saw, you would."

"I was once a man!" the great wolf snapped. "Let it go, Luthiel. It served its purpose."

Luthiel looked at the great wolf through eyes glistening with tears and anger. "My sister was Chosen to be food." She turned to the Vyrl. "I fed you."

"You saved us," Ecthellien said.

"Only so long as you eat a part of me," she snapped in reply before turning back to Othalas. "Am I no better than food?"

"Of course you are!" Othalas growled. "Only you can give what the Vyrl need."

"The best food. But food still."

Othalas snarled and shook his great body. "It's pointless talking to you. You're not thinking."

"When you just know something, you don't have to think," Luthiel whispered. "You don't understand. I *was* the owl."

"Luthiel, you shared the owl's sight, its dying moment," Mithorden said. "It makes sense you would sympathize with it. But Othalas is right, you must let go. There are more important things going on here."

"I can't!" she said through her tears. "You don't know what it's like to share a life—only to witness it snuffed out like that. To know it was for you. Important things? What could be more important?"

"The message it died to deliver. Would you dishonor its death by overlooking the reason for it dying?"

"It was a pointless death!"

"Only if you didn't receive its message." The sorcerer said firmly. "Think Luthiel! What did the owl see that was so important? Important enough for it to die trying to tell you?"

Luthiel shook her head and felt her heart pounding in her chest. It was all too difficult to think about. "I can't. I don't know."

"Remember or the owl dying was pointless."

"They were angry I escaped," Luthiel said slowly. "I should have died a babe. They were plotting to kill me. The dragon. They sent the dragon to kill me."

"They sent the dragon to kill the owl," Othalas growled.

"I was the owl!" Luthiel snapped back, then turned to Mithorden. "I can think of no good reason for it to have lost its life for me. There is *never* a good reason for such things."

Othalas leveled his great head and stared her straight in the eyes. "This way of thinking is madness. Some things must die so that we should live. It is the way of things. You know it."

"I knew it once. But now I wonder. Why must there be so much killing?" She stood up, Stone still held in her clenched fist. "So I have all these great things? My father's Stone, his sword, his *Dreaming*? But what are they good for other than getting things killed?"

They all stared at her. She was angry now, eyes flashing in the morning darkness. "They're weapons. That's all," she said with both anger and sadness.

"More than just weapons," Mithorden said. "Consider what we've learned. You've spied on the secret council of our enemies, listened on as they plotted against you. Without your father's gifts we would stumble blindly into a trap. Now we are forewarned." He looked at the Wyrd Stone in her hand. "They are objects of power. They bring dreams to life."

"How? Force innocent animals to serve as my eyes? Put them in danger?"

"You did not kill the owl," Othalas growled.

"I know it to my quick. He died for me. He knew me as I knew him. In his mind he called me *mistress*."

Again there was a long silence. Finally, Mithorden spoke.

"The owl will not be the last to die for you, Luthiel."

His words made her tremble and the anger inside grew hotter. "Make dreams come to life?" She shook the Stone at the sorcerer.

He slowly nodded, giving her a wary look.

"Then I will use it to make a dream. One to stop the killing."

"Impossible!" Othalas snorted. "Today we go out to war. There was never a war without killing."

She shook her head. "If I must fight, then I will. But fighting isn't always about killing. If I could make a dream real, I would not kill anything unless it could never be changed at heart."

"And if you must kill to survive? What then?" Othalas rumbled.

Ignoring the great wolf, she wrapped her bed sheets around her, walked over to the mantel and picked up the hilt of her father's broken sword—*Cutter's Shear*. In its place she left her Stone.

"Not unless there was no hope for good in a thing," she continued. "Even then, only with sadness." She looked at the sorcerer. "Can I make such a dream real if I swear in Father's name?"

"Would you take on an impossible restraint?" the sorcerer said, ignoring her question.

In answer, she brought the sword to her hand. Mithorden moved to stop her, but she backed away.

"Careful! It will slice flesh as easy as water," the sorcerer said, holding up a hand in warning.

He was right. She'd only touched her hand with it when blood appeared. But the sharpness made it easier. The cuts were painless. Carefully, she drew the shape of her father's name rune—a ᛪ—into her flesh.

She saw their looks. Realized they thought her mad and might try to stop her. "Stay back!" she shouted to them.

Lifting the Stone in her bloody hand, she sang aloud *Luthiel!* Light erupted from its heart, filling the room, making all seem to stretch and waver. In the World of Dreams her companions seemed to change. Othalas' eyes danced like great yellow flames. At his heart she could see the shape of an elf, curled in slumber. The Vyrl's mouths gaped with hunger as their bodies filled with golden blood. Yet from their hearts and eyes came light. Mithorden grew tall and rays like a pale sunrise seemed to crown his head. Last, her eyes fell on Vaelros, whose brow shone with a golden star. But something dark and hard to see lurked behind him.

She tore her eyes away from her companions and gazed deep into the radiant heart of *Methar Anduel*. The blood flowing over her Stone burned away in golden wisps. It seemed to feed the light and the Stone's brilliance slowly increased.

"*For my father! For the owl!*" she sang out, nearly shouting. It was defiance to Mithorden. But she didn't care. She wanted to be heard. The louder the better. *"I swear to harm only the heartless and hollow! Let no innocent die for me again!"*

Her Stone grew brighter still, blazing through the glass of Ottomnos, turning it into a palace of light, burning through the thinning mists, so that far away, many saw the glow against the sky and thought Soelee had risen early. Even the Fae army, gathering near the Vale for war, wondered at a sky turning to the blue of day. A passing cloud cast its shadow up toward the gray moon Somnos. Yet as brightness sprang up, a darkness in the sky seemed to gather—pressing in from all around.

Mithorden noticed. But Luthiel did not, for she was startled by something unexpected. Bathed in her Stone's light, the shards of *Cutter's Shear* chimed with a sound like breaking glass. The sound slowly changed. Growing clearer, it became like music. Then, some of the shards flew off the mantel. They shot toward her like knives. As a reflex, she lifted the broken blade in defense. The shards collided with it.

Light flared again—this time, blinding her. She tried to stop singing and found she couldn't. Slowly, the light dimmed down and she could see the sword glowing softly in her hand. More than a foot of blade had somehow reformed. The cracks between each shard were still visible—joining together in the shape of a ᛉ rune.

Over her song, she could hear a far-off roar. Puzzled, she turned from the sword and looked about, straining her ears at the sound. It growled and grew, becoming a rushing wind. She could hear trees groaning as it spilled into the Vale. It ran out over Miruvior toward her, troubling its surface with whitecaps. It cleared the Vale pushing its mists up against the west Rim Wall so the stars of early morning gleamed down like a million diamonds. Then the wind was roaring through the window, blowing around her. With it came a feeling of warmth and a smell like rain in summertime.

As I sacrifice, so shall others, whispered a voice in the wind. *Until all my blade is remade whole for your hand.*

The wind rushed out again. The light in her Stone grew dim and the World of Dreams fell away. She blinked her eyes, the sheets had fallen to her feet and she stood beside her bed—sword in one hand, Stone in the other.

The air was familiar—reminding her of The Cave of Painted Shadows. Of the tomb. But there was no comfort for her. Only terrible sadness.

"Father?" she whispered into the darkness. Nothing. She looked at her hand running a finger over the cut. What remained was a silver scar.

"Why?"

The sword vibrated in her hand, singing out a soft reply. Captivated, she listened as it hummed to her. A vision came to her of worlds like drops of dew on a field of endless night. Of stars like campfires scattered away throughout the blackness. Of the ever-bending horizon—Oesha's boundary between earth and sky. Of the great emptiness and its blessed silence. Of life itself—endlessly growing and changing.

The sound swelled, growing loud and majestic. It broke into two songs, then four, then a thousand. The music remained in harmony even as the songs continued their endless multiplying. Gradually, the noise faded returning to its first hum and then just a vibration. She could no longer hear it. But she trembled. It was as if she stood at the heart of a vast bell still quaking with the aftershock of that first great shout that called all the world to be.

Comfort deep as an ocean swept over her. Then came unexpected joy. The sword's song rang through her now and she felt certain her call had been answered. Standing, she held the sword up, eyes tracing its length. It was elegant—different from the *Cutter's Shear* she'd seen in paintings. Clear as crystal and filled with a warm light. A flowing shape graceful as a wave with an edge so sharp it cut the white out of light and left behind a fan of color.

"Did you ever sing before?" she whispered. The sword hummed in reply. If not for her sadness for the owl, she would have laughed in delight. Instead, she managed a smile. "Then I shall call you *Weiryendel*—a bright song. For you have answered my call with music and are now made as real as my promise. A promise against the darkness that is death." *Weiryendel* sang and grew bright in answer. She held it up for a few moments, then slowly let it fall. The song became a whisper and her sense of comfort faded. Luthiel fell back to bed, sword cradled in her hands. When she looked up, she wore a brittle smile.

"Why must good things always come at such cost?"

THE MAGIC OF SACRIFICE

The sword was short, and many pieces both large and small still lay in her pouch. She looked from the pieces to her sword and then turned to the sorcerer.

"'As I sacrifice so shall others? Until all my blade is remade whole for your hand?'" she wondered aloud. "What does it mean?"

Mithorden took her hand, eyes searching her and the sword. He paused and his face fell into a curious frown. "It seems the sword can be remade only when others sacrifice for you," he said at last.

Luthiel felt fear tightening in her throat. "Like the owl?"

"Like you feel about the owl," Mithorden said with a solemn nod. "To sacrifice," he continued, "To give of or risk your self, even your life, for the right reasons can awaken the strongest kind of magic." He looked back at her sword, eyes examining every crevice. "You should know."

Luthiel thought of her sister, of her own willingness to feed the Vyrl in her place.

"I don't want others to risk for me as I did for Leowin." She watched her friends but felt her stomach lurch when she saw their faces.

"I would," whispered Vaelros.

"And I," said Melkion.

"I as well," growled Othalas.

As one, the Vyrl nodded.

"All here would," said Mithorden evenly, "and many more who just don't know yet." He stared in solemn admiration at both her and the sword. "You set the example. It's a powerful thing you've put in motion."

Even though Luthiel stood on solid obsidian, she felt as though she'd tumbled down a bottomless well. "Death? Sacrifice? For me?"

"All magic, all power, comes at a cost," Mithorden said.

"It's not worth it. What if the next one is you? Or Othalas? Or Melkion?" She wanted to throw the sword away. It was supposed to be her promise against death, sacrifice. Instead, sacrifice had become a part of it. But it was a link to her blood father. Even now, its song hummed just beyond understanding. *Was it his voice that made the music?* she wondered.

"The risk was there already," the sorcerer replied, lifting a hand to gesture out the window and toward the Rim Wall.

"It needs death to come back together. There's something wrong with it." *Weiryendel* vibrated in her hand and she couldn't help but feel comforted. She looked at it and shook her head. "I just don't understand."

"I would spend years teaching you a thousand things and more. But we must make ready. Our enemies do not rest and wasted time plays to their favor. The Widdershae are ever at work thickening their webs. With each passing moment the army of elves draws nearer to the Vale," Mithorden's voice strained with urgency. "Yet I will say this—though Death has taken too much from this world and others, there is still such a thing as a good death. The ending of a life lived long and fulfilled that gives peace. The ending of a terror that gives hope. The merciful end to suffering. And the sacrifice of one's life to save another—that is the ultimate gift of love."

"But if Gorthar is Lord of Death, isn't he Lord of these things too?" Luthiel asked after pausing a moment to take in the sorcerer's words.

"No more. He gave up his fair gifts long ago when he became a tyrant."

Luthiel shook her head and looked at her sword. "I am of two minds. I can't understand how death is a good thing. But when I look at *Weiryendel* and am comforted by its music, I *know* this sword is a good thing."

"Accept the sacrifices of those you care for and mourn their passing," Mithorden said solemnly.

"But to make the sword whole others must die for me. I want the sword to become whole. I don't want them to die."

"A sword is death," Othalas growled. "A sword is defense against death. The thing it stops it causes. If you don't want others to die, then hope for peace. I am not optimistic. If I die in battle to defend you then at least my death will amount to something!"

Luthiel looked at the wolf, dumbfounded.

The sorcerer laughed and shook his head. "You should listen to Othalas. But for now, if we are ever to help the elves, we must make ready to leave. We are losing time." With those words, he, Vaelros, and the Vyrl started out of the room.

"But I still don't know what to do about it." Luthiel held out *Weiryendel.*

"Would you throw away your father's sword?"

Luthiel clamped her mouth shut, then shook her head.

"Good. We'll meet in the courtyard as soon as you're ready," The sorcerer said as he passed into the hall. "Be swift."

"Don't want to be caught below the Rim when night falls," Othalas growled after them. "Here, gather your things. Rendillo is coming to help."

She set her Wyrd Stone on the mantel and walked over to Othalas. Resting a hand upon his broad neck, she threaded fingers through his jet fur. The sword hung in her left hand humming quietly as she peered out her slit window and over the Vale. Below, Miruvoir had calmed and cast back a perfect reflection of the clear, predawn sky. Little lights filled the woods beyond. On the lake's far side, where it backed up against the Rim Wall, she thought she glimpsed the sickeningly crooked shape of a shadow web. She stared at it for a moment and a shiver passed over her before she lifted her eyes up over the Rim Wall. There was an army of elves out beyond that cliff. They'd gathered for one purpose—to rid the Faelands of the Vyrl. Her eyes scanned the cliff's top. Unlike the spiders, there was no sign of the elfish army. Still she knew they were there—sure as moons followed suns, sure as wolf-scent.

To the east, the green and golden Tiolas was rising. A slim crescent pointing the way toward her home—Flir Light Hollow. There, just weeks before, she'd struggled to find her way to the Vale of Mists and save her sister. Now, she was trapped inside by hundreds of giant spiders and a thick fence of their terrible shadow webs. Yet she'd promised the Vyrl to journey out through those webs to ask the elves for forgiveness.

She touched her Crown of Light—the thin weave of moonsteel and gems that gleamed with the brightness of stars if she were to hold a finger to it and blink her eyes. She turned her left hand, glancing down at the ring they'd given her and thinking of the wealth and power it symbolized—a quarter of all the Vale's riches and an equal rulership to the Vyrl themselves. They'd given her these things and others too, all for the gift of her blood. The blood that saved them from the terrible hunger that made them monsters. But it didn't make her ready to fight wars or to confront armies. It didn't give her the wisdom to be a Faelord or to know if to ask for the Vyrl's forgiveness was even good or just.

On her journey to the Vale, her aim had seemed so much clearer. Saving her sister was just something she must do. But saving Vyrl? Even though she was bonded to them, she was still faced with an awful truth—they had devoured the blood of hundreds of elfish children. Had Luthiel not come in her place, Leowin would be among them.

They did it to survive, she thought against her sadness and anger. *But it still doesn't change how the fae will see it.* Touching Ecthellien's mind, she knew he still thought of elves as prey. *And elves think of Vyrl as murderers.*

Do I know enough about them to defend them? she wondered unhappily. *And is it even right to?*

She let her eyes rise again to the Rim Wall and the unnaturally dark forest beneath it. Looking a second time, she knew her eyes weren't playing tricks, for in the growing light she could clearly see a patch of woods far darker than the rest. A place where shadows bent at impossible angles—turning and twisting so that not even the oncoming dawn could make sense of its madness. The Vale's mists and lights kept well away, as did all creatures not so unfortunate to have blundered into it.

Fighting down a rush of fear, she looked away from the window and turned to the werewolf standing beside her.

I'm off to beg pardon for monsters, she thought, *but only if the other monsters don't get me first.*

"Can we do this?" she asked.

The great wolf snorted. "Not likely. The shadow webs about the Vale are thick as deep winter's night. Impossible passage. But convincing elves to make peace with Vyrl is worse."

"Small comfort," she said.

"Is truth ever any comfort?" the werewolf replied.

Luthiel frowned and shook her head. "Not recently."

GIRDING

The door to her room opened and she blinked her eyes as Rendillo, leader of the grendilo, entered. Rendillo lifted his six-fingered hand to her in greeting. To Luthiel, he appeared to be half missing, for his body only had one arm and one leg. Odder still was his hand—large as a paddle, it boasted six fingers, and moved with an agility to put any two-handed creature to shame. Despite his awkward body, the grendilo's grace was without equal. Each movement seemed connected. Walking one-legged on his two-segmented foot made him look like a thin wave rising and falling toward her across the darkened chamber.

With Rendillo came a number of other grendilo she didn't recognize. Three fanned out across the room, tapping charred glass globes set in the wall with thin rods of the same material. With each touch, there was a chime and from within the globes bloomed bright blue light. The light advanced and soon the room was free of any shadow. Another two grendilo stood behind Rendillo. In their arms were her weapons and armor. They held them with care—like sacred things. Walking to her mantel, she picked up her Wyrd Stone and put it back in the pouch around her neck as she turned to greet them. When her eyes fell on them, the grendilo bent like moonflowers at sunrise, bowing silently before her.

"We've come to make you ready," said the grendilo to Rendillo's left.

Luthiel smiled thinly at the grendilo. "I hope you can," she said.

"Lady Luthiel, " Rendillo said, bending with his fellows, "let us gird you."

"We've brought arms and mail worthy of our Lady," Rendillo added. "It is a matter of pride we send you off with Ottomnos' finest." He waved his hand at her gear. "Much here is yours already. We've added a few things to help you. In the girding, resolve is given too—and strength unseen."

"Then gird me, Rendillo. For I could use both."

With a second series of bows, the grendilo approached her. Their movements were slow—as ones who perform a ritual. Each item was attended to with reverence but nothing more than Luthiel herself. They bathed her in scented oils, wrapping her wounds in fresh bandages. One brought scissors and made a motion at her hair.

Luthiel gave Rendillo a sharp look.

"So it won't get in your way," the grendilo responded. She lifted a protective hand, then lowered it, frowning as they cut and snipped. When they were finished, her hair was trimmed back to shoulder length. They handed her a mirror and she inspected her reflection. The grendilo were very skilled and the fresh cut was flawless. But she missed her long tresses.

A grendilo washed the remnant hair from her body as others came forward with clothes. The undergarb they gave her was of silk emblazoned with the Vale's sign—a silver swirl of mists surrounding tiny green gems in the design of a star. Overtop of this fine cloth was laid one of her Vyrl's gifts—the coat of armor made of the moonsteel *Lumiel*. To it were added a pair of ornate *Silen* shoulder guards. The grendilo slipped them over her coat and gently, but firmly, tightened the straps. The guards were done in an ancient mode she wasn't familiar with—each displaying a design of twelve stars running down the back of a dragon. The dragons curled around a larger star bearing the rune: ⚡. She moved her shoulders, testing the weight.

"We had to change the fitting, " Rendillo said. "But you wear them well enough."

"Does it come from father?" she asked with a shiver as she glanced at the tiny scar on her hand.

"We recovered some of his armor. This was made from what remained."

Her breath caught as Rendillo tightened a strap.

"There, how does it feel?"

Luthiel walked around the room in her father's armor. The armor that protected him against Vyrl and a thousand other troubles. Armor the Dark Forest's lord shattered when he broke her father's body. *Girding me for strength?* she thought numbly. *So they dress me up in the mail my father was destroyed in?*

She lifted her arms, testing the weight and range of motion. It was light and the straps didn't confine.

"Heavier in the chest than on the shoulders," she replied.

Mistaking her, Rendillo moved forward, then, with a look at her, seemed to realize what she meant and stopped—bowing his head in silent condolence.

"You'd best let me help you," he said at last in a soft voice. Rendillo motioned to a chest where the other Grendilo had laid out her weapons—bow, knife, a strange looking baldric, a scabbard, and two quivers filled with arrows.

She nodded.

He slung her bow and arrows to the baldric, looping it neatly over her shoulder and across her back. The baldric was of an odd make. For fasteners of wood delicately carved in the shape of hands were placed up and down the baldric and along the edge of the quiver. Their wooden fingers intertwined holding both bow and arrows.

"Watch me," he said.

Rendillo held his hand out to grasp the bow. There was a creaking as the wooden fingers released. Her mouth fell open. Before she could say a word, he placed the bow back in the hand. Fingers creaked again and the bow was held firm. Then he raised a hand over the arrows. Another set of hands, these much smaller, lined the edge of her quiver. One gracefully unthreaded its fingers, grasped an arrow, and lifted it toward his open palm.

"You see?" the Grendilo said.

"How —?"

"A bit of my people's magic." Rendillo replied with a little smile, then flexed and uncurled his single hand at her as if to demonstrate. "We don't use bows. Only darts and javelins. But the quiver works just as well. Now you try."

Luthiel shook her head and, despite herself, smiled as she practiced taking both bow and arrows from the hands. It was remarkably easy. They seemed to sense where she'd reach and adjusted if she missed a little, lifting bow or arrows till they touched her fingers.

"You're a wonder," she said. But the grendilo had already moved on and seemed not to hear her. When he turned toward her again, he held the scabbard. It was long and gently curved. Fashioned of gray *Sorim*, all down its length and on both sides were rolling waves of blue *Marim*. The top foot was covered in glistening scales.

Melkion, who was sitting in the slit window, whistled when he saw it. "That's dragon scale," he said.

"It's the scabbard for *Cutter's Shear*," Rendillo replied, holding it out to her in his single hand. "I thought you ought to have it."

"It's *Weiryendel* now, " Luthiel said. "Besides, I'm left handed,"

Rendillo bobbed his head and shifted the scabbard to her right side. It came with a belt of matching dragon scale, its buckle wrought in the shape of Oerin's Eye. Last came the trusty *Cauthrim* knife uncle Hueron had forged for her as a birthday present. A little more than a foot in length, the blue and red tinted metal was hot as an ember. It had already seen battle both against the Widdershae and the Vyrl when she first came to the Vale. She could feel its heat as Rendillo fastened it to her belt.

Tense and alert, she placed a hand over her knife and shifted her bow so it rested more comfortably on her back. There was a creaking as the hands adjusted.

"Made for killing," she whispered as she slid *Weiryendel* into the scabbard. It fit snugly.

"Lady?" Rendillo asked.

"Something a teacher of mine used to say. I think it went—'never carry a weapon without understanding the thing you hold is made for killing.'" It was a lesson she never thought she'd need.

"A wise thing to remember," Rendillo said.

"Wish I remembered more."

"You look fierce. Like one who goes to battle."

"Aren't I?" she replied. As she spoke, she trembled and her voice broke. Thankfully, Rendillo bowed and looked away, saving her from embarrassment.

"So it's finished? You've made me ready?" she asked the grendilo.

"Almost. There's just one thing more." Rendillo then opened a little brown pouch and from it pulled a tiny black potion bottle. Bending toward her, he uncapped the bottle, placing it in the palm of her hand. A foul stink rose up from it.

"What's this?" she asked, holding the thing away from her face.

"It's made from spider venom. Weakens Widdershae poison."

Rendillo's matter-of-fact manner chilled her.

"Oh," she said. "Thanks."

"It's best if you take it now," Rendillo said.

Luthiel looked at Rendillo in disgust. "You drink it?"

"What else would you do, Lady?" Rendillo's face revealed no emotion but Luthiel felt he was mocking her.

With a sniff, she raised it to her lips. The smell grew and her eyes watered. Stopping her nose, she forced herself to bring it to her lips. With a quick motion, she tossed it into her mouth and swallowed. It stung her tongue and throat as she choked it down. She wiped her mouth and coughed.

"It's awful," she said. Some of the stuff stuck to her teeth. It made her tongue curl.

"Should help if you're bitten," Rendillo said, handing her a cup of honeyed water which she gratefully drank. "No more than one bottle a day. Any more and you may as well be poisoned."

"It's worse than poison," she said, making a face.

"Poison and cure are often quite close," Rendillo replied. "And Widdershae venom is deadly. Makes you bleed, inside and out. Turns your guts into a bloody mess. That's what spiders like to eat."

Luthiel shuddered, trying not to imagine.

"It's just enough to keep you alive," Rendillo said, handing her a small pouch filled with vials of the stuff. "Use more only if you're bitten. But remember, one drop of Widdershae poison will still make you very ill."

She took the pouch and tucked it in her belt. "Thank you, Rendillo. Thank you all."

"My pleasure," he replied with a bow. Behind him, the other grendilo bent low.

"I guess that's everything," she said, taking a last look at the chamber. *Strange how it feels so familiar.*

Melkion leapt from the window and, in a wing flap, was perched on her shoulder.

"Best we go," he hissed.

"Fair fortune, lady," Rendillo said. "Hope you return soon. The place is kinder with you here."

Luthiel took Rendillo's single hand in both of her own. It was larger than the two of hers combined. "It is you who have been kind to me, Rendillo. Thank you." She kissed his hand and he bowed deeply.

"The lady's blessing," he said smiling at his hand. He bowed again before spinning on his only leg and gracefully hopping out of the room. Just as graceful, the other grendilo followed. A few turned to steal a last look at Luthiel before they, too, were gone.

SECOND WARNING

Ready for war, she let Othalas lead her out. Melkion perched on her shoulder, picking dried blood out of his claws and licking it off his jowls with his raspy tongue. The remnants of last night's hunt. Luthiel shuddered and thought of the owl.

One by one, she counted the lights of Ottomnos' halls as they made their way down to the courtyard. Her eyes held onto them the way an unsure swimmer might hold tight to a boat. She'd grow accustomed to Ottomnos' dangers. Now, the way ahead of her seemed far worse than even the charred glass palace—where she was now a queen. How might elves welcome a queen of Vyrl? How might she even reach them when the terrors of Drakken Spur multiplied and set a nightmare fence across her path? When they walked out into the morning, they found the pre-dawn sky filled with crows. They flew about recklessly and those upon the battlements cawed. The flapping of wings filled her ears as three spun about her head.

"What's made them so frantic?" she asked Melkion.

"Don't know," he replied. "I can't understand what they're saying."

She saw one that pulled away and immediately recognized Mindersnatch—leader of the great crows of Ottomnos. She watched on as his large, silver-feathered, body winged toward her. She held her arm out as the elder crow landed.

He preened his feathers for a short time before croaking—

"Re – port?"

"Yes, I'd like to know why your friends are so disturbed," she said uneasily. "What happened?"

The crow hesitated for another moment before squawking his message.

"Spiders! One flock, two flocks, three flocks—a hundred! Crept over the rim! An hour after midnight! Struck the elves. Many are dead! Many more, the spiders took! Back to the Vale!"

Luthiel's breath caught in her throat. She stood still and stared. For a moment, *The Dreaming* returned and she could again hear the clicking of spider voices along with a soft-spoken reply.

"What must we do?"
"Tonight, strike the elves. Then, draw the noose tight. No one escapes the Vale."

"Luthiel?" Melkion hissed in her ear. The sudden sound made her start and Mindersnatch flapped his wings to regain balance. She could feel Melkion's claws digging in.

"What's the matter?"

"It's just what the owl overheard," she said trying to compose herself.

"You're pale," Melkion sniffed near her face, "and you're terrified."

Luthiel fished a biscuit out of her pack with a shaking hand and offered it to Mindersnatch.

"Thank you, Mindersnatch," she said. The crow bobbed his head, then gently plucked the biscuit from her hand before flying off to the battlements.

Melkion was still looking at her.

"So I'm scared. You should be too. They *planned* this."

Smoke curled from Melkion's nostrils and his wings stiffened in anger. "Spiders," he hissed.

She nodded. A thin sweat had covered her and now she shivered in the cool air.

"Elves will think the Widder are with us," Othalas growled.

Luthiel frowned. She was still thinking about her *Dreaming*.

"I wonder how many spies the spiders left behind?" she said. "It would only take a few hidden in a thicket or some dark, out-of-the-way hole waiting to creep back with news of when and where and whom to snatch."

Melkion hissed and Othalas growled but neither they nor Luthiel spoke any more as they waited for Mithorden, Ecthellien, and Vaelros.

VEILING

Wights stood along the battlements or scrambled back and forth. As she walked into the courtyard, their eyeless sockets followed her and they tilted their heads back to sniff the air. Their bodies twitched and trembled but the wights who once had tried to claw out her eyes kept their distance, held back by the Vyrls' iron will. Grendilo also filled the courtyard. They wore their strange armor of overlapping bands and intermittent spikes. In their strong hands were greatswords, shortswords, or spears. Towering over them were giants. One was busily loading boulders into an insect-like contraption; another was bending a bow the size of a tree. On his back—a quiver of shafts the size of long spears.

"We should attack the spiders," she said finally. "Show the elves we aren't with them."

Othalas snorted.

"What if the spiders run before us, attacking the elves?" he growled.

Luthiel pursed her lips. "Then we'll catch them between us."

"Wouldn't work," the great wolf grumbled.

As she stood there, Vaelros strode through an archway. He wore an olive cloak over his armor and his golden Wyrd-Stone was set in the pommel of his sword. It gleamed dimly in the half-light and the glow spilled onto his face. Green eyes reflected the Stone's light back at her and his brown hair sparkled with shades of flax and russet.

"Is it wise to?" Luthiel asked, gesturing toward his Stone.

"I'll cover it when we enter the woods. For now, it gives comfort," he said. His eyes lingered on her.

Luthiel nodded. She understood. There were many times when she'd sought comfort in *Methar Anduel*'s light.

Reaching out, Vaelros took her hand, pressing something there.

When she dropped her eyes, she saw a star shade. The flower's blue petals seemed to glow in the pre-dawn.

"I wanted to give you something," Vaelros said warmly. "Something that might suit you. I found this. But it doesn't seem to match up."

Luthiel looked up and found Vaelros' eyes.

"What I saw this morning was far more lovely than any flower," he said.

Now Luthiel flushed.

"I hardly thought about it," she said through her embarrassment. "Please. Stop staring."

Vaelros' eyes dropped and he was about to turn away when she grabbed his hand.

"Thank you," she whispered, giving it a little squeeze. Before he could reply, she bounded off for Othalas. The werewolf had laid down and set his great predator's eyes on Vaelros. As she came to him, she could hear the low rumble of a growl.

"Stop," she said to the wolf. "He's no harm."

"Is he?" But they said no more about it as Vaelros stood awkwardly on the other side of the courtyard, picking through the petals of a second flower he'd found.

Minutes later Ecthellien broke the tension when he entered the courtyard. Hair the color of blood spilled over a cloak like a rain cloud and armor of midnight. On one hip hung his longsword; on the other dangled a horn of bone and a metal. Vyrl's eyes, black with small specks of swirling light, stared out at her through the dim morning. The sight, though one she'd grown used to during the time she'd spent in the Vale, put her ill at ease.

Are you ready? he thought. She must have still looked afraid, for she could feel his concern.

She grimaced. *Ready as I can be. How is someone ever ready to go out and meet such danger? How is someone ever ready to face the almost certain hate of their people?*

Vlad Valkire was a hero for turning Vyrl, Ecthellien thought.

A hero for turning tyrants against one another, Luthiel replied. *I'll offer excuses for children lost and beg elves to believe it will never happen again.*

You will offer yourself in the place of children that it may never happen again.

Luthiel tensed and her brows lowered. She didn't like thinking about it that way. But it was the truth.

Would it be enough? After all your crimes? Would it ever be enough?

Ecthellien was silent and she chided herself for seeking sympathy from a Vyrl. It was like asking a wolf to understand what's wrong with hunting and killing the sick and young. She glanced at Othalas and wondered what he would think about such things. Might he understand, once being an elf himself? Or had he lived a wolf for so long that all sympathy for them was erased? She shook her head and sighed. If morals weren't good for protecting one's own kind, then what were they good for? She sensed her actions estranged her and, being a little different all her life, knew well the likely fear and hate she would face.

Finally, Mithorden entered the courtyard. Her eyes and thoughts turned to him and away from her worries. His worn traveler's clothes were the least splendid of any in their company. But the look of him was greater than his clothes could tell. Brows like a painting of fire rose off eyes that seemed to shine out in the darkness, and a crest of dark hair as noble as any crown pulled back from his forehead. The broad frame of his shoulders put his cloak in a shape that reminded Luthiel of wings, and his sword seemed to float more than hang from his hip. Staring at him in the pre-light, Luthiel was reminded of a bird of prey, still sleek with the brightness of youth, but old beyond even the telling of elves. In that moment, he seemed grand and there was little she could do but stare.

"Vaelros," he said, gesturing to the naked Wyrd-Stone, "it is wise to keep hidden."

"I already told Luthiel. I'll cover it once we start."

Mithorden nodded, but his face was troubled.

"Best not be reckless," he said. "They attract attention."

With a sharp look at Mithorden, Vaelros pulled a leather wrapping over the Stone.

Luthiel noticed that the Vale's green lights were coming out. Contained in those tiny sparks were lost spirits robbed of both body and memory by the Vale's mists. Ever since she'd come to the Vale they'd seemed attracted to her. Now three swirled 'round her head, crowning her with their eerie glow. It made her feel a thrill to have them close and she wondered if they found comfort in being near her. With the feeling came a sense of melancholy. The Vale was so full of changed and lost things. It had even almost changed her. Without the protective magic in her Wyrd Stone, Luthiel had little doubt she would now roam the Vale in a shape far different from her own. Her eyes returned to Othalas. Long ago, the Vale's Mists had changed his body—leaving him in the form of a great wolf. She wondered if he was happy or if he missed his lost life.

Turning to Luthiel, Mithorden handed her a bundle.

"You should wear this."

"What is it?" she said, eyeing the bundle.

"Your disguise," Mithorden said.

Luthiel opened it. Underneath was a veil, a big gray cloak with a deep hood and a pair of long gloves.

"You were too careless when the Seven came. For now, I wish you to remain hidden. There's a subtle magic on the garments that will disguise your voice and mask your features."

Luthiel looked at the veil with distaste. "Why should I hide?" Even as she asked the question, she dreaded the answer. It had worried her all morning. Worried her since she'd decided to help the Vyrl. Elves would hate her for what she did. Mithorden's disguise only served to prove her fears. Despite her doubts, she did not like the idea of hiding. Her face fell into a frown as she stared at the clothes in her hands.

"To confuse our foes. But, far more important, the elves aren't yet ready to know you. It's well you stay hidden until they are."

"Mouthy today, aren't you?" Othalas growled to the sorcerer, who ignored him. Beside her, she could hear Vaelros chuckle. Grudgingly, she donned her disguise. But she tied the veil around her neck without using it to cover her face. It could wait.

LEAVING OTTOMNOS

Oerin's Eye slowly rose as they made ready to depart. Mithorden and Ecthellien took turns checking to make sure packs were full and weapons secure. No mounts could make it through shadow webs. So they would travel afoot. All but Luthiel, whom Othalas ordered to ride him. She smiled at the wolf's gruff command and knew he was only concerned for her safety. As they readied, Melkion sprang up to a high battlement and peered out over the Vale. Luthiel watched him, feeling tension settle on her like a heavy weight. Everything, all their plans and preparations, would now be put to the test. She wondered if it would be enough.

At last there was a shriek of chains and the grinding of wheels. The spiked portcullis and toothed draw bridge opened, revealing the path leading away from Ottomnos. Ahead of her were the standing stones where she'd slept the night before the Vyrl rode out to claim her. The path wound past them and on to Miruvior before plunging into the Vale's dense woods.

Mithorden took a step ahead of her and then turned to look her directly in the eyes. "Are you ready?"

At a loss for words, she nodded. But her heart thumped as she thought again of Mindersnatch's news. It was something Mithorden should know. "Did you hear about the spiders?" she asked at last, almost flinching. She dreaded to even talk about them. Poison to make you bleed everywhere. Slinking around to snatch and murder.

"More crow's news?" Mithorden asked.

She nodded.

His brows lowered and those sharp eyes took her in with frightening seriousness. "What did they tell you?"

She could tell by the subtle touch on her mind Ecthellien was also troubled. At first she couldn't say anything. It was too awful to imagine, much less speak of.

"It's terrible," she finally managed. "They attacked after midnight. Many elves were taken prisoner."

Mithorden's brows overshadowed his eyes and he frowned. "Widdershae don't take prisoners. Only slaves and food. The elves will think Vyrl sent the spiders."

Othalas rumbled in affirmation. "It will provoke them."

"We must reach the elves before they act," the sorcerer said.

"When?" Luthiel asked.

"Possibly today," Mithorden said.

Luthiel didn't like it. "So soon?"

"Possible. They should send scouts first."

It was almost as bad. She wanted to call back Mindersnatch. To have him send the elves a warning. But what would happen to her Khoraz friend? Would the elves shoot him from the air?

"Scouts?" she said, almost pleading. "But spiders will catch them!"

Mithorden gave Luthiel a look of concern. "Careful as cats, quiet as owls, the scouts of Ithilden are not ones to be misestimated. Many of those sent will return. They may even send Blade Dancers."

Luthiel felt her throat tighten.

"Vanye?" she asked.

"Perhaps. Unless he's still waiting with your sister for Othalas," Mithorden said.

"I hope he's not in danger."

"Blade Dancers are always in danger," Mithorden replied, putting a comforting hand on her shoulder. "Vanye's ready for it."

"Far more than I," Luthiel said. "What if it's just to set a trap for the elves?"

Mithorden looked away into the lightening sky. "It is almost certainly a trap. All more reason to hurry."

The sorcerer looked at each of them in turn and, as if by an unspoken signal, they made their way out through the gate of Ottomnos. Mithorden led the way, his sharp, hawk-like features undulled by the soft light of Oerin's Eye. Luthiel followed atop Othalas, his vast body giving some sense of comfort. Vaelros came after her and as he passed the gates he set a hand to his sword, looking left then right. Ecthellien strode behind them, standing head and shoulders above all but Luthiel upon Othalas. Hair the color of blood framed eyes like a black sea beneath a starry night.

For the first time since the reign of Vlad Valkire, a Vyrl set out to depart the Vale of Mists. Never was there a time more dangerous for a Vyrl to leave. And for the first time in an age Ecthellien recalled remorse and compassion. Yet the old predator's instincts did not ebb away. If anything, they were more urgent now that his only lifeline to reason and goodness lay in the frail girl before him.

Grendilo, giants, and a thousand strange and colorful beasts stopped to watch them as they passed. A horn sounded from the fortress behind them. Luthiel turned to see Elshael, Ahmberen, and Gormtoth standing atop the out-er wall. The Vyrl both wore armor of the darkly glistening moonsteel—*Sorim*. Ahmberen had a greatsword as tall as Luthiel strapped across his back and Elshael held a spear tipped with a shining blue head. Gormtoth was a giant and even made the Vyrl seem small. His wrought-iron armor gleamed dully from the inferno it encased. Thin streams of smoke leaked out the cracks and from the mouth of his great dragon helm. Through the helm's opening, Luthiel could see his fiery eyes following her as she passed the standing stones.

Oerin's Eye cast his soft light down upon the great castle which seemed to be sending off a cloud in farewell. She felt her breath catch as the light gleamed from battlements and glittered off crenellated towers so each seemed capped with a star. Though still gray, Ottomnos threw more of the light back than she remembered. In places, the glass seemed clear and clean. Another note sounded and the two Vyrl lifted their hands.

Keep her safe, they thought to Ecthellien.

I will, he thought. *I must.* Lifting his horn, he sent a peal up in answer.

Luthiel realized this might be the last she saw of Ottomnos for a long while. It was odd, but she felt a twinge of regret along with her fear.

For all the death and danger that surrounds it, I've grown accustomed to this place.

She realized, though, that she must return.

If I live.

In silence, they passed into the woods and Ottomnos was soon lost behind the trees.

SORCERESS

Mists lay thick over the forest floor. Looking about her, it seemed the wood rose up from a sea of smoke. It was so dense they couldn't see the path and many times wandered off the road. Even Othalas grumbled. There was little they could do but pick their way, taking small turns and switchbacks. Soelee's rise did little to disperse it. Instead, the mists turned dull red, then yellow, and finally white as Soelee began her climb toward mid-sky.

"Never seen it like this before," Othalas said, "It's not normal they lay so low and thick."

Despite the slow going, they made their way toward the Vale's east rim. At first, the land dipped into a marshy place, then it rose up toward the cliffs. From Othalas' back, Luthiel could see the rounded caps of the Mounds of Losing. Somewhere beyond those hills lay Flir Light. With the thought came a tugging in her heart and, for a moment, she forgot her fear and longed for her family. For Kindre's gentle licks. And for Leowin.

I'll see her again, she realized. It gave her a thrill of happiness that faded just as fast as it came on. *If we make it.*

A flock of crows gathered above them, flying escort as they continued on toward the cliffs. The birds wheeled and swooped, combing the land before and around them.

They stopped for a brief lunch at midday. Shortly after, they noticed the first web. In the distance, a great tree cast shadows that lay strangely about it. Like broken bits of a black egg. Looking at it, she lost all thought of home and wondered if she'd even see tomorrow.

I was lucky the first time, she thought with a shiver, remembering the two spiders and her near death. *If I'd blinked, it would've gotten me.* It was

32

enough to make her wish she could keep her eyes open all the time and never blink again.

Mithorden gathered them around him and, one by one, laid hands on them, saying the word *Ethelos*. After, they seemed to fade before her eyes. She had difficulty finding them even though they stood beside her or, in the case of Melkion, sat on her shoulder. Even Othalas was difficult to see.

When Mithorden came to Luthiel he stopped.

"Now you try," he said.

For a moment, she didn't understand. Then, slowly, it dawned on her that he meant her to do magic. "But I don't know how," she replied.

"Just do as I say and we'll see what you know and what you do not. Are you ready?"

"How could I be?" she said, feeling embarrassed.

Then Mithorden took her hands and looked her straight in the eye. "Just this morning, you did high magic," he said.

"That wasn't —"

"Oh it was!" And Mithorden gave her such a serious look that she immediately shut her mouth. "Now clear your mind and think of what it's like not to be noticed. Once you've gathered all your notions of solitude and of stillness, then speak the word *Ethelos*—which means secret—and touch your finger to your garments."

Luthiel took a deep breath and nodded.

"I'll try," she said.

The sorcerer clapped her shoulder.

"Then do it," he replied.

She took another breath, then gathered her thoughts. It wasn't difficult for her to think of what it was like not to be noticed. As an orphan, she'd grown used to it. She knew Glendoras and Winowe cared about her, they just focused on their own children more. And why shouldn't they?

When Luthiel was satisfied that she had the right feeling, she touched her cloak.

"*Ethelos*," she whispered.

There was a twinge, a slight tingling in her skin and a distant rushing in her ears. Then it was gone.

She frowned.

"Did anything happen?" she asked.

Mithorden looked at her curiously. His eyebrows furrowed and he seemed to consider her for a moment. Everyone was looking at her.

"Nothing happened," she said with a sigh. It was strange, but she felt disappointed. "I told you. I'm no sorcerer."

"No, nothing happened," Mithorden replied. "But I don't know why. Did you think of solitude like I told you?"

She nodded.

He stared at her for a few more moments and then his eyes brightened.

"Ah yes!" he said finally. "How could I be so thoughtless? It's been so long since I taught anyone. I simply forgot."

"What are you talking about?" Luthiel asked.

"The Wyrd—it's different for everyone. Most find it easier to speak the words. From time to time there are some who draw them. Even more rarely, you'll find someone for whom it is entirely natural to *sing* them. The words aren't necessary; they're just a focus."

Luthiel blinked her eyes. It made sense. Singing was how she awakened the Wyrd Stone and, at some deeper level, she realized she thought of magic and music as related. Again she wondered at what the sorcerer was saying.

Could it be true, after everything else that's happened?

She thought of *The Dreaming* and remembered her struggle to turn Vaelros' Stone. She thought of her battle with the Dimlock in the Cave of Painted Shadows. She thought of *Weiryendel*.

It was sorcerery. I thought it was the Wyrd Stone all along.

It was you, Ecthellien replied. *Only a sorcerer can use a Wyrd Stone.*

"Go on, try again," Mithorden encouraged.

"All right," she said, still somewhat doubtful.

Luthiel took a deep breath and thought of what it felt like not to be noticed. It was harder to find the sensation this time. The others were still staring at her. She closed her eyes to shut them out. In that moment, she wished she *could* hide. It was hard enough to concentrate without their stares. Finally, she was able to settle her mind and recall the safety of solitude. It was a different feeling from the loneliness she'd felt the first time.

At last, she was satisfied. She was about to sing *Ethelos* when an inspiration took hold of her. The memory of her struggle with Vaelros' Wyrd Stone suddenly came back to her. In that moment she realized what she must do. She opened her mouth and began to sing softly. Without having to think, the words flowed from her lips.

Softer than the lightest breath
That silent over waters blow
Dimmer than the dimmest shade
That rests in twilight fair
Untouched by motes
To light I'm lost
Where no eye turns
Ethelos!

For a moment, the world seemed to blur. Then, the feeling of solitude slid over her and she had a sense she'd slipped into a blind spot in the world's eye. It was an unremarkable place; one happily overlooked.

"Good!" Mithorden said. "Very good! For someone who's not a sorcerer."

"You were right," she whispered, not wanting to disturb the silence.

"It was well done." Vaelros said. "Now I can't see you at all."

"I'm here," she replied.

Vaelros turned his head. But she could tell by the look on his face he stared through her.

"We'll have to link hands," Mithorden said. "Otherwise, we're likely to lose each other. I'll lead, followed by Vaelros, then Luthiel, next comes Ecthellien and Othalas will take the rear.

"You can see us, can't you?" he asked the werewolf.

"I can," the great wolf rumbled. "Though I might see Luthiel better."

"I was counting on your hunter's eyes," Mithorden said with a nod. "The charm will last for a number of hours. While it covers us, we will be very difficult to see or hear. We should go quietly all the same and if we can, stay out of sight. Is everyone ready?"

They nodded.

With a whispered word, Mithorden faded and then they set out again—making their way deeper into the forest.

WEBS OF SHADOW

Shadow webs began to come into view. At first they appeared overhead—running crooked through the tree canopy and casting all into an unnatural twilight. Further on, they shot down from the treetops or jutted over the ground at odd angles, twisting in such a way as to make even sunslight seem wrong. To Luthiel, it looked as though the world had cracked. Running through everything were thin fissures of darkness. Where they walked at the border between webs and open land, light and color streamed through those dark lines. Further ahead, the shadow webs grew thick and flowed together—cutting off the rest of the world before tapering into a great black clot in the distance.

Worst of all, nothing the webs touched could escape. Creatures of every kind from the tiniest insect to the greatest beast were trapped—most already dead. All the rest just hung there, bleeding from every part. The whole mess of it smelled like nothing in all her experience. Once, she'd seen a herd of sheep driven off a cliff by wolves. There were so many the pack couldn't eat them all. Hundreds of bodies lay rotting. An odor rose on the wind and carried for miles until all of Flir Light stank.

The smell here was far, far worse. Even carrion birds and insects were caught. So there was nothing but rot to feed on rot. The whole place seemed to fester and that uncanny chill Luthiel had noticed upon passing the webs going into the Vale was far deeper and clammier than she remembered.

"The venom causes it," Melkion whispered, pointing at the bloody bodies with his tail.

"I saw a bear caught in their webs once," she said. "It was crumbling to dust."

"It turns the guts to liquid. When the work's finished, the spiders return. They drink it all through a hollow tooth."

Luthiel's stomach bound itself up in a knot. She regretted eating. One of them—a cat-like creature with a mane of white and rose feathers—looked at her. Its eyes leaked blood.

"Rendillo told me," she whispered. "Can't we do something?"

"Only a few things can break a shadow web." He stared at her with his violet eyes. "Fire will burn through it. But it takes time. Your father's sword may cut it quick. But even if you could part the web, it might bring spiders."

She stared up at the poor creatures. They looked so terrified. She couldn't imagine what it was like, dangling upon a shadow web, knowing there wasn't a thing you could do other than wait for death. But if she helped them and the spiders noticed, it would likely mean that it was she who dangled on a strand of shadow.

"How do you know so much about them?"

"Told you before. I lived in the mountains."

"Did they trouble you?" she asked.

But Melkion didn't reply. He just sat on her shoulder, swinging his silver head back and forth, keeping alert to every sound and movement. Soon afterward, they encountered a great shadow web hanging across the trail.

Mithorden turned left into the wood—making his way deeper into the webs. At first, it was easy going. They set a swift pace toward the Rim Wall. Small animal paths made for fast travel, and as the rock walls grew Luthiel's heart swelled with renewed hope. *It's getting closer,* she thought, stealing another look through a gap in the canopy. *We might yet make it.* But, less than a half mile further on, the gaps in the webs overhead slammed shut and she could no longer see the Rim at all. The land became rough—shot through with crags or littered with rocks that had tumbled, ages ago, from the cliff face. At the same time, the shadow webs pressed in from all sides—filling the gaps between trees and boulders and even overlaying gullies or other places where the land fell. So they had to go very slow—walking in each others' footsteps to make sure they didn't stumble into the ever-thickening webs.

As they picked their way through, Luthiel noticed it was easier to see her companions. They appeared as indistinct against the dark background, drifting like spirits through the misty wood. She realized her eyes were growing used to the enchantment.

Shadows pressed in, the chill deepening until her breath blended with mists. She kept looking for clear swaths—straining to see the Rim. It must be near, but webs drew closer with each step, forcing them to turn away. Gradually, the webs blocked out the light. Twilight dimmed into false night and finally, though it was still mid-afternoon, black of first winter.

"What happened to the mists?" Melkion hissed in her ear.

Luthiel looked around her. They were gone.

"Don't know. They were here just a moment ago," she said. Her eyes scanned the darkness. "Strange. Can't see them at all." Webs hung everywhere—tree to tree, rock to rock, crag to ground and in thick patches over the earth. Now and then, she noticed lights shining far off. Yet they reminded her more of the Vale's lights than spider eyes.

"Mithorden?" she whispered past Vaelros.

"Yes?" The sorcerer spoke without taking his eyes from the path. He seemed in deep concentration.

"Where are the mists?"

The silence carried on for a few heartbeats.

"I'm not sure," he said finally.

"Look at that patch of webs along the ground." It was Ecthellien who spoke this time. "See, beneath the denser webs?"

They all stopped, scanning the darkness near their feet. Luthiel saw nothing but more shadow webs. Then, just as she was about to give up, she noticed it. Below the webs lay a dark fog.

"It's in there," she whispered.

"Spider Wyrd," Vaelros hissed. His voice sounded distant. His face grew tight and his eyes glazed.

He's remembering, she thought. *It hurts him.*

"They're gathering the mists," he continued.

"You *knew* about it?" Othalas growled.

"They've used mists before."

"What for?" Luthiel said. She grabbed Vaelros by the arm and pulled him closer, forcing him to look at her directly.

He blinked his eyes and then shook his head as though coming out of a stupor.

"I only remembered it just now," he said through lips blue as though with cold. He put a hand to his head as if straining to remember. "How were they used? I just can't recall."

Luthiel trembled. She met eyes with the sorcerer. He frowned at her. Then he gripped Vaelros on the shoulder.

"Enough for now," he said.

Vaelros looked at the sorcerer and lifted a hand to his eyes. He let out a long sigh.

"Let's get moving," he said.

Mithorden nodded and continued on through the shadows.

Luthiel squeezed Vaelros' hand. He turned around. This time his eyes were clear. In them—concentration, anger. The pain of a moment before now gone.

She sighed. Though she didn't believe it possible, with each step, the darkness deepened until she was reminded of mid-winter when stars grow dim and moons have color but give no light. For the first time, she began to doubt.

What if Mithorden was right?

She looked over her shoulder to Ecthellien, but the Vyrl just shook his head.

Luthiel was so lost in worry she didn't notice they'd stopped. She walked headlong into Vaelros, pushing him into Mithorden. The sorcerer shot an angry look at Luthiel as he leaned back hard—inches from a web. Slowly, he drew away.

"Cunning weaver," he whispered. When he was a safe distance back, he sat down.

"What are you doing?" Luthiel whispered.

"Looking for a clear path," Mithorden replied. "It seems all ways are blocked. A little light would do us good. But it's certain to bring spiders."

Luthiel let out a fearful breath. She could no longer see webs—only dark-ness. But she imagined them strewn about in mad tangles. She shivered. When she drew her cloak close, she noticed ice crystals in the weave. She wanted nothing more than to turn back. Beneath the shadows, she despaired of ever seeing sky again or walking free on the untainted grass. The stuff beneath her feet was dry as straw.

Vaelros squeezed her hand.

"You all right?" he whispered.

"It's the webs—they're getting to me."

"Me too," he said with a nervous smile.

"I feel like running fast and far. All the same, I'm terrified to move," she said. "I can't even see them all. Can you?"

He shook his head. "Hope *he* can," he said with a jerk of his head toward Mithorden.

Mithorden sat on the log for what seemed like hours, staring into the deeper shadows. Finally, with a shake of his head, he stood and walked toward Luthiel.

"I cannot find a clear path," he said.

"What now?" Luthiel whispered.

"As far as I know we only have two choices. The first is we go back and try the way to Cauthraus."

At that moment, in that dim and colorless place, her fear of the Red Moon seemed far away. She felt a strong urge to leave, to abandon these mad webs and face whatever danger it held for her.

Anything is better than this. We are like flies in a maze of spider webs.

"What's the other choice?" she whispered.

"You have the sword?" he asked.

"I do," she replied.

"Well, you could use it to cut a path for us."

"*Weiryendel* will cut the shadow webs?" she asked.

"I told you it might," Melkion hissed in her ear.

"I haven't seen it," Mithorden replied. "Nor have I known a thing *Aeowinar* couldn't cut."

"But won't breaking webs alert the spiders?" she said, remembering Melkion's warning.

"There's a danger it will," Mithorden said.

"Do you think we should press on?" she asked.

"I leave it to you," he said.

Luthiel's heart quailed, but despite her fear, she drew *Weiryendel*. The blade sang as it cleared her scabbard and tiny lights seemed to gleam in its glass-like crystal. Just this morning those flecks had turned to suns. Now they were like motes that drift through water and only shimmer when the light hits them. A sound like breaking whispered around her. With it came the new sound—the bright music. Melkion crouched beside her, staring at the blade. There was a look in his eyes she couldn't read. She felt protective, thinking that the dragon coveted it as dragons covet all precious things. Melkion swung his head toward hers and looked into her eyes. His jaws unhinged as if he were about to say something. Then they snapped shut and he looked away.

Shaking her head, she wrapped her hand tight around *Weiryendel's* white and silver hilt. Lifting it, she held the new sword before her eyes. Calling it a sword wasn't quite right. It looked more like a big knife. But to her mind, it was a sword—fresh and keen as on the day of its first making. She thought also of the other pieces that lay secreted in her pouch and of what terrible things must happen for them to be added. It was enough to make her hand tremble. Eighteen inches of crystal blade rose from that curving hilt. In the darkness, it seemed to gleam with a clear light. Staring at its tiny stars, an odd feeling came over her as she was suddenly reminded of Vyrl's eyes.

I wonder if they have something to do with Valkire? His magic?

She looked closer at those barely visible sparks. But she dare not use the Wyrd Stone—even though its light would be as welcome as a coat filled with warmly buzzing flir bugs on a deep winter's night.

"There's more than enough to do the trick," she whispered, and brandished the little sword. "Let's try it. Which way to the Rim?"

"The dragon's eyes are keen," Mithorden said. "Let him guide you."

Melkion pointed toward the deeper shadows. "The Rim is that way."

Wrapping her hand tightly around *Weiryendel*'s hilt, she walked into the gloom.

"Careful now," Melkion hissed. "Go slow and I will show you."

Luthiel took one step and then another.

"Stop," the dragon said.

He pointed with his tail.

"There, do you see it?"

Luthiel focused her eyes on the space just beyond the tip of Melkion's tail. Nothing. Just darkness. She kept staring, holding the sword up next to Melkion's tail. A thin shade slightly darker than the gloom beyond slowly became visible.

She slashed it.

The crystal blade sliced through air and shadow with equal ease. For a moment, it seemed as though nothing had happened. Then the shadow parted like a ribbon sliced in two. It fell. It faded. And just before it struck ground it disappeared.

Luthiel breathed deep and took a few steps forward before slashing to clear the path again.

With Mithorden and Melkion guiding her, she sliced through the webs. The blade sang as it parted shadow and seemed to give a self-satisfied hum at the end of each swing. As she made her way deeper her relief slowly changed to fear. Some of the webs held mists. Soon they filled the air making it even more difficult to see. She dared not even breathe as she picked her way over animal carcasses and through mounds of spider spoor. Further and deeper she cut as the shadows grew and her tiny pool of light seemed about to be swallowed up.

Sometimes when she cut a shadow it would cling to her before fading. In those moments, she feared she was trapped. But the blade was true and no more than two cuts were needed for a strand. She concentrated on clearing the path, on making it large enough for Othalas, and on moving where Melkion and Mithorden guided. She'd lost all sense of direction and her only reassurance was the sorcerer's hand on her back and the dragon's voice in her ear. Then, she cut through a web and it fell away, leaving only black openness behind.

It took Luthiel's eyes a moment to adjust; for even elves and angels have difficulty seeing in utter darkness. Through the small opening, she could see shadow webs bending into a spiral—forming a great chamber that tapered into blackness. To Luthiel, it seemed she stared down a well and into a place that had lost all memory of light.

They made this in only a few days, she thought in dread.

It is said there are passes in the Drakken Spur, Ecthellien thought, *miles upon miles like this. No light has touched the earth there for three hundred years.*

Luthiel didn't know why at first, but she felt as though she were staring into a place of death and pain. Her eyes caught glimpses of wicked shapes hovering among bundles of shadow.

Melkion hissed softly and her sword gave off a low, angry, ringing as it vibrated against her palm.

Slowly, her eyes rolled back the shadows and she began to see them—spiders among bodies hanging in the darkness. It was terrible. It was something she didn't want to see.

She jerked her head away. But it was too late, the vision had burned itself into her mind.

"What did you see?" Mithorden whispered.

"You were right," Luthiel said. "We should never have come this way."

"Tell me!" Mithorden insisted.

Unable to speak, or even look, Luthiel grabbed his wrist and pulled him forward. Vaelros scrabbled up behind him.

They stood staring in silence.

"This is what they would do to us all," Mithorden whispered.

Luthiel still couldn't look. It was too terrible.

"You may as well see them," Melkion said. "Turning away doesn't change what's happened."

She nodded. Slowly, she raised her head.

There in that warren of shadow, strung up by the webs, were hundreds of elves. Those she could see were covered with blood. It filled their mouths till they choked, oozed from their skin in angry splotches, or seeped from their eyes, gumming them until they turned black. A few had burst and all that remained were dripping shreds of skin and pieces of bone.

There were spiders among them.

She could see one creeping toward an elf along a thin strand of shadow. As it approached, it unhinged its mouth and from out of it came a long, dripping tooth. The elf screamed as it drove the tooth into her body and began to devour her. A hissing sound issued from out of the spider. All the while, the elf's cries continued—slowly growing fainter and shriller. Then, the cries ended and an awful silence fell. The spider dumped the sagging bag of skin and bones that remained and made its way to another body.

Luthiel reeled and fell to her knees. She retched but nothing came up. Behind her, she could hear Othalas' low, feral growl. Melkion hissed and blew smoke. Mithorden gripped the hilt of his sword, eyebrows lowered in anger. Vaelros held a hand over his face and even Ecthellien looked troubled.

Her heartbeat pounded so loud she could hear it in her ears. She was at once enraged and terrified. Gathering her legs beneath her, she slid *Weiryendel* into its scabbard and lifted her bow. Her quiver was guiding an arrow to her hand before Mithorden noticed what she was doing.

"Luthiel! They'll see us!" he whispered.

"I can't let them do it," she said quietly as she notched the arrow.

The spider had reached another elf and was wrapping its legs about him. She drew the arrow. Mithorden put a hand on her shoulder.

"Do you think you can kill them all?" he said in a low voice. "For every one you see, there are at least ten more hidden away. You'd bring every one to us."

Luthiel aimed. The bow trembled. The spider unhinged its jaws. A tear ran down her face.

"I know how you must feel. But even if we could fight off every spider, the best we could give most of these elves is comfort and a swift death. Some might live, but most are already dead."

She let the bow drop slowly and turned her face away. Then the screaming began again.

Luthiel couldn't help herself. Tears of rage streamed down her face. That elf could have been a friend. It could have even been Leowin or Winowe. She wanted nothing more than to kill the terrible creatures. It made her question the vow she made just this morning. She shook her head against the thought. *No. This is wrong. Such cruel things don't deserve life.* All the tales of ruin she'd heard the night before came rushing back. She wondered if this is what happened to those who lived on Eledweil. She had the sinking feeling it was worse.

She turned her face to Ecthellien.

You were with Ingolith? she thought.

He nodded.

Were they like this?

He stood silent.

How could you be a part of it!?

I was mad, and very sick.

"I'll kill them if I can," she whispered, motioning through the narrow opening toward the Widdershae. There was a coldness in her voice she couldn't recognize. "If you ever do something like it, I'll kill you too."

The lights in Ecthellien's eyes swirled and then it was he who looked away. "I cannot change what I did," he said softly.

"Then you'll spend the rest of your life trying to make amends," she snapped.

"Luthiel, what are you doing?" Melkion hissed. "Standing here bickering will end us up with *them*." He pointed at the dangling elves with the tip of his tail. "Let's get out of here." His tail swished back and forth in agitation. Tiny blue flames rimmed the corners of his mouth and flickered in his nose. She'd never seen him so agitated. But, for the moment, her rage was far greater than her fear.

"We have to fight them *sometime*," she said.

"Now would be *suicide*," the dragon hissed. He seemed distracted. His head swung back and forth, eyes staring into the darkness. "They're close," he whispered. "Let's leave while we still can."

Mithorden and Vaelros both laid hands on her shoulders.

"You're right to be angry," Mithorden whispered. "But remember what we're trying to do."

Vaelros' hand tightened.

"Once we have the elves with us," he said, "then we can deal with these spiders."

Slowly, she returned both bow and arrow to her quiver. The wooden hands quietly put each in its proper place. She drew her arm across her eyes to clear the tears. Then, grudgingly, she nodded.

"We'd better start now," she said softly. "I don't want to stay in this larder one moment more than I must."

She pulled her hood over her head and was about to slip into the black chamber when there was a tremor in the shadow webs.

THE WYRD OF SAURLOLTH

"What was that?" she whispered.

Melkion stared at the webs. Mithorden gazed into the darkness at the chamber's far end.

The webs trembled again, this time jerking urgently.

"We stayed too long," Mithorden said.

Then, from the blackness at the chamber's end, there came two loud shrieks.

"*KAAAAREEK!*"

"*KAAAAREEK!*"

A chill wind blew down the chamber, through the small opening, and into her face. Clusters of lights appeared in the blackness and from it emerged two great spider legs, each the size of a small tree. Coming after the legs was a vast, pointed head, lit by clusters of eyes. Two were larger than the rest, green glowing and almond-shaped. Where ears might have been, a pair of spines protruded from its head. The body was a polished black beginning with the rounded point of a head, then narrowing into an hourglass waist before bulging again into a crescent abdomen. The forelegs tapered into tips like swords. It took Luthiel a moment to realize that, by some art, the great spider had fastened these weapons to itself. The black swords each ended in a barb and glistened with venom.

After it emerged from the darkness, it stopped, crossed the sword blades, then rubbed them together.

"*KAAAAREEK!*"

"*KAAAAREEK!*"

"It's Saurlolth!" Melkion hissed. "Queen of the Widdershae."

In a great rush the Widdershae surrounded their queen. There were hundreds and they came from everywhere. Some dropped down from the webs above. Others sprang out of burrows. Still others slipped out of the shadows.

"She's calling them for something," Vaelros said.

Then Luthiel saw ten elves hanging at the warren's center. Saurlolth stopped beneath them. Widdershae crowded close. Beneath Saurlolth were large bundles of shadow web and jagged symbols were on the ground in a ring around her. From what Luthiel could tell, they were the runes of her language— broken beyond her ability to understand. Something about their crookedness made her head ache. She turned away in disgust when she realized the symbols were made of bones, entrails, and caked blood.

Luthiel could feel the anger rising again. She guessed something even more terrible was about to happen. But she also knew now Mithorden was right. There was no way their tiny band could stop the hundreds of spiders gathered here. So Luthiel swallowed her anger and watched in horror as Saurlolth raised her forelimbs to scratch the air.

At first it seemed as if she were unwinding some invisible strand of thread. Then she stooped down and slashed one of the web bundles. From it rose a curl of mist. It grew and changed, making a web pattern. The mist-web rose and as it did, it drew in more mist—expanding beneath the prisoners who looked down on it, fear in their eyes. Then came lights. They shot from the bundle, rushing for open darkness. Saurlolth was too fast. As they fled, her legs worked and, one by one, she plucked them, threading each into her mist web.

Silence fell over the spiders as Saurlolth seemed to tense. Then she struck the lights. With each jab came a burst of glowing goo. Soon, the whole web dripped with it. Some of the elves moaned and lifted their hands to shield their eyes. In the glow, Luthiel could see the poison affected them less. A few even struggled—kicking, or swinging arms in desperation.

With a final push, Saurlolth gathered the web and shoved it up toward the elves. The web grew as it rose, then folded over them, covering them all. Moans turned into cries of alarm. For a moment, the light lingered. Then it faded and all was dark.

Luthiel couldn't see them. But she could hear noises. Shrieks changed. Growing thin. Turning to alarming rattles. No elf she knew could make such sounds. She jumped when she heard sharper noises coming from their throats—wet popping and hissing. Slowly, the darkness rolled back. The webs seemed drawn up inside them. Bodies twisted and grew, bursting clothes, ripping arms and legs end to end like paper shreds.

Something, she thought it was blood, fell off of them. Horrible snapping sounds—organs breaking and reforming, joints dislocating and relocating—filled the warren. It was as if some awful invisible hand had taken hold of them and molded their flesh as a child might mold clay. Black gloss appeared in splotches on the skin, then grew to cover them. New eyes opened in their heads. The arms split, thinned and moved backward. Legs came forward. The abdomen bulged and elongated.

They've become spiders.

As Luthiel watched in horror, Saurloth reared up and cut them down. No sooner did the new-made spiders hit ground than the others were on them. They swarmed over them, striking out with their forelimbs, scoring shells with fangs, torturing them into compliance. After about a minute of violence, the Widdershae who were once elves rose on beaten legs. They were horribly battered—bodies cut in a hundred places. A few were missing eyes. A tall Widdershae reared before them and snapped its forelegs like whips. The new Widdershae huddled together. But the large spider kept snapping its legs as it moved forward, driving them on. They scurried off into the shadows.

Luthiel let out the breath she didn't realize she was holding.

Mithorden turned to her. "We must go back *now*," he said.

Before Luthiel could even nod her reply, Othalas let out a fierce growl. There was a crash and when she turned around she saw the werewolf wrapped up in the legs of a Widdershae. The spider's teeth flashed. But Othalas rolled underneath the terror, clamping his great jaws over its head.

A shriek and then a crunching sound. Black fluid and spider eyes fell to the ground.

The spiders froze at the sounds. The queen turned, green eyes gleaming at them, then clapped her forelimbs together.

"Klingaklingkling!!!"

A moment later, a hundred Widdershae were scrambling toward them. But the queen sat still—eyes glaring in the darkness.

Though it seemed to Luthiel that the queen could see them, the other spiders were having trouble.

"Vvrrerrre itch itttt?" One rasped.

Luthiel drew her bow and let fly. The arrow spun wide, lodging in the shadows, and the spider, seeing her for the first time, scrambled toward her.

Remember what Hueron taught you! she thought desperately to herself.

She fumbled with her arrows as it drew close. Finally, her hand touched one lifting from her quiver and she snatched it. She missed the bowstring once, twice. The arrow rattled against the bow. In a surge of rage and fear, she willed her hand to move. At last, the arrow slid into place. She could see the spider— very near now. Pouncing from only thirty feet away. The fear of a moment before disappeared and a strange sense of calm came over her as she recalled her uncle's words.

"Breathe in steady as you draw in one motion,
   Eye to arrow tip,
   Arrow tip to target,
   Feather to lips—
   Kiss the feather as she flies."

She sighted down the shaft and into the spider's green eyes. Its movements seemed to slow as she aimed, drew, released. Her bowstring thrummed. The arrow flew. She could see the triangle pattern of its feathers glide away from her and toward the spider. Its path was smooth, its flight graceful. The arrow hung in the air for a moment between her and the spider. Then it seemed to leap away from her, plunging deep into the spider's head.

With a shriek, it crashed to the ground. The momentum carried it forward and she had to scramble away. Its legs twitched, wrapping around its body. Then it was still.

The death only seemed to anger the others. They shrieked and twittered and ran faster.

"We must go back!" Mithorden cried. He grabbed her, pulling her headlong through the hole.

Othalas growled in answer and, spinning around, bound back down the path Luthiel had cut through the shadows.

Mithorden pushed Luthiel ahead of him and they scrambled over the still twitching body of the dead Widdershae. A great stench rose up from inside the creature and by the time Luthiel managed to scramble across it she was gagging and covered in its blood.

"Run!" Mithorden cried. "Back to the open wood!"

Luthiel spun, running as fast as she could to catch up with Vaelros who was jogging, sword in hand, behind Ecthellien. The Vyrl raised his horn letting out a loud peal. After another few strides he sounded the horn again. Its echoes rang out and, far away, she thought she heard an answer.

She ran hard, glancing over her shoulder to make certain Mithorden was still behind her. Because of the magic, she could only see his sword flashing around and the indistinct blur of his movements.

The spiders were close behind and they made it no further than the end of the tunnel before another three had caught them. One was scrambling toward Mithorden when Luthiel let an arrow fly.

"*Cauth!*" Mithorden cried, throwing his hand high. And no sooner had the arrow left her bow than it burst into brilliant light. For an instant she was blinded and she stumbled backward, shielding her eyes. But through her fingers she could see the arrow as it flew from her. It gleamed like a star and from it hot sparks fell. The heat was so great that the feathers had already burst into flame and the arrow left a trail of blue smoke along the path of its flight. Then it struck among the spider's legs. The head showered sparks and smoked for an instant before flaring as the monster caught flame. With a scream it lurched into the spider behind it. Their bodies merged, legs flailing, mad teeth flashing. Over and over they rolled; one struggled to disengage from the other who, in its fear, only clung tighter. Soon they were both covered in bright sparks and burning. They fled, but it only fanned the flames.

The third spider hung back, lurking behind the webs. They could see its green eyes watching them.

They turned to run again. Luthiel sprinted, breathing heavy and then had to scramble as she ran headlong into Vaelros.

"It's the werewolf! He's stuck!" he cried.

Luthiel rushed forward to find Othalas bound up in a mass of spider webs.

"They're new!" he growled. "Didn't see them soon enough."

Sliding *Weiryendel* from her belt, she made hasty work of the webs. Her hands trembled, and she kept glancing over her shoulder. But within a few moments, she was finished and the great wolf bounded free.

"Be more careful!" she scolded.

"Harrumph! *You* be more careful," He panted in between great strides. "We might be past them—if it weren't for your temper!"

It stung but Luthiel was too afraid of the spiders to be cowed.

"Might be!? Might be that we'd have been found as we tried. *She saw us!*"

Othalas growled again, but didn't reply.

Afraid that someone might stumble into a web, she ran with *Weiryendel* in her hand and, wherever she could, she cut trapped creatures free. Many simply fell to the ground with wet plopping sounds. Some, though, possessed enough life to stagger for freedom. Her heart sang when she saw their eyes fill with hope. *Some may live now,* she thought. But her thoughts always returned to the elves.

Many more times, Luthiel had to cut herself or her companions from the shadow webs. Each time the spiders came closer. She could hear them scrambling behind and around them.

Othalas slowed down to let her catch up.

"Get on," he snapped.

She sheathed her sword and was putting her hands on his flank when she noticed the bite marks. They were side by side pits in his neck. Black stuff seeped from them and his teeth were already caked with red.

"You're hurt," she said.

"It's nothing," he growled. "Now get on."

She grabbed fistfuls of his hair, pulling herself up. They were starting to get clear of the webs. But they still had to move with care. All around, Luthiel could see the green eyes of spiders. She readied an arrow but held onto it, waiting for a clear shot.

Ecthellien ran beside her, blowing his horn. The answering peals were much closer now and flocks of crows circled above them. In the distance, Luthiel could see flickering lights. It reminded her of sunlight reflecting off of water. But these lights were above and coming closer.

Strange, she thought, wondering what they were.

Vaelros and Mithorden ran behind. Both held naked swords in their hands. Occasionally, one or the other would glance nervously into the shadows.

Finally, they came to a clearing. The trees of the Vale rose before them. Its mists swirled up in columns and through the wood she could see Miruvoir sparkling. Though some Shadow Webs remained, they were thin and sunslight filled the glade. The chill had lessened and a fresh wind blew about her. She breathed deep. For a moment, Luthiel thought they'd escaped.

Then the spiders made their attack. Scrambling up through the trees or lunging across the earth in great bounds, the spiders rushed toward them. Three pounced upon Vaelros from the darkness. One wrapped a shadow around his legs. A second beat him to the ground with its forelegs. A third rushed in with dark fangs flashing. Together they dragged Vaelros back toward the webs.

Not an instant later, Mithorden was there, his sword gleaming in the light of Oerin's Eye. It leapt through the air in a great arc. There was a shriek. One of the great spider's heads rolled free.

From beneath the spiders a cry emerged.

"Luthiel! Luthiel!"

It was Vaelros and he sprang to his feet with such ferocity that the spiders who held him stumbled back. In one hand, he held his Wyrd Stone which flickered with orange fire. A tongue of it shot out, setting the shadow at his legs aflame. At the same time, his black sword snaked through the air. A second spider crumpled, two legs in ruin. The third scrambled away into the shadows.

But now the danger had grown. For no sooner was the one group of spiders defeated than a second and much larger one rushed upon them. In a glance, Luthiel saw ten leaders, but behind them and everywhere in the woods, she could see their black shapes.

Frantic, she drew her bow, took a shot, missed. In a rush, she let fly again and struck one through the gut. It stumbled and fell to the ground, then kept dragging itself toward her on three working legs. The spider behind it leapt over its struggling body and lunged for Luthiel. Othalas caught the beast in his mouth. There was a crunching sound and the great wolf shook the spider like a toy before tossing it to the ground where it crumpled and lay still. But another had seen Luthiel and came at her. She saw it too late and held an arrow before her in a vain attempt to ward it off. It grasped a shadow between its legs and she knew it would snatch her up if it could.

Ecthellien leapt between her and the spider. Sword held high, in both hands, he brought it down on the spider with enough force to knock the beast to its belly. Its shell collapsed like an egg under a boot and a rush of black liquid spilled from its mouth.

They turned and formed themselves into a rough crescent. Luthiel and Othalas stood at its center with Mithorden and Vaelros to their left and Ecthellien to their right. Melkion had taken flight and spat fire at any who came near. Already two lay on the ground, their heads burning.

The spiders gathered into two large mobs. One was rushing them en masse as the other moved behind them. Luthiel drew her arrow.

Before she could aim, Mithorden let out a great bellow. *Soris!* he cried. There was a blinding flash of light and a shower of sparks seemed to rain down from Oerin's Eye and onto the spiders. They screamed as the sparks alighted upon them, burning holes into their shells or lighting fire to their legs. Great billows of smoke and a terrible reek rose from the burning creatures. The spiders fell to the ground, pulled legs into bodies and grew still. The fume stung Luthiel's eyes; the stench made her choke.

The rest, cowed for the moment by the ferocity of their quarry, melted back into the woods. They were still near enough for Luthiel to hear their pained shrieks and furious chittering.

Mithorden grabbed Vaelros by the elbow.

"Hurry!" he cried. "They'll soon return!"

Vaelros was quick to cover his shoulder with his cloak but Luthiel could see, in places, where his armor had broken. Blood and a black fluid oozed out of the holes.

"You're bitten!" Luthiel cried.

"Nothing to do about it now," he said through clenched teeth. "Come on, let's get out of here." He drew a pained breath and started jogging toward the open forest. The shadow at his legs snapped in half as it burned.

Ecthellien ran up beside him and grabbed his arm to help him move faster.

They rushed down a long slope and into open forest. The webs faded behind them. Still Luthiel thought she could see black shapes creeping along the ground or inching up the trunks of trees. Except for these, most hung back, lurking among the shadows. An angry clamor rose from the darkness. From the sound Luthiel guessed that spiders were gathering for another attack and in far greater numbers than before.

A horn rang out nearby and Ecthellien answered with a peal of his own.

Mounted on their terrible horses, Elshael and Ahmberen broke through the woodline. Beside them loped Gormtoth. As he ran, his feet impacted the earth, leaving a trail of smoking holes behind him.

A column of grendilo followed. They bore spears or greatswords. Luthiel was astonished by how rapidly they could move on one leg. With their narrow whip bodies covered in strange, spiked armor, they looked fierce, flowing over the land like an army of thorns.

Among the grendilo strode giants. On their hips they carried barrels of burning pitch and in each hand was a spear with a flaming head.

The light in the sky grew. It flickered vaguely through the mists, turning them yellow and orange. She began to make out forms like a thousand candle flames flying low over the treetops.

They were birds! Birds with flames for wings! Each bird was large—about the size of an eagle. Their bodies were covered in green shaded scales the shape and size of feathers. From their shoulders erupted membranous wings that blazed with fire. They had noble faces and hooked black beaks. The only true feathers were the azure crests at their heads.

They rushed low over the wood casting wild light and dancing shadow.

At first sight of the fiery birds, a great shrieking rose up from the spiders. Then, all grew silent. They were gone—melting back into the safety of their shadow webs.

Luthiel felt a wave of relief rush over her.

"It's going to be all right now," she whispered to Othalas, slapping him on the neck.

Othalas growled his reply.

She glanced at his wound, but did what she could to hide her concern.

The werewolf bounded toward the Vyrl.

"You were almost too late," he growled.

"We came as soon as we could," Elshael said, having to look twice to see through the spell. "We'd moved as far along your path as we dared and when we heard Ecthellien's horn, we rushed in toward the shadows."

"You're very fortunate," Ahmberen said.

Luthiel's face flushed with shame and anger. "It was my decision. I was wrong," she said.

Mithorden looked up at her with fierce eyes. "Now the only way is Cauthraus."

Luthiel nodded. But as she did, a deep and unreasoning fear took hold of her. She wanted to say something but her mouth didn't seem to work.

"If we are to have any hope of making the journey, we must leave at once," Mithorden said. He turned to the werewolf. "Can you carry three of us?"

"This girl only counts for half."

"Then you should have no trouble managing with Ecthellien and me too."

Othalas looked at the sorcerer and, for a moment, Luthiel thought she saw doubt in those great yellow eyes. Her mouth moved but nothing came out. *There must be some other way.* But there wasn't and she found herself faced with a terrible reality.

I'm going to Cauthraus. In her mind, she could see its burning face like a vast red eye. A tremor of fear ran through her and she felt her skin grow hot despite the day's pleasant coolness. Her breathing quickened, but she couldn't seem to get enough air. *Why am I so afraid?*

"I'll manage," Othalas growled.

"I'm coming," Vaelros said through clenched teeth. He was leaning against a tree and it seemed to take nearly all of his effort to stand.

Luthiel looked at him with concern. He'd seemed strong only moments before.

"Vaelros, you're hurt," she said. "The poison—"

"I'm fine! The potion!" he snapped.

"It may save your life, but you must get to bed immediately," Elshael said. "Widder poison is deadly."

Vaelros opened his hand. In it was his Wyrd Stone.

"The Stone will keep me safe."

"No," Mithorden said. "The poison will hurt you in dreams or in life. Listen to Luthiel. Rest. We will return for you."

Vaelros looked first at Mithorden, then at Luthiel. There was a too-strong intensity in his eyes. "I don't matter."

She felt a pang in her chest as she remembered the owl. *He'd die for me too! What would I do if someone else died for me!?* "Vaelros, listen to me," she said. "I want you to stay here."

Vaelros slid down the tree to the ground. He made a second effort to stand, but failed. A grendilo helped him up. When he finally stood, Luthiel could see blood running from his nose.

"I'm sorry, lady. I convinced you."

"It was my choice. My failure." She looked away, wondering if she could go on. "We haven't even left the Vale and already there's so much violence." Vaelros shook his head. He was about to say something. Struggling to maintain her sense of calm, she quieted him with a gesture. "Say you will stay with the Vyrl."

"If anything happens to you—"

"That's enough," she said, with almost too much force. "Othalas, Mithorden, and Ecthellien are coming."

Vaelros looked as if he might argue. Then, he grimaced and clutched at his shoulder. When the pain passed, he nodded.

"I will stay," he said at last.

Luthiel breathed a sigh of relief. Only an instant later, the worry came flooding back. She could see his eyes growing more bloodshot by the moment. His tongue was unnaturally red and little flecks of blood appeared under his finger nails. It was uncanny how fast the changes were coming over him and she wondered if he'd live.

"Next time we meet, I hope to see you well," she said in the strongest, most hopeful, voice she could muster.

Despite the pain that was taking an ever stronger hold on him, Vaelros could tell Luthiel wavered on the verge of control. He watched her fists involuntarily clench and unclench as she prepared herself for the dangers that lay ahead. He wondered if it would all be too much for this fifteen-year-old girl. She'd surprised him before and, as the pain slowly overwhelmed him, he hoped she would again.

"And I you," he replied.

There was something in the way he said it that made her laugh nervously. Vaelros nodded and, with a grunt of suppressed agony, held his sword up.

"May your feet always walk in the light of two suns."

Luthiel's breath caught for a moment as she remembered Vanye's salute.

"May the moonshadow never again fall upon you," she whispered.

THE LILANI

"Are you finished?" Othalas growled.

"Yes," Luthiel whispered.

"Then get that sorcerer and Vyrl over here!"

Mithorden heard the werewolf and climbed up behind Luthiel. Ecthellien soon followed.

"Are you ready?" the werewolf growled.

"Yes," Luthiel said.

"Farewell, Luthiel," Vaelros said.

"And you, Vaelros," she replied.

The Vyrl, grendilo and giants saluted them as Othalas bounded through their ranks. As they rode away and into the open wood Ecthellien sounded his horn—once, twice, three times. Three peals from Elshael's horn rang out in reply.

Othalas loped through the forest. Trees flashed by. Soon, they cleared the woodline and were running along the shore of Miruvoir. Its waters sparkled with the light of Soelee-set. On the far shore mists gathered in great billows, piling up against the Rim.

"Mithorden," Luthiel said as they came within sight of Ottomnos.

"Yes?" the sorcerer replied.

"You're certain about Cauthraus?"

"As certain as a sorcerer can be. We lost a few hours. We must hurry but we should still have time."

Luthiel looked at the bite mark on Othalas' shoulder and shivered.

And what of the wolf's hurts? If he can't make the journey—what then? She didn't want to say it aloud. She didn't want to let the werewolf hear her doubts.

Let's not think of such things, Ecthellien replied. *The werewolf is strong. He will not fail.*

Despite Mithorden and Ecthellien's assurance, she felt doubt. "I wish there was some other way."

Mithorden nodded silently. "As do I," he said. "But there's none I know of."

"Nor I," said Ecthellien.

"I don't know why. But I dread it," she said.

"The red moon claims wary and unwary alike. It is a very dangerous place," Mithorden said. "I wish I knew a safer road. But I think we just escaped from far greater danger."

"I hope you're right," Luthiel said.

They continued on in silence until they rode through Ottomnos' gaping gates. Rendillo was waiting for them in the courtyard. Before him lay a pile of bags.

"Rendillo!" Luthiel called, surprised by how happy she was to see the grendilo. Slipping off Othalas' back, she rushed up to him.

"Lady," he said with a bow. "The Khoraz told of your return. I thought it would be best to bring your supplies."

He had extra water skins ready. These he slung over Othalas' back. Then, he gave them each three small pouches full of crystals.

"What's this?" Luthiel asked.

"Salt," Rendillo said. "You'll need it on Cauthraus. It'll be very hot. If you eat this, it will keep you from losing water too fast." He held one up to her. "Place it on your tongue," he said.

She did as he instructed. The salt tingled as it dissolved and the taste was unpleasant. She washed it down with a big gulp from her waterskin.

"Eat one every hour and it will help you. It should keep you feeling thirsty. But even if you don't, keep drinking water. You'll lose it as fast as you can drink it."

She nodded as he tucked the pouch into her belt.

"Is it really so hot on Cauthraus?"

"From what I know, it is hotter than even the deserts in the far south past Rimwold and the ebbs of Felduwaith."

"Ecthellien says the air burns," she said with a glance to the Vyrl.

"When Soelee rises," Rendillo replied with a nod.

"But why is it so hot? It is no closer to Soelee than Oesha. And why does it burn?"

"It is said that the air of Cauthraus is much thicker. It traps the warmth. And something in the air burns when exposed to great heat or flame. In some places where the ground is hot or rich with the caustic metal—*Cauthrim*—there is always fire."

Luthiel tried to imagine but could not.

"Also, the moon turns much slower than Oesha. So the day there lasts for a hundred of ours. The heat and fires build until sunset. But the air is so thick that even in the long night it doesn't get much colder than early springtime here."

Rendillo gave her a bag filled with narrow wads of soft paper.

"What's this for?"

"Nosebleeds. The air causes nosebleeds."

"What a terrible place!" Luthiel said.

Rendillo nodded.

Then he seemed to notice Othalas' bite marks.

"You're bitten," he said to the werewolf.

"What of it?" Othalas snapped.

The grendilo drew back from the werewolf. Rummaging among his bags, he pulled out a vial of black liquid.

"Here, this will help," Rendillo replied.

"I don't need your potions," the werewolf growled.

Undeterred, the grendilo moved closer, holding the vial up to the great wolf's mouth.

After a few more angry mutterings, the werewolf finally opened his mouth and let Rendillo pour antidote onto his tongue.

The wolf coughed and licked at his jowls.

"Fouler than the poison, I think."

"You might not feel the same way in a few hours," Rendillo replied. "Here," he said, handing the vial to Luthiel. He motioned with his hand for her to lean closer.

"If he starts to bleed, give him more of this," he whispered. "But only use one vial at a time. Understand?"

Luthiel nodded. She wanted to ask him if he thought Othalas could make it. But she kept quiet fearing the wolf, who stood only a few feet away, might overhear her.

"I understand," she said.

"Best wishes, lady, masters," he said with a bow.

"Thank you again, Rendillo," she replied, letting Ecthellien help her back onto the werewolf.

Then Othalas was walking again, padding silently into the charred glass fortress. Othalas' powerful body rippled beneath her. With each step, her tender muscles throbbed and she was reminded of her hurts at the hands of Vyrl only days before.

I am fortunate not to have suffered more, she thought as she glanced again at the bite on Othalas' shoulder.

The great corridor wound deeper, spiraling down into bedrock. Mists rolled up from somewhere far below like smoke rising in the throat of a dragon. It took Luthiel only a few moments to realize that they were heading toward the springs.

How do you feel? Ecthellien thought.

Achy. Tired. Afraid, she replied.

Conserve your strength as best you can.

They rode on in silence for a few moments.

"Is the Lilani near the baths?" she said.

"It is among them, a special pool separated from the rest," Mithorden said.

They passed the lighted area and then traveled deeper. Luthiel touched her finger to her forehead and blinked her eyes. Starlight bloomed from her *Netherduel* and flooded into the chamber, reflecting off the water and glistening upon the walls. Farther down the passageway, she could see light flickering off the springs. Soon, they were riding through the pools, making their way deeper into the caves beneath Ottomnos. Othalas waded in and soon steaming water was lapping against her legs.

"Isn't it dangerous, having a Lilani beneath your castle?" she asked.

"It only opens from this side. Those on Cauthraus can't use it to come here," Othalas growled. His voice was tense. To Luthiel, it sounded as if he were in great pain.

"Ah," she said hoping all the while that the wolf's strength would hold. "But doesn't that mean we can't return once we're there?"

"Once we go through, there's no coming back the same way," the werewolf growled.

They continued through the water, coming to an island surrounded by springs. At the island's center was a bubbling pool that shone with red light. The light had no apparent source, seeming to come from the water itself. They came to a halt directly above the pool.

"Have you ever used a Lilani?" Mithorden asked.

"No," Luthiel replied.

"Do you know how they work?"

"I only know they are connections between two distant places."

"That's mostly right. The moons and Oesha itself are criss-crossed with lines of energy. In these places Wyrd is stronger, flowing like rivers from point to point. Sometimes the river is so strong it will push through into our world. In these places, Lilani form. You can use them to travel to distant places that are in the direction of the Wyrd's flow. All you need do is step into the stream."

Luthiel nodded. "I understand." Even as she said the words, she wasn't certain she did and she wondered where all the Wyrd came from. Why did it emerge here beneath Ottomnos? If you mapped all the flows what would you find? Would they all eventually lead to some hidden place? *Now I'm thinking like Leowin,* she chided herself even as she wished she had time to ask her questions.

"You'll feel cold at first," The sorcerer continued. "Next comes disorientation. It might make you a little sick. But it's over soon. Travel happens in an instant."

"All right," she said.

Despite her outward calm, her heart was pounding in her throat. It didn't seem natural to travel to a place so far away in so little time. All her life she had gazed on the moon Cauthraus. Now, in little less than an instant, she would set foot there. She'd heard tales of Lilani and of great travelers using them to journey to the moons or to the other side of Oesha. But she didn't consider herself to be one of them.

What talent have I for survival and adventure? she thought to herself.

More than most, Ecthellien replied.

Startled by the sudden intrusion of his thoughts, she jumped.

"Are you well?" Mithorden asked, giving her a concerned look.

"Yes," she replied. "It's nothing."

Mithorden nodded, then dismounted, walking over to the pool. Rolling up his sleeve, he stretched out a hand and lowered it so it barely touched the red surface. His eyes closed and he murmured in concentration.

What's he doing? She thought to Ecthellien.

Looking through the pool to see if there's anything on the other side, the Vyrl replied.

Luthiel felt her muscles tense at the Vyrl's thoughts. She hadn't considered that something may be waiting in ambush for them.

Finally, Mithorden stood up. "It's clear," he said with a nod to Ecthellien. Then he climbed onto Othalas' back and spoke in a low voice to the great wolf.

Othalas started into the water with a growl. When it touched her legs, she gasped at the cold. It felt close to freezing and was much thicker than normal water. Any movement she made met resistance. It sucked at her legs. Despite its thickness, there was a noticeable current pulling slow but strong toward the Lilani's center. Soon the frigid water was rising up to her waist.

She looked down and realized she couldn't see her legs. She couldn't *feel* them either. It was as if they didn't exist. A panic rushed through her as the waters rose to her waist, chest, neck.

It's devouring me!

But seeing no way to escape without legs, hips or stomach, she sat there atop a disappearing Othalas, sinking into the Lilani. As the waters advanced up her body, she lifted her arms above her head.

"Don't worry," Melkion said. "You're going to be fine. It's easier if you go all at once."

With that, he leapt off her shoulder, plunging himself full-bodied into the water.

But Luthiel didn't hear him. The panic within her was overtaking her reason and she struggled to escape. Then the waters rose over her head and she felt nothing.

THE AIR BURNS

There came a jolt and a feeling of spinning round and round at impossible speed. Almost as soon as the terrible spinning had begun it stopped with another jolt. An instant later, her head broke the water and she was rising out of a pool at the center of a rocky hill top. The first thing she saw was an endless expanse of sky. To her left, one horizon burned with a hellish glow. On her right, storm clouds ran away toward the night. The storms marched off on legs of lightning, their tops rimmed with violet.

Hot wind gusted out of the red horizon, blasting into her left side. It swept past her—rushing away toward the storms. On it, she could smell smoke and burning life. Wispy things blew about her. One stuck to her cheek. She pulled it away, looked down, and saw a flower petal. When she looked up again, they had risen completely out of the pool. Othalas stepped out, claws clicking on hard rock.

She gazed out at the land around her. Before them a mountain rose up. Its top, a great gaping maw, vomited a cloud of smoke and fire. The cloud swirled into the sky. Up and up it climbed, spreading into a roof of yellow, orange, and black. Fire seemed to flow through the smoke like lightning. Awful and beautiful at the same time, it meandered and swelled, seeming to claw at the stars. She stared for several heartbeats before tearing her eyes away. When she finally did, she saw rivers rushing through the landscape, winding away from beneath the storms. All about her, plants and animals floated and flew, rolled and skittered. Plants were brown, red, or yellow—possessing none of the greens of Mother Oesha. Animals all seemed hard and hairless with skin like gravel. Those who couldn't escape gave up their leaves, seed, and tiny eggs to the hot wind. All fled in the same direction—toward night.

Mithorden looked left, his face lit up by the fiery glow. "Soelee has yet to rise but already the eastern sky burns."

She turned, following Mithorden's gaze. A wind like air blowing from an open oven blasted her face. She choked. That oven was all the eastern sky and in the distance, she saw a rim of tiny red feathers and cloudy puffs marching across the edge of the world.

"Still far away," the sorcerer said.

She took another breath and choked again. The air was too thick, too hot to breathe. She tried to take shallower breaths and after a few tentative tries, was able to hold back the choking. Still her lungs felt heavy. Her chest burned and her limbs tingled with strain even though she was only sitting on Othalas' back. Sweat started to flow down her brow, into her eyes, over her nose—falling off in large drops.

It is worse than I imagined, she thought.

Ecthellien handed her a dripping cloth.

Tie this over your mouth and nose. It should help.

She did as Ecthellien instructed and the burning sensation in her throat and chest subsided a little.

Mithorden also tied a wet rag over his face.

"Your lights—it may not be wise to show them here," the sorcerer said. His voice sounded muffled from beneath the cloth.

He was right. They must move through the land like ghosts. There were trolls here and worse things, or so Gormtoth said. She raised her finger to her forehead and blinked her eyes. The starlight faded and the harsh light seemed to creep closer.

"Drink water whenever you can," Mithorden said. "The road will be hot and hard—hotter and harder as we near its end. Are you ready?"

She nodded.

"I'm ready," she whispered. But she didn't feel ready. The caustic air seeped through cracks in the rag—stinging her tongue and the roof of her mouth. She choked, cursing herself for speaking.

Talk only when you must, Ecthellien thought.

Let's start, she thought. *I don't want to stay here one moment more than I have to.*

Without another thought, Othalas turned from the Lilani and wound his way down the rough path that led from the high outcropping. Once they reached the valley floor, he broke into a run. His great muscles moved like a wave rolling beneath her. She hung on. But her arms and hands were already beginning to fatigue. She didn't know how she was going to keep it up for the next half-day or more.

They burst out onto the plain with firewind in their faces. Othalas' tongue hung out—a splash of red among the black. Melkion launched himself from her shoulder and flew before them, flapping his gossamer wings through air rippling with heat.

To their left, a ridgeline fell steadily into plains revealing another expanse of sky. Luthiel stared in awe at the vast horizon before her, its tiny tongues of flame hugging the world's edge, casting all in a pale glow. The dim light flickered beneath an orb of pitch squatting above the horizon. It was black and deep red. Like a ball of iron stained with old blood.

Despite the heat, Luthiel shivered.

Gorothoth.

She quailed and buried her face into Othalas' fur.

Can it see me? she thought, remembering the black mote in the sky. *Does it know I have the Stone?*

But she felt no cold finger probing through the heat and, slowly, she raised her head from Othalas' back. The black moon was still there, terrible and dark. Yet whatever wakefulness it possessed when she'd used her Stone before was gone. She glanced at the sorcerer, wondering why he hadn't warned her. He, too, was staring at the black moon. Perhaps he didn't remember it would still be in the sky. Then she realized it was *rising.*

On Oesha the black moon comes with chill, the Vyrl thought. *Here it comes with burning.*

It was difficult for her to grasp. She'd always associated the black moon with things dark and cold. It came first at Summerdark—appearing for only a few hours before setting. Then it returned, weeks later, for just a few days as summer failed. By late autumn, it was a constant feature in the sky. A chill fell over all lands and darkness ate up the stars. Day by day, it deepened. Until everywhere the world lay dim and frozen.

But here the black moon was rising before the coming of the greater sun. A sun that, on this world, brought fire and death instead of the life-warmth of summer.

She wondered if this was a world that loved the gentle light of Oerin's Eye.

It must be enough in the thick air. Here, Soelee is the tyrant.

They rode on into the heat. Occasionally, they would come across animals—wild packs of black-skinned dogs or strange herd-beasts with three horns rising from their heads. Once, they came within sight of a tribe of trolls. All stopped and stared at them, watching dumbfounded or jeering as they rode on toward the blazing horizon.

They must think we are mad, she thought.

Everything here flees the fire, Ecthellien replied. *They know they must keep moving toward night to escape it.*

What happens to those who cannot keep up?

They fall behind and are left to thirst and fire, Ecthellien thought.

It is awful, she thought.

They rode on. The land flashed by as the fires ahead slowly grew. After a while, the burning in Luthiel's hands and arms became too much. She couldn't hold on to Othalas any longer.

Enough! Enough! Let's stop for a short while, she thought.

Tired so soon?

I am. And if you want me to stay atop this wolf, then you'd better let me take my rest.

"Othalas, stop, Luthiel needs to rest a moment," Ecthellien said.

The wolf snorted, then jogged behind a rock outcropping so Luthiel could sit in the shade. His body trembled as he lay down behind the rock and his breath came out in hoarse pants. Luthiel felt too weak to move but forced herself to climb off the wolf's back. Walking around his front she looked at him.

His tongue and teeth were caked in blood, and with each pant ropes of red and black dripped from his mouth.

Luthiel stumbled back.

"Not pretty is it?" Othalas growled.

Luthiel shook her head. "No, it's not so bad," she said, doing her best to reassure him.

"You're a wretched liar," the wolf said around a cough.

She fumbled with the vial of antidote. "Here take some more of this. Rendillo said it would help."

"Stupid grendilo and his potions," the wolf snapped. Despite his complaints, he let Luthiel give him more of the foul stuff. The wolf choked the antidote down and with each cough more blood rose into his mouth. It dripped from his tongue until the ground in front of him was covered with red splotches.

He can't continue like this, she thought.

He will and he must, Ecthellien replied.

Mithorden noticed her concerned look and put a hand on her shoulder. "Don't worry," he whispered. "The wolf is strong." But when he glanced back at the wolf, she could see the fear in his eyes.

Realizing it was better for Othalas if they pressed on soon, she decided to make do with only a little rest. Taking out one of her waterskins, she took several long drinks before eating another one of Rendillo's salt crystals. She grabbed a fistful of nuts and ate what she could. The hot air ruined both the food's taste and her appetite. But she knew she must eat something to sustain herself on the long journey.

Then she climbed onto Othalas' back and they were running out over the low hills and into the blazing horizon. Before them, the black moon lorded over a ruined waste. Everywhere Luthiel looked she saw shriveled plants. Withered orange grasses, bushes heavy with wilted leaves and thorns, and strange plants that looked like yellow pine cones growing straight up out of the ground rushed past her. As they journeyed, even these became sparse, giving way to a heat-blasted deadland. Luthiel gripped Othalas with all of her strength. She didn't look into the burning horizon or the land that was rushing by on either side. She only concentrated, trying to force her muscles to work.

Her nose began to bleed. First a trickle and then a deep, rich, flow ran from her nose, onto her lips and down her chin. She could taste blood in her mouth as well. She pulled the nose-plugs from her pouch and stuffed them in. But now she was forced to breathe through her mouth. Her throat and lungs burned all the more, growing rawer with each breath.

Othalas' breathing became labored as they continued, and twice he stopped in his tracks to vomit red and black upon the ground. At these times, she fed him more of the antidote which the wolf choked down even as he complained.

Time was difficult to measure. If the moons moved in the sky, it was too little for Luthiel to notice. Her world became one of burning heat and breath, of aching muscles, and of bleeding. The heat was unbearable and sweat flowed over her body in a torrent. She drank water continuously but she couldn't quench her thirst. The salt stung her mouth and throat but she forced herself to eat it—noticing when she didn't she began to feel dizzy and her heart raced in her chest. Her skin became red and irritated in patches, splotching in the heat and the caustic air. She wondered how anything survived in this place.

The creatures here must be made of tougher stock than elves or anything else on Oesha, she thought.

Trolls were such creatures. Troll-skin was as thick as leather and studded with bits of bone and gristle, giving it the consistency of gravel. If they took a cut or even lost a limb, it would grow back over time. The only sure way to kill a troll was to burn it in white-hot fire.

This world must be filled with things as hardy as a troll, she thought.

For all she and Othalas suffered Ecthellien and Mithorden seemed implacable and the dragon untouched.

"They are made of stouter stuff than you or I. No vapor or venom, not even fire will harm a dragon," Mithorden had said.

Other than the odd drop of blood on the mouth or nose, neither sorcerer nor Vyrl showed any signs of fatigue. It embarrassed Luthiel that she was in so much pain. The hot, caustic air took a terrible toll. Parts of her body were still recovering from her ordeals. The Vyrl, the Dreaming, the spiders' ambush and almost twenty hours of journeying added to her pain.

She held on, pushing herself as hard as she was able, and slowly the fires on the horizon grew until they become tall tails of flame spreading up and up. It seemed to Luthiel that she stared into a storm front where the clouds were made of red pillars of fire that climbed to the very roof of the sky. The flames fanned out as they rose—blanketing the blue in roiling yellow and red.

The fires drew nearer, until when she looked up, it seemed they had covered a quarter of all the sky.

She felt as though she were standing in a pottery oven. Two of her water skins were already empty and she was halfway through the third with only one full skin left. Looking again at the flames, she hoped fervently that they were nearing the far Lilani.

Suddenly, Othalas stumbled, then vomited again onto the ground. She dismounted and emptied her full waterskin into his mouth. The wolf's legs collapsed beneath him and he fell. The corners of his eyes were caked with blood and long ropes of it oozed from his mouth. She had used up the rest of her antidote or she would have given him more. He blinked his eyes. But to her, he seemed both confused and angry. He snarled at Melkion as the dragon flew by.

"I don't think he can hold out much longer," she said, glancing at Ecthellien and Mithorden. "The poison is tearing him apart. Can't you see—he's killing himself to carry us."

Then, the werewolf's eyes seemed to clear.

"Stupid elf," he growled. "What do you know of the strength of werewolves?"

He stood and shook himself. But his legs trembled beneath him.

"You're shaking!" Luthiel cried.

"So would you if you'd run three hundred miles, even without a burden!" He coughed and more blood came up. Luthiel was splattered by it. She was terrified by the amount coming from him. It permeated the air, making him smell like a slaughterhouse.

"But—"

"Get on!" he growled. "We've not much further to go. Then I can rest while this silly spider venom runs its course."

More blood was flowing from his mouth. But she did as he said. She couldn't see how he was still standing, much less maintaining the strength to run. Yet, as soon as she, Ecthellien, and Mithorden had clambered onto his back, he sprang forward, shooting like a bolt toward the towering flames.

"Don't worry!" Ecthellien cried. "The strength of werewolves is the strength of life itself. If anything can survive harm it is Othalas."

Luthiel nodded but she feared for the great wolf nonetheless. She wrapped her arms around his broad neck and whispered into his ear.

"Come on! You can make it!"

But tears ran down her cheeks. It seemed to her, with each choking gasp, the great wolf was dying.

Still he ran and the fires before them grew until the sky was covered in flame. The light and heat were so intense that she was forced to hide her face from it. Blisters formed on the tips of her fingers, nose and cheeks. Smoke billowed from the land around her and she choked on its stink. The sound of burning grew until it filled her ears with its endless roar. Flames sprang up. At first, there were only a few. Then more and more until Othalas ran side to side around long walls of dancing fire. Thin wisps of smoke rose from their clothes and off of Othalas's fur.

"The fires are upon us!" she yelled.

"We have a few minutes more!" Mithorden cried. "We're very close."

He frowned and his eyes scanned the landscape.

"There!" he said, pointing toward a tower of rock a half mile distant.

Othalas sprinted for the rock. But as they neared it, Luthiel's heart froze, for she saw draped along the shoulder of that grim spire a massive bulk in the shape of a serpent.

Dragon at the Gate

Luthiel watched on, entranced. This was no wyrmling like the one sitting on her shoulder. Here was a great dragon vast as the spire on which it rested. She'd heard many tales of the great dragons. Stories told to her in the deep winter by flir-bug glow. Born of Wyrd itself, growing larger by sleeping, the dragons were rumored to live forever unless killed by some violence. As the ages passed they were said to became awesome as dreams, terrible as nightmares. Lorethain had once told her of their deep kinship with the forces of air, earth, water and fire. Hueron had spoken of how they could fly and swim, eat rock and breathe fire, and survive even the utter chill of the void between worlds. The greatest dragons could shoot a line of fire a thousand feet long, Galwin had once boasted. And then there were the legends she'd known since childhood. In one, a dragon ate all the inhabitants of some far away village and lived there still, brooding over bones and treasure. In another, a great drake devoured a Tree of Life and was locked away by mighty enchantment, held prisoner in a mountain's heart. Valkire slew a dragon once, and then he tamed another.

Luthiel would never have believed any of these tales, until now. For all the grand stories of these great and horrific monsters could not make words believable enough to match the thing that had coiled up around the huge mound in front of her.

It was long—longer than the tallest trees of Minonowe—and its black and brimstone body looked tougher than iron. Great wings like those of a bat gathered at its flanks within a sheaf of spines. Spikes ran in a ridge from tail to head before ending in a crown of horns. Sunken in that terrible head were a pair of lava-splash eyes and from its mouth streamed smoke.

74

It was a dragon and, judging by its size, ancient in dreams. Yet for all the terror she felt rising in her chest, she could not flinch or look away. Its eyes drew her in. Held her.

Othalas skidded to a stop, claws making gouges in the steaming ground.

"Narhoth," he coughed through the blood.

"You know its name?!" Luthiel shouted.

"The mate of Desire whom Valkire slew an age ago," Mithorden replied. "A terror as ancient as hills that were mountains."

Narhoth was the dragon's name and long she had lived upon the worlds in hunger. She had fed, from the hand of one or another, but she was too proud and too great to serve any master for long. In her black thought, she was queen and all should bend before her terrible will.

Now that will reached out over the blasted plain and Luthiel strained beneath it. The dragon's eyes settled on her. The air around her grew heavy. Her vision blurred. She reeled and a hissing sound filled her ears.

There you are! a voice called through the hissing.

Luthiel knew it was the dragon. Somehow, in her mind.

The one he spoke of! the voice continued. *Who turned Vaelros. Who fed Vyrl. Daughter of my love's slayer!* Like a great crocodile, the dragon opened her mouth. Drool leaked out between the teeth.

Terror rushed over Luthiel. *She means to eat me,* she thought even as she struggled against the force that had slipped around her like a coil, pulling her toward the dragon.

You will come to me!

It took all her effort to sit still and not leap from the werewolf. She struggled. Each instant stretched out. Sweat dripped from her nose and turned to mist before it touched the ground. Dragon eyes shone down and down. Seeming to grow huge as volcano mouths. She pushed back, fighting desperately to break the Dragon's hold. It felt like pushing against a horse, a hill, a mountain. She quavered. Then she crumbled. As she failed she felt her limbs spasm and then jerk as one toward the monster. She lunged, her feet pushing away from the wolf. She felt as if some thread was reeling her toward the dragon who'd stretched itself out on the hillside, mouth agape to receive her. She felt a foot touch ground and tensed her muscles to sprint toward it. But Ecthellien caught her, gripping her by the mail coat. She kicked then struck at his hand. His grip seemed to slacken. She felt herself slipping away. Then, his fingers tightened and he drew her in, hauling her back onto the wolf. She struck at Ecthellien's face. It took a shout from Mithorden to revive her. She sat dazed, panting through her rags, Ecthellien's arm around her chest.

Still, those terrible eyes reached out to her. But their spell had broken. The dragon's will seemed to hiss in the air, but it no longer held her. Before she could catch her breath, another dragon thought came.

Very well. Then I will come to you.

Luthiel trembled. "Let's get out of here!" she yelled.

"Our way is blocked!" Melkion replied. Uncertain, they paused as the fires grew and the monster reared before them. Then, as if by a silent signal, Mithorden and Ecthellien drew swords together.

In response, the great wyrm unfurled her wings. The motion made a clap like thunder and the wings spread out wide as a storm cloud. A gale rushed out on a spray of flame. The fires surrounding the drake swelled with a howl. With a single wing beat Luthiel could feel as much as hear, Narhoth launched from the spire and swooped toward them.

It seemed impossible that something so large could move so fast. Some nightmare marriage between volcano and tornado, rushing at her. *Nothing can fight this! If only we'd made it through the webs!* she thought bitterly. *If I'd only controlled my anger!*

Then, with the dragon nearly on them, Mithorden thrust his sword high chanting —

Nani Lumen! Eleth Eshald!

Which means: "Here is light! Let it be my shield!"

With his words, brilliance shone from his sword's tip. The light grew into a globe surrounding them. The air inside felt cool.

The horror bore down on them. Its eyes so bright Luthiel had to squint to look at them. The violence of her flight so great it sounded as though the air was ripping. A feeling of awe settled upon her and she wanted to do nothing more than stand and stare. Shaking her head, she closed her eyes.

More dragon magic! she thought. Frantically, she reached for her bow.

The dragon rushed on. It cried out again and this time she trembled, fighting down a sudden panic and an overwhelming urge to run. Melkion let out a cry in answer and Othalas howled with him as they turned to face the drake. The sound echoed through the waste only to be drowned out by the noise of the dragon. Then Narhoth breathed and in front of her a flame built up like a wave pushed ahead of a great ship. Luthiel drew her bow and let her arrow fly. It was caught up in the fire and cast away like a burning twig.

"We don't have time to fight her!" Mithorden cried. "The fires!"

"Leave me!" Ecthellien yelled.

Before anyone could speak another word, dragonfire was upon them. Mithorden held his sword up and the light at its tip filled the globe with brilliance—walling out the flames. It surged over them, but was flung back.

Then the dragon was on the ground before them, claws ripping rock and stone.

I will eat you.

Dragon eyes shimmered with hunger and Luthiel knew Narhoth would never give up the hunt. Not until she drank her blood, cracked her bones.

"You will not have her!" Ecthellien cried. He leapt from Othalas's back and pointed his sword at the dragon. "Stand aside!" With his left hand he pulled a dagger from its sheath. *Give me your hand,* he thought to her.

There was so much force in Ecthellien's thought that she extended her arm immediately. Hot pain erupted from her hand as Ecthellien expertly cut it. She cried out, but before she could draw her hand back, Ecthellien slid the blade of his sword over her wound. Blood flowed and from it a golden light seemed to rise up, wreathing Ecthellien and his sword. Then he sprang away from her rushing toward the dragon.

"Liel! Named and marked! Rune of Luthiel! Give me strength to defend her!"

Ecthellien collided with the dragon and the crash, for an instant, drowned out the fires' roar. Ecthellien's sword flashed—once, twice. Where it fell dragon scale shattered. The dragon, whose eyes for the first time were drawn away from Luthiel, struck back. Fangs flashed and a great clawed hand lashed out. Ecthellien leapt aside.

Luthiel drew her hand back. On it was a cut in the shape of a ᚱ rune. Golden blood spilled from it, covering her hand.

He marked me!

Without another thought, Luthiel drew an arrow. Blood spilled from her hand and onto the shaft. Tipped in *Marim*, the arrowhead gleamed blue.

Blue for my mother!
Blue for her moon!
Blue for water!
Water for fire!

She sang it all in a rush as the arrow seemed to leap from her hand and onto her bowstring. The bowstring felt light as wind itself beneath her fingertips and the arrow flew from it, then disappeared into the dragon. A shudder passed over Narhoth as she let out a terrible cry. The sound of it made Luthiel's ears feel as though they crumpled and then were made to turn inside out. When the dragon faced her again, Luthiel could see the arrow protruding from a bloody eyelid. It gathered for a lunge and Luthiel fumbled with her second arrow.

I don't have time.

Othalas was faster. She felt him tense beneath her. There was a sudden scrambling and a jolt that almost flung her from the werewolf's back. The world seemed all a blur of fire and rock. When her eyes grew clear again she saw that the wolf had, in a few great bounds, taken them around the drake's left flank. They were rushing up the path toward the Lilani! The dragon lurched but was unable to spin fast enough to follow the wolf. Fangs snapped, claws cut but each met only air. Then the great beast rolled, turning so her spines faced them and lashed out with her tail. Luthiel could see it, large as a wall, rushing toward them. But again, Othalas was faster. He gathered himself and, stretching his great legs, leapt through the air at the last moment. Both tail and spines passed beneath them.

"Hold fast!" Mithorden yelled.

Luthiel, who still held her bow in her left hand, was forced to grasp with only her right. They landed hard and she felt herself falling. Then, Mithorden's hand was on her back. Holding her down. She looked up. In a few bounds, Othalas had carried them to the spire's far side. Luthiel watched on in terror as the dragon turned to follow.

Suddenly, there was a loud cry of *Luthiel! Luthiel!* and she saw Ecthellien rush forward, striking the dragon on its flank. A long gash appeared and blood fell. The dragon screamed and drew back, clutching at its wound. Luthiel felt its gaze leave her. But her dread came back when she saw it turn on Ecthellien. A deep rumble sounded in its throat. It reared, spreading its wings wide. A shadow fell over him. Beneath it, he looked tiny and alone. Then it crashed down on him—biting, tearing, spewing fire.

"No!" Luthiel said. "We can't leave him!"

"We must!" Mithorden yelled back at her. "The fires!"

As they climbed the spire, Luthiel could see them joining together in a great blaze. Even the air was beginning to burn as columns of flame stretched up to the sky.

"The firestorm is upon us!" Mithorden shouted. "Let the Vyrl fight!"

Ecthellien's sword flashed, breaking Dragon scale. Narhoth cried out. Still the mighty fangs snapped and still Ecthellien leapt aside. From the pits flames belched and a cloud of smoke rose up.

She could no longer see him.

"Ecthellien!" Luthiel yelled.

Then they were on top of the rock. All around them the lands burned. The light hurt her eyes. She saw the pool, untouched by fire. Two bounds brought them plunging into it. This time the change was instant and the chill welcome as balm.

BOOK IV:

AGAINST THE SPIDERS

A COMPANION LOST

They rose up from a scarlet pool. Above, Silva shone in fullness and Merrin waned gibbous. Othalas collapsed and she rolled on the ground choking and crying.

"He's gone," she sobbed. "He's gone." But more terrible was the unspoken thought—

It was my doing. My anger caused this.

Mithorden put an arm around her. For a time he just stood there, letting Luthiel cry on without saying a word.

"If he is, then we should honor him by not giving up."

"Could he survive?" she sobbed. "The fire, the dragon?"

"I don't know," he replied grimly. He pulled a jar from his steaming pack and motioned to her.

"Come here, you're burned."

He smoothed the cool stuff over patches of her burned and blistered skin. It tingled and some of the pain dimmed.

"I was afraid something would happen. The moment you mentioned Cauthraus, I dreaded going there. And now, Ecthellien's lost. We should never have come!"

She grabbed Mithorden and looked him in the eyes.

"The way was guarded. You didn't know?"

Mithorden met her gaze, his bright eyes flashing. Gently but firmly, he lifted her hands from his robes.

"All ways were guarded," he said in a soft voice. "And no, I didn't know. I feared it." He looked away and then spoke more firmly. "We may see worse things than dragons before the end."

"Worse things than dragons?" Melkion grumbled. "Not all dragons are like Narhoth. It's her kind that made the elves fear dragons in the first place." He landed on the ground beside her and ran his tail-tip through her hair as he hissed. The sensation was oddly soothing. She glanced at the dragon and was shocked to find fierce concern in his eyes.

"Here, I'll give you a chance to do some good," the sorcerer said, placing the balm beside Melkion. "Smooth this on her hurts."

He handed her one of his waterskins. "Drink too."

Melkion dabbed his tail in the fair-smelling stuff and began spreading it over her burns. She lay still, allowing the dragon to tend her, taking small sips of the hot water. Her throat was raw and cracked. The water stung terribly as it went down. Mithorden stood quietly by with his arms crossed. He glanced at the werewolf who'd sprawled out on the ground, taking long, deep breaths.

"Luthiel Valkire," Mithorden said. "I will not have you speaking this way. Do you think Ecthellien would have put himself at such great risk only to see us give up now? We are here for a reason. And there *is* still hope. If not for Ecthellien, then for Elshael and Ahmberen, and for elves too. Do you understand, Luthiel?"

She shook her head and guilt flooded into her.

"I don't know," she said. "The terrors he allowed! I couldn't understand. Now he's gone."

"I remember what you said," he replied. "Do you think now, that he's earned his forgiveness?"

Luthiel shrugged struggling with herself. "I—sometimes I can't believe I'm even trying to help them. When I saw the Widdershae —" she broke off, shuddering at the memory. "It gave me a glimpse of what the Vyrl did long ago. Of what they did to children too. Can you ever forgive that?" She looked back at Mithorden, anger and grief waging a silent war inside her.

"Most Vyrl did not choose their madness," he said. "They are a fallen race. When the eldest of them decided to serve Gorthar, their descendants fell under a curse. One wrong choice that echoed down through the ages, leaving no Vyrl or other dreaming race untouched. Before your father came, Ecthellien never had a chance."

For a moment, she looked into Mithorden's sad eyes. She saw her grief reflected there and had to look away.

"The Vyrl did what they thought they had to," Mithorden continued sadly. "To survive."

"How could there ever be an excuse?" she said, shaking her head again. The scenes of Ecthellien facing the dragon flashed through her mind alongside the terror of the Widdershae feeding on elves. One did not fit with the other. Yet the Vyrl was a part of both.

"How would you have him make amends?"

"I don't know," she said, barely holding back the tears. "I just want him back."

Mithorden nodded grimly. "It is a hard, hard thing, Luthiel," he said more softly. "Ecthellien is guilty of terrors. And he fought to save us from the dragon. What does he deserve? Blame or forgiveness?"

"Blame?" Luthiel croaked, looking up at the sorcerer.

"Yes blame," he said firmly. "That's your choice Luthiel. To blame or to forgive."

Luthiel took a deep breath and tried to steady herself. With the loss of Ecthellien, she felt as if something had been ripped out of her. There was hope for good in the Vyrl. She'd reawakened it. And now, for Ecthellien, there would never be another chance.

"How can I judge?" she said at last. "To me, he is a hero. To the world a monster." She let her head fall into her arms and started crying quietly. "I miss him! Curse him! I miss him!"

Mithorden put a hand on her shoulder and let her cry for a few minutes. A sad smile slowly spread across his face. "I'm glad you can forgive him," He said at last.

Luthiel lifted her head. "How do you know?"

"Because you miss him."

Luthiel blinked, then slowly nodded. A part of her was still angry with Ecthellien but the other part wanted him back, wanted him to have the opportunity to make amends.

"It *is* hard."

"It is the best and most difficult thing you will ever do," the sorcerer replied.

"I just wish I had another chance with him," she said.

Mithorden looked away. "At least you can do for Ahmberen and Elshael what you would have done for him."

Luthiel nodded sadly, then glanced at Othalas who was lying on the ground, panting.

"Poor, brave Othalas," she said. "I cannot imagine how he bore us even as the poison was running through him. Do you think he will live?"

Mithorden smiled.

"It would take more than Widder venom and a hard run to kill that wolf," he said.

"I wish we could stay with him, for tonight, at least—to give him comfort."

Mithorden shook his head. "We will—he's coming with us."

"But he's too weak to walk," she said.

"Not yet, I think," the sorcerer replied.

Mithorden stood.

"We'd best be moving. If the drake survived, then she may come after us. Othalas!"

The werewolf grumbled but managed to stand. The smell of blood rose off him and Luthiel shuddered at how gruesome he looked. Yet he stood and walked regardless.

Mithorden picked up the jar of balm and put it back into his pack. He held his hand out to her. She took it and soon she was standing on her feet again.

It hurt to walk; her blistered and cracked skin protested with each step, but she made her way as best she could. She followed the sorcerer down an animal trail. Melkion landed on the werewolf's head, perching there instead of on Luthiel's shoulder, which was covered with splotches of burned skin. He settled down into the fur and looked warily about.

The werewolf didn't even seem to notice.

Slowly, and painfully at first, they made their way away from the Lilani. The pool dropped out of sight as they plunged through a dense patch of woods and made their way into a grassy area beyond. If anything rose up from the Lilani that night, neither she, dragon, werewolf nor sorcerer heard it.

The silence in her mind with the Vyrls' absence was like a hole in her head. She felt surprised at how lonely she was without their thoughts. It made the loss of Ecthellien that much more unbearable. She kept thinking things and expecting those thoughts to be heard or expecting to hear the whisper of thoughts in return. When she was in the Vale with them it was as present to her as a heartbeat. But now there was nothing.

She remembered longing for such solitude. Now she feared it.

In a haze of exhaustion and pain, Luthiel walked on. Occasionally, she would lean against Othalas for support. But it seemed the great wolf was faring worse than even she. When she touched him, blood oozed up through his fur and stuck to her hand in greasy clumps. He walked with an awkward gait, as if afraid of breaking something inside him.

The smell of blood filled the air. Having ridden on the bloody werewolf for so long, both she and Mithorden were covered in it. She wondered if she would ever get its stink off of her.

I bet we make a gruesome sight, she thought wryly.

But worse than the pain, the blood, the exhaustion, or her worry for Othalas was her grief for Ecthellien.

"No one but the Vyrl and I will mourn him," she whispered. "But he is as great a hero as any I've heard named in legend."

"What's that?" Melkion hissed.

"Nothing," she said.

"I miss him too," Melkion whispered.

She nodded, walking on in silence.

A Secret Return

The land rose and fell gently. Here and there she could see wild flir-bug bulbs glittering among the trees. She let her hand trail through a velsoph, sighing as its soft petals brushed her sore fingers. Above her, the three sisters shone down—Merrin's blue crescent seemed to smile, and the pair of Lunen and Silva glistened like white and silver coins among a diamond blaze of stars. The ribbons of summer's night threaded on through midsky and then fell away eastward, lit by strange flickers and soft glows. Their shadow sides trailed into the north where barely-visible fingers of blackness edged the night. In the Vale, she could seldom see much more than moons at night as the mists would obscure all but the brightest stars. But here the sky had depth and she felt she could reach out and touch the luminaries. Luthiel smiled at the sight despite herself. There was a sense of home about these woods, this sky, and she knew as much as felt that she was traveling through some part of the Minonowe.

As they crested one of the gentle rises she caught a glimpse of a sparkling river to the south. It dipped east then west before disappearing between the arms of two hills.

"Is that the river Rendalas?" she asked.

Mithorden nodded. "We're north and east of the Vale. It and the Mounds of Losing stand at our right shoulder. The elves have gathered away from the hills and the Widdershae webs."

"How far to the Vale?" she asked.

"No more than a day's march."

Luthiel felt her skin prickle. It was closer to the spiders than she liked.

They continued on into the night and she descended into a state of numbness. Her body hurt in more places than she could count and the silence in her mind seemed to gnaw at her. After a while her sense of desolation lessened as she became aware of the peaceful wood. A small brook trickled beside her, leaves whispered a lullaby, her feet made soft crunching sounds in the underbrush, and great wolf's feet plodded beside her. The sounds lulled her and soon she began to feel her eyes shutting. There was peace—more than she'd felt since leaving Flir Light. She began to wonder about sleep and sighed as they passed a comfy patch of moss beneath a whispering willow.

"Here, this will do nicely," Mithorden said suddenly and turned away from the path.

"Where are you going?" Luthiel asked, a bit startled by the sorcerer's sudden change of direction.

"We're getting close to the elves. I don't want to be found looking like we've been bathed in blood. They may forgive *me*. But if they saw *you*—" he motioned to her shredded and bloodstained clothes.

She laughed nervously. She'd been so worried about escaping the Vale she'd barely had time to get used to the idea that she was coming home.

"I guess I don't look very nice."

"You look like something scraped off Othalas' better side," Melkion quipped, pointing at Othalas' rump with his tail.

"Careful, dragonfly, I saw that," the werewolf grumbled. "Wouldn't want to end up squashed by the big nasty wolf." Othalas shook his head and the motion seemed to take Melkion by surprise as he almost fell off. The dragon hissed, flared his wings, and scrambled to gain purchase on the wolf's matted fur.

Luthiel grinned. This was the first time she'd heard the wolf talk in hours. She felt relieved to hear his voice. To her ear, it sounded a bit more like the old Othalas—not so muffled and gurgling as before.

"So how are we going to clean up?" she asked.

"I smell water." Mithorden stretched out his hand and parted some branches. Beyond lay a pool glimmering under the moonlight. The water was clear and little flower petals danced on its surface. Luthiel pushed her way in front of Mithorden.

"I'll go first," she said with a smirk at Melkion. "I don't particularly like resembling something from a werewolf's backside."

This brought a grin from Melkion and a cough from Othalas. She turned, slipping through the branches and on up to the spring as the others sat down to wait. With a few quick flicks, she loosened her pack straps and let it slip off her aching shoulders. It stung and as she went to open it she noticed blisters on her fingers. Inside, she found a fresh set of clothes that didn't smell too smoky. She laid these out on a stone, found some soap, and then went to work on what she was wearing.

This part wasn't easy, as there were places where the garments had burned and stuck to her skin. Some would have to be cut away. She drew *Weiryendel*.

When the blade cleared its scabbard, it made an odd chiming. The sound was at once sad and insistent. As if in answer, a tiny light flickered through the pouch that hung at her neck. Her Wyrd Stone was awakening! With trembling hands, she opened the pouch. Immediately, the light swirled about her and she was plunged into the World of Dreams. It was the sword's music that did it this time, for not a sound slipped through her parted lips. The music grew, as did the light. A wind began to blow, bending the trees and rippling the lake's surface. Her belt and pouches, which also lay on a rock, began to rustle. Then as if touched by unseen fingers, the pouch that contained *Aeowinar's* shards began to unravel. A few fragments flew out and began to swirl around the sword. There was a burning in her hand and, flinching, she held it up before her. The ᛈ rune Ecthellien had cut there felt hot and shimmered with the golden color of Vyrl's blood—her blood.

The light grew and the fragments swirled faster. Tears fell. It was all too plain. Ecthellien was the second sacrifice.

No sooner did the recognition fly swiftly through her than the sword began its change. The shards seemed to merge with it and the blade grew yet again—this time a full six inches. As it grew, the shape changed, seeming to become elongated and graceful. A keyhole appeared at the blade's base and through the guard. It widened until it was large enough to hold *Methar Anduel*. Then she was lifting her Wyrd Stone, bringing it up to meet with the blade. When the two touched there was a flash of light as bright as when the Wyrd Stone first awakened, and for a moment it seemed a small sun shone in the night. It was so bright, she had to turn her eyes away—but the song rang in her ears even as the dreaming world swirled about her.

The wind suddenly gusted into a gale. On it, her father's voice returned to her.

To live is to lose, it said. *For all things fail in the end. I am sorry for your lost ones, my daughter. But even they had more chance to know you than I. A blessing on you Luthiel, so you may begin to undo the terrible work of my father.*

Then the light dimmed and she let *Weiryendel* fall to her side. The music faded into silence as she slipped from the World of Dreams. For long minutes, all she could do was sob quietly.

"He's dead. Oh, he's dead. I threatened to kill him and I did."

A sense of heaviness settled over her and she felt again the desolation of the night she left Flir Light. Gazing at the remaining pieces of *Aeowinar*, she held back an urge to fling them far into the forest. As pieces of the sword fell back into place, bits of her life were being ripped away—never to return. Each time loss. Each time changing. Each time a hint of her father's presence on the wind. There was still this sense of *him* about her. Something she could feel. Like the clean in the air after a storm. She stared at the blade again.

"Somehow, he's bound his will into it," she said with sadness. "I should honor it."

With numb fingers, she gathered the remaining shards.

"Oh Ecthellien," she whispered. "I would not have had you make amends like this. If you can hear me now, I forgive you."

For a moment, the wind seemed to rise again and all the branches in the trees about her swayed. It blew on for only a few moments. Then the night was still once more.

Having gathered all the remaining bits, she sat for a few minutes in silence to honor the dead. Then, she returned to the painful business of removing her clothes. She lifted the blade and noticed her Wyrd Stone still rested in the keyhole. She poked at it to see if it was stuck. At first contact there was a small shock in her fingers and the Stone came free. Curious, she placed the Stone back in the hole and felt the shock again as it reattached. To test it, she swung the blade. No matter how swiftly or forcefully she swung the sword, the Stone stayed firmly attached. When she went to lift the Stone out for the second time there was another strange shock as it slid into her hand. Satisfied, she returned it to her pouch and used the sword to cut the tattered rags off her. It was starting to look like a proper sword blade now and she guessed fully half its length had reformed. She looked at the changed shape and wondered if it would still fit the scabbard.

While musing, she cut herself in a careless instant. The blade had no more than rested upon the skin of her forearm when it slid into her flesh as easily as a reed through water. She shivered as she felt the cool crystal passing through her. But when it exited there was no blood, only the tiniest white line. A soothing numbness entered her arm and she felt her drowsiness deepen. Shaking her head to clear it of stupor, she continued with care wondering if more than the blade's shape had changed.

After a few minutes of cautious cutting, she was finally rid of her clothes. She looked over her skin. It was a patchwork of tiny red burns with small blisters mainly at her fingers. The Vyrl wounds were still visible but seemed to have been scorched shut by the heat of Cauthraus and the dragon. She grabbed the soap and made her way to the spring.

Thankfully, the water was cool, but not unpleasantly so. As she entered, her skin came alive with pain. She could feel each burn and bite. Even the place where the Dimlock had tried to strangle her when she and Othalas had sheltered in the Cave of Painted Shadows seemed to ache as she immersed herself. She knew Dimlock hurts were slow to heal. Winter wounds, they were called. For their only cure was time and long days basking under the suns of summer. She counted herself lucky they hadn't done more damage. The Vyrl's bites puzzled her, though. *At least the other injuries have healed. Mithorden's Yewstaff fruit was good enough for those.*

Once her skin grew used to the water, she began to work with the soap. As she washed, she found comfort in the sights and sounds of night. Nearby, she could hear the call of a bird answering a mournful song in the distance. A family of voles came to drink by the water in which she bathed. They paused to watch her for a time before scurrying off to the protective brush. At last she was finished. Feeling clean and somewhat refreshed, she rose from the water, dried herself and put on her new clothes. She also put on the cloak and veil Mithorden had given her. Inspecting them, she found that they were in excellent condition. With a few quick brushes they seemed in even better shape than the clothes from her pack—which stank of smoke.

"Newspell," she whispered. She'd seen her foster brother Lorethain use it to keep clothes fresh and undamaged. She assumed Mithorden had cast it to protect the other enchantments.

Still hesitant to lift the veil over her face, she let it hang as she made her way back to the others. As she walked, she noticed a few soft notes rising up from the wood. Following the music, she found her companions beneath an old pine. Othalas sat on his haunches, great yellow eyes scanning the night. Melkion had coiled round one of the pine's lower branches. His eyes drooped as he blew a half-hearted smoke ring. Mithorden leaned against the tree, a flute in his hands, playing a soft tune. She stopped and stood listening. The tune was both full and sorrowful; exultant and touched with grief. Melkion and Othalas were silent and solemn. About halfway through, she realized it was Ecthellien Mithorden played for. The thought came to her with a pang and she bowed her head. Finally, the flute song ended. Mithorden stopped and returned the flute to a polished case.

Luthiel drew *Weiryendel*, letting them look at the remade blade.

Melkion let his long neck drop and he hung his head. "Ecthellien is dead," he said mournfully.

"The air is restless with the spirits of the lost," Mithorden said softly. "Peace then."

"The spring's yours," she said to Mithorden after a long silence. With a nod, the sorcerer slipped through the brush and made his way toward the pond. She watched him go, then sat down with her back to the tree.

"Might not want to get too comfortable," the great wolf rumbled. He lifted his chin and sniffed the air. "Elves are near."

"I couldn't get comfortable if I lay on the finest bed in all of Oesha," she replied. "I'm just too beat up."

Melkion stared down at her, concern plain in his violet eyes. "It's a mad quest. Far too much for one of fifteen years—Valkire's blood or no." ·

"She's done well enough," Othalas growled. "We'd all be worse off, but for Ecthellien."

"You're both right," Luthiel said with a sad sigh at the mention of Ecthellien. "I'd much rather be playing tap-and-turn with Leowin than fighting Widdershae and dragons. Now I've got to convince my friends the Vyrl had a change of heart."

"And that Othalas is a kitten," Melkion quipped.

"It gets worse," Othalas joined in.

Melkion looked at Othalas. "The enchantment?"

"What else?" the werewolf grumbled. "I was wondering when the sorcerer would tell her. Seems he doesn't think it's important."

"What are you talking about?" Luthiel asked, uncertain if she really wanted to know. "There's even more bad news?"

"It's not exactly bad," Melkion answered. "Just a little odd."

Othalas growled his disagreement.

"You may as well just say something," she said.

"It's about your disguise," Melkion said. "It's meant to make you look different. Nothing too noticeable. No facial hair or anything so distasteful."

"What do you mean?"

"It was Mithorden's idea," Othalas grumbled. "Although, with the way elves act these days, I'd say it's a good one."

Luthiel would have thrown her hands up in exasperation if it didn't hurt so much. "Are you going to tell me what this is about or are you going to keep talking around me for the rest of the night?"

The dragon and wolf eyed each other. Melkion looked sheepish enough for both of them.

"It's bound up in the veil's magic," the dragon said, pointing his tail at her disguise. "When you put it on there's some kind of spell that changes your features."

"Changes?"

"Yes," Melkion said. "It won't even be plain that you're a woman."

"Well, that's not so bad," Luthiel said.

"No, it wouldn't be," Othalas said with a gravelly chuckle.

"Except that Mithorden plans to introduce you as a man," Melkion said.

Luthiel stood up, restraining a surprised outburst. She took a few steps forward and then put a hand on Othalas' flank. Some dried bits of blood crumbled away at her touch but the flesh beneath seemed to have mended. "Clever sorcerer," she said finally.

"This way you could give news about yourself with less danger," Melkion said. "You wouldn't have to return as someone who broke an unbreakable law. A woman many among the Fae would fear."

"If you're a man," the wolf continued, "few would question that you were the Vyrl's messenger."

"They would fear me?" Luthiel said, staring into the night.

Both the wolf and the dragon were silent.

"But how will I convince them if I cannot speak of the Vyrl's change? How if I'm not speaking from experience?"

"You must convince them," Othalas replied as he swung his great head toward her. "There is a lady of the Vale of Mists. She saved the Vyrl from madness. Her name is Luthiel. That is what you must tell them."

"And when will they find out who I am?"

"When they need most to know it is you." Mithorden spoke from not far off in the wood. As they talked, the sorcerer had returned and come upon them unawares. Now he stood at the edge of the wood watching them. His skin shone from what must have been a very quick bath and his garments seemed new and unmarred. "If they saw you as you are now, it would be too much. It's likely you'd bear the brunt of their hatred for Vyrl. You may still—but only as an anonymous messenger."

"It's a lie," she said.

"You're just hiding from their anger," Melkion said.

"They'll find out eventually. We'll have to tell them."

"We must be careful to choose the right moment," Mithorden said.

Luthiel paused and looked at each of them. She didn't know why, but this seemed an important moment to her. She was about to hide her identity by playing the part of a man. It seemed strange and unnatural to her. Though she'd never really known where she'd come from or who her parents were, she'd always had a strong sense of who she was. It made disguising herself as a man seem even more awkward. "So I must hide that I'm a woman?" It still didn't seem right.

"They know you as Luthiel and as a woman," the sorcerer replied.

Luthiel nodded and frowned. She sensed Mithorden wasn't telling her everything. It didn't quite seem complete.

"I don't like it," she said. "Not at all."

"It is for your safety. Otherwise, I'd never ask."

Luthiel put her head in her hands. She'd looked forward to returning home. Why come home if no one knew it was her?

"There's more to it," Othalas growled. "It has to do with being a woman. Some elves are threatened by women with power. Ashiroth and Rimwold are the worst. There, sorcery is banned to women and those who practice it are outlaws—named 'witches' or fouler things."

"There's nothing wrong with witches." Luthiel said with a frown.

"You might not think so," Othalas said. "But there are many who do."

There was something in what the werewolf said that deeply disturbed her. It was something she'd overlooked or happily ignored.

"I'm not really very powerful. What have I done that's so fearsome?" Even as she asked the question she realized how silly it sounded. She'd broken the most perilous and long-kept law in the Faelands, freed and become a friend to the monstrous Vyrl. She'd come to possess objects and weapons of might, Wyrd, and legend. She was a sorceress and the only daughter of Vlad Valkire. It made her sad to think the werewolf was right. To do all those things would make her seem both terrible and powerful to some of the Fae. But to be a woman? What was the wrong in that?

As the thought passed, she realized Othalas was right. For most who lived in Ashiroth and Rimwold and even for some who lived in Ithilden, Minonowe, and Himlolth the old myths were changing. It was something Leowin had tried to talk about many times. How many fae were taking Ëvanya out of the Ebel Kaleth. How they were beginning to believe that the world was created by a lonely act of will from Ëvanyar and not at the moment he discovered his love of Ëvanya. How when the myths changed, their treatment of women changed. It was something so dreadful Luthiel had done her best to ignore it. Could this be what Mithorden and the others were afraid of? Not just that she'd saved Vyrl. That some would see her as a witch and hate her for it?

Othalas watched her, taking in her changed expressions. "You know it's not true. You are powerful."

"It all has to do with the changing myths, doesn't it?"

Mithorden gave her a considering look and nodded. "Yes. That's the root of the trouble."

"I still can't believe what they've done. Our world began with Ëvanya and Ëvanyar falling in love. Who would want to change a myth so beautiful as the Ebel Kaleth?" For so long, she always thought it a silly tale. But she realized that, now, for reasons she was just beginning to understand, it was important to her.

Mithorden's look was sad. "The Ebel Kaleth is fading from the world. Many just don't believe any more."

"Why?" Luthiel asked.

Mithorden blinked his eyes and slowly sat down. Even the sorcerer seemed battered by their hard journey. "I don't rightly know the whole story," he said. "What I do has been pieced together over years of patient watching." With one hand, he unclasped his cloak. With the other, he pulled a little pouch out of his belt. Gathering the cloak in his lap, he opened the pouch and pulled out a long needle and a spool of fine thread.

"To my best guess, it started long ago," Mithorden said as he threaded the needle, "during the time when your father was coming up. He had just become my pupil, in fact. But he wasn't my first. My earliest and most promising was a young and powerful elf by the name of Zalos."

As Mithorden spoke, he began repairing his cloak. Looking closer, Luthiel noticed there were many stitches. They were so fine she hadn't seen them before and she wondered why he went to the trouble when he could mend it with a spell. The needle flashed and Mithorden continued his tale.

"He was bright, cunning, and ambitious. His ambition was so strong, it concerned me at first. But I saw good in him as well. So I continued his training. Under my direction, he bloomed into a powerful sorcerer and Blade Dancer. Though Zalos was my first pupil, your father and Merrin soon followed. Each, in their own way, were talented, powerful, and nearly a match to the other. Soon, they became close friends and energetic rivals."

Mithorden paused in his sewing and looked away. His expression seemed pained and he licked his lips. "I should have noticed it, but I didn't. Looking back, I think Zalos pursued your mother even then."

Luthiel felt her breath catch but she kept silent, drinking in everything she could about her father and mother.

"Things were not so certain then, for I think your mother also felt for Zalos at the time. For a long while, Vlad and Zalos competed for your mother's attention. It wasn't until the War of Dreams that her relationship with your father bloomed.

"I think it is both this competition over Merrin and Zalos' feeling of inferiority to your father that eventually pushed him to begin studying the darker arts. I suppose he intended to prove he was superior to Vlad Valkire both to himself and your mother. Though he seemed fair, Zalos' pursuit of power was both cruel and impatient. Clear-minded Merrin noticed what was happening to Zalos and found it ugly.

"In time, Merrin and Valkire fell in love. They became companions both in their fight to save the elves and in their passion. Zalos grew distant. But, for a while, he seemed to accept their love. I suspect, now, he was only biding his time. His opportunity came just three weeks before Merrin and Valkire's wedding day. Merrin had returned to her city of Eddendell on the watery moon to prepare for the ceremony. Zalos followed her. Finally finding her alone, he confronted her. He kissed her, telling her to cast aside her love for Valkire, to take him instead.

"But Merrin did not return his kiss and pushed him away, ordering him to leave. Zalos' demands frightened her and, for the first time, she saw the darkness of evil in him.

"So spurned, Zalos left, returning to his home of Ashiroth where he was welcomed as a hero and eventually made its lord. Merrin and Valkire married. Time passed. Three hundred years they ruled the Faelands in peace until Valkire's father—the Lord of the Dark Forest—came and destroyed his son.

"Again Zalos went to Merrin, this time commanding her to marry him. Now he could see no reason for Merrin to refuse. But Merrin fled and, returning to Eddendell, fell into a centuries long sleep of grief. In her womb, she bore Valkire's only child.

Luthiel shifted uncomfortably against the tree.

"During her long sleep," the sorcerer continued, "Zalos grew ever more bitter. He took on wives. But though he knew passion, he never showed love, and they seemed to him little more than playthings. He still desired Merrin. Each year, he sent an emissary to her moon. Each year, the emissary was turned back."

Mithorden set his needle aside and looked at Luthiel, eyes gleaming in the starlight.

"It was during this time that the new religion began to appear. It started in Ashiroth and then quickly spread to Rimwold. In these places, it took root, stretching branches wide like some great, dark tree. It also surfaced in Himlolth, Minonowe and Ithilden but never in such force as in the realms of Zalos and Thrar Taurmori." As he spoke, he resumed his sewing—the swish, swish of the needle punctuating his words.

"Their teachings were simple. There was only one god and his name was Ëvanyar. Ëvanya was his consort but never more than a side note and often seen as an inconstant temptress. They stopped teaching women sorcerery. Then they outlawed it for them altogether. A new name was made for any girl or lady who practiced the art. And they were ever-after called witches. The punishments were harsh. Soon, women with magical power had disappeared from those lands.

"Zalos had embraced the new religion and he hosted a school in his capital of Arganoth. With the new religion came new laws. Women weren't allowed to own land and had lesser rights than men. In courts, the testimony of one man was equal to that of two women. Men were allowed to have many wives and these later became little more than property.

"In Ashiroth and Rimwold, many began to see the ways of the old religion in the other Faelands as heretical. They planned and fought wars. They sent emissaries out to gain converts."

"Like Elag," Luthiel whispered, nodding her head.

"When Merrin returned," Mithorden continued, "Zalos immediately arrested her, holding her on charges of witchcraft and keeping her first as a prisoner and then as a wife. He said it was for her protection. But he could never convince her to love him and has not yet become so terrible as to force himself on her. So, she became his wife in letter only—but she never took him into her heart or bed. Many have wondered how Zalos could keep Merrin bound in Arganoth—for she is powerful and no walls of stone could hold her for long. Some have suggested that Zalos tricked her with a spell and this seems most likely. But I know Merrin and wonder if she stays there willingly—to watch and learn about her enemy."

Mithorden put his needle down, inspecting his mended cloak. "That, to my best knowledge, is the history of the new myth. I don't know the extent of Zalos' involvement, though I guess it must be great. I am afraid it grew up out of Zalos' rage at being spurned by your mother and from a pride so great an injury to it would not heal. Not a happy tale at all, but I hope it helps answer your questions."

Luthiel felt a deep sadness welling up in her and she wondered what might have been if not for Zalos. "It does," she said, blinking her eyes. Luthiel set her hands on her knees and squeezed them in frustration. "Can't elves see it's a trick? Can't they know what they're losing?"

"It's always been a struggle to keep true to the old ways," Mithorden said sadly. "Clever folk *know* the impracticality of a sacred union. Hard decisions are necessary to survive—they *say*. Hard hearts are needed to make these decisions—they *think*. A person can truly trust no one, truly partner with no one, truly love no one. So if love in the world is impractical, why should it be a part of their myths?"

"Impractical? Love brings life to the world—makes those who live by it strong and fair."

Mithorden looked at Luthiel and gave her a proud smile. "You are more wise than you often act. Can you tell me then what this new religion follows, if not love? What happens to creation if women are taken from it?"

Luthiel frowned, trying to puzzle out Mithorden's riddle. "There is no creation," she said finally.

Mithorden nodded again. "The new religion is the religion of death."

"Death?" Luthiel said with dread. "They worship Gorthar?"

"Yes, but often without knowing what they do. They fill their minds with threats, fears of what may come, dark prophecy. Over time, they come to live by fear of death and so to worship it. Yet they also hate and subdue women—if only for the memory of love lost or the subtle power of creation within them."

"To think that all this came from jealousy?" Luthiel shook her head, still unable to believe.

"It is often from those denied love that violence comes," Mithorden replied.

"So my mother is responsible?"

"No. Zalos thought your mother could give him something that was taken from him long ago."

"Who were Zalos' parents?" she asked. "Were they cruel?"

"I do not know, Luthiel. Zalos kept his family secret. But I guess by the way Zalos acted and by his hardened heart that he first came to me out of adversity. He does not understand love, only power, which he desires as much as he desired your mother."

Luthiel sat looking into the sorcerer's eyes for a few moments longer. She could feel her heart beating in her chest. "So I must hide from him. From those who believe the dark myth?"

"You are a powerful woman. Someone they would hate and fear."

Luthiel's mind was in turmoil with everything Mithorden said. But there was one thought that came out more clearly than the rest. "They live in fear. Why should I do the same?"

A surprised smile spread over Mithorden's face. "You do not fear as they do. That is why we must protect you."

With the sorcerer's words, something shifted in Luthiel's mind. It was like the falling of a great beam in a bonfire which will set off hundreds of sparks into even the blackest night and briefly illuminate it. "How would *they* see me? How would *they* view what I did?"

"How would they see a sorceress? Someone who turned the Vyrl? The daughter of Vlad Valkire—unafraid of terrible laws and willing to do right despite fear of death? To those we will face, you are the most dangerous kind of person. You are someone they would claim was *evil*."

"I broke the law. The law says that only Chosen go. I chose despite threat of death..."

"So you understand."

Luthiel stood up and walked over to a gap in the trees, looking out into the night. "They won't even see the good thing I did."

"They would overlook it in the face of what they consider to be hard truths. Do you know, now, why you must hide at least at first?"

"If I was truly unafraid, I'd never use a disguise."

"You are a threat to the King of Death and all who live by fear of him. All his servants in all the nine worlds will know you and call you enemy. Who you are puts you in danger. So we must hide you. Keep you safe. Reveal you only when it will help us most. Until then, among the elves, you must be seen as a man. Yet keep safe your woman's heart as though it were the most precious thing in all of Oesha. For it is."

Luthiel took a deep breath and let it out. The way the sorcerer spoke and the thought of elves so near made her tremble. "Though it is not an easy thing for me, I will do as you ask."

"I know, Luthiel," the sorcerer said softly. "It wouldn't be you if it was."

"When should I begin?"

"Before we travel any further. If you like, you can wait until Othalas is finished at the spring."

THE UNWELCOME MESSENGER

The wood about them was quiet, as if expecting a storm. Though she couldn't see them, she could sense the forms about her as they barely whispered through the forest. They'd passed the night under the suspicious watch of the giant wolves and elves of Ashiroth—Urkharim and Gruagach. Despite her exhaustion, she'd slept only fitfully—face buried in Othalas' coat. Mithorden had left as she slept. She awoke with a start before first light, fearing the Gruagach would do some dark business. Their eyes flashed at her. Hands never strayed far from weapons. She'd been an object of ridicule and scorn before. Never hate. It wasn't something she was sure she'd ever get used to.

At Oerin's dawn, the sorcerer returned with company. Luthiel felt her breath catch when she saw Vanye, and then again when she noticed the Gruagach's hardness reflected in his eyes. He was as she remembered him and more. His face was angular without being harsh and his gray-blue eyes were filled with distant flashes—like a far-off but violent summer storm. His black hair seemed to roil on his brow, spill over his ears before stopping just above his broad shoulders. He stood tall without towering and was strong without bulk. What skin she could see was lightly kissed by the bright star, making that red splash of lips stand out all the brighter.

In all, she found his qualities, both physical and otherwise, to be held in a perfect, if tenuous balance—like a string that, drawn taught just to the point of breaking and plucked, will sing a note so pure the fair call it music. Today his was the music of war.

He wore the leaf scale armor of a Blade Dancer like a second skin. His Cat-o-Fae flexed wickedly on his shoulder. A ring of blades. Strong and sharp as moonsteel. Forged in dreamfire, it was both weapon and defense. Yet it also held a fragment of the Blade Dancer. It could sense the world, protect him from danger and on its own leap into the air—flying with far greater speed and violence than any bird. At his hip rested a Wyrdril—a dream sword. Also a part of the Blade Dancer. Also forged from his dreams. A mate to his Cat-o-Fae. It was said a Blade Dancer could feel as much through the point of his Wyrdril as through the tip of his own finger.

Luthiel remembered her first meeting with Vanye. Remembered the threat she felt from him. Now she felt it all the more. For he looked at her like an enemy. And when he did, she looked to his weapons and worried what they might do to her if she misstepped.

"So this is the Vyrl's messenger?" He asked sharply.

Mithorden nodded grimly. "He is."

The Blade Dancer stepped closer and looked her up and down. His face bore a look of stone. It was the same look he'd given her when he'd come with news about Leowin.

"Mithorden already told me. But I want to hear it from you. The girl, Luthiel, she's alive?"

Luthiel did her best to remain calm. There were tears forming in her eyes. She felt a strange urge to reach out and embrace the Blade Dancer.

"She is." She half choked the words.

"She'd better be. The Fae have not been so united since the Age of Dreams. It's the last great effort against the Vyrl and, all hope, an end to their trouble."

"I understand," she said. "Who better to know the Vyrl's terror than I? Now things have changed. I can hardly believe it myself." She was dancing around with words. It felt wrong to lie and she'd resolved herself not to un-less she must. "With what's happened, I think it neither wise nor fair to meet violence with violence."

Vanye stood still a moment and the only way she knew his surprise was by his momentary pause. "Well said. The Vyrl have never treated us with honeyed words before."

"Things are different now," she replied.

"The news is both strange and welcome. But there are few who will see it as I do."

Luthiel was silent.

"Best we move on. There's little time," Mithorden said. He was looking at Luthiel with a strange gleam in his eye. She couldn't tell if it was curiosity, surprise or a mixture of both.

"It may be too late," the Blade Dancer said. "The army is ready. It is only hours before they move."

Othalas stood, great muscles rippling under his sleek fur. The transformation over only a night was alarming. His wounds of the days before had completely healed, leaving no sign of past damage. Melkion flexed his wings and hopped onto Luthiel's shoulder. The motion drew Vanye's eye. He stepped closer to Luthiel and looked her over once more as if seeing something he hadn't before. "Why do you wear a mask?"

"The magic of the Mists is strange," Mithorden replied. "It is for his protection and for ours as well."

"I see," said Vanye with a look on his face that showed he did not.

Luthiel stood still, holding her breath. *Did he notice me?* she thought. The moment passed as fast as it came and the Blade Dancer turned away from them.

"You'd best follow me. Keep close. Wolf riders and Gruagach archers are not known for discretion." With that, he stepped into the wood, taking a winding path up a ridgeline. The ground steepened for a bit and then fell before them. All about, great trees loomed, casting long shadows in the twin light of Soelee and Oerin's Eye. The foliage became dense and seemed to rise ahead like a wall. She had to hold a hand up to keep the branches from her face as they pressed on into the ever-thickening wood. Othalas labored and limbs snapped as he pushed through. Vanye sprang from limb to limb and she almost made the mistake of jumping up with him. The brush became impassible and at Othalas' growled order, she climbed onto his back. He lunged, using his bulk to smash through. Mithorden followed in the path he made. Everywhere, Gruagach archers were slipping through the trees, arrows to strings, waiting for any hint of violence. The wolfriders formed into two files, one on their left, one to the right. Luthiel had little doubt that any misstep would mean her death.

Gruagach use poison arrows. For an odd moment she longed for her room in Ottomnos with its blue lights and slit windows that seemed to follow the suns as they rose and fell through a misty sky. Hope though she might, she was coming back to the world of the elves. Vanye had reappeared and she was going to meet with the faerie army's leaders. Had the Faelords come? What would they look like?

Finally the trees gave way—opening to a valley. It was as though they'd suddenly entered a vast chamber. Trees formed a great wall behind them and on the valley's far side. The wall stretched in either direction for what seemed like a mile. The valley itself looked to be about a quarter mile wide. A small stream trickled through it. Long ago, it must have been a much greater flow, for large boulders of granite and quartz were strewn all about. They were covered in green and blue moss.

On and around them, file upon file, rank upon rank, were thousands of Fae. There were green skinned Gruagach and great Urkharim, wicked red and blue Goblins and fair Ithildar, graceful Valemar and Tyndomiel in both elf and animal form, heavy-set moonhounds and lithe faenmare. They were all girded in armor—fine and terrible—and bristled with weapons according to their kind. Horned axes and curving greatswords for goblins; longbows, spears, and straight, double-edged, swords for Ithildar and Valemar; recurved bows, lances, and cruel shortswords for the Gruagach. Some of the Tyndomiel had taken animal form, and giant beasts—bears, boars, wolves and eagles were scattered through the host. One of the noble faenmare, horses of distant relation to unicorns, let out a cheerful trumpet upon seeing Luthiel. It shook its mane and pawed at the ground as though restless to join her. For a moment, she saw its face. In it there was recognition. But the faenmare's rider—an Ithildar knight—held firm to the reigns as he looked on them with anger and no little fear.

I was scared too, seeing Othalas for the first time, she thought.

A similar reaction spread through the fae and all turned angry and fearful eyes toward her. Some fingered weapons or notched arrows as she rode the great wolf down toward them with Melkion on her shoulder. So they were confronted with both Melkion, the bearer of Vyrl's demands, and Othalas, the collector of children. The veiled rider they didn't know. But that she rode Othalas and had Melkion perched on her shoulder was enough. Elves gave quiet and deadly stares, goblins jeered, and faerie frowned.

So Luthiel Valkire, who'd made herself a Chosen, became the first to ever return from the Vale of Mists alive and unchanged. Hidden from the sharp eyes of fae by veil and enchantment, they thought her only another Vyrl's servant. They believed Luthiel a victim, still imprisoned in the Vale of Mists. Yet here she rode before them triumphant and they didn't know it. They had come to put an end to the bloody sacrifices. To at last put down the ancient enemy. As she rode down the hill and came to a stop before them they pointed their weapons at her and swept around, cutting off all escape. Luthiel did her best not to waver. These were her people. This was her homecoming. She tried to hold her head high. But beneath the veil she could feel hot tears streaming down her cheeks.

A group of knights and wolfriders encircled them, lowered lances and advanced. Othalas tensed, Melkion spread wings wide. A lance head touched Othalas and he snapped it off with his teeth. Luthiel gripped *Weiryendel* tight.

Is this it? I've come home only to be killed by my own people?

Then came a loud cry from the Army's center. On a small hill were five figures. One was a unicorn with her head raised to the sky.

"Hold! The order is hold!" she shouted. The unicorn's command stopped them. She pranced, catching them in first one eye and then the other. A silver horn crowned her head. It spiraled out of a mane that seemed like wave crests bending beneath the moons. Sunlight seemed to fall on her like rain and her feet danced in a way that put the brook to shame.

Upon her back sat a rider in silver mail. He held a spear with a tip like a star. Upon his shoulder perched a Cat-o-Fae, its ring of blades flashing in the twin light. A third eye, black as polished onyx, split the center of his forehead. Seeing it, Luthiel was reminded of a Vyrl's eye without the swirling lights.

To their right a stately lady rode a giant lynx. She was clothed in leather armor and bore a longbow. In her face, there was both wisdom and sadness. Luthiel felt her throat tighten when she realized it was the face of one who kept hope despite hopelessness, love despite lovelessness.

Beside her stood a towering giant. Thirteen feet tall, it was covered from head to foot in a cloak of dragon scale. Beneath its hood, she saw a face engulfed in flame. Two eyes like white-hot coals blazed out at her. Smoke and fire leaked through cracks and from beneath the cloak. The dragon scale itself looked like cooling magma—black with splotches of red and orange. In its right fist it bore a great hammer licked with blue flame. In its left it held a black sword. Both hands were cased in lobster-like plates.

Last of all was a figure on a great wolf. The wolf was massive, nearly the size of Othalas. He sat on the great beast's back as if born there. His face was fair, like that of an Ithildar, and even for an elf it seemed young. Yet in the eyes there was age and enchantment. His armor was golden and set with gleaming crystals that seemed to hold both power and light. On his arm was a great shield bearing the crimson crown wreathed in flame and in a sheath at his side was a graceful longsword. Everything about this man—his movements, his posture, his voice—spoke of power and lordliness.

They are the Faelords! she thought. Elayethel of the Tyndomiel in her unicorn heart-form. The High Lord Tuorlin of Ithilden with the third eye in his forehead. Belethial of Minonowe—the melancholy lady. Thrar Taurmori of Rimwold—the fiery giant. Last of all Zalos of Ashiroth—who seemed so fair. On Zalos her eyes lingered.

She felt both anger and awe. Here was the greatest companion of Vlad Valkire and his best friend; a Faelord who'd ruled for thousands of years. Here was the monster who'd imprisoned her mother, forced her to live as an orphan, and set a black curse on Vaelros and his companions. Beside him stood the demon, Thrar Taurmori, who'd first served Gorthar the great himself, then Vyrl, and at last Vlad Valkire who turned him. When their eyes fell on her—and there could be no doubt who they were watching—she felt her legs become weak and she had to lean into Othalas for support. There was a pause. All fae in the great gathering seemed to take them in. Then Zalos raised his hand and motioned to an elf who stood before them.

"Please, lord Wisdom, continue," he said. His words were oddly amplified. It took a moment for Luthiel to realize the trees were rustling their leaves together and that it somehow increased the sound. "This new arrival makes your words and blessings even more important."

The Wisdom was a tall elf with a pointy nose and severe features. His white hair was pulled back into a braid that emphasized the sharp widow's peak upon his brow. His cheeks were russet and his thin lips curled into a smile as he saw them. With a show of mock humility, he gave a bow.

It's Elag! she realized.

"By my lord's favor, I will continue," the Wisdom replied as he turned to address the army.

"Companions in arms! We gather to confront the Vyrl!" he shouted to them. "So we ask Ëvanyar, father of all things, to guide and protect us as we move to strike down those that robbed us of our children! Year after year! Age after age! Now the days go down into darkness and the suns are in peril. Vyrl send messengers like crows before the storm to sow confusion. I assure you, what they will tell us is false. The bargain they offer—foul. They will ask for peace, but we will have war the moment we let down our defense. Why let these liars speak?" He drew a finger across his neck. "Silence them, I say. Better we do justice on them now! Let us do it and show the Vyrl our resolve is strong."

There was a rumble from the assembled host. At Elag's words, the Goblins and Gruagach let out cries of assent. Even among the Ithildar and Valemar there were tight knots who cheered Elag on. Others looked at these zealots with discomfort; but she could tell their anger was also aroused by Elag's words.

What has Mithorden led us to? They'll tear us apart!

"I say let them speak!" The High Lord shouted. His eyes were on Mithorden, who held up an open hand. The High Lord seemed to understand the gesture and he spoke with authority. "You've overstepped your bounds, Wisdom. You were here to give comfort and to bless us before battle. Now your words incite violence. Perhaps they are here to surrender."

"I warned this council before," Elag replied with a bow to the High Lord. "A greater terror now rules at the Vyrl's side. The Blood Witch of prophecy. I tell you as I am Wisdom. I saw her in dreams. Beautiful. Terrible. She is here. Darkness follows her."

At the Wisdom's words, elves shouted at one another, goblins bellowed and animals roared. None seemed in agreement. Some looked on the messenger with fear, others with hope.

"Who's this Blood Witch?" she whispered to Melkion.

"Don't know. I'm not much for religious studies. Prophecy is especially revolting."

The unicorn Elayethel seemed to agree with Melkion. "What is prophecy but a glorified wish for disaster?" she said once the noise died down. "The Blood Witch is among the worst. Oesha's end brought on by a woman? What rubbish. It's an offense to the great lady."

She drew herself up tall.

"*Ëvanya!*" she cried. The word echoed in the valley. Gruagach and Goblins flinched at the sound. A few made signs of warding. Other Fae frowned. "Have so many forgotten the magic of her name? You goblins once loved her. But adoration turned to anger. And you Gruagach abandoned her long ago." She said this with an angry glance at Zalos. "Now you curse her as wicked—a temptress and beguiler of men. Too many believe the lies. Women are flawed and evil. Sorceresses are foul witches, the servants of Gorthar. Blood Witch? Wisdom, do you know her? Or is she just a phantom of your hate?" She glared at Elag who opened his mouth to reply. Luthiel could see it wasn't going to be kind, but Elayethel interrupted him before he could. "I say let the messenger talk," she said in a voice that was like a clarion. "We do not know what he will say."

"Yes, let him talk," said Zalos with a clever smile. He seemed to be enjoying Elayethel's display. "Although I don't agree with your words on Prophecy. Those who ignore the future do so at their peril."

"Prophecy isn't about predicting the future," said the Lady Belethial. "It's about controlling what people believe about it. But at least in this I agree with you, Zalos. Let the messenger speak."

Where at first there was general uproar, now an eerie silence fell over the army. Luthiel felt her skin prickle as thousands of faces turned to her. She felt her head become light and her stomach fluttered. She'd never had so much attention directed at her and it was almost enough to make her sit down. Mithorden intervened, grabbing her by the elbow and marching her to the top of a nearby boulder.

Now every elf in the world can see me, she thought. The sorcerer gave her a wink.

"I'm going to say something first," he whispered. "Then it will be your turn. Are you ready?"

"I guess I'd better be," she said.

He gave a serious nod, then turned toward the elves.

"My friends," he began. "Many of you know me well." A number of Fae smiled when he spoke; but for each one that did, there were at least two that scowled. "I have just returned from a dangerous journey to the Vale of Mists itself." At this there was a general uproar; the suspicious Fae scowled even more and the ones who had smiled seemed shocked and surprised. "I did so because I recently had an exceptional visitor. It was a young girl who did something unheard of. She decided to go to the Vale of Mists in the place of a Chosen."

The response to this statement was even more extreme. Some jeered, while others nodded with open and solemn smiles. A few raised their voices to shout—"She broke the law! She should be punished!"

"Now, I agree with you. A law was broken. But maybe it was something that needed breaking long ago. I see some ten thousand Fae gathered together today to break another law. Yet I will not defend her actions other than to say I decided to help her."

Grumbling, head-shaking and a few more smiles followed.

"I gave her an enchantment to help her pass the Widdershae who'd invaded the land around the Vale. After meeting with the Faelords in Ithilden ten days ago, I went to visit her in the Vale of Mists. What I discovered there was extraordinary."

More mutters, deadly looks and a few hushed whispers.

"I won't say what. That is for our messenger. But it was so important I have risked my life to return here. All ways to and from the Vale were guarded by monsters. Six set out from Ottomnos. Four are here. Vaelros was wounded by a Widdershae and Ecthellien, a Vyrl of the Vale, was killed."

Mithorden was greeted with cheers and dark smiles. Even those who seemed to support the sorcerer were happy. Only a few held back from the general revelry. After a minute, the sorcerer raised his hands to quiet them. It took another minute before he was able to speak again.

"Many of you are not old enough to remember the Vyrl when Valkire turned them. If you were, then you would not cheer. This Vyrl died a hero. On Cauthraus, we were attacked by a dragon. Desire's own mate: Narhoth. To protect us, Ecthellien challenged her to single combat. He did not return."

Luthiel could feel a knot forming in her stomach as Mithorden spoke of Ecthellien. She wondered if she'd ever get used to the empty feeling his loss had left inside her. But it reminded her of the journey's purpose. Ahmberen and Elshael. They were tied to her now. In some ways it was a deeper bond than family. If they were monsters, then perhaps she was a monster as well. It didn't matter to her. If Ecthellien's loss had cemented one thing in her mind, it was that Vyrl deserved a chance to live.

"Would be better if the dragon got you all!" a goblin bellowed. There were shouts of assent and cries of anger among the other Fae. Too many raised voices in agreement. Too many lifted clenched fists to the sky.

"Listen to the message," Mithorden said. "You may not think so after you hear it."

"Then let him speak and we shall see!" the same goblin shouted.

"As you wish," Mithorden said with a bow. He nodded to Luthiel and gave her a tight grin. She didn't fault the sorcerer. She knew this was going to be difficult and he had spoken as well as could be expected. Better, in fact, than she thought she could ever speak to such a group.

What has happened to them? she thought. *They're so full of rage. Why?* She glanced suspiciously at Zalos and Elag. *It's been building for years. Those two are just riding it.*

With a deep breath she stepped forward. The veil lay over her face. A thin strip of fabric the only thing between her and ten thousand swords. She stood on top of a boulder, yet she felt is was only a pebble cast in an angry sea. The fae pressed in from all around. Though she searched and searched, she couldn't find even one friendly face. Her hands trembled. She clasped them together to keep them still.

"Greetings from the Vale of Mists!" she shouted. It was eerie how the trees seemed to catch her voice and throw it out across the valley. Worse was the roar of jeers that answered her. She resisted the urge to stumble back. Melkion blew an angry cloud of smoke and hissed. The display only incited the Fae.

"Give us the dragon! Give him to us! We'll make him pay for all the bad news he's brought!"

Finally, after a good minute of shouting, the elves seemed to have spent enough of their rage to quiet down.

"I bring tidings of joy and an offering of peace." She spoke the words with caution, doing her best to sound gracious and unassuming. *Did I say it well?* she worried. *Does it even matter?*

There were some more cries and angry shouts from the crowd. But most sat still with blank faces or looked at her suspiciously. Among the Faelords, the unicorn Elayethel, the Lady Belethial, and the High Lord Tuorlin seemed to be giving relieved yet cautious smiles. Zalos' face seemed one of open consideration but his eyebrows were raised in surprise.

Probably plotting even now, she thought to herself with grim satisfaction. *I've put you in a bit of a spot, haven't I, Zalos? Bet you never thought I would return to give the Vyrl's offer.*

Then her eyes fell on Thrar Taurmori, towering over the army. She could see his face—eyes white hot and awful. Burning bright at her. She wished for Gormtoth strong and tall beside her. But even his great presence was no match to the lord of fire demons. The distance between them seemed little protection. He was terrible, tall, dangerous. She forced herself to look away.

"A Chosen like no other has come to the Vale," she continued. "Luthiel of Flir Light Hollow. The adopted Valshae. She lived among you for years and you did not know her. She must not have seemed like much for she was only an orphan. Yet there *was* something special about her. Her blood was enough to sate even Vyrl's hunger."

Now there was complete silence except for the voice of one small Red Cap who asked, "After so many years? How can it be true?"

"I don't know," Luthiel replied. "It is as strange to me as it is to you. Yet believe me when I say the Vyrl were restored."

Now one of them is dead.

"They have agreed to surrender and pay homage to all families who lost loved ones. To each disfigured by Mist. They only ask they be allowed to remain in the Vale and to have the girl, Luthiel, return once each year to feed them—keeping hunger and madness at bay. As a sign, they granted her equal lordship over the Vale. She would be the first Faelord to rule there in nearly three thousand years. The first since Vlad Valkire."

Now there was murmuring among the Fae. Some seemed suspicious; others shocked, and a few were relieved. Luthiel felt a little relieved as well.

Tuorlin raised his spear and shouted out in a clear voice. "By what right does Luthiel claim rulership of the Vale? To be the first Faelord there since Vlad Valkire?"

"Luthiel is no Valshae. She is the daughter of Vlad Valkire," she said it softly and as she did a breeze whispered around her. The trees picked up her words, carrying them to every corner of the fae army. If there was silence before, now the only thing she could hear was her heartbeat pounding in her ears.

I might really do it, she hoped. But she dare not believe it was over. In thousands of faces she saw doubt. *The daughter of a faerie tale returns? How convincing could I be?* Widdershae still surrounded the Vale. She wasn't certain how to talk about *them.* But she stood firm and waited for the question she knew would come. It was Zalos who finally raised his voice.

"The daughter of Vlad Valkire has returned?" His voice held a hint of mocking. "How can we know it is true? And what of the gestures of war the Vyrl have already made? Just two nights ago, Widdershae came and attacked us. They kidnapped a number of elves. Some were soldiers. But the rest were camp followers who never saw battle."

Luthiel looked down at Zalos. *I bet he knows more than he lets on,* she thought. For a moment, her nightmare came rushing back to her and she wondered again about The Dreaming. *The dragon was there and she became real enough. His six captains were there too. They would have told him.* She was careful with her words, fearing any misstep might lead to disaster.

"Only the blood of Vlad Valkire can restore Vyrl. Do not doubt that before Luthiel came they would have happily fought and killed you. Now they ask for peace. What better proof can I give? As for Widdershae—they are invaders of both Vale and Faelands. Vyrl are gathering an army to fight them and will not rest until the spiders are driven off. If you are wise and accept our offer, you will gain an ally against them. If you refuse, you must move through the spider's webs to fight the Vyrl. Can you make it? Or will they ensnare you all?"

It was the demon and not Zalos who answered her. It took her by surprise and the great sound of his voice—like a bonfire roaring in the wood—was enough to make her skip a half step back.

"What is the wisest course? Listen to the enemy that has eaten our children?" She could almost feel the heat radiating from the demon. But even worse was the spell of rage and anger it seemed to cast over the Faerie host. Where many had seemed to consider her a moment ago, now hands leapt to weapons and angry faces turned toward her. "I say strike now as the Vyrl beg for mercy," said the demon lord. "If we take this messenger, his wolf and his dragon, they will not know what we plan."

At this, the unicorn leapt onto a nearby bolder and let out a great cry. The sound was unlike the neighing of any horse. It was more like the sound of a trumpet that is followed by the clear ringing of bells. "My lord has confused cunning with wisdom, I think. It is never wise to have enemies where one could have friends, or to face two foes when you could turn one to your side."

The unicorn's words seemed to make the Fae pause. They turned on one another. There were shouts and even a few blows. Weapons flashed. A group of wolfriders formed to rush up at Luthiel. No sooner did this happen than a motley group of Fae led by the Red Cap who had spoken earlier, formed in front of Luthiel.

"For the lady!" he cried. In that moment, Luthiel's heart went out to him and she felt hope. *There are some who were inspired by what I have done. They'd even protect a hated messenger of Vyrl.* But the thought was short lived. Goblins and Gruagach alike were forming behind the wolfriders. Even a few Blade Dancers joined them. A Cat-o-Fae rushed at her. She saw its spinning blades catch the light only a moment before it plunged to her. It was far too fast for her to move in time. There was a ringing of metal on metal and a flash in the sunlight. Without her seeing it, Vanye's Cat-o-Fae had rushed up from behind and met the other Cat-o-Fae mid flight, deflecting it over her head.

Again and again, the Cat-o-Fae collided in the air like two great metal birds. Finally, as if by unspoken agreement, each returned to its Blade Dancer.

A battle line came together in front of her. Soldiers milled about, confused when a sergeant shouted one order and a captain shouted another. Ranks formed, then broke, then reformed as soldiers ran back and forth pulled in a tide of changing orders and loyalty. Some were paralyzed—unable to move or decide. She was surprised when a few hundred came to stand with her. Sergeants and captains saluted her.

"Brice, Captain of the Bonegrinders, at your service!" A redcap with a proud, flame colored, mohawk and teeth the size of pocket knives shouted.

"Hueron, Captain of the Warriors for the lady Luthiel!" Luthiel felt her eyes tear as she recognized her foster uncle at the head of Flir Light's fighting militia—a mix of archers, spear, and sword.

"Vanye of the Blade Dancers!"

"Jaedos, Captain of the Knights of the White Rose!"

The shouts continued and Luthiel looked over those who came to help her. Most were Valemar and Redcap goblins. There were also a surprising number of Blade Dancers and Knights of Ithilden. Before the greater army, they were a feeble force terribly outnumbered. She wondered how anyone would support her. *This is to be my journey's end? I'll never see Leowin or the others again? I've done my best. Even that isn't always enough.* In one hand she gripped the hilt of *Weiryendel*, in the other the bag that held her Wyrd Stone. If it was going to be a fight, she'd give these Fae something to remember.

It was then the High Lord Tuorlin finally acted. He'd been holding back, watching the gathering with growing anger and unease. He knew he must use the power of his rank now, or risk losing it. His hold over the Faelands had been sliding away from him for the better part of three years now and he wasn't going to let it go further without making a stand. As Luthiel prepared to struggle for her life, Tuorlin made his first move. Though his act was likely to bring a bad end, something about this messenger gave him hope. He saw her with the gift the Vale's Mists gave him long ago. They'd rushed him in much the same way they'd rushed Luthiel. Lacking any defense of Wyrd or song, he succumbed to their touch. The Mists tore the skin of his forehead, boring a hole through his skull as he cried out in pain. When they receded, from his open wound grew a third eye. With that eye Tuorlin could see things hidden—past, present, and future.

What he saw now was a great lady veiled by magic. He could see the marks of power and grace upon her. He had little doubt that this was the lady who'd delivered the Vyrl from madness. He knew, unless he did something, she'd be killed or taken. So he raised his great spear above his head and let out a loud cry.

"Stop! In the name of Ëvanya and Ëvanyar stop! In the name of Elwin stop! In the name of all that is good cease! Halt! Arrest!" As he cried out, a great light arose from his spear. It was more brilliant than a sun—shining so bright that it left all who stood in the valley reeling and blinded.

The light overwhelmed Luthiel and she fell. For a moment, she thought she was struck down by a great blow. Then her eyes cleared and she saw that everyone in the valley had fallen or stooped with hands over faces. Weapons lay dropped or discarded and most stood or sat in a daze.

"Wretches! Rabble! Fools! Hate has brought you here and made you think you were united. Before the battle is even made hate has broken your ranks and turned you one against the other. It is not this messenger, who brought an offering of peace, who should bear the blame. It is yourselves! I have said that this war is folly from the start but was turned when all the Court begged me for vengeance. Where is your vengeance now? Who will you avenge when you have killed your own brother? Fools every one! And they call you the fair race! I see no more than squabbling children!

"Ithilden! To me!" he cried. The great host of Ithildar broke rank and withdrew. Reforming around the High Lord. Tuorlin didn't wait for them to finish.

"By right of High Lord, I call a council. We will consider the words of this messenger. The Widdershae have taken as many lives in one night as these Vyrl have in centuries. Who now is the greater danger?"

Luthiel had finally found her voice.

"My Lord, if I may say one more thing?" she called out.

Tuorlin raised his hands and made a sharp gesture to quiet the fae. This time, discipline held. "Speak, but be quick!"

"Yes lord," Luthiel said with a bow. "It's about the spiders. We tried to pass them on our way to meet you. We saw some of the elves they'd taken. Most were being eaten. But some —" It was hard for her to continue. The images played over and over in her mind, making it difficult to keep her head together. "They used black magic. They turned elves—elves into spiders!"

The trees picked up her words and whispered them out to the Fae. They all fell silent and there was horror in their faces. A few of the Gruagach turned and shook their heads, but the rest stood in shock. She'd finally gotten the elves' notice. All eyes were on her and where she saw hatred before, now there was fear and confusion. She didn't know if she liked it any more than before.

A Welcome Surprise

"Make a way for them!" the High Lord shouted. "The council will be here and now for all to see. The Vyrl's messenger will speak for the Vale." Before her, the Fae parted, leaving a long aisle up to the Faelords.

Mithorden helped her down.

"You may take your veil off now," he whispered. "The magic has taken hold. They will see you, but only as they expect."

Luthiel nodded and, somewhat relieved, somewhat terrified, lifted the veil from her face as she walked down the lane through the army. As she passed all eyes were drawn to her. She could hear them whispering or speaking to one another in low voices.

"Look at the eyes," one said. "Those aren't the eyes of a killer."

She noticed she was moving through ranks of Valemar. Unlike the Gruagach, they were a mixed force with an equal number of men and women.

"He's beautiful," she heard one of the women whisper to another, followed by, "...and so young."

Vanye turned to Mithorden. "Marred by the Vale's magic? A fairer face I've never seen, Mithorden. Perhaps you should have spoken of the dangers of your messenger's charms."

Then Luthiel heard a voice that made her heart swell up in her chest.

"Messenger! Messenger!"

Could it be? With equal parts dread and anticipation she turned around. At first all she saw were hundreds of elfin faces staring back at her. Her eyes caught movement. There was a rustling as elves made way for a lady, hardly old enough to be called such, moving toward her. In her hands she held a great bow and at her hip was a long, thin, Faewand—the light and deadly swords of expert Valemar archers. Hueron's training had done her well, for she carried both sword and bow with an ease and grace that even Luthiel envied.

"Messenger!" she cried again, then gasped as Luthiel met her eyes.

"Leowin," Luthiel whispered. Behind her, she could feel as much as hear Vanye tense. The look in Leowin's eyes was one of both fear and wonder. But along with the wonder was a flash of open admiration. Leowin shook her head as if to clear it, put on that determined look she got when she wouldn't be denied, and set one foot in front of the other on her way toward Luthiel.

Luthiel couldn't believe what she was seeing. She'd seen Leowin approach boys in this way, but never thought she'd be the object of one of those considering looks.

"Messenger," she said again with a smile as though she liked the word better now. "Is it true? Is Luthiel really coming back to us?"

Luthiel felt a number of emotions she couldn't name flood over her. She wanted to reach out to her and give her a big hug and then say, "It's me, silly!" She wanted to scold her for joining the army and putting herself at such risk. She wanted to laugh like they did when they were six or ten and forget all about wars and Widdershae and other nonsense and get down to the important business of some good fun. Last of all she wanted to run far away from that look Leowin was fixing her with. "She'll come when she can," she said in a low voice.

Leowin fell in beside her, looking both relieved and intrigued. "She's not hurt? She's not changed?"

"Neither," Luthiel replied.

"Are you sure?" Leowin asked.

"She's as whole as when she came," Luthiel said, and couldn't help but let a cunning smile touch her lips.

"How do you know?"

"You're not the only one who knows secrets," Luthiel said as her smile broadened.

"Some would say she's far more," rumbled Othalas from behind them.

Leowin started and turned a wary eye to the werewolf.

"Othalas?" she said, suppressing a tremor of fear. "I thought you would show up at any moment." Her hand fell to the hilt of her sword and her eyes grew fierce despite her fear. "I was ready for you."

"Leowin, I presume. A very lucky girl. It wasn't too long ago that I promised I'd see Vyrl drink your blood."

The color that had risen into Leowin's cheeks suddenly drained away and she looked more like the scared ghost Luthiel remembered on that terrible First Summer's Eve night.

"Where is Luthiel?" Leowin said sharply. "Why isn't she here?"

Othalas bristled and gave a gruff chuckle. He lowered his massive head to look Leowin directly in the eyes. "I give you my word. Luthiel is alive."

"Your word?" Leowin snapped, taking a half step back. "The word of a servant of murderers?"

Othalas showed his great fangs. "No more," he growled, "I serve Luthiel now."

Leowin blinked her eyes, a little taken aback. "You could be lying. What proof do you have?"

Othalas' growl deepened and he fixed his great yellow eyes on Leowin. One snap of the werewolf's enormous jaws would easily have made an end of her. Luthiel grabbed Leowin's wrist and pulled her away from the wolf.

"Easy," she said to Othalas and the great wolf looked away. "Leowin," she said, looking her sister in the eye, "we have proof. The Stone saved Luthiel from the Mists. The one you gave her on her birthday. The magic. The song. *More graceful than willows...*"

Leowin fell to her knees and clutched herself. In that moment, Luthiel wanted more than anything to embrace her. To give her some comfort. But she stood still and did her best to keep from showing any of the emotion that was tearing through her.

"She's alive," Leowin whispered.

"Alive and coming home," Othalas rumbled.

"Home?" Leowin stood sizing the great wolf up. She turned back to the elfin host and shouted while thrusting her arm into the air, "See! Even Othalas says it's true! Hueron! Lorethain! Luthiel's coming back! Three cheers for Luthiel!"

The Valemar in this area all seemed to be from Flir Light. Luthiel recognized faces even where she couldn't remember names. Leowin thrust her arm into the air with each shout.

"Luthiel! Luthiel! Luthiel!"

The cheers were infectious and soon a good part of the Valemar host were cheering as well. Luthiel wanted to cry and laugh. Instead she shouted along with them. Melkion took up the cry and flew a merry jig above them, drawing her name in flaming letters till the host of Valemar were hoarse from shouting. Even Mithorden and Othalas joined in. The other Fae watched on, and the display seemed to have an effect on even some Gruagach.

They moved on past the Valemar. The faces around them grew somber again and the cheering died down. Melkion returned with a big grin on his face but performed no more tricks. Luthiel looked sideways at Leowin. She half expected her sister to return to the Valemar. She didn't want her to go.

"Why are you still here?" Luthiel asked.

"Well, I thought you might need me." She looked around at the fae army. "Besides, it's dangerous here."

"I think it would be best if you went back," It hurt Luthiel to say this, but it was probably true.

"Besides," Melkion said proudly, "we're here to protect the messenger."

"One more won't hurt," Leowin said with a determined look and marching off with them toward the Faelords. "Another council! It's all so splendid!"

Mithorden looked down at Leowin with his eyebrows raised and exchanged a look with Luthiel as if to say, *is she always like this?*

Luthiel only shook her head. She wanted to laugh, but they were getting close to the Faelords now, and the weight of the whole event was again beginning to fall upon her. As she approached, she could see their eyes following her. For the first time, Luthiel wished she still had the veil.

BATTLE PLANS

As she approached them, she found herself in the shadow of Thrar Taurmori. His eyes fell upon her and where his gaze touched her, she felt uncomfortably warm. He stood stiff and seemed to tremble, as though holding back violence.

Far worse was the speculative and oddly magnetic gaze of Zalos. His face was angular, crisp, young, and when he smiled at her she found it difficult not to smile back. Everything about him radiated confidence and power. He looked every bit a hero of legend. In his face, she found resigned conviction. It was as though he'd come to some momentous decision long ago and now was at peace with himself about it. She had to keep reminding herself that here was the lord who'd used black magic to enslave Vaelros, imprisoned her mother, and likely ordered her death as a child. Looking at him, though, she could understand why elves loved him and followed him blindly.

"Welcome messenger," Zalos said. "Do you have a name? Or should we call you by your title only?"

Luthiel tensed but didn't hesitate.

"I am called Valas," she replied without thinking.

Beside her Leowin gave her a look of surprise. Luthiel silently cursed. Valas was the name she used whenever Leowin and she pretended they were knights. Leowin had always chided her for the name, which she thought was pretentious.

The exchange wasn't lost on Zalos, who grinned at both the surprised look on Leowin's face and the uncomfortable look Luthiel gave her in return. "Well met then, Valas. A brave speaker. Still, words and swords are quite different things. I hope you survive the day."

He said it as politely as if he'd asked her to a cup of tea.

"To just survive?" Mithorden asked. "We should hope for far better things."

Zalos leaned forward and looked Mithorden directly in the eye. There was a flash of something like anger between them and Luthiel wondered if Mithorden's words weren't part of an older argument. For a moment, she thought of her talk with Mithorden. She wondered if the sorcerer had told her everything. For the warm and friendly smile Zalos gave now was enough to make her doubt.

Remember, Luthiel thought to herself to keep from smiling in return. *Remember what he did to my mother.* Luthiel was so caught up in her thoughts she didn't realize Zalos was speaking again.

"What good is life if it has ended? There's no opportunity for joy in death. The day is coming, Mithorden, when survival will be the only concern and joy a half-remembered fancy. It's not far away."

"More prophecy, Zalos?" the sorcerer replied.

"Call it what you like. Have you heard the Blood Witch prophecy, then? Maybe you should. The warning is there in the sky."

Mithorden didn't reply this time, he only looked at Zalos with a puzzled expression. He seemed taken off guard. There seemed to be something he didn't expect in Zalos' argument. Finally, he replied by saying simply, "The best lies hold in them a seed of truth."

"So you've heard of the Blood Witch? Have you seen her too?"

"I know of no Witch. In fact, I dislike the word altogether, the way *you* use it. But I am aware of signs in the sky, if that's what you're talking about."

To this Zalos nodded. "We've always been more alike than you realize, Lord Mithorden." When Zalos said it, a look fell over Mithorden's face that seemed alien. In his eyes she could see a bit of the bright being she'd seen in the light of the Wyrd Stone. But it was only momentary and this time it seemed far stranger.

"You would see it that way," Mithorden replied. He looked at Thrar Taurmori and seemed to shake his head sadly, then returned his gaze to Zalos. "We become what we do, Zalos."

At this, Zalos' face became glazed and momentarily very intense. "I do what I must to survive. I help others to do the same. Some of what you advise would kill us."

"I would rather live than die. But I would rather die than survive as a monster," Mithorden said, his sharp eyes locked on Zalos.

The other Faelords had watched this exchange with interest. "Practical is what we must be now," Lord Tuorlin said, with an eye to Zalos. "Any misstep might cost more lives than we've lost in an age. I am of a mind to take the Vyrl's offer. The Widdershae have become the greater danger. We should use our strength to drive them from the Faelands."

Belethial and Elayethel nodded their assent. Zalos frowned and Thrar Taurmori just loomed.

"So you would risk trusting Vyrl?" Zalos asked. "What if it's a trick?"

"We'll send out scouts," Belethial said. "We'll know well in advance if the Vyrl and Widdershae are mixing forces. We've seen none of it so far. Two days ago there was a report of the Vyrl's Firewing attacking Widdershae. We thought it an odd incident. But what the messenger says rings true to our sightings."

"You are all in agreement?" Zalos asked the other Faelords. His eyes cut from one to the next, summing them up.

Tuorlin, Belethial and Elayethel nodded.

"Then I will fight with you," Zalos said. "Yet I fear this is a ruse the Vale's new power has cast over us."

Elag's face became grave. "Lord, it is also my fear the elves will come to regret this choice. The Wyrd about the Vale has been disturbed. I can sense the new power reaching out. Was it not said she would seem fair?"

Mithorden and Tuorlin met eyes.

"Now is not the time to bandy superstition," the sorcerer said.

"We must strike the spiders fast," Tuorlin said, turning to Luthiel. "The Vyrl will give us aid?"

"They will," Luthiel said with a nod.

"You must send word. It is known to us they communicate using birds. Great talking crows. They should be sent for immediately so we can coordinate an attack. If the spiders don't expect us to act together, then we may catch them unawares."

As Tuorlin spoke, Luthiel felt a grim smile creep over her face. After seeing their treatment of elves—as slaves and as food—she'd found herself wanting to kill the spiders. There was a battle lust inside of her now. She reveled in rage and it left her hollow. *I want to kill them and I don't regret it.*

She turned to Melkion. "Will you fly to them?" she asked.

Melkion also seemed to be infected with a killing lust. "Gladly," he replied. "What shall I tell them?"

"Tell them to bring their main force to bear against the spiders at first light tomorrow," Tuorlin said. "At the same time, we will strike them from the cliffs. It will take a day for us to move and prepare. But no more. Already, our scouts have burned paths through the shadow webs and work to keep the ways open for us. If the Vyrl can drive the spiders to the Rim Wall, we can rain fire and death down upon them from above. A force of cavalry, knights and wolf riders, will sortie around the spiders and into the Vale to join with the Vyrl. This combined force should be enough to drive the spiders into our trap—shadow webs or no."

If Zalos seemed troubled by this plan, his face didn't show it. Luthiel expected more argument but was pleasantly surprised when he offered none. He just nodded and gave the necessary orders to his Lieutenants. The Urkharim would journey south along with a force of Tyndomiel in animal form and the knights of Ithilden riding Faenmare. Zalos himself would be the leader of this sortie. The rest would stay with the main force which would consist chiefly of archers, the slower, sturdier animals, infantry and ballistae. The Vyrl would also be asked to contribute Firewing and any other flying beasts able to attack the Widdershae from above.

When all plans were made, Melkion spread his rainbow wings and lifted himself into the sky.

Be careful! Luthiel thought to him as he slowly faded into the blue.

TO WAR

Like waves gather ahead of a storm, the army formed. Sword and spear came together before columns of cavalry backed by archers. Everywhere she looked, sunlight glistened on helm, arrowhead, lance, and sword.

Zalos rode out to his wolfriders. They gathered beneath Ashiroth's banner. A ring of gold with crystal thorns in fire. Luthiel wondered if Zalos wore the awful thing even now.

How can he even think? Yet there he sits— authority itself.

Coming to the standard, he took it in hand and thrust it high. A breeze caught the cloth.

"Wolfriders!" Zalos cried out. The riders raised their closed fists and answered with a cheer. The Faelord paused, meeting the eyes of each of his captains. An aisle parted in the group and Luthiel's breath caught as she saw the six captains approach Zalos, then surround him in a protective ring. A few cast looks her way, cold eyes making numb assessment of her and Othalas. One gathered up the banner staff. In a moment, the colors were gone and her eyes were drawn to the dulled armor, to the bits of cloth tied to weapon and harness.

"To the Vale!" Zalos commanded. Then, they drifted up the hill. Like a cloud, they passed into the trees and melted out of sight.

"Just like that," she whispered to Othalas, making a snap with her fingers.

"Ashiroth's pride," Othalas replied. "Silent and deadly is the wolfriders' attack. Take care where you sleep if you want to keep your neck."

"I'm not sleeping more than arms length away from you."

Othalas gave a low rumble.

Beside her, Tuorlin shouted orders and knights on Faenmare rode up to join him. Among them were Blade Dancers. Cat-o-Fae shifted, spun or flexed their blades. A few drifted above them—flitting through the air like metallic birds. Thrar Taurmori remained so close she could smell the burning and Elag lurked nearby. Trying not to stare, she kept her eyes ahead. All around, horns blew and the army moved. But she stood still, rooted by a demon's glare. Remembering Gormtoth, she wondered how well Mithorden's spells kept her secret.

Troubled, Luthiel looked away.

"I'd rather be in a Widdershae den than to have *them* know where I'm sleeping." She nodded toward Elag and Gormtoth.

Othalas nudged her.

"Get on," he growled. "Best stay with me now."

Glad to be near the big wolf, she sprang to his back and found herself surprised and somewhat pleased to be looking down upon the Faelords and their army. What she saw made her breath catch. Where before there was bickering, now an eerie silence lay over them. She could see fear in their faces. They'd heard the old tales since childhood. For all knew of the eastern mountains' danger. The terror that consumed the Delvendrim. An army sent to face it disappeared. All but one—driven mad by the fear.

"May I say something to them?" she asked the High Lord.

"What will you tell them?" Tuorlin's third eye was like an oval of night in his forehead—absorbing everything, revealing nothing.

At least I need not hide from everyone.

"Something to give them heart," she replied.

"You may. But be brief and have a care what you say. Many still think you're the enemy."

With a nod, she turned Othalas to face the army.

"Fae of Oesha!"

Picked up by the trees, her call rang out. In a moment, all eyes were on her. There was something in the sunlight. It splashed like a rain of fire-drops and graced her brow with a shining ring. In that instant, they saw a fierce and heavenly warrior. One recalled from tales of Oesha's making and the great wars fought in the void. Wyrd shining through her, the enchantment touched them all. Though she didn't know she used it.

Mithorden chuckled to himself. "Daughter of Valkire, indeed," he said softly.

Silence carried through the wood and seemed far louder than her shout. The whole place was listening. Even the trees held their breath.

"I did not just come to give a Vyrl's message. I also came to bring news of hope!"

She paused and the silence stretched on again but this time it was pierced by a proud voice. A Tyndomiel in the shape of a bear lifted his growl in answer.

"When has hope ever come from beyond the Mounds of Losing?"

"When Vlad Valkire ruled," she replied, "beyond the Mounds lay the only hope. Or do you not remember?"

She paused again and this time all were silent.

"You do not face this danger alone or without aid. The Vyrl you once feared have become your friends. As proof, I will ride beside you on great Othalas! But I am not your only new ally. A force from the mighty fortress Ottomnos is coming to help you. We of the Vale are strong! We of the Vale are with you!"

With her last words, Othalas bounded in one spring to the top of a great boulder. His claws scored the stone as he lifted his head high and let out a great howl. The trees echoed his call. In answer, the fae gave cry. The sound rose and became so loud that beasts for miles around stopped to listen. Gone was the apprehension of a few minutes before, gone the fear. They were ready. Othalas sensed it too. The fae were going to war.

"Now you've got them raring for it," The great wolf growled.

"I hope I did the right thing," she said grimly.

"We'll soon find out."

With a number of whispered commands and hand signals, the elves began their march.

Since the lands' forming, fae honored their dead at the Mounds of Losing. Later it became the point of no return for Chosen. As they entered the mounds, many touched their foreheads out of respect or bowed, whispering prayers for their lost. Even in normal times it was an eerie place. The land rolled and jutted, seeming to take on strange and elusive shapes. Beyond, the Vale of Mists was crowned in ever-shifting cloud. Shadows danced over rolling hills, taking on shapes that tricked the eye. Further in, they began to see threads of darkness bending at impossible angles against the dual light. But as the webs grew thick about them, their path remained clear—the work of goblin scouts and their trained salamander.

The elves traveled in loose formation. In front, lines of swordsmen were backed by spear. Behind were great ballistae among knots of the small but vicious Red Cap. These fae wore studded leather coats but bore no weapons. Their teeth were enough—able to smash a sword or crack the thickest armor. In a lane through the middle were what remained of the riders. They formed in a wedge with five Blade Dancers bearing Cat-o-Fae and longspears at the point. She rode along with Vanye, three more Blade Dancers, and the Faelords at the wedge's center. Archers looked down from the trees and the air was filled with Tyndomiel in hawk and eagle form. In their talons, they each bore a javelin and among them flew pixies with tiny crystal wands.

Luthiel watched the army in wonder. She never thought the Faelands could gather so much power in one place. Riding at their center was heady. For the first time since she left Ottomnos, she felt secure.

"Impressive isn't it?" Mithorden said to her. The elves had given him a great gray Faenmare to ride, but he still had to look up at Luthiel. "Don't be fooled, armies far greater than this have come to nothing in a matter of moments."

Luthiel blanched.

For a time, they rode on in silence. They were in a region that gradually rose before meeting the Rim Wall. Though spider webs surrounded them, they still seemed sparse and haphazard. The spiders who made these webs must have fled or hidden at the army's approach. For Luthiel could see no sign of them. But the creatures trapped—some still alive, some dead and sucked dry—bore gruesome testimony to the danger closing in about them.

Overhead, there was a chirping and commotion among the hawks and pixies. A few archers stopped to look skyward. In the distance, what seemed like a small cloud appeared. Slowly, it grew until Luthiel realized it was a flock of birds. They were tiny mu-sparrow with azure and golden feathers. They flew high, well away from any shadow web, then coming abreast of the army, dove down upon them. As they approached she could hear excited chirping. They paused above the army as though looking for something then shot down again, rushing directly toward Luthiel. In an instant, the flock was upon her. It shot overhead, banked left, then turned to plunge again. On the second pass, the flock swirled around her and Luthiel had the odd sensation that she sat in the center of a whirlpool as the birds swirled and dipped. The excited chirping grew even louder and a few whizzed by so close she could reach out and touch them. After only moments, the flock lifted off and was flying away—back toward where the land was free of shadow webs.

Luthiel felt breathless.

"Why did they come? Why so many?"

Othalas gave out a gravelly chuckle. "Tuorlin isn't the only one gifted with special sight. Birds can see the very forces of Oesha. The force that binds the moons to her, the force that pulls a loadstone north, even rivers of Wyrd are visible to birds in colors more vivid than we could imagine."

"So what does that have to do with what happened?"

"They came to see *you*." The werewolf replied in a much softer voice.

She leaned forward and bent over his ear before whispering "they can see *me?*"

Othalas nodded. "Oh yes, probably better than anyone save Tuorlin."

"But why would they want to?"

"Rumor spreads among beasts and birds fast. It's seldom they care about elves, but they do take an interest from time to time. It definitely seems they have in you."

Leowin, who'd been riding a Faenmare beside Mithorden and asking him an endless battery of questions suddenly turned toward them.

"Why would so many birds come? Why would they be so interested in you?" Leowin's question seemed to be echoed in the eyes of all who surrounded her. Indeed, the entire army had turned to look. It seemed to pause. But when Luthiel was not forthcoming with any answers, it returned to the march and the battle ahead.

Othalas tilted his head and let out a low growl. "Keep your nose to yourself. Mithorden may humor you but I have a temper. If you become too annoying I may eat you and solve two problems in one—your constant twitter and the rumbling in my belly."

"If there's a secret here," Leowin said, "I'll find it out."

"Good at getting into trouble, I'd imagine," Mithorden said with a smile and a twinkle in his eye.

This only seemed to egg Leowin on. "You don't know how much trouble I can be. You're not telling me everything about my sister. Seems she's done something extraordinary. But she's gotten herself in even deeper trouble. She broke a terrible law." Leowin lowered her voice and shot a glance at the Faelords who rode less than twenty feet away. "Tuorlin, Elayethel, and Belethial are fair. But law is law. There's always consequences."

Luthiel couldn't resist. "As I recall, you're the reason she journeyed to the Vale in the first place."

Leowin hung her head. "I know," she said. "I kept saying there was something extraordinary about her. I just didn't expect her to prove me right by going to the Vale of Mists. Then getting the Vyrl to ask for peace! This will upset a lot of powerful fae who like hating Vyrl. The trouble's just started and I need to find Luthiel before it gets even worse. You should have heard all *his* talk about Witches!" She nodded her head to Elag who'd ridden a little ways off but could probably still make out bits of the conversation. "Wisdom?" Leowin whispered. "They mistitled him. Should've made it Deceit."

"So you're not angry with Luthiel?" she asked.

Leowin looked up at her.

"Why don't you come down and ride with me for a bit so we can chat about it, Valas?" There was that twinkle again. She said the words plain and open but the invitation for more was in her eyes. Luthiel could feel her cheeks becoming hot. It was infuriating! Sometimes Leowin could be such a fool. Luthiel stole a glance at Vanye. His face was as impassive as ever. But, now and again, his eyes stole over to Leowin. *He does care for her. But he keeps it under tight guard.*

"He's staying put," Othalas replied. "Things could get dangerous fast and battles have too many accidents."

Leowin shrugged her shoulders, then gave an even bigger grin. "Maybe after, then?"

Luthiel nodded. "Maybe after," she said evenly. What Othalas said struck her and she glanced anxiously at Thrar Taurmori who was striding lazily beside them. His pace was slow and his body language spoke of boredom and contempt. Watching him made her feel like she was riding beside an executioner. It was more than just the heat coming from him that made her sweat.

SPARRING

They continued to travel throughout the morning and into the afternoon. It was nearing Soelee set when they finally drew to a halt. They were on the edge of much denser webs and not far beyond lay the Vale itself. Some parts of the army had encountered spiders but any violence was limited to small skirmishes. True to the fae, the army had moved to mask its size, using the land between it and the spiders as a screen. The only difficulty was with the goblins. A constant clamor rose from their ranks and they seemed intent on breaking everything they passed. Bits of leftover meals and other trash marked their passing. A group of pixies had to be sent behind them to pick up. The goblins only laughed when they saw this.

"Let the spiders come!" they would say, and some were even so bold as to bang weapons against shields.

Despite her hard living over the past few weeks—which was slowly encasing her body in lean but nearly invisible muscle—she felt tired and sore after the long march. Othalas' size made it difficult for her to hold on with her legs. The result was an almost constant strain on her whole body. *I'd rather run than ride*, she thought.

The Faelords had made camp beneath a great tree which was mostly free of shadow webs. Despite the scouts' hard work and that of the pixies—who used their wands to shoot burning sparks at the shadow webs—many webs remained, and inevitably someone got caught. The army was already busy burning the odd bear or goblin out of the webs. But for every one set free, it seemed that at least one more stumbled into another snare. Soon the camp was filled with muffled shouts and shuffling. Luthiel wondered if moving an army in after the spiders was such a good idea.

She didn't have long to think, though, and she'd barely had a chance to let her muscles unwind before Vanye came to where she was sitting against a tree and tossed something down to her. A padded practice sword and a bag bulging with food plopped at her feet. Upon seeing the food, her mouth immediately began to water.

"That's for after," Vanye said as she grabbed the bag. His voice was even but his eyes were stern. He motioned to the practice sword. "For some reason, Mithorden seems to think you need instruction. I volunteered."

Luthiel sized him up and immediately disliked the idea. She remembered sparring with Hueron and the beatings she used to get from it. She got a lot more than she gave. She was certain the Blade Dancer would be far worse. Then there was also Leowin to consider. Would Vanye hold a grudge? Seeing no alternative, she flipped the practice sword into her hand and sprang to her feet.

"Mithorden says I need practice?"

"It's as strange to me as it is to you. Let's get this over with."

So Vanye isn't excited about the idea either, she thought. He turned and began leading her to an open area. He walked with a relaxed gait, his practice sword held loosely in his hand. Without looking at her he began talking.

"How experienced are you?"

"Not very. I'm best with a knife or faewand," she replied.

He glanced over his shoulder at her. "A luneblade would be better for someone of your build." Without warning he spun at her, bringing his practice sword around in an arc that made the air hiss. She was taken completely unawares. Her practice sword was held point down in her right hand, which was also her bad hand. She didn't have time to reposition, by reflex, she lifted her practice sword to block. She never made it in time. Vanye's sword pounded against her forearm making it sting with pain. Without the pads, a loud crack would have reported through the woods. Now the sword made only a muffled thud. She flinched at the pain. But the Blade Dancer wasn't finished, with flick of his wrists the practice sword had switched direction and was whistling toward her legs. She lowered the point and pivoted. Thud! This time her block worked.

Did I actually do it? she thought.

Unable to retaliate because of the speed with which each blow fell, she jumped, shifted, and danced to block each one. After about a minute, Vanye stopped.

"See what I mean?" he said. "Holding it back hand is natural for you."

She nodded and wiped the sweat from her lip.

"You're tall with long arms and a deceptively slight frame," Vanye continued. "If you keep the blade backhand, it brings your opponent closer and increases the likelihood he will overstep." He grabbed her sword wrist. His hand was there before she knew he'd moved. Firmly, but gently, he guided her hand in an arc. "Your speed and reach make for a vicious counter. Attack by making arcs, whip strikes, or by a back hand thrust." He demonstrated each attack with a new motion. "Now let's try it full speed."

Full speed? She'd barely had time to think before Vanye's sword was hissing through the air again. She did manage the first block but the force of Vanye's blow left her arm numb and the second blow caught her across the chest, toppling her onto her back. The air rushed from her lungs in an explosion. She gasped for breath. The tip of Vanye's practice sword lowered, hovering over her neck.

"So what interest do you have with Leowin?" There it was sudden and straight as an arrow flies on a windless day.

She gasped a couple more times before she was finally able to form words.

"I saw her looking at me, if that's what you mean. I'm not interested." The tip of Vanye's practice sword lowered and he helped her stand. Then, he began lazily swinging at her. He wasn't moving fast at all. But somehow, he managed to keep her on the defensive despite his seemingly slow swings. She felt embarrassed—like a child being tossed around by a grown up for fun. She prided herself on her speed. But it did little good when matched against Vanye's efficiency.

"She's very lovely," he said as he brought a blow down on her that would have split her skull—sword padding or no.

"I thought Blade Dancers weren't supposed to fall in love," she gasped. Both her hands stung terribly. *How can he put so much force behind his blows? He looks strong, certainly, but it feels like I'm fending off a tree trunk!*

"Happens from time to time. It'll ruin your *li* then you'll go insane as the Wyrd tears you apart from the inside out." He swung again and this time her practice sword did break. His sword continued and knocked her sideways. She fell to the ground, did a somersault, then sprang up. *I'll be lucky if I'm not torn apart by this sword practice.* Her hands smarted and she shook them to ease the sting. Vanye grabbed another practice sword that was leaning against a tree and handed it to her.

"Does it happen to everyone?"

"Not Zalos, Valkire and Tuorlin. Here, relax your hand a bit." He moved her hand to a place on the hilt that felt much more comfortable. "Keep your wrist loose. When the blow falls let it give a little and then do the same with the rest of your body."

"Only three?"

"Slim chances." Vanye's sword lunged deceptively at her face, then, as she countered, slipped by her guard and raked her ribs. But she blocked two more blows and managed a counter attack. She gritted her teeth against the pain as she fended off more of the Blade Dancer's awesome blows. He was moving faster now and more of his strikes were finding flesh. Each blow stung enough that she knew it would leave an angry bruise. *If it keeps up for much longer, he'll beat me to death.*

"I've thought about it and am no longer worried," he said between sword strikes. "Come what will, I'm happy to have felt love." His face got a strange look to it. "Luthiel would understand."

Two successive blows knocked her off her feet once more. She came up with her lip bloody. She spat on the ground. The punishment was really starting to make her angry. She was being whipped around like a rag doll and Vanye hadn't even broken a sweat. She stayed on her knees for a few moments while she caught her breath.

"I understand," she growled through clenched teeth. The odd thing was, despite her anger, she did. She couldn't imagine how lonely and terrible a Blade

Dancer's life must be. "Always fighting. Never knowing love or companionship. It's a wonder you don't all go mad."

With those words, she sprang to her feet and whipped her sword at Vanye. She attacked time after time, doing her best to hold onto her practice sword as Vanye delivered block followed by bone-jarring block. Vanye countered and she began to feel as though she were about to be tossed through the air again. Then, she saw something that made her smile. She angled her practice sword so that Vanye's blade went over her head. For a moment, he was exposed. She made a quick slash at his open side. Vanye saw or sensed what had happened and sprang back. In an instant he was out of reach.

Luthiel felt her heart sink. "You're just too fast," she growled in exasperation.

Vanye stood still, dropped the point of his sword and raised his hand. He stared at it. "You touched me," he said. The words were direct and without wonder. But the way he turned his arm you'd think he'd discovered treasure. "That hasn't happened with a new trainee in two years." His eyes lifted, appraising her again. "You're quick." He lowered himself and delivered a series of strikes so fast she couldn't see them at all and had to rely entirely on intuition. The first one she blocked but the second two stung her arms and the last one hit her throat.

She fell to her knees wheezing for air.

Vanye came over, knelt beside her and massaged her neck. In a few heartbeats, air was flowing again. Finally she was able to speak.

"You're not treating me rough because of Leowin? If so, maybe I need another practice partner."

Vanye looked at the ground and let out a laugh. "Perhaps. It did make me angry. But I feel less that way now after we've spoken. It's more Mithorden. He said to give you a tough lesson."

Luthiel nodded. "I hope the rest aren't so bad."

For the first time since she'd been with him that day, Vanye grinned. "It only gets worse."

SPIDERS AND MISTS

He led her back to the tree and handed her some Yewstaff fruit, then left her alone to eat. She smiled as the coolness swept through her, mending her hurts. She'd almost finished her meal when she noticed a small group of rats in front of her. They'd sifted through the grass, poking out long, twitching noses. Heads, bodies, and feet followed. They sat in front of her, bringing their little hands up to their faces and making gestures as if washing. Then, from behind them, a large, white rat came forward. He carried an aelberry in his teeth. The fruit was full and round—bursting with ripeness. He brought it directly in front of Luthiel, and then, in an almost dainty motion, placed it on a smooth rock. He sat back, making the same washing gesture with his paws. Luthiel looked at the fruit. Despite herself, she smiled at the rats. She loved ripe aelberry. Could they have brought it for her? Dropping her hand, she slowly picked up the berry and brought it to her mouth. When the juice touched her tongue its taste was perfection. She savored the berry, taking little bites to make it last. All too soon, the berry was gone. Still the rats sat before her, small eyes twinkling in the moons' light.

"Thank you my little friends," she whispered to them. Suddenly, the rats became agitated. Their whiskers twitched and they crouched close to the ground—small bodies trembling in fright. With one last look at her, they bounded into the grass.

What a strange and wonderful thing! she thought, still tasting the aelberry on her tongue. Her skin prickled and she noticed a slight breeze disturbing the still air. Looking skyward, she saw a mercury body born aloft by a pair of rainbow wings threading its way toward her through the moonbeams.

"Melkion!" she cried. "You missed it! Vanye nearly killed me."

"Hssst!" the dragon replied as he alighted on a low-hanging branch. "No time for joking! I need to talk to the lords now!" Then he froze. A still had settled over the wood. Moonlight fell through the crooked shadows. Over the hillside she saw a swaying as long arms of mist reached down into the camp. Melkion spread his wings wide, feeling the slight movements of air with their sensitive membrane. His tongue slipped out, tasting the wind. "I'm too late," he said finally. "They're here."

Luthiel fell into a crouch and rushed to gather her things.

"Here? Now?" she asked as she buckled on her sword-belt and slung her quiver. "Where could they come from?"

Melkion craned his head, peering into the darkness. "With the mists!" he hissed. "I can feel them around us."

Luthiel scanned the darkness. "I don't see anything."

"They're masters of stealth. They've even come upon dragons unaware. See them? Look to the mists!"

Luthiel's eye peeled back the darkness and she saw places about the camp where the mists had formed into pools. In one, she thought she saw a spider flexing its legs. Her skin quivered. The thing was easily within jumping distance. She started to run.

"They'll see us!" Melkion hissed, and he was off, flying through the air beside her.

"Better we who know than those who do not." Without a thought she drew *Weiryendel*, holding it backhand as Vanye had instructed. It hummed through the air as she ran, giving her an odd sense of comfort despite the coming trouble. When she neared the center of camp, she held her hand high and sang out —

Lumen! Unmask, illume, reveal!

The Wyrd came to her easy as breath this time and her hand erupted in a flower of light. A thousand rays seemed to shoot out and each one found a Widdershae, outlining it in a brief silvery glow. They were everywhere throughout the camp. Those that saw them stared in shock. Luthiel was fast to follow up.

"To me! To me!" she shouted, waving her still-glowing hand as a signal.

In camp, the force had made guard and fortification. A full half stood alert with weapons at the ready. They formed a rough circle with sword and spear on the outside, archers and horse to the center. More archers perched in trees along with rookeries of eagle, hawk, and pixie. Bear and wolf Tyndomiel prowled both in and along the outskirts of this woodland fortress. Small groups of Blade Dancers roamed through the camp, talking to captains and checking to see if the positions were secure. Only the goblins were belligerent and many had simply dropped to the ground and fallen asleep then and there. The exception was a small group of Red-Caps who stood away from their fellows and whispered among themselves of dark dealing and betrayal.

That the spiders had slipped into the faerie host was no small feat. Some may think it bad luck that Tuorlin had chosen this time to rest—sitting eyes closed and back to a great tree. But the spiders had sent their scouts to climb to the very tops of the highest trees. From there, ugly eyes could see far and it was easy for the long-legged things to swing out to other tree-tops for a better view. In this way, they had watched the elves move, using their strange Wyrd to stay hidden. If Tuorlin had flown with the pixies he would have seen the danger. But, land-bound, even his great sight was limited. For he could not see through miles of leaf or wood. On his return flight, Melkion saw the spiders moving in. So he flew ahead of the Khoraz and Firewing to warn Luthiel and the Lords.

At Luthiel's light, both forces stood frozen—taken by surprise. Spiders readying to pounce were suddenly revealed, rimmed in an eerie glow. There were many—nearly one for every two fae inside the camp—and more had gathered about it. Most had long shadow threads stretched between their forelimbs. They appeared ready to snatch away fully half of the faerie host and scamper off into the darkness. But they were caught! Seeing what the spiders were about to do, the fae let out a cry of anger and leapt into battle.

All fell into a bloody chaos. A rain of arrows, javelins, and fiery sparks fell where the spiders had gathered into large groups. Cat-o-Fae sang through the air and came away wet with spider blood. Blade Dancers were not far behind and they came together in front of Luthiel before sweeping into the spiders with violence. But the spiders were still the more ready to fight and many snatched up the nearest fae in a shadow web before springing outside the ring. Still others fought directly with the fae in a great melee. Soon the bodies of both fae and spider lay on the ground.

It happened as suddenly as everything else. But it was the thing that stuck most in Luthiel's mind after. For the goblins, as one, stood, picked up their gear and walked through the spiders. The spiders let them pass, rasping with shrill laughter as they did. All except the Red-Caps, who broke from the flee-ing goblins with a yell and fell pell-mell on the spiders, biting through legs and bodies like land-bound piranha. Some elves shouted in anger and a volley of arrows left a score of the goblins dead before they slipped away into the wood and out of danger.

So, in a few moments, nearly a third of their force was lost.

Thrar Taurmori watched them go and his burning eyes seemed to laugh with the spiders. The elves of Rimwold had retreated to him and fought only those spiders that came near enough to threaten but, for the moment, gave no more than token aid to the larger force.

A great rage began to build in her. Around her, foot soldiers had gathered and many of them looked to her for word. Melkion perched on her shoulder and the fire rimming his mouth reflected her anger. A light grew above them and Luthiel realized the Firewing had come. Melkion launched into the air with a cry and flew with them—the fires of his mouth adding to their wing flames.

Raising *Weiryendel* she let out a visceral cry and charged into the largest group of spiders. She'd seen Othalas and Mithorden coming with a force of cavalry but she couldn't wait and watch any longer. In her rush to the spiders, she drew her *Cauthrim* knife. So with a blade in each hand she met them. At first they attacked her with glee, thinking her easy prey. But she blocked any fang, claw, or leg-blade with *Weiryendel*. The edge was so fine it cut through all it touched—flesh, metal or bone—with equal ease. Soon, her attackers found themselves missing teeth and limbs—their weapons cloven in half. Through the gaps, she thrust the smoking knife and soon their bodies burned as well.

All near her were inspired by her fury. They saw an angel of vengeance fighting beside them. And, one by one, her foes fell and the force before them wavered in fear. Overhead, the Firewing shot down like a gale of flame touching the spiders and setting hundreds alight. Melkion was with them shooting lines of fire into the faces of spider after spider. Soon, ten lay on the ground, their heads burning. Inspired, the fae followed her and drove deep into the spiders. Though she defeated many, she was untouched by gore, for those she slew seemed to wither to dust or fell with strange silver cuts instead of scars and balled in upon themselves in a death-like sleep.

Othalas, Mithorden, Tuorlin and a large group of riders charged into the spiders' flank. Mithorden was shouting something to Luthiel but she couldn't hear it through her rage and the din of battle.

The combined onslaught was too much for the spiders. Their force broke and they fled. The elves paused, but she urged them on with a yell. Her frenzy fed by memories of elves dangling, then eaten.

Never again. Never again. Never again.

It became a chant in her head and kept her moving long after as her limbs grew numb with exhaustion.

In her mind, she felt she must do everything she could to keep the fae from being taken again. But already hundreds had been snatched. So the fires of her rage grew—fed by desperation.

"We must defeat them now and hunt down each straggler till every captured fae is saved!" she shouted to the elves around her. The words seemed to spread her fury on to the elves and with a cry they ran after the spiders. They passed outside the camp's protective ring and under the overhanging shadow webs. The cavalry stopped but Othalas and Mithorden rushed on, still shouting something Luthiel couldn't hear.

It was then that the trap was sprung. The spiders before them stopped and were suddenly joined by hundreds more of their fellows. Then, with uncanny coordination, they each drew a shadow from the air and flung it. Spiders were also above them and from everywhere the webs fell on her. She cut them with *Weiryendel*. But there were too many and soon she became hopelessly tangled, and finally buried. She tried to hack with her sword but her hand was pinned and she had to work her wrists and fingers to get the blade moving. It only had one edge. So she could only move it so far in a certain direction before she had to spin it around and work it the other way. The *Cauthrim* knife was even slower. It wouldn't cut the shadow webs, but the hot metal did slowly burn through. After short-lived thrashing she set about the slow and careful work of cutting herself free.

Separated from everyone else, she could only hear what followed. With their hero and all around suddenly caught in a mass of shadow webs, the faerie charge wilted. She could hear calls of 'retreat!' and 'fall back!' through the cold press of shadows. All around her, other elves groaned as they tried to breathe through the dark mass or stay warm. The shadow seemed to suck heat from even the small patches of flesh it touched and leave the rest of her body trembling. If there were any light, she was certain her breath would have misted.

Nearby she heard Mithorden raise his voice. "Hold fast!" he shouted. Then, she saw the flickering of dream-light through the shadows and she knew he was using his Wyrd-Stone. Some of the shadow webs melted away. And a few of the elves closest to Mithorden sprang free. But the spiders rushed in and the press of their massive bodies drove Mithorden and the others back. There was a howling and she thought she heard Othalas break through but, in the end, there was nothing he could do for the shadow webs so he was forced to run back or be overwhelmed.

The sounds of battle raged at first and she slowly widened her range of motion. There was little she could do but make a tiny pocket for her hand to move in. She had to be careful or she'd cut the other elves trapped beside her. It was agonizing, as she was forced to work even more slowly. The minutes passed and the sound of battle dimmed.

They must be retreating!

There was little she could do except carefully cut the shadow webs. Often, she thought of using *Methar Anduel*. But she discounted it. She'd have to reach it. Even if she could, her disguise would fail when she awakened the Stone. As she thought about the disguise she wondered if it was still important. *At such desperate times, would it even matter?* It was all just thinking and worrying, though, as she could no more get a hold of her Stone than she could scratch her head.

She'd cut for about ten more minutes and had finally worked one of her arms free when she heard a familiar voice nearby.

"You wanted me to tell you where the Vyrl's messenger fell? I saw it happen there."

Luthiel's ears pricked and she gasped. There was no mistaking the snide voice.

Vane???

But before she could think any more, her question was answered by the scraping twitter of a Widdershae.

"You're certain, boy?"

"Yes, mistress." She flinched at his familiar, gloating, tone. Vane, Elag's apprentice. The bully who tried to take her Wyrd stone when she first set out for the Vale.

Vane's helping Widdershae? Is he captured or inspired?

"Step back, unless you want it to happen to you." Then, to someone or something else she rattled—"Draw the circle, bring the mists. We'll catch the leader along with the rest." The screeching racked her ears and she didn't have to think hard to figure out what the voice meant.

Saurlolth! She's going to use the mists to change us.

She had to move fast now. She knew she had only one chance and it lay hanging in the pouch at her neck. *Weiryendel* was just slicing through the webs at her right wrist when she heard another sound that made her heart quaver.

It wasn't the scratching around her that she knew were Widdershae making the crooked symbols of the dark spell. It wasn't the terrible screechy chanting Saurlolth had already begun. It was a voice mixed with the groans and terrified mutterings of the elves around her.

"Dear Ëvanya, she's going to change us into spiders!" it said. The voice was one she'd known all her life. It was that of her sister Leowin.

She followed me in my charge?? At that point, she realized how reckless and foolish she'd been. She wasn't certain she could counter the magic even if she got hold of the Wyrd Stone. She might well be able to stop it from affecting her. But what of the other fae? What of her sister?

Desperately, as the chanting built around her, she cut away the thick strands that covered her chest. A green glow had begun to fill the shadows around her and she knew she only had a few moments left to act. She cut so fast she almost dropped *Weiryendel*. Then she shaved the bag in half but the blade turned aside when it touched the Wyrd Stone. It fell from the bag and she made a desperate move to catch it.

Then the sickly green mists began to take hold of her. Everything seemed to slow down. The Stone fell past her chest. She felt her body begin to ripple and bile filled her mouth. There was a convulsion. The Stone fell past her belt. She was sure her eyes were about to be squeezed from her head. Then the Stone fell into her open palm and her shortening fingers hammered shut around it.

She opened her mouth and the dream light erupted in the Stone. She sang and the terrible convulsing stopped. Like a mist burned off by morning sun, the shadow webs drew back and the elves around her were revealed. Even touched by *Methar Anduel's* light they were still changing. Their bodies beginning to become twisted and misshapen. In reflex, she turned and saw her sister. Leowin was in pain but there was recognition on her face.

"I knew!" Leowin shouted in the sound and light.

And then the change took hold. The first wave made her skin become red as the veins pushed close to the surface.

"No!" Luthiel sang out and before she knew what she was doing she pushed the Wyrd Stone against Leowin's chest. Singing louder, she tried to fight it, for she could see the awful nightmare forming within her. Taking hold of both thought and body. But already she could see the light of *Methar Anduel* was having an effect. Heartened, she sang louder even as the terrible chanting rose to shrieks and screams.

The battle raged now inside Leowin's body. Luthiel could see her blood, muscle, and organs trying to move, trying to break, trying to reform. But she sang to them of stillness and healing.

The dark thing began to fade but as it did it fell inward trying to take hold of blood, then bone, then, at last, it wrapped around her heart, attempting to rip it in half. But Luthiel's song and the light of *Methar Anduel* were too potent and the shadow fell away, leaving her sister whole. She trembled but still stood, and in the dreamlight Luthiel could see Leowin's love for her burning like a warm fire. She could see other things too. Her dreams, her lust for secrets, and a smug sense of knowing much more than anyone else. Not a few of the dreams involved Luthiel. Hopes for what she might be. Though tempted to explore it all, she turned away and instead drew her attention to the other fae around her.

They were all changing into spiders and were too gone in form for her to undo the curse—arms and legs now split, bodies blackening, fangs swelling up out of their mouths.

In sudden inspiration, she sang against the terrible magic, protecting all she could from it and reworking some of the damage into unique forms. She sang of love and healing and of the good things spiders did. Of weaving gossamer that was so much like moonbeams, and so in them was born the power to shape webs of light and not of shadow. Of snaring evil insects that bore illness and of stilling them to sleep with their venom. So their poison was changed from one of terrible bleeding to one of merciful sleep as their bodies were built to prey on the monstrous things of the world and all that is born of nightmare. Of the understanding that comes with the art of web craft—and so their minds were enhanced and they gained rather than lost in wisdom. She sang of the light of Lunen and how she would grace the orb weavers at night—and she changed their shell from black to silver-white.

So the spell was done. Both she and Saurloth stood in silence regarding their handiwork. For the most part, she was the victor. For the elves, though changed, had retained their good hearts and become a new race of spiders.

I name you Senasarab—the good weavers! She cried out in dreams and across the Faelands a thousand sleepers heard her and were comforted. The Senasarab answered by rubbing their legs together and the sound was a gentle whisper in the wood. They were great and truly beautiful creatures. Their eyes shone like gems. The twin horns on their heads curled like those of unicorns and their bodies were covered in soft and beautiful fur. Each had a shape on its back that looked like a sunburst and their faces looked kindly and genteel.

Luthiel turned to Vane, Saurloth and the Widdershae, raised *Weiryendel* high and sang out a challenge. But the dark spiders had seen enough and, as one, they melted back into their shadow webs.

You did this Saurloth! She sang out to the shadows. *Had you not cast your horrible spell this would have never come to pass. For without the mists, I cannot change a thing. Now it is done! Ever will the Senasarab be a bane to you and weave the light against your darkness!*

In the darkness, though, she could hear loud shrieks and angry calls. The spiders had not withdrawn. They'd just slipped back as more rushed in to swell their numbers. For they saw in the Senasarab a terrible danger and they trembled with anger and fear. More than anything, Saurloth was stung by the surprise of Luthiel's song magic. How had she taken control so easily? How had she shaped their flesh and spirits so well against the plan she'd laid out for them? How, in everything, had she managed to create them into a new race—deadly and dangerous to the Widdershae? Here was a threat the spider queen had never encountered and she saw the chance to end it now.

She drew up her weapons and let out a cry to all the spiders gathered nearby. There were hundreds and they rushed to her call, gathering in the woods nearby to pounce upon Luthiel, her sister, and the Senasarab. For they were still only few—no more than a hundred in all.

Vane had run into the shadows with Saurloth but not without a backward glance at Luthiel. The magic had made him smile. He didn't quite know why, but there was comfort in it. With it came jealousy and lusting so deep he felt as if his guts would turn inside out. *He* was the name-son of Tannias Rauth, a Lord of Rimwold. *He* was Elag's apprentice. And yet he was never allowed to do anything of consequence. Treated like a servant instead of being imparted with the glory he deserved.

It didn't matter if he was late to show talent. What mattered was his lineage. They should have treated him with respect. Even their enemies received more than he. As he looked at her, he thought of the day it all had changed. When he had touched the Stone and felt its energy run through him. It was exquisite. Hunger, pain, joy. Ever since that day, he had been able to use magic.

Again bathed in her light and music, his eager sorcery fed on her glory as a dark and hungry thing might also feed on something full of life and energy. His feet flowed over the ground as he reluctantly ran from her. Breaking through the trees, he nearly tumbled head-long into a swarm of spiders gathering to attack. He shouted in surprise, and his little cry was enough to alert Luthiel and her companions.

Upon hearing Vane's cry, Luthiel began to sing her song of Ethelos. Yet now she held *Methar Anduel* and now the great magic of dreams swirled around her. Even as she sang, bits of mist were drawn in as a great storm might draw in a lesser one and explode in intensity. So the power of her spell was far more than the one she cast before in her escape from the Vale. First she faded then she disappeared utterly. Then Leowin, then the Senasarab. They made no noise; they cast no shadow. The light of *Methar Anduel* only visible to them and then only as a spark. All they heard was the voice of Luthiel as she directed them. She did not think to pause or question. She knew right action and acted.

"Follow fast!" she sang out. "We must make our way to the treetops and then back to the elves!" Then she was springing away and up the branches. Leowin and the Senasarab followed even as the Widdershae rushed in. They screeched with anger as they found no sign of their quarry and even Saurloth's pale eyes could not see them.

In anger, the great spider lunged at Vane and, were it not for the one who held him in thrall, would have torn him in half. Instead, she punted him with one of her great legs as she made her way back to the shadows. Vane was carried about ten feet by the force and lay sprawled on the ground not daring to move. But the thrill of Wyrd was still strong within him and he lay there with a big smile on his face. Vane's magic had awakened and was strengthening. Though rare, the way was not unknown among the wise. But it was unsavory— for Vane's was nothing without the talent of others to leech from.

As Vane lay laughing in the grass, Luthiel sped away through the trees, jumping from limb to limb, making her way through the night as she sang. Overhead, the moons of midsummer gleamed and the air was filled with light. What few shadow webs she came upon she slashed with *Weiryendel*. The Senasarab seemed impervious to them and walked along the strands of shadow as well as a Widdershae might. What's more, they could spin the moonbeams out into strands and bridges if they came upon a gap too great for them to cross. In little more than an hour they had sighted the elves and were rushing toward them from the treetops.

What Luthiel saw made her breath catch. For the faerie host was terribly diminished. Still pressed by the Widdershae, they fought them on land and in the trees. The force seemed to have shrunken to half its previous size, and all about, elves were strung up in shadow webs or being borne off in the clutching forelimbs of Widdershae. The Firewing still aided the elves but it seemed that far too few flew about them. Here and there she could see Widdershae burning but she also noticed the spiders clinging to tree limbs, ready to snatch the birds and crush them in their metal tipped forelimbs. The elves were beating a fighting retreat out of the woods. Far away, in the distant hills, she could see the banners of Ashiroth.

The Wolfriders! They're trying to reach the Wolfriders! But even as Luthiel saw them, her throat tightened in dread and she wondered if it would all come down to Zalos. Shaking her head, she sprang still closer to the furious battle, stopping just beyond the fighting.

"We can help them," she sang in the darkness. "But we must have a plan." Motioning with her Stone, she pointed toward the mists. A thin finger of light shot out in the direction she pointed. "There lies the Vale and somewhere a great army moves toward us. Even now, they may be making their way through the darker shadows. We must find them and bring them here."

She raised her head and scanned the air above. Sure enough, above the Firewing flew the black specks of Khoraz—the great talking ravens of the Vale of Mists.

"I wonder," she said to herself.

"Wait here," she said to Leowin and the Senasarab.

Springing up the branches and onto the tallest treetop, she let the enchantment fall. The light that surrounded her fell over the battlefield and illuminated the sky. She waved *Methar Anduel* above her head like a beacon.

"Mindersnatch!" she shouted to the birds wheeling above her. "Mindersnatch!!"

It was a reckless gamble. But upon seeing her light, the birds wheeled and dove falling upon her with cries of welcome. They flocked around her and, for a moment, the lights of the moons were blotted out by their feathered bodies.

"Luthiel! Luthiel!" they called out into the night.

Then a bird much larger than the rest flew toward her. Grinning, she gave the great Khoraz a nod of greeting as she held her arm out for him.

"Mindersnatch! I knew you'd be here."

"You! You! We were looking for You!"

"Well you've found me and I need your help. Where are the Vyrl? Where is the Vale's Army?"

"Coming! They've crossed the Rim. They burn the webs. Spiders leave them alone for now. Too busy snatching elves."

Luthiel felt a pounding in her chest. "How far?"

"Two miles into rising Silva."

"Will you lead me?"

"I will! I will! But there's more! More to tell!"

"Then tell me quick!"

"The beasts have gathered to help you. Bird and bear! Rat and rabbit! Hawk and hedgehog! Othalas was cut away from the elves. He searched for you. To aid him, he called the werewolves. Now they run with the other beasts. They are coming!"

Birds and beasts gathered to help me?

"Where are they?" she sang to him.

"One mile toward Merrin's setting. But you can see them from here if you look. Glimflirs light the sky above them!"

Luthiel turned her eyes and sure enough she saw the warm yellow glow of Glimflirs not far off. They were rising up like streams of sparks into the night sky. If she didn't know better, she would have thought the forest burned. But the light of the Glimflirs was a sign of the seasons—the Flir Bugs had left their homes to mate on the winds of summer. Even now, that hot wind blew upon her, making the tree tops sway like the waves of a great green ocean.

Some of the Widdershae had noticed her and were climbing up to investigate—their long forelimbs questing in the darkness. She sprang away fast and as she did the Khoraz dove upon the spiders in fury. Beaks rattled upon shells like rain and pecked at tender eyes. One spider, flailing to protect itself with its legs, fell from the trees and the other two shrank back. In the distance, she could see more on the way. So she rushed to explain what she'd just heard to Leowin and the Senasarab.

"The Vyrl's army is coming from that direction." She motioned with her hand. "And Othalas has gathered the werewolves together with a group of other animals over there." She pointed toward the light of the Glimflirs.

"Animals?" Leowin asked.

"Mindersnatch here says they've come to help us."

"They came for her!" Mindersnatch cawed.

Leowin looked at Luthiel and despite the terrible danger of the night grinned at her.

"The spiders are in for a surprise."

"That's the idea," Luthiel said with a smile. As ever, Leowin's spirit was infectious and Luthiel felt glad to be with her again. "But we've got to move and I need your help. I want you to take half the Senasarab and find the Vyrl. Mindersnatch will guide you."

The crow let out a loud caw in affirmation.

"Where are you going?"

"To meet Othalas and this army of beasts. If what Mindersnatch says is true we may be able to help them reach those hills." She pointed to where the Wolfrider banners waved.

Leowin looked down at the fighting and grimaced.

"I hope so. Lore, Hueron and Vanye are down there."

Luthiel glanced at the dwindling army and frowned.

"Let's go. Or there won't be anyone left to help."

LADY OF BEASTS

With half the Senasarab behind her, she sprang through the trees, making her way toward the rivers of light rising into the sky. Beside her, they glided through the branches without a sound. She wondered if they had even needed her enchantment. Khoraz broke into two flocks—one following Leowin and the other escorting her. Mindersnatch launched off her shoulder and flew in the air beside her as she sprang.

"Have you seen Melkion?" she called to the crow.

"With Mithorden! He's spending all his fires burning spiders. He hates them!"

Luthiel nodded. It was something she'd never wondered about before. But Melkion did seem to have something personal against the spiders. She laughed silently to herself.

As do I. But my anger comes from seeing my kind poisoned, tortured, eaten.

Did Melkion have such a sense of kinship with elves? How could he having served the Vyrl so long?

Seems more personal.

Luthiel mused about the dragon as she sprang but was unable to puzzle out the little Dragon's rage. She left it and turned to other matters.

"And Vanye?"

"Fights like a demon. He leads the other Blade Dancers. They fight to defend Tuorlin. Spiders have nearly killed him twice."

"You mentioned demons. What of Thrar Taurmori?"

"Rimwold fights if it must."

Luthiel gave a grim laugh as she jumped to the next branch. "Their goblins deserted. He and his elves may as well have done the same."

"They wait."

Luthiel didn't have to wonder much about what for. Even she realized what the demon Faelord might gain in Tuorlin's death and Ithilden and Minonowe's weakening. "The spiders let the goblins pass. It's treason."

"Thrar remains. His captains betrayed him—he'll say."

Luthiel frowned. She didn't like this business with the Faelords. It seemed a rotten union. Ashiroth and Rimwold were busy playing empire and seemed ready to throw the rest of the Faelands to the spiders in order to increase their power.

After what Zalos did to Vaelros, should I be surprised? And yet, tonight, all may rest on him and his wolfriders. The more she thought about it, the less she liked it. The war against the Vyrl was some thing of vengeance. The spiders would have let them pass to fight the Vyrl and then fallen upon both armies after they had broken themselves—one against the other. There would have been little left of either army and the spiders would have been fattened both by the feasting and in numbers through Saurloth's mastery of the mists.

Could Zalos have planned it? But her thoughts returned to her Dreaming and she knew it must be so.

Then how can I trust him to act honorably now?

She neither spoke nor thought through the rest of the journey. She would do what she must to help the elves. She felt caring for them as one might feel toward extended family. And even though she now knew she wasn't one of them she loved them deeply and, strangely, felt responsible.

It was with these thoughts drifting through her mind that she came upon the oddest assembly of creatures she'd ever encountered.

The birds were the first to see her and hundreds—from the tiniest flitswa to the greatest eagle—flew to join her. There were thousands more, and she could barely see the sky through the thick of them. It didn't take long for the other animals to notice her arrival and, of these, Othalas was the first.

Upon seeing her, he let out a great howl and the wolves about him—a hundred other werewolves, all great and terrible, but none so great as he—picked up the call. Then the bears growled and the great cats roared—ligers and tipards nearly as big as the werewolves. All the other creatures paused, some of them resting on their haunches as they watched her descend from the trees.

Othalas padded up to greet her with a bow.

"All of wilddom has come to aid you, Lady," he said with a formality she was unused to. But her Stone was afire now and the lights about her head gleamed bright as stars. In her left hand *Weiryendel* sang with lights and rainbows. Her disguise cast aside, she looked in every part a great Faelord, if not something greater.

At his bow, all the other creatures bowed as well. There was a hush and Luthiel's breath caught when she saw love plain in the animals' eyes.

Oh what have I done to earn it? I, who would hunt them and eat them? With animals bowing before her, she recalled Mithorden and his principles and she wondered if he had the right of it. For she saw in each of these creatures great heart and spirit even to the tiniest among them.

They all love life and will fight for it as I have.

She did not need to speak. It was as though the animals heard her thoughts and gave silent affirmation.

"We are ready to help you!" Othalas growled. "All you need do is give the word."

"Then the word is forward! I would save as many elves as possible. Will you follow me!!??"

The responding roar made the wind in the trees seem a whisper by comparison. Even the Glimflirs seemed to glow brighter.

"The wild has answered," Othalas growled.

Luthiel sprang to his back and the Senasarab gathered with the host. Othalas gave them only one questioning glance. But knowing they were with Luthiel was enough. Now was not the time for questions. That would come later. The wolf was built for action and this was the time for it. Woe to the Spider who stood before him or threatened his mistress.

With a final howl, he was off through the woods, the great horde of woodland creatures surging in behind him.

ZALOS' CHOICE

Upon Othalas' back, she rushed through the wood. Light spilled from her Stone, making all seem to sway and waver. Even the animals looked like a great pack of spirits rushing through the woods. Trees flashed by as the animals ran or flew beside and above her. Werewolves were intermixed with native wolves and foxes. Badgers ran with porcupine and hedgehogs. There were faenmare, and Luthiel even saw one unicorn. The air was filled with birds of every kind. But borne aloft on the hot summer air, Glimflirs rose up above them, making the sky shimmer with a million false stars. A great wind was howling, fanning the trees, running ahead of Oerin's dawn.

Othalas found a low spot, making a riverbed his road. They ran along, masked by hill, tree, and rushing wind. But the cloud of Glimflirs must have made a disturbing spectacle as it grew and loomed over the spiders. Two of the rear-guard twittered uneasily as the cloud drew near. The plan hadn't gone quite right and though the elves were losing, this night's events made them want to slip off into the shadows. Too many had felt the bite of faerie sword, arrow, and Wyrd. Many more lay burned to ash. Now the wood was filled with strange sounds. It made them long for the mountains—the shadowed valleys no sunlight could touch. They'd caught enough to last for a good while and the greedy, lazy, spiders were ready for a feasting well away from the struggle. Were it not for *her* they'd be gone in a moment. But the Spider Queen was not to be argued with. So the spiders held tight to the tree limbs and quivered in anticipation of what dawn might bring.

Less than a mile away, a desperate struggle was taking place. The elves had fought their way to the hills. The spiders threatened to overwhelm them.

Again and again they were thrown back. The battle raged on the ground and in the trees. The air was filled with birds and pixies on the wing.

Saurloth sensed the changes. The Vyrl were coming. Beasts were gathering. Luthiel's magic was at work. Were it not for her, the battle would be won. The elves—slaves and food.

A group of least Widdershae lined before her. There were about three hundred in all. Quivering legs seemed barely able to hold up the awkward bodies. Once elves, now no better than slaves. With her approach, they gave a collective moan. The only part of them still elfin—two eyes—showed hate. But fear kept them better than any chain. Whatever courage they'd once possessed was broken by the long days of dangling poisoned, of listening to their kindred cry out as they were eaten, the terrible transformation and then the abuse. You or I might think that at least one would show courage and put up a fight. But neither you nor I have suffered as they, and even we have born witness in silence to lesser ills under less dire threat. Yet, in the face of evil, to sit silent is an even greater evil. Complacency is ever the enabler of darkest deeds; so it was with the Widdershae who once were elves. Though they didn't realize it, had they acted at that moment, they could have saved a great many lives. But the moment passed and with it any chance for heroism.

Dumb with terror, they watched Saurloth wave her gangrel forelimbs in wicked ritual. Metal screamed and sparked. Dark Wyrd rose in answer. Cracks began in the ground at her legs and shot out toward the spiders. Though terrified, they were unable to move. Their fear of Saurloth held them fast. The cracks drew nearer. Smoke spilled from the openings. The ground bulged. A hissing as from a hundred snakes filled the air. Then, out sprang red worms. They were large—as long as an arm. And the air around them smoked with the heat of their bodies. They surged forward, fiery mouths questing. Still the Widdershae couldn't move. Fear had overcome them. Rather than giving them the will to fight or flee, it crushed their spirit, leaving only panic and disbelief. They could no more move than they had will. And the will had left them days ago. So clumsy as the fireworms seemed, they met no resistance. They were slithering over the earth. They were arching up, reaching for the spider's underbellies. Then, they were burrowing through shell and flesh. Shrieks filled the night.

The worms worked in and, as they did, strange magic took hold of the Widder. Cracks gaped in their shells. A poisonous reek belched out. It filled the air with venom. And its merest touch was enough to make a man bleed. The undershells cracked too and great bags hung out. They ballooned and squelched—working like a bellows. Poison filled the air.

The night was filled with the gasps and moans, the awful cracking, the reek of poison and of searing flesh. The Widder convulsed, driven insane from the pain of it all. Their eyes dulled to red as the fire began to burn them.

"Tuorlin!" The great spider shrieked. "Kill him and it will end!"

As mad as any poor creature burning from the inside out may be, the least Widder flooded down the hill in a rush, drowning all about them in a cloud that ate flesh. All who tried to stand before them fell in the dire charge. Even Blade Dancers were forced to flee. But Vanye called on his fellows and they set their Cat-o-Fae upon the surging spiders. Together, the archers shot into the mad Widder. But neither arrow nor blade did much to slow them. The deadly hurt was already done. All that remained of life was pain and a terrible need. Only Mithorden and Melkion seemed unharmed by the poison. The Sorcerer flashed like lightning through them—striking again and again. Where he passed, spiders fell. Melkion flew behind—burning out their eyes. Yet he and the dragon were like pebbles tossed into a raging tide. It flooded around them and up the hill toward the High Lord.

The other Widdershae gathered for one last rush. The charge had left the elves in disarray. Before they could recover, Saurlolth meant to finish them.

It was as the spiders gathered for a final strike that two things happened.

The first was a charge of grendilo, wights and giants. The wood rumbled with great blasts of Ahmberen's horn and with the footsteps of Gormtoth. Norengar, tall as trees, lead a charge of giants. Vaelros sat upon a great steed of the Vale, its twin horns gleaming in the light of Oerin's Eye. Behind him came Grendilo. Elshael led the wights and the terror of their eyeless faces even made the Widdershae tremble. Fresh Firewing and Khoraz filled the sky. So the left side of the spider force faltered and many were drawn away from the charge. But it was still too few.

Then Luthiel appeared from out of the wood.

Borne upon the back of Othalas, the Wyrd light surrounded her. It danced about her and Othalas like a ring of silver flame. In her left hand she held *Weiryendel* and in her right *Methar Anduel*. They gleamed brightest—twin beacons casting their light up against the clouds. Lesser lights like small stars ringed her head and all around her Glimflir lifted up like rivers to the stars. The first dim rays of Oerin's Eye seemed pale and wan by comparison. Beneath her light, the werewolf stood out blacker than the corners of night. His yellow eyes were the only lights visible in that darkness. With thousands of beasts behind them, they fell like a tide upon the spiders' rear.

Such was the spectacle that elf and spider, Vyrl and grendilo, faerie and goblin all stood stunned. The battle seemed to sigh and the great lady rode through the gap. Only the tortured Widder rushed on, desperate in their need to reach the High Lord. The animals surged over the spiders in a great swarm. Even the tiniest mice joined the fight. They surged in, searching for a tender spot. But she drew Othalas up short. For she saw the Widder scrambling madly toward the High Lord with murder in their eyes.

Two hundred yards away, Zalos brought his line of wolfriders to a halt. They lowered lances and bore fang. They were ready for the charge. But Zalos held his hand high, waiting. A few Gruagach gasped at the sight of Luthiel and some made the sign of Soelee against evil.

"It's the witch. She's here." The whisper passed swiftly among the Gruagach. Zalos scowled. The prophecy was coming to pass—but in disturbing and unexpected ways. This night had brought far too many surprises and now it seemed possible that his most careful plans would come to nothing. But the war to rule must be won. For not long after, the greater war—the war to survive—would come. And everything, all of Zalos' plans and effort for hundreds of years, was bent on winning it.

As if a herald to Zalos' thought, Oerin dawned on a day wet with blood. First light was always painful for the Faelord. Thorns bit. Fire burned. More than anything, the pain was his discipline. It sharpened him. Gave him rage. Beat him into a deadly shape. He must watch and wait. If he committed now, he would turn the tide and Lord Tuorlin would be saved. So he stood his ground.

Luthiel saw the mad Widder in her dream sight. She saw the terrible worms that burned through them, filling their guts with fire, poison, and pain. She saw them rushing up the hill to overwhelm the High Lord. She saw the Widder and animals all about her fighting and dying. Even Thrar Taurmori was fighting but she guessed this was because the spiders in their madness were lashing at all around them.

She cast about. But there was nothing, no way for her to reach the High Lord in time. And then she saw them, a thousand wolfriders standing in a line before the field—waiting. Zalos stood at their head with his hand held high poised to give the order but holding it. Here was the rescue. Here was the High Lord's hope. And it rested on a thousand Wolfriders with Zalos to lead them.

Luthiel didn't hesitate. With a yell to Othalas, she was riding toward them. A group of animals and Senasarab, who acted as honor guard, broke off to follow her. She held her sword and Stone high and as she came close, she sang out all the louder. Her song filled the air and when it reached the wolfriders' ears they seemed to fall under enchantment.

Blood of sap and flesh of wood
Brothers of great Ashiroth
Give your aid now, it is time
To heal the hurts to pay the cost

Of bitter deeds done in the dark,
For power's sake and on to woe
But choose right now and it will break
Upon the back of this our foe

The Widdershae and others too
Shadows in a greater game
A shade that comes to each and all
Mortal child and elf to claim

With violence for the world is full
Of larger things than you and I
That violence sets us man 'gainst man
Burns the earth and breaks the sky

It draws a sack-cloth over day
As suns go out then all are slain
A world made barren—nothing left
Only the ice rime will remain

But you may end it here today
You may save the great High Lord
You may turn our path away
From a road that's paved with swords

I sing a song that you should know
Since Zalos shamed me in a dream
And set the blame upon my back
For a thing that he would bring

Come with me now—save the High Lord
Free his life and all his land
For the victory of death is no victory at all
Only woe for each woman and man.

Her spell reached out, spreading over his force with a light and power that touched even the hardest Gruagach heart. The words had flowed through her like a river. She hardly understood them. It was as if some deeper dream had taken hold of her. The wolves heard her loudest and a few raised cry to this queen of beasts who rode out on the greatest of all wolves. Seeing them waver, she let out a final cry singing out —"Wolfriders! To me!! The High Lord Tuorlin!!" And with a faith in her Wyrd born of her long struggle to save her sister, to survive the Vyrl and to forge an alliance between Vyrl and elf, she turned to lead them up the hill.

With a grim smile on his face, Zalos watched them go. The display had shocked him. For this was High Wyrd and Luthiel had slipped into the deep dreams that touched all things. He would as soon stand against such a force as he would an avalanche. But Zalos was wily, for he knew the hearts of Ashiroth's kin and the other deep dreams that had taken hold there. The dreams he be-gan to lay so long ago. No, he would not face the magic of a Valkire again, he would let it break itself on forces far greater and deeper running than the truth Luthiel revealed. For there were deeper and uglier truths at work. So he stood firm and held his hand high. The command itself was enough to keep much of his force. But a full third broke rank to follow the Witch. Another third struggled to regain control of their wolves who fought hard to follow her. But, in the end, rider won out and the hard training and discipline of the pack set in. The wolves looked to Zalos and knew him the alpha.

Zalos almost smiled as he watched her go, leading a third of his force to save Tuorlin. It might have been enough. He turned to his riders.

"The Blood Witch is revealed! More than three hundred of your brothers have fallen to her craft! Now she threatens the very life of the High Lord!"

Confusion stirred in the elves' eyes. He would have to be careful and not push them too hard.

"You must do everything you can to take her alive. Go now and bring her back. We have seen enough hurt this day."

There, the old law was taking hold. He could see it in their eyes.

With a yell, he was leading them up the hill behind Luthiel. She rushed through the faerie host driving for Tuorlin. Though Zalos knew she meant to defend him, he also knew her charge could easily be misread.

The Mists of War, he thought to himself and laughed as he charged behind.

THE MISTS OF WAR

Upon Othalas' back, Luthiel led the charge. Funneling in behind and beside her, wolves, werewolves, and foxes leapt to aid her. In front, she could see Mithorden. He stood before a force of archers and Blade Dancers protecting the High Lord. Arrow, fire, and Cat-o-Fae plunged into the spiders. But the tide surged up the hill. Mithorden shouted and the sky opened. From above, a great wind rushed down, blowing the poison back as the Widdershae rushed forward. The wind held and the air remained clean enough for them to stand and fight. They drew swords and knives while others lined up, spears pointing outward. The spiders came on and didn't even pause to fight in their rush. Some were speared. Others were cut down. But the rest climbed over their fallen fellows and elf alike as they made for Tuorlin. He stood beside Mithorden, his white-tipped spear held high. The first spider that came upon him fell, pierced as if by a thunderbolt. Then a second and a third.

Luthiel was nearly upon him. The riders lowered their lances, ready to plunge into the spiders surrounding Tuorlin. She pointed *Weiryendel* at the High Lord.

"Protect him!" she shouted in the din. Most could not hear but the motion was plain enough.

It was then that Zalos plunged into them. The wolfriders leapt in front of their kinsmen and came to a halt, forcing them to stop. Wolf collided with wolf, riders fell to the ground.

Out of the corner of her eye, Luthiel saw it. At first, it seemed strange to her—as if the whole host of wolfriders had collapsed into one another. And then, in an instant, she realized.

My song only reached some. The rest —

It was then that Othalas turned with a great growl. For Zalos was upon them, his wolf snapping at the werewolf's flanks.

"Defend the High Lord!" Zalos was shouting.

"Defend?!" Luthiel shouted in fury. "You would let him die! We went to save him!"

Zalos pointed his sword at her.

"Liar! Lay down your weapon! You are overcome!"

"*You* should call me a liar! Who would have murdered me but a babe! Who kept my mother all these years! Against her will!!" Faced now with Zalos and the prospect of her imprisoned mother, tears of rage streamed freely down her cheeks. Her impulse was to urge Othalas forward and to strike him down. But the High Lord was behind her. What would happen to the Faelands if he died? Who would replace him? She sang loud and angry as Wyrd built up around her like a storm of light.

The wolfriders had circled round, barring her path to the High Lord. Behind, she could see the six captains draw up in a line. Darkness streamed from the boxes at their chests and their naked swords gleamed like winter ice in the pale light. In dreams their flesh seemed almost transparent and their shoulders hunched unnaturally as if something rather large had eaten a hollow in their backs and now lived there. Shuddering, she remembered the thing she flushed out of Vaelros' Stone and wondered for an instant what it could be.

"Let me pass!" She sang out. The werewolves gathered around her in a tight knot. Foxes and wolves flanked them, growling at Urkharim and wolfrider alike.

"Let me pass!" She cried again and this time, slid her Wyrd Stone into *Weiryendel's* eyelet. The light spilled into the blade and her song seemed to ring through the crystal. It thrummed in her hand like a heartbeat, sang out with a voice like choirs.

Zalos also held his sword high, Wyrd Stone burning with gold and red fire at its hilt. She could see his crown of crystal thorns now. It clutched his head like a great claw, points digging through his flesh. It seemed to touch his mind and the look in his eyes was filled with a will both greater and more violent than that of any elf. In his gaze there was ruin and behind his eyes—emptiness.

She drew in a breath and in that moment was certain of what she faced for she remembered Mithorden's words well.

We become what we do.

In dreams, she could see Zalos and his six all the clearer. They were consumed by the dream of death. They bore it, housed it, fed it on blood and dreams. She had a name for this death dream—nightmare. But in the tongue of Elohwë there was an older name for it. Ming. It was a name that recalled the first ending in all the worlds. The first great loss that was to herald all loss and terror to come.

Ming. They serve it.

So she named the six *Mingolë*—servants of nightmare. And Zalos was their chief—the *Morithingol*. Deathlord.

"Mingolë! Baby killers! Mother takers!" she sang mockingly at Zalos. "I know who you serve! Let me pass or, by my hand, fate will send you to meet him early!" She drew the *Cauthrim* blade and Othalas showed him his teeth.

Zalos was laughing for this was his language. With one eye, he was watching Tuorlin's struggle. It was mighty. It was hopeless. And he'd cornered her. Now for the bait.

"You forgot one thing." He spoke the next words slow and with emphasis. "Father betrayer."

It was enough. Her mind leapt the gulf in an instant. *Weiryendel* shuddered in her hand as her song turned into a howl.

Too much! It was all too much!!

The rage filled her and the next thing she knew she was charging Zalos. Othalas sprang muscles exploding forward driven by her anger and all the hot rage of his kind. He raged now for Luthiel. Her loneliness. Her terrible sense of loss.

Zalos saw her coming and his smile broadened. They were in full charge and a mongrel pack of animals followed them. With a shout to his wolfriders, they drew tight and held out their lances. He lowered his own wolf into a crouch and waited. When Othalas was nearly upon him, Zalos' wolf sprang. The collision was so violent that both Luthiel and Zalos were flung free as the wolves tore into one another. Fangs flashed and red sprang up on their coats.

Had she not been in the World of Dreams the fall might have broken bones or at least winded her. But in dreams she barely felt the impact. As soon as she hit the ground she was rolling and then standing. It took her only a few moments to find Zalos again. With a yell, her sword and knife raised high, she charged him. There was nothing in her other than the urge to kill this villain. The drive came deep. Her mother. She must protect mother. She must free mother.

That it was a mother she'd never known made the drive all the stronger. Here was the one who'd separated them. Who'd tried to kill her. Who would force Merrin to marry him. Who by his own admission had betrayed her father.

It all flashed through her mind as she charged. And with each step. With each heartbeat. Her rage grew.

Zalos stood in a slight crouch, sword held low and to the side. There was something deadly in the stance, the way he let himself be open to her with sword out to the side ready to come slicing in. She focused on the sword. He may well have more skill than her. But all she had to do was touch the blade with *Weiryendel's* edge and she could break it. So she struck with both knife and sword at his weapon.

Zalos had fought in the great war against the Vyrl and a hundred wars after. He had sparred with Valkire and was among the first Blade Dancers. Though Luthiel didn't know it, he was a legend even to the most highly skilled of swordsmen. His discipline in the art was without compromise or compare. He knew well enough the power of *Aeowinar* to cut a thing. Even his moonsteel blade would be parted like grass. But there were ways to position and strike that did not require blades to meet. In this swift and deadly art, Zalos held the mastery. So as Luthiel struck for his sword, he flicked it down and away. Continuing in an arc, he came up under her guard and struck her square on the chin with the flat of his blade.

He was tempted. Oh how tempted!! To turn the edge in and remove Luthiel of head and himself of a major problem in less than a blinking. But he also knew, if he were to hold the Faelands in his power he would have to do more than kill Luthiel now. She had come with Vyrl and animals to defeat the Widdershae. Even now, the tide of battle was turning. No, there were many who would see her as a hero. Before he could kill her, he had to kill her character.

The blow caught her hard on the chin. The moonsteel was both real and solid in dreams. Its force lifted her from her feet and laid her on her back.

"Protect the High Lord!" Zalos shouted to the wolfriders.

Luthiel scrambled to regain her feet. The fear was in her now. There must be little hope for Tuorlin if Zalos was moving to protect him. She rolled onto her heels and into a crouch. Her vision was blurred and she could taste blood in her mouth. Zalos' sword lashed out. She caught the blow on her knife and it flew from her hand. In that instant she knew she'd lost. Zalos was far too skilled. There was nothing left but desperation. She did the first thing that came to her. Had she tried it with a normal weapon, the act would have been futile. But all things perished at *Weiryendel's* edge. So she did the only thing she knew might surprise the Faelord. She threw the sword.

It lifted through the air and cut toward his face. Nothing but reflex and three thousand years of constant training saved Zalos from decapitation. All he saw was the rapid flick of Luthiel's hand and then a strange glimmer of light upon the crystal blade as it sliced toward him. He ducked and swatted at the flat part with his sword tip. There was an odd humming sound as metal met crystal and the reflexive block caused *Weiryendel* to spin wildly. It lifted over his head, but as it did it sliced clean through his crown's crystal. One great thorn fell to the ground.

Weiryendel landed point down and slid into the earth.

Sudden and intense pain filled Zalos. It brought him to his knees. The crown on his head seemed afire and for a moment he was filled with doubt. What if he was wrong? What if all he'd done would amount to nothing? In a flash he had a vision of all his power crumbling to naught. And then the death-fear was upon him again. This time more intense and powerful than ever.

No, he would survive. There was nothing else. Kill or be killed.

When his vision cleared, she saw Luthiel scrambling across the ground for her sword. He beat her back with the flat of the blade and struck her open-handed across the face. She fell and he dragged her away by the hair.

She kicked, struggled, bit. But there was nothing she could do. Strong hands were on her now. They were binding her arms, pulling a bitter cloth over her mouth. The dreams were wrenched from her and the Stone went out. She didn't have to try to close it. It was as if some oppressive hand had snuffed it out. The dreaming left her and she was only Luthiel. Tears streamed freely from her eyes as she watched Zalos in rage. How could she have been so stupid! How could she let him bait her!

Beside her there was a snap, then a growl, then silence. The body of Zalos' wolf fell limp to the ground. Othalas' eyes focused on Luthiel and he sprang toward her with a forlorn howl.

"Kill the werewolf!" Zalos shouted.

Lances lowered. Urkharim barred teeth.

But Othalas knew well he couldn't save Luthiel from Zalos, the six, and a thousand wolfriders all alone. Even he could not match such might or numbers. But he still held out hope and his eyes fixed on a different prize. In his great jaws he snatched up the hilt of *Weiryendel* and he sprang away—tearing off through a gap in the wolfriders. The other wolves gave her one last sad look and rushed out behind Othalas—heads and tails low, shoulders hunched. Then they were gone and she was left alone with the Lord of Ashiroth.

TUORLIN'S STAND

The monsters rushed all about Tuorlin, grasping with their great legs, lashing out with their terrible fangs, belching poison. It didn't help that with his third eye he could see them as they once were. Here was an elf who'd served him well for three centuries. There a young warrior freshly recruited to Ithilden's army. All turned to spiders. All broken by pain, fear, madness.

He struck with his spear and another spider fell, fire licking through the cracks in its shell. Mithorden and Vanye fought beside him. Melkion flew above, spewing long streams of fire in the spider's faces. Cat-o-Fae swished through the air, forming a deadly cloud around him. But the spiders came on heedless of all defense and soon he knew he'd be overwhelmed.

Then he saw Luthiel charging—the white rider on the black wolf—and he thought he would be saved. The wolfriders had joined her and they flowed like a tide up the hill. With a yell, he struck out with renewed fury. Melkion took up the cry.

"Luthiel! Luthiel is coming!" His rainbow wings flared in the sunslight and fire surged from his mouth with each shout. Beside him the Firewing gave out an eerie cry. It rose and wavered, taking up a piercing note that made Tuorlin think of ghosts and wind howling over a barren crag.

Then the charge crumpled and the hope vanished.

The spiders surged in and he was unable to see her anymore. But what he'd glimpsed was enough.

"Zalos has betrayed us!" He yelled to those around him even as he fought desperately for his life. He knew these were his final moments so he chose his words carefully. Three spiders rushed upon him and he let one spit itself on his spear. The other two pulled his shield away before he could turn his spear to them.

"Listen all who can hear me! For I would name my successor!" There was something in the wind that carried his voice and all the Blade Dancers around him as well as much of Ithilden's host heard him shout.

"I name Luthiel as High Lady of all the Faelands! I name Vanye Faelord of Ithilden!"

Then the spiders bore him down. He speared one and Vanye cut the legs out from under a second. But where two fell, ten more surged in. They gathered around him, pinning him to the ground. Legs flashed and his armor broke. More were felled, but still more pressed in. They beat him into the ground. They bit his head. His blood spilled on the earth and his breath rattled. The Blade Dancers rushed in and pushed the spiders away.

He was covered in blood and his body trembled. He opened his mouth and struggled to draw a rasping breath. Ugly spider bites covered his head. But he still kept the power of speech and he struggled to shout.

"I refuse Ashiroth and Rimwold!!" he croaked. "They are henceforth rebel provinces and will be until their lords are removed from power!!"

He lifted a broken and misshapen arm to Vanye who'd knelt beside him.

"Grandfather," the Blade Dancer whispered, tears streaming from his cheeks.

"I've failed," Tuorlin choked. "In my wanting to keep the land whole I abided a cancer. Now I fear there will be nothing but violence and terror. I go into darkness, but I leave a greater darkness behind me."

"No!" Vanye shouted taking his hand. "You have given hope."

"Too little! But I must go." His ruined hand lifted to Vanye's face. "You are a good man of great heart. You've made me proud beyond imagining. Remember. When all other stars go out, *she* will give light."

Then the light in his own eyes faded and the single eye in his forehead grew milky.

"I will remember, grandfather," Vanye whispered. "I promise."

STRIFE

The battle ended strangely. The moment the High Lord died, the cursed spiders were consumed in gouts of flame. The fires roared high, spilling black tails into the clean air. Seeing this, the other spiders fled into the wood. Senasarab stalked after them, catching a few stragglers in webs of light and mists. Animals, The Vyrl's army, and those fae who could still fight gave chase and paid the spiders back terribly for the night's killing. But many escaped into shadow and waited for the cover of night even as the webs were burned around them.

After the spiders left, a general confusion fell upon the fae. The Vyrl had come to help them, but none wanted to approach the terrible rulers of the Vale of Mists. They stood off and eyed the Vale's lords and their strange army with suspicion. The animals moved in among them, and those who would let them near found their wounds licked by tongues great and small. It seemed a wonder to even the Fae who'd kept close ties with all things of earth and air, of wing and paw. Many attributed it to Luthiel, and depending on whom you spoke to this was either a good or bad thing.

And there lay the point of strife.

Many had heard the High Lord's proclamation. Many had also seen Luthiel's charge up the hill. Some believed she meant to save the High Lord. Others to kill him. Worse, Ashiroth and Rimwold, who almost wholly believed Luthiel to be an evil witch bent on destroying the Faelands, were labeled rebels by the now deceased High Lord. Even Ithilden's force had fallen into confusion and bickering spread rapidly throughout the entire Faerie army.

Mithorden, Vanye, Melkion and Othalas moved through the confusion like an island of calm. Behind them were a score of the Blade Dancers. They were focused on one thing and one thing alone—Luthiel had been taken by Zalos. Vanye had taken *Weiryendel* from Othalas. The crystal blade swung lightly in his left hand. Its music whispered in his ears and he wondered at both its sadness and its strange comfort. Still agitated, his bloody Cat-o-Fae swooped around him like a deadly bird. Elayethel had joined them and a train of Tyndomiel in bear form followed in her wake.

"The damned liar," Othalas growled. "I'll bite his head off. He broke her heart. Then he beat her to the ground."

"We're fortunate she's not dead," Mithorden said. "But Zalos plays a deep game." He looked out at the army. "Still thinks he can win them. When he realizes he can't, things will get dangerous."

"They're not now?" Melkion hissed. "Spiders, dragons, wolfriders, the lord of Rimwold lurking like a vulture. What's not dangerous?"

"What's not dangerous is that Zalos hasn't reached the point of desperation," the sorcerer said. "I told her she'd best stay hidden. She revealed herself too soon. Now we'll have trouble."

"She's not good at hiding," Othalas growled. "You wronged her by trying to make her."

The sorcerer nodded sadly. "I had to choose between two wrongs. Last night we almost lost her to the spiders and this morning—Zalos."

Melkion laughed out a cloud of smoke. "You said it yourself. She's dangerous."

"I did?"

"When you were talking about what some Fae fear," the dragon said as he lowered his head. "When you were talking about her."

"Well, I meant how they would see her," the sorcerer replied.

"They're right, you know. But she's dangerous for the right reasons. They just don't see that part."

Othalas was growling now, for they'd reached the line of wolfriders. Mithorden raised his sword and spoke out in a loud voice that all around could hear.

"Let us through! In the name of the Queen of the Faelands, let us through!"

There was a growling among the wolves and a whisper as the riders loosened swords in sheaths. Zalos stood up and a thin aisle parted in the wolfriders so he could see them. Luthiel was on the ground beside him. Bound and gagged. But her eyes spoke volumes and there were tears streaming freely down her cheeks. There was a stunned silence as Zalos looked them over.

"Queen of the Faelands? Has Tuorlin named Elayethel then?"

Luthiel had sat there in stunned silence for what seemed like only a few minutes. There were flashes through her mind of terror. But the thing that overwhelmed the fear, the thing that kept playing over and over in her mind were Zalos' words.

Father Betrayer. Father Betrayer. Father Betrayer.

The Vyrl were nearby and they picked up the strand of her thought. There were no words, only a sense of sympathy and deep loss. Of any creature, the Vyrl knew betrayal. The first betrayal was Gorthar and then, age over age, an endless string insults. When the surge of grief and anger subsided a few words drifted through.

Help is coming.

Beside her, Zalos stood looking on. His eyes were stern, calculating. The Gruagach had encircled her and Mingolë lurked nearby. The terror in them was so strong it made the air smell of cold and ash. She could sense a decision coming. They were going to do something with her.

"Quickly now —" Zalos said. But before he could continue, a runner approached.

"Lord! Elayethel and the sorcerer are here. Othalas and the Blade Dancers too."

Luthiel's eyes lifted and she felt a flash of hope as she saw her friends moving toward them. But it was a dirty hope, tainted by the morning's revelation. In her mind she kept seeing glimpses of her father, of the terrible hands that crushed the life from him. All brought on by a trusted friend. Luthiel felt hollow, as if someone had set a stone in place of her heart. But despite the emptiness she knew resolve. Her life had purpose now. It was to kill Zalos.

Zalos looked down on her and there was a strange look in his eye. There was calculating. There was calm. But there was also regret. Sadness. The dream returned to her in a flash.

You! she thought. *You were the figure in black! The one in my dreaming!*

Zalos nodded as if he could hear her. But it was only coincidence. Perhaps he had seen the recognition in her eyes and mistook it for something else.

"Aye, Luthiel. We would not have come to this. But your mother is too clever by far. Why could you have not stayed quietly in that happy no-where—Flir Light—for just another few months? Then it would be done."

She watched him with a mixture of hatred and amazement. His eyes had glazed as if he saw something very far off. But there was also a terrible sense of immediacy.

"Then it would be done," he repeated at almost a whisper and he laid a finger on her gagged lips. "Silent. So it should be. You have no place in this world, Luthiel. And there is no other." Zalos reached out and lifted a few strands of her hair. "Bright songs and the magic of hope are but a dangerous illusion. The fake comfort of witches charms."

If she could, she would have stood and struck him.

"A shame. A lovely face and form. Made well for treachery."

She saw pity in his eyes and for it she hated him all the more.

"Now Merrin will never know love for me," he said and looked away as if reconsidering an impossible puzzle.

This was too much, she growled and struggled against the hands and bonds that held her.

"That won't do any good," Zalos said with a laugh. "But your friends are coming. We'll see if they can help. Who knows, they may even hurt." He said the last in a mocking tone and there as a twinkling in his eye.

Then her friends were there before her and she felt hope as she heard Mithorden speak.

A new queen? Elayethel?

In the few moments Luthiel had known her, she'd felt reassured by her grace and wisdom. She would be free. She would have her chance against Zalos. She would have her chance to free Merrin.

"No, Zalos," Mithorden was saying.

No?

"No?" Zalos echoed and a shadow seemed to fall over his face.

The world seemed to slow down. She had that same feeling of disjointedness she'd felt when Vanye had come to name the Chosen. When she thought it was her and found out that it was Leowin.

Who else could it be? Belethial of Minonowe? Yes. It must be Belethial.

But even as her mind groped, Mithorden spoke.

"You see, Zalos," Mithorden said. "You've attacked our new High Queen and, through violence, taken her against her will. Release *Queen* Luthiel immediately."

There was no question in Mithorden's voice. Only resolve and a threat.

Queen Luthiel??

She had a dizzy feeling and were it not for the hands that held her, she would have fallen.

It cannot be!

The Vale of Mists was enough. The Vyrl were enough. But not Queen!

I'm only fifteen! She wanted to shout at the sorcerer. To scream at him. To call him a liar. Her childhood was somewhere back there at Flir Light. She fully intended on having it and sharing it with a real mother and the best sister in the whole world.

Then the hands were lifting her up, taking her gag off, cutting her bonds. The Gruagach looked at her uneasily. But in Zalos' eyes she saw only satisfaction.

The trap! The trap! It's still there!

"Very well," Zalos said to Mithorden. He was actually smiling. "You may have your queen." His voice dropped so that only he and those nearby could hear. "A *witch* to rule the Faelands? What was Tuorlin thinking? The poison must have addled his mind." Then louder. "And she was coming to kill him herself!"

"Cut out his lying tongue," Melkion hissed.

There was a *whisk* and spears and sword points seemed to form a hedge around them. The Gruagach had brought their weapons to bear and the Blade Dancers had answered.

"There is no need," Mithorden said calmly despite the tension around him. "For, by the decree of Tuorlin, Zalos is also no longer Lord of Ashiroth. He is bereft of title and all who serve him are now rebels."

At this, Zalos' face fell becoming both sad and angry.

"Bereft?" he said. "I doubt such a wrong would come from our High Lord." Then he turned to Luthiel. "This *queen* will be lucky to rule through summer. The fae will see to her justice."

At his words, a hundred spears drove toward Luthiel. Zalos lifted his hand to stop them.

"No!" Zalos cried. "Would we prove them right? If we were rebels, couldn't we kill her now?" He held his sword up, towering over Luthiel. "Do any doubt we could?" There was a pause in which all seemed ready to explode into violence. Weapons were naked. Cat-o-Fae twitched in agitation. It would have taken only one lunge. A single mistaken move. Luthiel gathered herself to spring away. But slowly, deliberately, Zalos sheathed his sword. "We will not kill her. Though it be just to. Let her rule. We shall see the truth for ourselves when the black moon rises. For she *is* the blood witch."

"Treason!" it was one of the Blade Dancers who yelled it. Had not Zalos acted so swiftly blood would have spilled.

"So rebel it is!" he shouted. And with that he turned and walked away. The wolfriders followed leaving Luthiel to her friends. "Under tyranny it is right to be a rebel!" he shouted back to them.

As they made their way down the hill one among them broke out into song. It was Elag. Luthiel would have recognized his scarecrow voice anywhere. At first he sang alone. But then the others picked up the song and it echoed hollowly as they made their way down the hill and into the mounds. The sound was like a dirge and the hollow mounds seemed to echo the music drawing it out, making it seem all the more harsh. Wicked. The sound filled the air and all around fell to silence.

> When Glimflirs golden lift and fly
> Like rivers run against the sky
> Upon the howl of rising air
> The Blood Witch comes--
> Beware, beware

On quiet feet she creeps in dreams
Of summer spun the wild Wyrd moons
Kissed by Merrin's cobalt beams
To Vyrl she's a bloody boon

Enchantress soft and seeming fair
A singer pure of eldritch spell
Beware! Beware! her soft spun snare
Pretender's tale is hers to tell

Beware the Blood Witch
That comes with summer
To unleash the wargs
Chained in the sky

Gorthar's pack
The black moon's get
Will eat the light
'Till all things die

Spiders black of Drakken Spur
Come with promise of a feast
On elfin flesh the hosts of war
That rose to punish Vale's worst beasts

Her mount a werewolf old and drear
Her allies are the ancient terror
For her sword a shattered Shear
Stolen from an honored barrow

Beware the Blood Witch
That keeps the council
Of the serpent
Great beguiler

She'll take the life fruit
Grant great knowledge
A hollow knowing
That calls the fire

So listen well unto her singing
If you wish all good to end
She'll tempt with freedom—a choice death bringing
As her form is sight of sin

As was once and now it shall be
Woman takes and woman mars
The weaker sex in strength corrupted
Will draw on us the wrath of stars

Beware the Blood Witch
Werewolf rider
Who'll open wide
The gates of dread

So death may come
To reign o'er Oesha
When horns grow from
The eighth moon's head

Others among the fae picked up the song and from each fae nation there were some that left with Zalos. All the rest of Rimwold marched off with him as well. Luthiel felt her breath catch when she realized that almost half the fae left to follow him.

When it was finished, Luthiel raised her hands to the sky in anguish. "Tuorlin! What have you done? Would you make me queen of death itself?" They moved in to comfort her. But she felt no consolation. The song was a doom and she knew well it was one she must face. She looked around and saw terror in many faces.

They'll believe in it. Make it real even if it wasn't before.

Othalas put his muzzle to her chest and Melkion landed on her shoulder, laying a comforting tail around her neck.

"You're safe now," he hissed.

But Luthiel knew he was a liar.

THIRD SACRIFICE

Vanye passed *Weiryendel* to her and when it touched her hand the song returned. This time it was soft, distant. For the Stone had gone out. Yet a thin rime of light remained, glittering at the edges. When she saw this, she felt her muscles tense and then a terrible sense of *knowing* came over her.

"I would like to see Tuorlin," she said when she was finally able to compose herself. But there was dread in her voice even as a certainty filled her.

They led her up the hill to the place where Tuorlin lay. As she passed, the fae watched her. In the eyes of some there was wonderment. In others dread. She did her best to keep her face forward and not blanch. She held her chin high and tried to look the part of a queen—though she felt it very little. Yet inside she knew, whether she liked it or not, she was in a terrible game and must play it as best she could.

I'm not made for this.

"You act like one born to command." Othalas growled.

His unwitting contradiction made her smile and she put a hand on his neck. The feel of his muscles rippling beneath the fur reassured her. Here was power, and by the way the fae watched them they knew it too.

But to be feared is one thing. Will they ever love me?

Yet that was what she must do. She must, somehow, make them love her. The thought made her sick and she almost fell. She had to lean against the wolf in order to make her way over the broken ground. When was the last time she'd truly had rest? She raised her hand to her lips and wiped away some of the blood.

Queen? More like a whipping girl by the look of it.

Tuorlin's body was placed on a bed of shields and his hands were crossed nobly on his chest. His spear was laid beside him and an effort had been made to clean the blood away. A helm had been placed on his head. It hid the ruin, the terrible wounds. The banner of Ithilden—a Tree of Life set on a field of blue, its leaves gleaming like stars, its root cupping a fire like the sun—draped over his legs and torso.

Kneeling before his body, she undid the pouch at her belt. The sound like breaking sifted out. There was a humming and her Stone awakened. Silver shot with red and gold. The flower of light burst out, making a small blaze on the hilltop. There was a gasp among the fae and many fell to their knees.

Her song erupted from her mouth and the shards lifted as if picked up on a swirling wind. They clashed against *Weiryendel*, rising up the blade and then fused to form another eight inches of length. The wind gusted over the hill. Another banner, this one of Minonowe—Tiolas in a circle of green stars— ripped from its pole and blew away on the gale. Then came the voice. But this time it was no comfort.

"*My craft to your protection. A weapon for your hand. The only safety I have left. The cutting edge of oblivion.*"

A final shard rose from the pouch. It danced over her palm cutting as gracefully as a stylus. The mark that remained was a golden ᚼ rune, even as the other scars blazed red and silver. Then the song was finished and the air grew still. The fae watched on in a mixture of anger and fear. Even Vanye seemed disturbed. When all was still he asked her in a low voice.

"Why did it happen?"

"The sacrifice," she said, trying and failing to hold back the tears. "The magic in the sword comes when someone dies for me."

The Blade Dancer's face grew impassive as he stood and walked away.

"Your magic feeds on death," he said over his shoulder and then he was gone among the fae. Luthiel watched him leave.

"I did not choose it," she said to his back.

A Necessary Parting

It was a beginning. Not the best by far, but a beginning nonetheless. Knowing she must make some kind of statement, Luthiel swung herself up onto Othalas' back.

A werewolf rider? Then let it be.

Above her, Oerin's Eye and Soelee blazed brightly. Even for High Summer, Oerin was larger than usual and the blue glow was pierced by a white fire nearly as bright as Soelee. The day was hot—hotter than she ever remembered even in high summer, and sweat streamed freely from her body. Briefly, she was reminded of the flames of the Red Moon and of the dragon. She glanced at Mithorden.

What had he said about reading the sky?

She shook her head to clear it. Being able to *sense* so much was overwhelming. It took longer for her mind to understand it all. A large group of fae were watching her and she turned her attention to them. They were mostly Ithildar and their noble faces turned toward her. There was confusion. There was awe. There was fear. In too many faces she saw anger, doubt.

They know that somehow I gained strength from Tuorlin's death. But how do I make them understand?

"The High Lord did not die needlessly," she said with resolve. "He has uncovered a great danger—Lord Zalos and Thrar Taurmori working with Widdershae. Zalos deceived us into entering a trap laid by his spider friends! If they succeeded our bodies would now fill their larders or be twisted by black Wyrd and by mists into spiders as well. To serve as food or slaves. And if we were defeated, do you think they would have stopped here at the mounds? No home would be shelter. No child would be safe."

Her own words made her tremble and she paused to gather herself.

"This threat has been with us ever since my father's downfall. I swear, by him and by mother I will set it right. We should not need to live in fear of Zalos or the monsters he runs with!"

The last words she spoke with a startling force. Though she hadn't realized it, she'd raised her clenched fist into the air. Many stared at her in amazement. Some of her friends looked at her as if she was a stranger. She didn't care. The anger had consumed her. She was faequeen and if she could use it to save mother, she would. If she could use it to bring Zalos to justice, she would. As sure as moons followed suns, as sure as wolf's scent—she would.

Silence fell on the host. Some watched her disbelieving, or glanced over their shoulders at the Vyrl's army. Rank after rank, the wights stood trembling. Fingers touching ugly weapons. Tongues questing for eyes. A vast force of dreamless slaves. Held only by Vyrl's will. Forever marked by Vyrl's tyranny. These were the soldiers of madness. Some among the elves still recalled the abuses. They knew friends or lovers who were devoured; who may now stand before them as a Wight. They would never forgive the Vyrl's age of terror or the blood tithe of Chosen.

"But Zalos is not the only one to hold to account." She felt guilty as she spoke the words. *Now how am I any better than Zalos? Asking them to suffer one evil and then to fight against another? Or am I just selfishly trying to use them to save mother?*

I promised the Vyrl, she argued against the dark thought. *They have changed.*

Despite her inward doubt, she spoke the words all the clearer. She was fighting with everything to save the mother she never knew. To save the idea of what they might be—the fragment of a family she might save. Her words echoed among the mounds in the heat of day. Burned hotter in the heat of her anger.

"In the name of Ecthellien, Tuorlin and Vlad Valkire. My bond, my High Lord, and my father, I call the Vale's rulers Ahmberen and Elshael come forward!"

There was a murmur among the elves. From the front of the Vale's army rode the Vyrl upon their eyeless steeds—bone and blackness. She recalled that instant not too long ago when three Vyrl had ridden to claim her as their prize and their food. Now they rode to beg for mercy.

Vaelros and Leowin followed. Vaelros rode his strange Vale-horse while Leowin sat on the back of a winged lion with ruby feathers instead of fur. Looking closer at Vaelros, Luthiel noticed he still appeared weak and his eyes were bloodshot. Yet it seemed he'd recovered from the worst of the poison. Leowin gave Luthiel a look of amazement and Vaelros' wan face was filled with relief and longing. Luthiel sighed. As a woman, she understood Vaelros' look. But she couldn't return the desire in his eyes. Instead, she gave him her best warm smile and turned quickly to the Vyrl. Though tall and riding great horses they had to look up at her. The werewolf was a giant and he made even the Vyrl's steeds look like runts. Melkion's chuckle whispered in her ear.

"So even a Vyrl may be humbled," the dragon mused.

Gormtoth had come behind them and across his great shoulders he carried a chest of black iron. It stood out wider than his frame and was fully three feet deep. Luthiel gazed on them with her best imperious glare. It shocked her how easily it came. *What's happening? What am I becoming?*

"I have bound you as my father did—by blood. Dismount and kneel before them." Ahmberen and Elshael hesitated. Vyrl did not like to be commanded. She felt their minds reaching for hers, but she walled them out.

"Do as I say!" she shouted. "You *have* wronged them. You *will* show apology."

Together and with some of the grace they must have once possessed, they swung off their horses and knelt.

Not to me, she thought to the Vyrl. *To them.* She pointed at the fae. Slowly, the Vyrl shifted to face them.

"Now speak after me," she said to the Vyrl.

The Vyrl looked at her and nodded. They did not like this public display. But they understood. She could sense hope along with humiliation and even a little anger. But there was no way she could overcome the pride of Vyrl. Hopefully, she could convince the fae to be merciful.

"We have wronged you," she said the words and the Vyrl spoke after. "We were driven mad by hunger but it is no justification. We were angels but we became monsters. We ask you to forgive us."

Brought low before the elves, the Vyrl looked out. There were many among the elves who fingered weapons and thought they could end the Vyrl here and now. But many also heard remorse in the Vyrl's words. These nodded and mumbled their forgiveness. At this Luthiel smiled grimly and continued.

"I know many of you do not trust the Vyrl. But there is no treachery left in them. My blood has driven out the hunger. They will be our allies. If they live long enough, they will become angels again. No more Chosen will be sent." She paused and spoke half out of dread, half out of her odd, happy, memory of Ottomnos. "I take their place. I will be both their sacrifice and their living law."

"And what if you die?" A fae among them shouted. Her breath caught when she saw he was a Gruagach.

Mithorden answered for her. "If Luthiel dies then there will be no more hope."

The elves looked at the Sorcerer in shock. It wasn't the answer they were looking for. But there was an awakening in some eyes and many looked on Luthiel in wonder.

"I hope to live," she said, then turned toward the Vyrl. "Now rise and return to the Vale of Mists. You are part of the Faelands, now. But you may not live with us three hundred and three years. A necessary parting. As necessary as the old wounds are deep and slow to heal."

Then Elshael motioned to Gormtoth who lowered the great chest. As one, they mounted their terrible horses. Ahmberen rode to the chest and lifted the lid. A riches of gold, gems, and the metals of seven moons gleamed beneath the lid.

"It can never equal the value of lives or vanished experience," the Vyrl said. "Give a portion to each family who has lost a loved one to our madness."

Elshael lifted her voice above the fae. "We hunt the spiders and will aid in the scouring of the mounds. Only ask, and we will hunt them across all the Faelands until they are dead to the last or driven back to their black mountains."

This brought a low cheer from the elves. Then the Vyrl were riding back to their army. Ahmberen blew his horn and drew his sword. There was a flashing beneath the suns as the army lifted all its weapons high in salute.

"To Luthiel!" The Vyrl shouted.

"Luthiel!" the army echoed. Then it turned and departed into the hills. As it went Luthiel could sense the Vyrl's bitterness at the humiliation. They were proud beings and shock and displeasure rippled back along her bond with them. *It was necessary,* she thought back to them. They did not reply.

She watched them go for some minutes before turning to Mithorden.

"No more hope?" she said.

In answer, the Sorcerer lifted his eyes to Oerin whose swelling orb seemed to crown his head in a blue and silver fire.

"Yes, I'll tell you more later."

A KINDNESS UNEARNED

The Vyrl's army sifted into the hills. She stood silent, watching. Their *thought* departed steadily as the distance increased and she was reminded of Ecthellien. *Three have died for me now.* Perhaps it was exhaustion, but the thought didn't hurt so much now.

Across the battlefield lay dead and wounded.

"Thousands of immortal lives were lost this day," she whispered. But these words also felt hollow and she knew events were finally starting to overwhelm her. *If I don't feel it, then what have I lost? Or is it just the capacity to feel so much?* She wondered if it was just a mercy of the heart that, like the body, when confronted with great hurt grew numb to it. *Beyond a certain point, the awareness of pain does no good.*

On her shoulder, Melkion hissed in reply. "They've descended into the dust. Never again will they see the light or *know*."

"It's just beginning," Mithorden added.

"If this is just beginning, my heart won't feel the light anymore and soon life will seem little better than the dust." Saddened and unwilling to hear or speak anymore, Luthiel urged Othalas away from the hillside. The others followed and stayed quiet as if sensing her need for silence. Without another word, she rode through the army.

Leowin looked up at her sister with a mixture of sadness and pride. Here was the orphan she'd loved as her own. Her eyes shone and she smiled at the thought she'd known her all these years—as a child, as a friend, and now as queen.

"You know," she said to Luthiel, "I thought I'd lost you? I was going to die in the Vale of Mists. You'd run away. At least that's what I'd thought."

Something in Leowin's voice awakened Luthiel to feeling again. Suddenly the sadness returned. But with it came joy as well. *Is this what it is to be alive? To feel such sadness and joy at once?* She looked at Leowin. "I know," she said simply. "I'm sorry."

Leowin stared into Luthiel's sad eyes. She wondered at their age and wisdom. These were no longer the eyes of a child.

"I didn't want you to die," Luthiel continued. "I would have rather lost myself."

Leowin couldn't keep back the tears any longer. "Well, you did, in a way," she stared into those eyes that were both so strange and so familiar.

"I lost my innocence," Luthiel said.

Leowin looked away. "I should thank you."

"I'd do it all over again."

"I knew *something*. The secrets, the Stone."

There was silence between them again. The others were quiet or held back out of respect as they continued through the army.

"You should rest some, Luthiel."

"I know. But I want to do something first." She wanted to see the wounded. To pay her respects and to help if she could. *I don't know what I can or cannot do anymore. It all seems so unclear.* So she made her way to where the fallen had been gathered together on the hillside. Elf and beast, faerie and goblin. All wounded. Many dying. Though it was terrible and the field seemed to go on and on, Luthiel knew it could well be worse. She climbed off Othalas, walking slowly through them, touching a head here, giving a whisper of comfort there. When she reached the center, she came to a stop and looked around. Healers drifted among the hurt, weaving their Wyrd, doing their best to mend the broken bodies.

"I hope things haven't changed too much," she said to Leowin suddenly. "It would make me very sad to have gone through so much only to have lost the sister I fought to save." In a short bound, she was standing beside Leowin's winged lion. She put a hand on her leg. "You're tapped," she said with a half-smile.

Leowin leapt off her lion and pulled her sister close. She laughed and the tears fell. Caught up, Luthiel laughed as well.

"It wasn't easy getting here. But it's good to finally be home," Luthiel said. Her eyes returned to the wounded. "Let's see if we can help them."

Leowin nodded and together they walked through the wounded. Luthiel had some idea of trying to use the Wyrd to heal them. But she didn't know where to start.

"Mother's bound to be here somewhere," Leowin said.

The word mother made Luthiel stop. It was amazing how much hurt one little word could do. But the thought of Merrin was enough to bring all the rage back full force.

"My mother's at Arganoth," she said numbly. "But I would be very glad to see Winowe."

Leowin frowned but kept silent. She was too glad to be back together to start a quarrel. But there was some deep pain in Luthiel and with it came a distance she couldn't cross. Half the things she said she couldn't quite follow. *Mother in Arganoth? What does she mean?*

Leowin shook her head to quiet these thoughts. *You're not giving her a chance,* she thought. *She's been through so much.* Leowin wondered how she would feel if her real mother —

"Luthiel!" Leowin shouted in realization.

Her sister turned with a start.

"What is it?"

"I'm a fool! I just realized something I should have known all along. Merrin's your mother."

Luthiel nodded. "I should have told you. I keep thinking people know things they don't. But through all that's happened it's hard to keep track." She grinned as she watched Leowin working it all out. *You've always loved mysteries,* she thought with a laugh.

"It makes sense now! I thought you may be related to Valkire in some way. But his daughter... and Merrin?"

"— is Zalos' captive," Luthiel answered before she could ask the question. "They say he's trying to force her to marry him."

Leowin's mind was still adjusting, still taking in all the new facts. They were so huge and at the same time so personal. The pain and anger in

Luthiel's voice shot through her like lightning. But Leowin couldn't help but be overjoyed at witnessing it. To think what secrets she may discover being so close to Vlad Valkire's heir! As soon as the thought came to her, she felt ashamed.

She's my sister!

But her excitement and curiosity lingered. Was it so bad to want to *know* about her? Was it wrong to want to witness incredible things? She's always lusted after the deep secrets. In Luthiel she'd found a way to uncover so many!

With an effort of will, she brought her excitement under control. *Luthiel is hurting,* she thought. *I'd be hurting too.*

Almost without thinking, she put her arm across Luthiel's shoulder. She felt Luthiel lean into her. Though taller and stronger than Leowin, she still felt surprisingly vulnerable.

Not much more than a little girl, really. Yet you've defeated great ones.

"Zalos will kill me if he can," Luthiel said. "He's already made me into some kind of monster to half the Faelands." She stared at her sister with those blue-green eyes that seemed both deep and yet full of light. "You don't think I'm a monster, do you?"

"Monster?" Leowin said as if the thought were the most ridiculous thing she'd ever heard. "You're a hero! You've got the blood of gods and angels in you!"

"Vyrl have angel's blood too. Look what good it did them. But they can also be heroes. I've seen it." Luthiel looked away and thought of Ecthellien. "Even Zalos was good once. Don't you see Leowin? It doesn't matter what we are. We're all capable of evil."

"But you mean so well."

"Mean well? I did with you, yes. But not with others." She thought of Zalos and how she'd kill him in a moment given the chance. "Sometimes I wonder if well meaning really helps so much."

"It *should* help."

"Don't you realize? We all do terrible things. We do them to survive. Even in day to day life. We eat animals—don't you think they see us as monsters?"

"But they're just animals. They don't think as we do."

"What did thinking ever have to do with being? They have lives. They have feelings. They have experience. It took me to see through an owl's eyes to realize it. And he died for me too."

Leowin frowned. She'd never gone so deep or put so fine an understanding to things. It was truth. It disturbed her. *There, Leowin. You wanted mystery. You wanted deep secrets. Now you're up to your neck in them!*

"But it's natural for us to eat them," Leowin said in self-defense.

"Why is it so? We have a choice. Long, long, long ago our ancestors chose to eat animals. Maybe they did it to survive through a difficult time. Who knows. But they stuck to it. Over time and generations we got better at it. But we're lucky. We can still eat other things too. We only subsist on death and suffering by choice." Luthiel paused and looked at the werewolf who walked a little ways off beside them. "Othalas has no choice. By his body he is forced to kill in order to survive. In a certain way, I am like Othalas."

Luthiel felt strange. It was almost like she was watching someone else do the talking. But it felt good to have these things off her chest. She'd always shared deep things with Leowin and having her near made her feel free to unburden her mind.

"Othalas? How could you be like him?"

Luthiel drew *Weiryendel*. Leowin took a deep breath and held it. The crystal blade contained beauty—both joyful and sad. Its music and light expressed it perfectly. She noticed small factures in the blade and its abrupt incompleteness. Its light gleamed through, drawing each imperfection in a tiny rainbow.

"Because people must die for me. This sword was broken. Now it is nearly reformed because three have died. It's like Vanye said. My Wyrd is feeding on death."

"Who's died?" Leowin said in a half-whisper.

"An owl. Ecthellien. Now Tuorlin."

"The High Lord didn't die *for* you. He died fighting spiders."

"No Leowin. He died because he went against Zalos. He died because he sided with me. His talent, Leowin! He saw me! I was the messenger, remember?"

Leowin stared in shock.

"How am I any different from Zalos?" Luthiel continued. "My Wyrd feeds on death. Zalos was right. I'm flawed."

Leowin had finally regained her composure. "I don't see it that way, Luthiel," she said quietly. "They all may well have died for you. But it seems that at least Tuorlin chose to. Maybe your Wyrd feeds on selfless sacrifice. On heroism. On unearned acts of kindness. It's in your nature. You did it for me."

Leowin paused and thought about what she was saying before she continued. "There's another word for a kindness unearned. It's grace, Luthiel. Your Wyrd responds to *grace*."

Luthiel lifted her arm and rubbed it across her eyes. When she'd cleared them, she looked at Leowin and then at *Weiryendel*.

"Grace? If so, then it's you who's to blame for it all." At this, Luthiel laughed. Its music made Leowin smile.

"How could I? It was your Wyrd."

"My Wyrd! My Stone! It all started there on my birthday. You said it yourself—with love and a song. You awakened my Stone with an act of selfless kindness. You awakened my Wyrd with *grace*."

"And you returned the favor by saving my life."

"One good deed in return for another," Luthiel said with a grin.

"Grace for grace," Leowin replied. "You know, I just thought of something. I know a little about how the magic of dreams works. Do you think it's possible your Wyrd is acting in honor of those who've been heroes to you? Do you think it's possible these acts make your Wyrd stronger? Strong enough to repair your father's sword?"

"I don't know. But one thing's certain. I don't like the idea of people dying for me."

"Then you should think twice before running off to do it for others!"

At this Luthiel laughed and Leowin grinned. It was good to be back together. It felt strong. It felt bittersweet. But there was something deeply right to it all. No matter what else happened in life, they were still sisters and that mattered most.

"I should get you in a chat with Mithorden," Luthiel said. "I bet you'd even teach him a thing or two." She shot a look at the sorcerer who appeared too occupied with his thoughts to be listening. With a last look at *Weiryendel*, she slid the sword back into its scabbard. It nearly filled the length now.

"The sorcerer?" Leowin smirked. "I bet I'd give him a good run."

"I'm certain you would," Luthiel said with a smile and then her face became thoughtful. "What you've said does seem to be possible. But I know there's darkness in me too."

Leowin nodded. "It's like you said. It's about choice. Sure, there's dark in everyone. It's how we handle it that counts."

"And handling it well once is no guarantee. Each time things work out it's like a small miracle."

"Like a gift unearned?" Leowin asked.

"Like grace," Luthiel replied with a pat to Leowin's shoulder.

HEALING

They continued through the field of maimed and dying. Elves lay beside goblins and animals. Here a faerie cradled her tattered wings—if they weren't mended soon she'd never fly again; there a red-cap sat still as an elf wrapped a bandage around a wound so deep it exposed his skull. His eyes were vacant and clear fluid streamed from his nose. Hundreds lay in the field. These were the worst of the wounded. Most suffered from poison as well as terrible physical injury. Too much of the bleeding could not be stopped. The life flooded out of them and even Wyrd did little.

Leowin walked alongside her—face pale, eyes filled with sadness. Melkion had sat silent on Luthiel's shoulder as the sisters talked. Now he flared wings, casting rainbows out over the dying as he bowed his head in respect. Mithorden, Vaelros, and Othalas drew closer. At the wolf's approach, many of the wounded moaned in fear. One watched him with mad eyes as he pointed and mouthed "Death! Death!"

The smell of blood and fear filled the air. Luthiel passed on, taking it all in, saying soft words of comfort when she felt she could. She watched as healers struggled to use both magic and medicine. It was such a helpless thing, walking through the field. As she continued she felt more and more ill at ease, more and more as if she must do something.

"Try to find Winowe," she said to Leowin. "If I can be of any help here, she's the one who'll show me."

Leowin nodded and scanned the field for any sign of her mother. After some time, she shook her head. "Too many," she said before breaking off and making her way to the nearest healer. Luthiel watched as her sister picked her way through the field of wounded. The healer looked up and Luthiel gasped at her sunken eyes. It was as if she were giving small shreds of her life to save them. Leowin spoke with her but Luthiel couldn't hear. The healer nodded and pointed further down the field. Luthiel didn't wait for her sister. She started at once along the way the healer showed and met Leowin further on.

On a nearby hilltop, an elf with a banner appeared. The banner was for all the Faelands. It was the High Lord's banner.

The queen's banner, she corrected.

It displayed a golden five pointed star on a field of black. The star's upper gap cupped a gleaming design of Oerin's Eye. Soelee burned at the bottom tip and the eight moons filled the spaces and capped the points in between.

It only took the banner man a moment to see her. His eyes found the great wolf and Melkion's rainbow wings first, then followed on to her. With a shout, he rushed down the hill and came before her. He dropped to a knee and put a closed fist over his heart. Luthiel felt a chill of recognition as she looked down at him.

"I've come to serve as your man, my queen," he said in a rush. "The other banner man fell with High Lord Tuorlin. I picked up the standard even as he named you."

She smiled at him warmly. Here was the same Galwin she'd known since childhood. The one who'd given her a pandur's box. The one she'd danced with. But here was also a blooded warrior. His heavy plate armor was caked in grime and gore. A wicked greatsword rested in a sling across his back. A flash of purple tinted metal above the scabbard showed a blade crafted of *Viel* moonsteel. His eyes were hard, still filled with the night's terrors. Yet there was wonder in them too and relief as well.

"I'm glad I found you," he said. "Now the captains will know where to send the runners. There's much still to be done. They're off to hunt the Widdershae. Already, Vyrl are starting to burn their webs. They have a demon with them— kin to Thrar Taurmori—who holds a terrible fire. He's leading the force."

"Gormtoth," Luthiel interrupted.

"My Queen?" Galwin gave her a puzzled look. To Luthiel, the words came too easy for him. She wondered with a sinking feeling if he'd always felt some sense of deference to her.

"Gormtoth is his name. He is Narcor—the opposite of Thrar Taurmori."

"I'm sorry. I didn't —"

"Don't worry Galwin, you wouldn't. But you may find it strange to know I think of him as a friend. You're my friend aren't you?"

"I'm proud to say I am."

"I wouldn't like it if someone compared you with a demon either."

Galwin opened his mouth, shut it, then opened it again. If he was out of his depth before with Luthiel, now he was entirely lost. Behind, she could hear Vaelros chuckle. But a glance over her shoulder revealed a jealous glare. Luthiel looked away. She didn't like being an object to such ugly looks or feelings.

"So this banner will help people find me and bring me news?" she said, running her fingers through its threads.

"That and bring runners to ask for orders. You lead the army now." Galwin looked away and over the wounded. "What's left of it," he said in a lower voice.

Luthiel nodded in sympathy. "Keep near."

Galwin flushed but quickly covered it with a bow.

They crossed the rest of the field in silence—each listening to the sounds of wounded all around. Luthiel took advantage of the time to get her bearings. The army was doing its best to reform around her. Fae were accounted for. Units were called to order. Above, faerie and birds still filled the air. She was reassured to see Khoraz and Firewing among them.

They've stayed for me. At least I won't be without some help if things turn bad.

So they followed Leowin down one side of the field and up the other. As Luthiel passed, she felt a growing sense of loss.

Hundreds dead. Yet I'm afraid it's just starting.

It was a dark thought and it drew her eyes to the sorcerer.

He keeps hinting of danger. As she drifted closer, she thought of his quarrel with Zalos. The more she thought about it, the less she liked it.

"I think I agree with you about prophecy," she said to Melkion. At this, the dragon snorted smoke.

She changed direction and walked closer to Mithorden.

"You were going to tell me something later?" she asked as she drew up beside him.

A dark look crossed his face and then was gone. Like some stray cloud that passes over the sun at noon and then lifts away.

"Yes. But not here. Not now."

"Can you at least tell me what it's about?"

He looked up at blazing Soelee and Oerin's Eye. "The dying of this Age. And how, for some, a time of trouble is also an opportunity for conquest."

Luthiel walked beside him in silence for a few moments.

"That is all?"

"For now, yes."

"It makes more questions than it answers."

The sorcerer nodded. "I didn't want to trouble you. On the road there will be time to rest. Time to think about what's coming."

"You sound like you're expecting something. A storm?"

At her words, the sorcerer's face darkened and his eyes grew distant. The change was startling. She'd never seen him act this way. It was almost as if a desperation and doubt had set upon him. It unsettled her deeply and she realized how much she'd come to trust in the sorcerer's optimism. But seeing this look on his face and in those deep eyes was like seeing the ending of comfort.

"A storm you say?" he replied with a grimace. "Yes, though I'd never thought of it that way. A storm then, but one that blows across all the sky. One with winds strong enough to extinguish the weaker stars and with clouds large enough to block out the strongest. If it's a storm then it's the one that eats worlds."

A lump formed in her throat and her mouth watered in fear. *A storm that eats worlds? What does it mean?*

"There are signs it's coming?" she asked.

"On the road to Ithilden. After all is finished here. I don't want you troubled now."

"Too late," Luthiel said.

"Luthiel! I've found her!" Leowin's shouting startled her enough to make her quiver.

"Go on," the sorcerer said. "We'll talk later."

Luthiel took one last look at the sorcerer before turning around and no-ticing Leowin guiding Winowe toward them. *Seems there's more to it all than he showed at Lenidras.* With a shiver, she realized he'd probably told her just enough to get by. *He's been around for a very long time. Might take years for him to tell me even a small part. He's just giving me what I need.* The thought stuck with her and nagged at her for a long time after. Even when danger seemed far off, the mystery of what Mithorden knew troubled her. From his manner and from his way of speaking, she sensed he'd experienced a thousand terrors over the ages. No one, no matter how good, could remain unaffected after so much. She didn't doubt him. Yet she feared what he knew and what he had yet to reveal. Deep truths. The ones that filled in the dark gaps in myth and history. Terrible and dangerous. For in a world where nightmare may become real, a terrible truth became an awful weapon.

Like Zalos. He uses truth as a weapon.

She stopped and drew a sharp breath. *He uses truth as a weapon. I wonder how many he learned from Mithorden or—or even father.*

Luthiel's thought was interrupted. Before she could think or say a thing, she was caught up in her foster-mother's arms.

"Thank you!" Winowe said to her as she clutched Luthiel close. Her arms seemed thinner than before and her eyes had that same hollowed look the other healers showed. But in them she could see joy.

She let Winowe fold her up and she rested her head on her shoulder. For a moment she felt she was home again in Flir Light. This time, she felt she belonged.

"What did I do?" she asked.

"What?" Winowe laughed and then choked on her tears. "First you took Leowin's place. Then you stopped us from going to war with Vyrl. We would have gone to the Vale. Dead or changed—that's what we'd likely be without you."

"Leowin was my sister. It was the right thing."

Winowe laughed and held her tighter. "You did it even though we didn't deserve it." Her face fell in shame. "Your Stone... we used it as payment for Lorethain's schooling." She looked away. "Now we've lost him."

Luthiel felt her belly tighten. When Leowin had given her back the Wyrd Stone she'd confided that it had come with her as a child. Instead of saving it for her until she came of age, they'd used it to pay for Lorethain's sorcery lessons. "It was wrong," she said after an uncomfortable pause. "But Leowin mended it. Now what's this about Lorethain?"

"Gone. Left with Elag and Zalos." Winowe looked small and afraid.

"With Zalos?" She blinked her eyes and felt the shock come on her. She had to lean into Winowe to steady herself.

Winowe nodded sadly.

"But I, *we*, may have to fight them."

This seemed to trouble Winowe. Then she did something that seemed very strange to Luthiel. She fell to her knees.

"I know you're queen now. But you are also a woman and may one day be a mother. So I beg you, who risked so much for your sister, to spare your brother."

Luthiel couldn't stand to see Winowe there beneath her. She took her by the shoulders and stood her up. Then, holding her at arms length, she looked her straight in the eye.

"I promise I'll do all I can."

Winowe leaned into her again. "After what happened with Leowin, I've come to think of you as a hero. I'm not fooled by the werewolf or what some of the others say. You're a good heart, Luthiel."

The words made Luthiel feel a mixture of joy and sadness. Here she was being recognized by one of the people who mattered most to her. To do a terribly hard thing and then to be acknowledged. It was overpowering. She almost lost herself in Winowe's arms. But a glance over her foster-mother's shoulder brought it all back—the dying, the reason she'd come in the first place. Gently, she pushed her mother away.

"The battle. The dying —"

There was a flash of guilt on Winowe's face.

"I've stopped for too long. They need me." She started to turn away.

"Wait. They're why I came. I want to help."

Winowe stared back at her with a blank look. Then she frowned in thought. "You want to heal them?"

"To try at least."

"But you've never —"

"She's a quick learner," Melkion interrupted. He'd flown about at a respectful distance while Luthiel and Winowe reunited. But now, he landed with a flare and a puff of golden smoke upon Luthiel's shoulder. Winowe watched the dragon with wonder.

"Few have the talent. I've never seen someone learn it in a day."

"She's a sorcerer," Mithorden said from a little ways off. He'd also followed Luthiel at a respectful distance as he took the fae army into account. Now he wandered closer and looked on both Winowe and Luthiel with interest. "And very strong at certain things. Healing may be one of them. I've taught her spells in just minutes. She made one of her own this morning and nearly stole all of Zalos' wolfriders from under his nose! She's like her father."

Winowe looked at Luthiel with an appraising eye and opened her mouth to say something. But before she could speak, Leowin stepped forward and put a hand on her mother's arm.

"I've seen her do it. A Widdershae tried to turn me into a spider with a spell. Luthiel stopped it! There were some more she saved. But they were already spiders. So she changed them into Senasarab—the good spiders who are helping us hunt Widdershae."

Winowe put a hand on Luthiel's cheek. "I've known you since a babe. It's hard for me to believe all this." She shook her head. "Valkire's daughter?"

Luthiel nodded. "It's been tough for me too."

"Then come and learn what you can. There are far too many wounded. Even just one more healer could save twenty lives."

She motioned to Luthiel to follow as she turned and walked over to the young fae she was tending. A beautiful Ithildarin archer. Her body lay crumpled beneath Winowe. In her belly was a great gash. Blood flowed out, running in small rivers over her skin and pooling in the grass.

"Her name is Lyra," she whispered so the wounded fae couldn't hear. "A spider cut her open. I could mend her flesh. But the venom can't be stopped and may still kill her."

"You don't have anti-venom?"

"No-one knows of an anti-venom."

"I do," Luthiel said. Kneeling, she rummaged through her pack and found one of the mostly empty potion vials she'd used on Othalas. She handed it to Winowe. "Give her what's left in this."

Then she turned to Melkion. "Can you find Mindersnatch?"

The dragon flared his wings. "In a moment!" he cried and then launched himself into the air. The suns burned bright through his rainbow wings. Then he was away—flying off toward the circling crows.

Melkion was barely gone before she wheeled on Mithorden and Vaelros. "Do you have any anti-venom left?" she asked.

Soon, she had five more vials to give Winowe.

"Use these," she said, as she handed them over. "One should be enough for each. Hopefully, Melkion will bring more. Now can you teach me?"

Winowe looked at the vials in her hand as if they were a miracle. "Yes, this will help," she said, her voice filled with gratitude.

She guided Luthiel back to Lyra then sat her down beside the wounded elf. "Watch and listen," she said.

She arranged herself into a kneeling position and tilted a vial into Lyra's mouth. Lyra choked the foul stuff down, made a face, then cursed.

"Much worse. I liked the other stuff better," she said weakly.

"Good, then maybe this will help you more," Winowe said with a reassuring look. "Just lay still and try to relax. I'm to give it a little time. Luthiel, here will be helping. So don't be alarmed."

At mention of Luthiel's name, Lyra became more alert. She shifted her head to get a better look at Luthiel and then smiled.

"The good spiders who came for me told me about you."

"There Lyra, just try to relax," Winowe said.

"I know it'll be well now," Lyra replied with a smile at Luthiel. Then, she shut her eyes and let out a slow exhalation. Her body, though stiff with pain, became more relaxed.

"Let's begin then. I'll explain as I go. Sometimes I'll have to shut my eyes and touch the Wyrd. Sometimes I won't be able to speak. Don't be alarmed."

Luthiel nodded to show she understood.

"Good. Now I'll start by touching her. The Wyrd of healing is best used through touch. It creates a connection." She placed a hand on Lyra's chest and closed her eyes. After a few moments of silence, she continued. "Now I can sense Lyra's life through the Wyrd. It helps me tell how she's hurt and where. It is all communicated through the bond of our touch. At first, all I feel is heartbeat and breathing. I put my breathing in synch and through the Wyrd my heartbeat falls into rhythm as well. When this happens, I gain a broader sense of her well being. I can feel the hurts as if they were mine and, in Wyrd, I can see them as well."

Winowe's face tensed in pain.

"Now comes the hard part," Winowe continued. "I can sense her pain and the broken parts inside her. To mend them, I send some of my blood into her. I share the wound as if it were part of my own body and then use the healing Wyrd to repair it. When this happens, I both see and feel the hurt. I must be careful. For though I can tap into Lyra's energy and life to help heal her, I also use up some of my own reserves. If I use too much, I could pass out or even die. This is the way life-Wyrd works. Life sustains life. But it always comes at a cost. So a healer must take care she does not overtax herself. She must pace herself. Eat, drink and take rest often. Women make better healers. Their bodies are more resilient to pain and they recover faster."

Luthiel watched as Winowe's concentration deepened. Her face became twisted with pain and the shadows around her eyes darkened. Lyra moaned. There were things moving and knitting inside her. Winowe coughed and some blood appeared at the corner of her mouth. It trickled down to her chin. The healing went on for some time. About a quarter hour passed. Then, Winowe finally removed her hands and rocked back on her heels. Her palms were bloody and she wiped them on a rag at her hip. Pain and exhaustion carved deep hollows in her face.

Lyra gave a contented smile and fell into a deep sleep. Her wound had closed and blood no longer flowed freely from it. Winowe put a fresh bandage over top. It smelled of herbs and flowers.

"She should live. The poison will make her bleed a little more than she should. But the anti-venom seems to have taken the edge off. At least she's whole on the inside now."

"You look exhausted."

"I am. I should stop. She's my twenty fifth since last night. More will die if I stop now. But I'll end up with them if I don't.

"I've shown you what I can. If you have the talent, you should at least be able to sense the hurt. A big part of healing is not drawing back from the pain. That's the reason it usually takes some time to learn—even for those with the talent."

"I'll try," she said.

Winowe smiled at her. "We'll see, won't we? Let's start."

Leaving Mithorden and the others behind, she led Luthiel down the slope to another wounded. This one was a Blade Dancer. His thigh-bone had fractured and fragments were sticking up through the flesh. Blood pumped out and his face had become white. He stared skyward with a blank look. If Luthiel could have described his expression with one word she would have said 'doomed.'

"Usually, we'd start with a less dire wound. But everyone on this field is either maimed or on the cusp of death."

"I understand," Luthiel said.

"We'll work together on this one," Winowe said. "I'll set the bone while you use the Wyrd to mend it and his other hurts. He's not poisoned so at least you won't have to worry about that." She turned and shouted to a girl of about Luthiel's age who was tending to another wounded. "Min! Take these vials! They're anti-venom! Pass them on if you can't use it all!"

Min raised her head and seemed to start.

"Luthiel?" she gasped as she approached. "Why? I mean, aren't you queen now?"

"Is there any reason why a queen should not also help with healing?"

Min shook her head. "Well, now that I think of it, it's good you're here. It should give confidence—to wounded and healers both. I'll spread word." She gave a curtsey to Luthiel and then she was gone.

"It's good to see her," Luthiel said. "Don't know what to think about the curtsey."

"You're queen," Winowe said. "Now let's see if you're also a healer."

Luthiel brought her attention back to the wounded Blade Dancer. His armor was covered in gore and marked in a hundred places by the violence of battle. His Cat-o-Fae was likewise caked in blood and spider flesh. By the look of him, he'd survived through the very thick of the fighting. Luthiel was shocked by his size. For he would have rivaled even Ahmberen. And a Blade Dancer too! She guessed it had taken quite a lot to bring him down.

"What's your name, Blade Dancer?" Winowe asked.

He clasped his hands across his chest in a brave effort to stop the shuddering. But his eyes were steady as he spoke.

"Balnos. And who are you?" His fingers lurched to give the sign for Oerin's Eye. "A blessing on you."

"I am Winowe. Queen Luthiel will help me. You will be her first patient."

Balnos' eyes fell on Luthiel and the shuddering grew worse.

"A healer queen? I wonder. I saw your charge. I was on the hill with the High Lord. Some say you rode to save—others to slay. But he named you queen. Was it glamer or honor that won you the throne? Are you an angel, as some say, or a witch?"

"Neither," she said with a shake of her head. "I've never wished for power and I'm not happy about coming to the throne. I fear it is only a short way from the tomb. Seems there are many who want me dead. More don't know what to think. I'm not here to convince you. I'm here to save your life."

Balnos laughed and she could tell it pained him. "Well said. You have a golden tongue, little queen."

Winowe looked at Luthiel and Balnos grew quiet. "We should start now. There will not be a later."

Luthiel nodded and placed her hands on Balnos' broad chest. She did as Winowe instructed—slowly matching the pace of his breathing with her own. She found it helped to imagine the tune of her namesong and to set it to the pace of his breathing. As a rhythm emerged, her heartbeat slowly fell into pace.

She felt Winowe's hand touch her arm and stay there. Then it suddenly happened. The world seemed to fade and she had this overpowering sense of *flesh*. There was terrible pain as well and the shock of it almost drove her out.

But her experience with the Vyrl had prepared her. To her, the gift of blood seemed oddly similar. As she'd seen with Winowe, blood oozed through her hands and into Balnos. It spread out, pushing through him and toward the damaged parts.

She could sense his shattered bone and the torn blood vessels around it. She could also sense Winowe pushing the pieces back into his body. The pain was intense but she shared it with him. Between them, it became easier to bear. Her blood mingled with his, restoring what he'd lost. It moved where she directed and, layer by layer, healed the damaged flesh. It was exhausting work. Yet, in the end, she'd mended most of his hurts. He may not walk for another week without aid. But he was no longer in danger of dying.

When she removed her hands, he was fast asleep and his face bore a contented smile. She looked at her palms and, like Winowe, there was blood. She found a cloth in her pouch and wiped them clean.

Winowe smiled at her. "I should have believed Leowin," she said with a shake of her head. "Elag was a liar. He tested you and found you lacking."

Luthiel didn't like the talk of Elag. "Perhaps it's because he's so wise. Better to keep a woman from the temptation of magic? Or as Zalos says—I'm flawed."

Winowe bowed her head. "I'm sorry," she said.

"Don't be. I'll have to deal with it—with them—sooner or later."

Winowe placed a pouch of Yewstaff fruit on Balnos' chest then tied a yellow ribbon around his head. "It's to mark him. I forgot to do it with Lyra. We'll go back." She gave Luthiel a serious look—"You saved his life, you know. How does that feel?"

Luthiel smiled. "Happy. But very tired."

"Can you try another?"

She gave a nod. "Wait," she said. "I think I see Melkion and Mindersnatch is with him!" She sprang up in such excitement that dizziness almost made her sit back down. She took a moment to steady herself. Spots floated before her eyes and, by the time they cleared, Melkion and the crow were flapping around her in a slow orbit. The dragon alighted on her pack and Mindersnatch perched on her outstretched hand.

The crow bobbed his head in greeting as he fanned his silver-feathered wings.

"A queen! A queen! But always one to me!" he croaked in greeting.

"Word travels fast."

"With wings! It does! It does!"

"I've a favor to ask."

The crow bobbed his head again. "Ask! Ask!"

Luthiel smiled. "Many here were bitten by Widdershae. Yet they have no cure for the poison. Can you find Rendillo and ask him to get as much anti-venom as he can? Then, will you and your sisters and brothers bring it here?"

Mindersnatch bobbed his head a third time. He looked pleased he could be of help. "I will! Vials! I'll bring them!"

With a flap of his wings, he was airborne again, his caws ringing out over the army. Soon a flock of excited Khoraz had gathered around him and were winging off over the mounds.

Winowe tried to smile, but on her exhausted face it seemed more like straining. "They'll need to bring hundreds of those vials," she said.

"I hope they do," Luthiel replied as they made their way back to Lyra.

When they returned, they found Galwin leaning on his banner, glowering at Vaelros. From the look of it, the two had been arguing. There was no sign of Mithorden and Othalas lay on his side pretending boredom. Leowin stood a ways off casting angry glances back at Galwin and Vaelros.

"Where's the sorcerer?" she asked.

"Riding here and there," Galwin replied. "A faenmare came and he rode off without a word."

"I think he's spreading news about you," Vaelros said. "Look!" He motioned to a nearby hill where a group of fae gathered. All faces turned toward her. Then, a rumble of hooves rose behind them. As she looked, she saw Mithorden leading a group of cavalry. The sorcerer pointed and spoke with the Captain.

"Let's show them what they came to see," Othalas growled as he stood and shook himself.

"What is that?" she asked the wolf.

"Their queen can heal."

Luthiel took a deep breath and then put a hand on Winowe's arm. "Take me to the next one," she said. "I'll do what I can."

They picked through the field and came next to a tiny faerie. She was less than half Luthiel's size but her beautiful wings lay around her like a strange and colorful sheet. In them nestled flir-bugs. Drawn by the warmth and life, they flooded light through the clear wings, revealing pink veins and gossamer membranes. She was perfect but for one terrible detail. A metal spike thrust through one eye and out the back of her head. Its two-foot length was covered in the broken writing of Widdershae. Blood and milky fluid stained her brilliant green hair.

Seeing her, Luthiel was amazed she still lived. But she breathed and her remaining eye roved here and there, taking in Luthiel and Winowe. It was wide with fear and tears streamed down the side of her face.

She can still think? She can still understand what's happening?

From watching, it was clear she did. She even acknowledged Luthiel's presence with a slight tick of her hand. One side of her mouth turned up. The movement was a sort of spasm and Luthiel's chest pounded when she realized the faerie was trying to smile.

Poor, poor thing. A shame I don't know more about them. Maybe I could say something to comfort her?

Faeries were from Ashiroth, mostly. Luthiel noticed, looking around, that many had stayed behind. Over the years, more and more had come to the Minonowe. But these were sad things for they missed the Tree of Life at the great forest's center. Luthiel wondered at how little she knew of faeries and their male counterparts the Qlune.

She fell to her knees before the little faerie and ran a hand over her cheek.

"She's very close," Winowe whispered. "You think you can do this?"

"I can certainly try." She felt the unnatural coolness in the faerie's skin, saw the overwhelming bloom of her pupil.

"It will be anything but easy. The thing has punctured a good part of her brain. You can never return what ability she's lost. But you can repair what's there. She will have to relearn things—even flying."

Luthiel looked at the glorious wings and bent over to whisper in her ear. "You're meant to fly," she said. "I promise, you will again."

The faerie's one good eye filled with hope and her hand jerked up to clasp Luthiel's arm. It squeezed and the grip was fierce.

Please, it seemed to say.

Luthiel lay her hands on the faerie. She was shocked by how large her hands looked against the tiny body. Heartbeats pattered against her skin. Faint, fast, hard to feel. Worse, her breathing came so fast it was tricky to match. She grew light-headed and, at last, had to sing out loud—matching the rhythms of her music to those of the little faerie's body. It took far longer than before, but after some time, her heartbeat fell into pace.

Now everything seemed broken and disjointed. There was less a sense of pain. Instead, she struggled with lost senses and feelings. It was as if the tiny fae's thought and body were covered in growing patches of nothing. As she touched the blank spots, terror shot through her. She recoiled. It took tremendous effort to keep her hands in place.

This is how death must feel. Little patches of nothing devour you. To Luthiel, it was far worse than pain. Trembling, she forced herself to sense the empty spaces. Blood seeped through her hands and flowed into those places. When her blood touched it, she was filled with a deep sense of cold and was forced to withdraw. She tried again and again. But it was impossible. With each new push, she fell deeper into exhaustion. Wet trickled down her neck from a re-opened Vyrl's bite and her senses began to fade.

I'm doing something wrong. The cold and fear seeped up from the faerie and into her arms. Heavy. They felt so heavy.

That dark thing. That death in her. It's eating me up. She almost lifted her hands. Almost let the little faerie go. Then she remembered her promise. So Luthiel clenched her eyes shut and returned to the bloody work of healing. She trusted her fear this time and avoided the empty places. Instead, she worked at the edges. With her blood, she built the faerie's body back. New life grew on top of the old. Filling the dark places. After what seemed an endless time, the emptiness was gone. So was her strength. She collapsed and lay beside the little faerie. She could feel Winowe touching her, hear her concerned voice. But she was too exhausted to answer.

Then she felt strong arms lifting her.

"You did it, Luthiel," Winowe whispered in her ear. Luthiel wanted to look but lacked the strength to turn her head or even to open her eyes. But she did smile. Then, she heard a familiar voice.

"I shouldn't have doubted." It was Vanye. Her last thought was of the Blade Dancer.

I'm the reason his grandfather died. Yet he came to carry me.

HUNTRESS

She slept. They carried her away and laid her on a bed of soft flir-silk and moss beneath the open sky. Soelee was at noon and Oerin's Eye just beyond. They were briefly obscured by a great flight of Khoraz. Hundreds swept in. The shadow beneath the flocks—a momentary respite from the heat. With a chorus, they settled upon the field. Beside each wounded, they left two vials. Then, with continued cries, they lifted away. A slight breeze rose, pushing them skyward.

Through it all she slept. Until day sank down and pulled the moons and stars behind. When she finally stirred, many hours of darkness had passed. Her wounds were tended with new bandages and fresh Yewstaff fruit rested on a folded cloth beside her. This she grabbed and greedily devoured. Some of the juice dripped down her chin. She hungered for the warm explosion inside her. The healing. The soothing of all aches and exhaustion. Fresh Yewstaff fruit was very rare this far from the Tree of Life—even more rare than dried Yewstaff fruit. And its healing was far greater. She plucked the crucis leaf from the top and laid it on her tongue, letting the mint taste fill her mouth.

She touched her hair and found it freshly braided. Tiny star flowers wove through it. A few soft petals tucked beneath her light crown, forming into a garland. Her clothes had been replaced by fine garments of Flir-Silk beneath her mail shirt and a green and silver tunic over top. Beside her stood a shield with the Vyrl's tabard fixed to it for a blazon. She stared at the spiral sign and thought sadly of the owl, Ecthellien, and Tuorlin.

Behind her, there came a "whoo, whoo." Turning her head, she saw a beautiful white owl. It curled its head into a circular dip, then spread its wings and lifted off.

"He brought the fruit," Melkion hissed dryly.

"They've been so kind to me," she said.

Melkion arched his neck "Sssssss??"

"Animals. Rats brought me something the other night."

The dragon nodded. "They followed you in battle. I've never seen such a thing."

"I wondered about it too. Where's Othalas?" she looked around and noticed the wolf had left along with the others. Only Melkion and a couple Blade Dancers she didn't recognize remained.

"Gone to hunt Widdershae. They all went. Fae and Vyrl burned webs all day. Then, just as dankness fell, the spiders started to slip out. At first, only one by one. Then a trickle. Soon they were flooding out—running for the mountains."

Slowly, but with limbs reinvigorated by rest and fresh Yewstaff fruit, she stood. Her sword belt lay nearby and she strapped it on. From it hung the silver horn Othalas had given her. She picked it up and placed it to her lips. At first, no sound came. Then, a high peal filled the night. It dropped in pitch sending its great bellow through the darkness. Trees around her seemed to echo the call back. Her wind finally gone, she lowered the horn.

In the silence that followed, she lifted her quiver and slung it over her shoulder. She noticed the arrows were replaced.

Khoraz? she wondered.

"Why did you call him?" the dragon asked.

"So I might hunt with him."

Quiet fell over the fae army. Many turned to stare up at their new queen. Then, far off, there was an answering howl.

Othalas, she thought with a grim smile. "Come then, my wolf," she whispered. "It is time to call your kin. Time to raise the hunt."

Galwin, who stood a ways off, shivered when he heard those words. To him, Luthiel's eyes seemed filled with a passion he could not understand. It was enough to make him step back and clutch his banner tight. She seemed strange to him then and, for the first time, his feeling for her was replaced by fear.

She reached for her bow. Her fingers surrounded the cold, white wood. The hands on her quiver lifted an arrow; she drew. Its *Cauthrim* tip shed a dim, red glow, casting tiny fires in her silver hair. Placing arrow to guide, she pulled it back. A 'click' and then all was set. She dropped to a knee, staring out into the darkness.

The wolf was not far away. After only a short time, he crested a nearby hill. His eyes blazing yellow fire. Fierce. For his mistress called. There she knelt. Queenly and yet so wild. Arrow set to bow—spilling out a bloody light.

At the sight of her, passion filled him. It rose in his gut, swelled his chest, then burst out of his throat. It overwhelmed the air and beat against the starry roof. The howl filled the mounds, rang out through the Vale and then rolled into Minonowe.

She had called him and here was his answer.

The spiders were out there. Running. With Luthiel, he would hunt them.

She heard the rush of blood in her ears as Othalas came up to her. With a spring, she was on him, burying her face in his soft fur. She could feel his great heart beating. Winding her hand through his coat, she found his hide. As Winowe taught her, she matched breathing and heartbeat to his. For a moment, she let their blood mingle through her touch. A thrill and a heat rushed through her arm.

"What are you doing?" the great wolf growled, feeling strength rush through him.

Pulling her hand away, she licked her palm. His blood felt like fire in her mouth.

"My dear wolf," she said, hugging him with both arms and legs. She held him tight for a few more heartbeats, then rose up, holding her bow high.

"Call them my hunter!" she cried. "Gather your brothers and sisters! Tonight we hunt the nightmares!"

THE GREAT PACK

Othalas tilted his head back and let out a call. It rose and it wavered. It dipped and it shuddered. Howl became growl and then howl again. Three times he lifted his voice. Three times the echoes filled the night. Then, other howls ripped through the air in answer. These were not the calls of normal wolves but savage cries. Luthiel added peals of her silver horn to Othalas' brutal answers as the werewolf sprang away from the elfin host and toward his kindred.

There, in the moonlight, they saw their liquid bodies streaking through the night. Their teeth gleamed like white knives. Their eyes like sparks filling the night. Hundreds leapt out over the Vale's steep walls and filled the mounds about them.

These were the kin of Othalas and none but he could command them—not even Vyrl. For he was the greatest and oldest werewolf, and they only hunted alone unless *he* brought them together. It was a very rare thing—this pack of werewolves.

They formed a large circle and joined their voices, howling out to earth and sky, showing their flanks out of respect to him and his fae mistress.

Still the werewolves gathered. Their large bodies flowed out of the night like great specters. Stranger and taller than Urkharim, these once-men were now the mightiest of wolves. Around Othalas and Luthiel, they came to order and by some unspoken command all fell silent. The Great Pack had formed.

Luthiel thumped Othalas on the neck and pointed with her bow. With a leap, he shot out into the mounds. Legs ate up the ground and the Great Pack silently and swiftly followed.

HUNTING NIGHTMARES

They ripped holes in the night filled with fangs and fur. Earth rolled away beneath them and the chill smell of Widdershae made a path as plain and bright as coldfire. Though the spiders were still miles ahead, the scent was strong and growing stronger. For few creatures possess the speed and endurance of a wolf on the hunt. Long striders they are called. And the greatest of these are the werewolves of Oesha.

Their senses were so acute that they did not need to call to one another. It was enough for one to lead and the rest to follow.

Night and lands sped on by. They reached the River Rendalas in less than an hour and made a sweeping left turn at its banks. Luthiel could now see the mud pitted with spider tracks. The pack stopped and growled to one another in low voices. They sniffed and ran about. Excitement spread through them and they glanced at Luthiel and Othalas for a signal.

"Looks like hundreds passed this way," she whispered.

"Yes. But not all continued. Look," the great wolf pointed with his nose to a tree at the bank. There was a large black shape that seemed suspended by glowing strands. Two furry bodies clutched at the shape. They were spiders too. But something in the look of their eyes seemed friendly.

"Senasarab," she whispered. "They've come far."

Othalas sniffed the air. "They have some of your smell on them."

"I —" Luthiel's voice fell off.

"Made them?"

She shook her head. It wasn't quite right.

"No. They were elves. I just saved what I could from Saurlolth. She would have turned them into Widdershae."

"Now they hunt Widdershae. Cunning revenge."

Luthiel looked at the dead Widdershae and watched the Senasarab eat it. A chill came over her at Othalas' words. *Did I do right? Or did I just match hurt for hurt?* She shook her head to clear the doubt. And gave a forced smile to the wolf.

"Never thought of it that way," she said.

She raised a hand and the Senasarab lifted their forelimbs in answer. The werewolves watched. A few growled at the fae spiders and then turned to follow Luthiel and Othalas as they moved on.

They picked up the stride again and the miles shot by. Now they were coming to the lands near Flir Light Hollow and Luthiel couldn't help but feel an aching in her chest. Yet they were on the north side of Rendalas and Flir Light was still some distance up and across the river. Part of her felt glad that it lay out of the spiders' way. The other part longed to see the home of her childhood.

No sooner did these thoughts pass than they came upon the first group of stragglers. They ran in fear, thin legs blindly questing eastward. Many were fat—their bodies bloated with feeding on those poor animals or fae they'd snared in their shadow-webs. These were also the most cowardly for they had avoided the greater part of the fighting.

Many of the fatter ones had fallen to the rear. Seeing them bloated from the slaughter, Luthiel felt anger rekindle and her pity was swallowed up by rage. She held her arrow until Othalas and the werewolves were almost upon them. The spiders must have sensed that something was wrong. At the last instant, they spun around and crouched low—screaming in their screechy voices when they realized the pack had caught them.

Luthiel shot one of the leaders with her *Cauthrim* arrow. The shaft hissed out and then seemed to dive into its body. It fell into a mass of thrashing legs and didn't get up.

Tiolas and Violen looked down as the wolves tore into the spiders. Some grabbed at their legs as others jumped on top to snap off the heads. Othalas rushed in fearless of tine or fang. The spiders had little defense for the great wolf and Luthiel. If they reared up she shot them full of arrows. If they pounced,

Othalas would swat them out of the air and then crush them in his great jaws. If they ran he would bound atop them and pull off their heads. Terribly out-matched and outnumbered, the Widdershae fell quickly.

About halfway through the fight, Luthiel put up her bow and drew *Weiryendel*. The sword sang out as she struck again and again. There was little happiness to the music now. Instead, its melancholy song filled the night. The sword passed as easily through flesh as it did through air and many spiders fell to her blows with some part of them cloven off.

But a few seemed unhurt and, instead, fell into what seemed a peaceful sleep. As the battle ended, Luthiel drew close to a sleeping spider and inspected it. There were no wounds, only a thin silver scar where *Weiryendel* had passed through it. *What has happened here?* she thought. When werewolves circled in to finish them, she called them off.

"Let them rest!" she shouted. "They'll do no more harm!"

At this, she got a few growls and angry looks from the wolves. But Othalas would brook no dissent and these he pinned or flashed his teeth at till they walked off—tails between legs.

"Why do you spare them?" he growled as the last few werewolves straggled off.

"It is my father's sword that does. I feel some part of his will lives on in it. I want to honor its choices."

The great wolf snorted at this and then they were off again—hunting the spiders as Oerin's Eye began to splash first dawn across the east.

As light grew, she began to notice more dead spiders across their path. Othalas approached one of these—sniffing and looking it over.

"Animals killed this one," he said. "Bears and maybe a wild Urkharim too."

Luthiel nodded. She was still puzzled about the animals. It was as if some strange will were guiding them to help her. For a moment, she thought of the owl. *It started with him. But I still don't understand.*

Othalas glanced at her and chuckled to himself. *Just when I think I know enough about this little one, she surprises me again.* Then, he caught a scent that made him lift his head. They'd made their way along a ridge that looked down on the river and the surrounding lands. As light grew, it gave them a wide view for miles around. What Othalas saw made even the great wolf's ears prick.

"Unicorn," he growled.

"I saw one with the animals who helped us —" Luthiel stopped short. Unicorn! More than she could count! They'd formed into a line and were sweeping over the land. Spaced about twenty feet from one another, their line stretched about two miles from end to end. They would surge forward and then collapse into bunches. Luthiel strained her eyes to see them attacking Widdershae.

"Ëvanya bless us, there must be hundreds," she gasped.

Othalas nodded in agreement. But the great wolf had noticed something else. "Look closer. There are riders."

At this, Luthiel's ears tingled and she started. She scanned the line again and, this time, she saw them—riders in glittering mail carrying bows or spears, swords and graceful axes. There weren't many. Luthiel thought she could count twenty.

"Daughters of Elwin?" she asked in awe.

"Valkyrie," Othalas growled in answer.

"Why would they come here? All the way from the Dark Forest?"

"I don't know," the great wolf growled. "Might have something to do with you."

Luthiel's brows lowered. "What would the Dark Forest have to do with me?" It was more a question out of fear than one of disbelief.

"You're the grandchild of Elwin and the Dark Forest Lord."

"Elwin sleeps and the Lord hated my father." Tears rose into her eyes but she quickly wiped them away.

Othalas could hear the distress in her voice so he stopped talking. Instead, he sprang down the slope and toward the distant black mass of spiders.

"That's enough tears," he growled. "Today's chase will be hard enough without them."

Luthiel sniffed and wiped at her face with one hand as she held tight to the wolf with the other. "Today only? I intend to follow them all the way to the mountains. I don't want them to ever think of returning."

Othalas snorted. "Don't you know me yet, girl? You ride with werewolves. We could make the mountains by nightfall in a straight run. Spiders are slower. My guess is we'd see Metheldras and the Gates of the East before next sunrise."

"Then we'll catch them?" she asked with a grim smile.

"Well before then."

They fell silent and Luthiel kept alert to what was going on around her. The werewolves fanned out in a line that stopped at the river. Between the unicorns sweeping down from the north and the werewolves coming in from the west, the Widdershae could either stand and fight or run in hopes of reaching the mountains before tooth or horn found them. They were strung out and only the lead group moved with any kind of coordination.

They'd taken terrible hurt in the battle on the first night. The following day, as Luthiel was sleeping, the Vyrl's army and many of the Fae had thinned them even further. Less than half the spiders who'd crept down from the mountains remained alive come the next nightfall. Saurloth knew if she had any hope of living she must run. The Vyrl's giants and grendilo were burning deep paths through her webs. Their wights were undaunted by pain or poison and the Vyrl themselves fought like demons. Joined by Blade Dancers, the fiery Gormtoth, and what seemed like every animal in all the Faelands, the spiders found themselves terribly outnumbered. Their usual tricks of snatch and kill didn't work when a hundred tiny birds followed each spider and made a ruckus that was impossible to ignore. There was simply no way to hide. Even worse, those who were caught in shadow webs were burned free by the strange fire-winged birds of the Vale. Khoraz could talk to birds, elves, and Vyrl, and they were soon flying everywhere with messages.

The cover of darkness gave them some respite. But the nocturnal owls quickly replaced the day-birds. These were much quieter. So quiet that they even surprised the spiders with their sudden hoots and shrieks. The spiders were in terror for their lives as, one by one, they were found and killed. Saurloth drew those she could together and fled en masse. Swift animals, elfish cavalry, faerie, and other creatures of wing gave chase. But the spiders quickly outdistanced grendilo, wights, giants, and those elves who fought on foot. Still, enough were able to follow the spiders to turn the flight deadly.

Then came the unicorn and werewolves. Saurlolth began to wonder if even she would escape the blood-letting. It had all gone so dreadfully awry. By now, they should have been feasting on fae blood. The armies crushed, all the Faelands would have become their hunting grounds. But there was this Luthiel. This daughter of Vlad Valkire and not yet much more than a girl. Somehow, she'd swept in and gotten elf and Vyrl to work together. Even worse, it seemed that all of nature had come to her aid. When her 'swift legs' came in to report of unicorn and Valkyrie, she understood that Elwin had become involved.

"She protects her granddaughter," the spider queen had hissed upon hearing the news.

For Saurlolth, the time for secrecy and hiding was finished. So she sent her 'swift legs' north and south to beg help from her allies. Of the north she expected little.

He is too deep in his game. Still thinks he can win. And he might! That deception with Tuorlin had sown a deep doubt and division.

She'd stroked her legs together in pleasure when she'd seen so many fae slip off to join the Faelord of Ashiroth—and not too few Blade Dancers! She'd also noticed that many who stayed were in doubt. She could taste it on the air as well as an ocean shark could taste blood in the water. But for the doubt to fester, they must leave. A visible enemy could unite the elves and spoil all of Zalos' work. So the runners she sent north were little more than a gesture.

But the ones sent south—on these lay her dark hope. There was strong darkness in her jagged mountain home. Masses of spiders and shadow webs and something else too—a bloody secret. There she could return and regroup. There she could wait for Zalos to do his work.

Not so far off, she could hear the werewolves' howling and the battle horns of the Valkyrie and not for the last time she wondered if her spiders would have to choose a new queen after today.

Luthiel let out a cry when she spotted a group of Widdershae running through a nearby thicket. The wolves howled in answer and rushed in to surround the spiders. It was only ten and they were quickly overtaken. The werewolves hemmed the spiders in and then attacked in a rush. A few scrambled into trees but Luthiel shot them with her bow. It was quick and bloody work. A few werewolves ran from body to body—biting to make certain they were dead.

It was past noon and this was just one of many contacts they'd had with stragglers. They were nearing the main group of Widdershae and, as they drew closer, other animals joined them. Wolves, bears, even horned deer ran with the pack. Some could not keep the werewolves' pace and these fell away. But more came than left, and soon there was an animal for every werewolf.

They'd come far now and Luthiel found herself in unfamiliar country well past Flir Light Hollow. The terrain became rougher; the hills carved out of steep ravines. Rendalas grew narrower and, in places, filled with rocks and rapids.

As they rushed away from their latest skirmish and ran up a hill, Luthiel noticed a big bend in the river ahead. It was wide—but shallow and filled with boulders cast down from the mountains in some past flood or other calamity. The mass of spiders was drawing near the river and the leaders were making their way across—swift spider legs clambering over boulders or picking through the shallows.

Close by, she could see the unicorn. A beautiful Valkyrie rider raised her sword in salute to Luthiel. Aside from the Valkyrie's blood-red hair, Luthiel was stunned by how much she resembled her. The Valkyrie could be her mother or sister. The shape of the eyes, the face, her height, her strong but streamlined body. Luthiel raised *Weiryendel* in answer and the lead Valkyrie let out a cry.

"Elwin! Elwin! Fair mother of dreams, fighter of Gorthar and nightmare! Hear me! I have found your grandchild!"

At these words, Luthiel trembled. But she wouldn't let herself be overcome by emotion. Instead, she leaned forward and whispered into Othalas' ear.

"Let's join them."

BATTLE AT THE FORD

Luthiel rode up to the Valkyrie. Because of Othalas' great height she looked down at her. Here was her *father's* sister. One of many who'd raised and looked after him in his youth and exile. For every Valkyrie was a daughter of Elwin—and Vlad Valkire was her only son.

She gave the sign for Oerin's Eye. "A heart-gift to meet you —"

The Valkyrie nodded and returned the sign. "A heart-gift to meet you, Luthiel. I am Elonwyn."

Luthiel couldn't help but smile. Elonwyn's assuredness and familiarity gave a strange sense of comfort.

"What brought you?"

"You," Elonwyn said.

"How did you know?"

"Elwin heard your Namesong. She comes to us in dreams now and then. The Dark Forest Lord no longer speaks to us—out of envy."

Luthiel swallowed but her mouth was dry. Elonwyn's words seemed to fall upon her like blows. *Who is this jealous Lord? So powerful and yet so blind?* Even deeper was her hurt for her father. *She knew his sword on sight. She must have known him well.* Luthiel wanted to ask a hundred questions. But with each moment more Widdershae slipped across the river. She sensed this was their best chance to catch them before they reached the mountains.

"I would like nothing more than to talk," Luthiel said. "But there's no time." She pointed down the hill with her sword. Nearly half the spiders were across with the other half scrambling toward the banks. Othalas growled and she could feel his muscles tensing.

Elonwyn's brows lowered and she nodded. "Hit them hard here." Her unicorn struck its hoof against the ground and raised its horn high in challenge.

Luthiel looked down the hill. "They're crossing. If we charge together, we'll catch them with their force split."

The Valkyrie held her sword high as she smiled bravely at Luthiel. "For Elwin!" she called out.

Cries echoed back as other Valkyrie picked up her call.

"Together then!" she shouted.

"Together!" Luthiel answered, lifting *Weiryendel* and turning to the werewolves. Othalas gave a howl and then they sprang down the slope.

Unicorn and werewolf swept down the hill, falling with fury on the spiders. The animals rushed in too—among them, above them, beneath them. Birds lifted out of trees and rodents rose from their burrows. Othalas let out a howl that echoed through the wood. Soon the werewolves' baying filled the valley. Unicorn and Valkyrie sang out their own battle hymn as they rushed in. The first spiders they came upon, worn out by the running and endless fighting, were too exhausted to react. Bite and horn, spear and arrow took them swiftly. A screeching rose up from the spiders. In fury and fear, they turned and fought back. Spiders slung shadows across their path and snared many werewolves, animals, and unicorn. Others gathered into large groups and pounced—punching holes in the charge. She saw one unicorn pulled down and bitten. Its terrified screams rang out. Then a werewolf was completely covered in shadow webs. He seemed to freeze as the hope drained from his eyes. She quickly found herself in a dangerous fight. Her quiver was empty but she didn't remember shooting her last arrow. *Weiryendel* sang in her hands, slicing through the nightmare webs.

A group of spiders rushed up the hill at her. She could see anger in their sickly fae eyes. In their forelimbs they clutched shadow-strands. There were about thirty all rushing toward her and she knew that even Othalas would be overwhelmed. She glanced up the hill, thinking for a moment of running.

It was then that she noticed the tree.

It was a dead tree—scarred by lightning but thick and tall with hundreds of spiky branches. Tilting slightly downhill, it seemed to lean out over the rushing spiders. She urged Othalas back and, in a quick bound, they were behind the tree. With two swings of *Weiryendel*, she cut clear through the dead wood. There was a groan and then a splintering. Finally, with a crash, the tree fell into the spiders' midst. Three were instantly crushed by the great trunk and branches. Many more were pinned. As swiftly as it had come on, the charge fell apart. Luthiel and Othalas rushed forward—sword and fang finishing those who couldn't flee. Then they sprinted on and down the hill, catching up to the charge of werewolves as another knot of defenders gathered against them.

Many spiders had turned to fight out of desperation. But others were driven by the whipping legs of overseers. Slowly the charge ground down into melee. They were still pushing forward, but the fighting allowed the other spiders to escape. She thought she saw Saurloth among a group of large Widdershae making their way across the river. Twilight was coming on, and now even bats were coming out to trouble the spiders.

Then, as if by some silent signal, all the spiders turned around and fled. Above, the birds and bats were joined by Khoraz and Firewing. Luthiel saw the flash of Melkion's mercury body winding through them. His violet eyes blazed with an insane fury as he shot long, blue streams of fire at his enemies. Even a few faerie had joined in. They shot burning sparks down on spiders, who dipped their bodies in the river for protection.

Luthiel cut through the shell of a Widder and it fell to the ground, asleep. The silver scar left by the blow seemed to gleam in the twilight.

She raised *Weiryendel* high and shouted "Valkire!" before leading the werewolves in a charge across the water. Above, a mercury shape shot down— borne on rainbow wings shaded pink by the twilight. She could hear the dragon yelling but couldn't make out the words.

She and Othalas splashed through the water. The great wolf pounced on another spider. He bit as she slashed down with *Weiryendel*. Though focused on her strike, she could see something moving on the far bank. When she drew her sword back from the fallen spider and shifted her gaze, her eyes locked and her stomach filled with terror.

"Back!" she cried.

Too late. For on the far bank she saw the demon lord Thrar Taurmori surrounded by giant trolls. They wore strange garb and their hair was braided and woven through with spikes that left tiny cuts as they passed over their face, neck, and shoulders. The great lord held a spear. This he hefted and threw. It leapt the distance between them coming directly toward her. The heat of the great demon's form caused the shaft to ignite and flames licked about the head. Othalas reared at the last moment—stopping the blow with his body. Its force pushing through him—causing the great wolf to fall. She found herself submerged and pinned beneath the werewolf to the river's rocky bottom.

She opened her eyes and through the water she could see other spears splashing down, other werewolves and unicorn falling. She struggled and Othalas thrashed about. Somehow, in the confusion, she came free. She stood and her head broke the surface. She gulped the air and found herself waist deep in the water.

Thrar Taurmori stood before her. Where his feet and legs touched the water, a steam rose up and, around him, the river boiled. In one hand, he held a great black sword. In the other, a blazing hammer. He'd cast off his dragon scale cloak and his naked body sweat brilliant fire.

Somehow, she'd managed to keep hold of *Weiryendel*. Now, she held it before her and shouted—"Betrayer! Demon! Return to Rimwold and trouble this place no more!"

The great lord gave a laugh that sounded like the heave of a bonfire. "Would you command me, little queen? Your words have no power here. For there is no true law but that of violence and I am its king!"

Hammer and sword lashed out. His weapons were massive—far too large to deflect—so she leapt away. The great weapons splashed into the water where she'd stood only a moment before—carving pits in the river bed, causing the water to boil.

Tap and turn had made her a stronger jumper than she knew. Up and back she sprang—clearing the water and coming down on a boulder ten feet behind. But a nearby troll caught her legs by the shaft of his spear and she fell. Thrar Taurmori pushed through the water flames screaming at its touch. Ponderously, he lifted his great hammer and brought it down on her. She could do little else. She held *Weiryendel* out in a vain effort to ward off the blow. There was a shriek and her arm jolted. But her grip held firm. Sword clove through hammer. Half glanced off her chest—knocking the wind from her and scorching her tabard before splashing with a gout of steam into the river. Then the werewolves were rushing over her, leaping upon the demon, pushing him down into the river. Some caught fire but they bore down on him, heedless of any pain.

Pushed beneath the water, his body flickered. Then the flame went out showing skin—hot red and white but covered in expanding black patches. From beneath the water he let out a cry and steam boiled up from the river. His great hand lashed out grasping then crushing the neck of a werewolf. While still on his back, he ran another through with his sword. Still more rushed over him, snapping at his throat.

She tried to stand, but her legs failed and she crouched on the stone, panting for air. Pain lanced through her chest and she could feel blood trickling down her side. Probing with her fingers, she pushed against her chest. Two ribs shifted unnaturally and she saw spots, almost losing consciousness. More werewolves rushed in, grasping at her arms with their mouths, pulling her back toward the riverbank. Arrows splashed all around her. One bounced off her chest, deflected by her *Lumiel* mail.

Othalas pulled himself from the current and followed. Though pierced in his flank by the great spear, he stood and lumbered after her through the bloody water.

Luthiel's head began to clear and she saw rank after rank of Troll and Goblin on the far bank. Luthiel coughed in pain and watched as unicorn, Valkyrie, and werewolf retreated with her toward the near bank and its relative safety. Thrar Taurmori had regained his feet and, lifting his arms to the sky, he let out a monstrous howl as fires reignited over his body.

"It's over," she whispered hoarsely to Othalas.

"Done," the werewolf growled through his pain. "We've hurt them badly enough. Look, they're still running."

Luthiel raised her head and noticed the Widdershae still fleeing up the far slope. If it didn't hurt so bad, she might have laughed at the sight. Instead she gave a grim smile and gulped more air.

"Let's go back. Can we run?" She asked it as much for herself as the wolf.

"Soon as someone pulls this pig poker out of me," he growled.

She ran her fingers through his fur in concern. The wound looked terrible. But after Cauthraus and the spider venom she knew better.

Do I?

She stumbled to his side and with both hands drew out the still smoking shaft. Blood spilled to the ground, then filled up the hole. Almost immediately, she could see clots forming, flesh weaving back together. She shook her head in amazement.

"Get on—before the fae start to miss their queen."

"I will. But ride easy. I think the demon cracked my ribs."

She'd only just clambered onto the great wolf's back when there was a flare of rainbow wings as Melkion alighted on a nearby branch. His eyes seemed sad as he looked her over.

"Wait," the dragon said. "It's time you remembered your promise."

MELKION'S DEMAND

Luthiel pushed some scorched hair out of her face and gave the tiny dragon a puzzled look.

"Promise?"

"You've forgotten?" Melkion asked. His brows lowered and his face faded into a pained expression.

"What's this about?" the werewolf growled.

The dragon shot Othalas an angry look as fire curled in his jaws. "Be quiet, Vale Wolf."

Othalas' answering growl was deep and primal. But, for the moment, he kept silent.

Melkion swung his head toward Luthiel. "I want you to come with me to the mountains. The spiders will be confused. It's our best chance. I know a secret way. If you will follow?" As he said that last, his voice seemed to drop and his eyes grew sad. But it was an intense kind of sadness—one clouded with anger.

"I remember promising to help you, Melkion," Luthiel said. A pang ran through her. She'd caught a glimpse, just then, of some deep and long-born hurt. "But I don't think it's wise to follow these spiders. They're wary from fighting and the hills are crawling with Rimwold's finest." She said the last bit with a hint of sarcasm. "Now what's all this about?"

Melkion's jaws fell slack and his wings crumpled. Fat dragon tears fell from his eyes and rolled into his mouth with explosive pops. Then, with a shake and flaring of wings, his body stiffened and his jaw again grew firm. "It's my father. He's trapped beneath a mountain."

Luthiel shook her head. "Trapped? How? I thought dragons could eat even granite."

The tiny dragon drew himself up and flared out his wings. His tail arched and fire crackled in his jaws. Luthiel leaned back. She'd never seen the dragon so upset. His rapid swings from mood to mood were uncanny.

"He was *imprisoned*. The Wyrd in that mountain is old and it is strong. Too strong for even a dragon to break."

For a moment, she didn't understand. Then, Luthiel felt her heart quicken. She'd heard of only one mountain that could trap a dragon in such a way. Heard of only one dragon imprisoned there.

"Which mountain?"

"Flower Mountain. The old pass." Now Melkion was hanging his head. "It doesn't matter! You gave your promise!"

Melkion's words seemed to come from too far away. *Flower Mountain! Faehome's Prison!?* She wanted to laugh and cry at the same time. How did the old rhyme go?

In elder days
With freedom yet fresh
Borne on a wind
Like burning breath

Lightning his fire
Soot his rain
Faehome the mighty
King of pain

Homes he's the wrecker
Tombs he's the filler
Army destroyer
The great tree killer!

The one Blade Dancers imprisoned in the mountains for devouring a Tree of Life?

"Faehorne the tree killer?!" Luthiel exclaimed without thinking. "*He's* your father?"

Melkion's plumed tail flicked in anger. "Faehorne *is* my father. But he is no tree killer. Narhoth ate out the roots. Of shadow, she made a shape like my father's to cover her. For nearly three thousand years, now, he's suffered for *her* crime."

Luthiel looked at the dragon under lowered brows. "I can see why you didn't tell me sooner. The son of a tree killer."

"As much as you're the Blood Witch," Melkion said acidly.

The gibe bit deep and Luthiel found herself shaking her head. "So many lies. I can't tell what's true anymore."

"Will you help me?"

Luthiel looked away toward the dark mountains. Oerin's Eye rested between two peaks, casting ghostly shadows out into the hills. Melkion's eyes filled with tears. Some rolled into his mouth, hissing where they met fire.

"You know I can't now. If I leave, this land will fall apart and Zalos will snatch up the pieces."

"The spiders came many years ago—to drink his blood." He looked away into the twilight as if seeing something that wasn't there. "You should see it. They swarm over him. Prying at the cracks in his scales. You must understand. He will die soon."

If it were my mother, would I go now? Luthiel shook her head, unable to answer her own question. *I must help him. And yet I cannot.*

"I promise, Melkion. I'll help your father as soon as I'm able. Can you reach him? Can you tell him to wait?" She couldn't even fathom what she was promising. Enter the heart of the spiders' realm to free one of the most hated dragons in all of history? *Maybe they're right. Maybe I am the Blood Witch.*

The dragon let out a tortured breath and slowly nodded. "I can't travel with you any further. A great spirit of Oesha is dying. If he dies I don't want him to be alone at the last. I must go. Send a Khoraz to let me know when you're coming. Just don't take too long." He spread his rainbow wings wide and gave her a bow. Then, with a single flap, he was lifting away. She watched him climb, shrinking to a speck and finally disappearing into the twilight.

AFTERMATH

"He's gone." She said hoarsely. One by one, it seemed she was losing the friends she'd gained in her journey to the Vale. At least she could hope to see Melkion again. But at what cost!? She wondered if she could even help him. *Free Faehorne?*

Othalas nodded. Despite his anger at the dragon, he seemed sad. He turned his great head sideways and looked up at her with one big, yellow, eye. "You were right to refuse. It's not time."

She patted him on the neck.

"I wonder if it'd be better for everyone if I just followed Melkion."

Othalas snorted. "After all you've done you still doubt? They need something to bring them together. What's better—you or Zalos?"

"That's just it. I'm not certain I can. You saw them."

Othalas shook his neck. The healing was making his ribs burn. "Wherever power's at stake, there's a contest."

"How can I win?"

Othalas gave a gravelly laugh. "Now you're thinking like a werewolf."

They padded back through the animals and Valkyrie. Dead creatures lay scattered over the ground and she turned her head toward them as she passed. *Death seems to follow wherever I go,* she thought sadly. Unicorn passed among them looking for wounded. When they found someone still alive, they would stoop, lowering their horns to touch the hurts.

Luthiel found a clear place to sit down and tend to her own wounds. Stripping off her tabard, armor, and silk undergarb, she untied her new pouch and pulled out her Wyrd Stone. Then she looked herself over. Fully half her chest was black and bloody from Thrar Taurmori's hammer blow. Probing with her fingers she felt again her cracked ribs. *All from a piece of his hammer falling on me.* She frowned and tried not to think about how much worse it might have been or how fortunate she was to be breathing at all. Singing in a low voice, she slipped into the World of Dreams even as she touched her skin to work the healing. Cool energy bled from the Stone and into her body. She worked slowly to mend bone and then moved on to repair even burns and bruises. She didn't know what new trouble she might encounter but she wanted to be unhurt and ready to face anything. Finally finished, she slipped from the World of Dreams and looked over her body. Her wounds were fully mended and her skin gave a healthy pink glow.

Donning her clothes and armor, she returned to help and give healing where she could. She moved through the wounded beside the unicorn and paused for a moment in wonder to observe the soft glow that seemed to come from their horns and heal almost any wounds they touched. Healing was exhausting for unicorn as well and, after only a few tended wounds each, the magical creatures had to rest. After mending an eagle's broken wing, she turned and noticed Othalas had grown impatient. He paced side to side and glanced over his shoulder at the stars which seemed much further on than she remembered. Oerin's Eye had dipped below the horizon. But he'd grown large, even for High Summer, and his light spilled over Oesha's rim, dimming down the moons and stars.

Elonwyn stood nearby. Luthiel hadn't noticed her approach. When she saw Luthiel raise her head she lifted her hand.

"Come Luthiel. The road calls."

Luthiel gave her a puzzled look.

"We're going with you," she said.

She motioned with her hand and a short distance away Luthiel saw two more unicorn—each bearing a rider. One was tall and willowy with short cropped hair of jet and brooding violet eyes and the other was smaller, a thick braid of blood red twining down from her head reaching all the way to her waist. "This is Athina and Elone." The Valkyrie touched their brows in greeting. Elone winked and gave her a conspiratorial smile. Luthiel grinned, flashing the sign for Oerin's Eye.

Othalas ran up beside her and she grabbed hold of his fur, pulling herself onto his back. They rode past animals, werewolves and Valkyrie. Goblin, spider and troll still held the river's far side. Now and then she could see explosions of fire—trees turned into massive torches when the Demon Lord touched them.

"Ugly lights," she said softly to the wolf. Then, she lifted her voice. "Kind creatures of the wild, cousins of the Vale and Dark Forest!" she called to them. "So many of you came to help without my asking! So many of you followed me into danger of your own choosing. Because of you, that danger is greatly diminished. But as you can see by the fires, we have merely traded one trouble for another. Though I must leave, I ask that you please stay here and guard your cousins who sleep innocent of it!"

Werewolves and animals looked on even as unicorn raised their horns. A flight of owls hooted in answer. *We will! We will!* they seemed to say.

When she saw that they would stay, she drew *Weiryendel*, holding it high as she chanted—"A blessing to you all! You are each, to me, a hero! May the great lady Elwin sing you into the never-ending dream!" At this, the werewolves lifted their mouths and joined their voices in an ethereal howl. Across the river, goblin and troll held their weapons close. For even the warriors of Rimwold feared the greatest of wolves.

With an answering cry, she was off, racing through the forest with three Valkyrie behind her. Overhead, the Khoraz, Firewing, and Faerie flew in escort. The luminaries of Firewing cascaded down, painting strange lights and shadows along the ground. They rode on for much of the night and well into the following morning before they reached the army. Exhausted and aching, she took brief naps. Othalas seemed to sense her sleeping and was somehow able to cushion her, keeping her upon his back. Though the sleep came in fits, she was almost refreshed by the time they came within sight of the army.

Above it all flew Mindersnatch. His great silver wings cupped the rising air of morning. It was a hot sky in a hot summer. Hotter than any he remembered. Strange it seemed to him, for the air didn't cool so much as he rose. And the sky seemed odd. The stars dimmer and more clouded—as if some fog or dust above the air obscured them. He doubted anyone but his Khoraz brothers had noticed. For even eagles couldn't see as far as a Khoraz. The Vale had been kind to their flock, granting not only the keenest sight but also speech and long life. For of all the birds, only Khoraz were immortal.

Mindersnatch let out a joyful caw. His silver wings spread wide, bearing him higher. For what better thing was there than flying? The world expanded and he felt he could see all that walked or crawled on the face of green Oesha. His mistress was below, borne on the back of great Othalas, and his lord and lady Vyrl too. They would want to hear his news. So he turned his keen eyes down, scouring the land about for signs.

Below him, the Faerie army had regrouped. Mithorden seemed to have taken charge and there was movement everywhere. Wounded were tended, the healed returned to their companies. For miles around, scouts moved across the land—faerie on the wing, elves on the soft-hoofed faenmare. The animals who'd come to help Luthiel had faded back into the wildlands. But Mindersnatch saw they kept a careful account of all goings on. The rats and mice seemed especially busy. They scurried to and fro, chattering out their strange messages for miles about. A combined force of Fae and creatures of the Vale had stopped at the banks of Rendalas. Their job was finished. For no more Widdershae could be found.

Mindersnatch looked further east where he found animals and werewolves, unicorn and Valkyrie facing a force of Goblins and Trolls led by the Demon Lord Thrar Taurmori. *Clever demon!* Mindersnatch thought as he looked over his force. *I saw the dragon who bore you east. And the goblins and trolls gathered there a week before. But I bet this wasn't what you'd have used them for!* To Mindersnatch it looked like a follow-on force, one equipped for conquest.

Turning his eyes north and east he saw Zalos' wolfriders just entering Arganoth. They'd ridden hard ahead of those who'd deserted the Faelands. These marched or rode in long lines raking out across the Minonowe and just beginning to enter Ashiroth's lands. At their front were the first goblins to leave and behind came those who'd believed Zalos. Those who feared the witch.

Further out, he saw Widdershae creeping back into the mountains' shadow. Atop a great peak, he thought he glimpsed a flicker of silver and rainbow wings. *So,* he thought, *Melkion has returned to his father.*

BOOK V:

QUEEN OF THE FAELANDS

DUST IN THE SKY

"We're nearly there," Othalas growled.

Luthiel opened her eyes. The first thing that struck her was the heat—strong even for High Summer. The light wasn't as bright as she'd remembered and she looked skyward expecting a cloud but only found a muddled blue. It was odd. As if the sky were dirty. Even the suns seemed a bit dimmer.

"Is there dust in the air?" she asked.

Othalas' nostrils flared. "Seems clear."

"It is dust," Elonwyn said. "But not in the air."

"Where then?" she asked.

"In the sky."

"Is it normal? I've never heard of such a thing."

"Not normal at all. It's a sign of trouble."

"What kind of trouble?"

Elonwyn exchanged looks with the other Valkyrie.

"Elwin is losing," Athina said.

"Losing what?" Luthiel asked.

"As Elwin sleeps, she dreams, " Athina replied. "Just as Gorthar dreams. She is fighting him there. Her dreams keep him at bay." Athina's bright eyes shone in fear as she turned toward Luthiel. "He's trying to blot out the lights. Not just in winter. But for all time."

Luthiel trembled as she remembered the song they'd made to mock her. *Will eat the light till all things die.* "Mithorden's skystorm," she whispered. "They'll blame it on me."

A Chosen of Sorts

In silence, they passed down the hill and into the Fae army. Looking around, she was stunned at its order. When she'd left only days before it had seemed a broken thing. Now it moved like a living creature—each part with its purpose. Bundles were packed, weapons stowed, faenmare fitted for riding. The wounded were now mostly healed. The few still too hurt to walk rested on bowers laid across giant, long-legged walking sticks that crawled throughout the army. A cheer rose up at first sight of her and grew louder as they noticed Valkyrie. Legends for their role in the War of Dreams against the Vyrl, the elves watched them and their unicorn steeds with reverence. Luthiel didn't expect the reaction but, as she heard the cheer rise up, she was doubly glad for their company.

Vanye, mounted on a black Faenmare, rode out to meet them. The horse wore *Silen* barding—silver in the sunlight. Twin horns of pale metal rose out of its faceplate, making both horse and Blade Dancer seem like strange angels. Luthiel involuntarily lowered her eyes at his approach. His face, always full of purpose, seemed even more stern than she remembered. His tenuous balance between grace and violence—on the verge of snapping. The Cat-o-Fae on his shoulder gave violent flicks and spins in mirror to his mood. When he pulled up alongside her, she fully expected to be berated for riding off to hunt. Instead, he surprised her with a bow.

"Queen Luthiel," he said, his tone formal. "Welcome back. I hope all went well?"

Surprised only for a moment, she followed his lead with relief. "Well as can be expected. We ran down nearly half. The rest escaped because of Thrar Taurmori. He had an army at the fords of Rendalas. They fought us."

"Khoraz told of the battle," Vanye said. "And of your new allies." He inclined his head to the Valkyrie and then motioned toward the cheering army. "They celebrate your victory!"

He turned his horse and led them toward the army's center. There five banners waved—four for the Faelands, including the Vale but missing Ashiroth and Rimwold, and one for the Faequeen. Mithorden stood beneath them surrounded by the army's captains. He spoke to each in turn and then to them all. At his words, she saw heads nodding, eyes gleaming with respect—some grudging, some outright. With a final word from the sorcerer, the captains dispersed—each with a mission.

"Mithorden held command. He said you left him with it," Vanye said.

Luthiel slowly nodded. It made sense. He was certainly the most experienced. But she'd left no instructions at all.

"Wiley sorcerer," she whispered to the wolf.

Othalas gave a gravelly laugh.

"He does seem to have everything well in hand," she said louder. "I'm glad he understood the spirit of my intent, if not the words."

At this Vanye gave a rare grin, which he swiftly concealed. "I should let you know, then, that we plan to leave for Yewstaff at first light. The fae lords want a proper coronation. They want to meet you." Then he lowered his voice. "Of course, Rimwold and Ashiroth will be absent. My coronation as King of Ithilden will be settled there as well."

"Yewstaff?" Luthiel asked. Even as she said the word, she felt uneasy. Though in Minonowe, and Belethial's capital, Yewstaff also housed The Seat of Dreams—a place where the order of sorcerers called Wisdom held regular meetings. There they were said to work to keep many ancient mysteries and beliefs safe. Elag was, until recently, their chief. "Do you think it wise?"

"Queen Luthiel," Mithorden interrupted. "I'm glad you're back!" He made his way toward her. Taking her hands, he guided her from the werewolf's back. Leaning close he whispered in her ear. "If we are to win hearts and minds, the Wisdom must stand with you."

"Must?" she whispered back. "I don't think it's likely. There's a reason Elag was elected to lead them."

"Many of those sorcerers are gone now," Mithorden said, even as he nodded approval. "How did you know?"

"I kept track. The sorcerer always scared me. Anyway, Leowin told me."

"You're wise to be wary. It's a gamble. But one we must make."

Luthiel felt as though the heat were draining from her.

Vanye, catching her terrified look, nodded grimly and whispered. "Welcome to rulership."

As Luthiel nodded, she saw Leowin walking toward her with Vaelros and Galwin.

Vaelros had pulled his cloak close, as if against a chill, even with the blaze of summer painting sweat on his cheeks. The effects of poison still lingered on his body and the memory of Ashiroth's captains was still fresh in his mind. But his beautiful face had brightened at her presence. He smiled and did his best to push them out of his thoughts.

In those chiseled features Luthiel could see the face of Zalos now, in those eyes that endless depth of passion. Yet, in that moment, she knew Vaelros to be a good heart. She wondered how it happened despite his terrible grandfather. The father he was forced to kill must have been a good man. And where was his mother? Why had he never spoken of her?

Galwin's face, though not so fine, was strong and earnest. She could tell by his look that he was glad she'd returned. There was worry and a deeper strain that she recognized all too well.

Leowin ran over to her, catching her up in her arms. "You dangerous girl!" she whispered in her ear. She pulled her close despite her anger. "Why must you always rush off into trouble?" Then she held her at arms length and looked her straight in the eye. "Next time, tell me? I might save your life one day."

"I might get you killed one day," Luthiel returned.

Saying these words aloud made her gut clench. She looked at each of them in turn, one to the other, and realized that here was her family. Not a family of blood, except for the Valkyrie, but a family of spirit. She looked away, wondering who might die next and if they would be the last before her sword was finished. Would it be one of these eight? Again, she felt the urge to fling the beautiful thing far away and run as fast as she could in the other direction.

But it was the strongest link to her past. To her blood father. She remembered Leowin's words but found in them little comfort. Whether it was because her magic gave the deaths significance by remaking the sword or by some awful curse, the result was the same. In order for the sword to be whole more people must die.

As much as she hated and feared how the sword was being remade, she loved the sword itself. The way its music rippled the air, the grace of its form, the balance and the vibrant hum in her hand, the way it sometimes granted mercy. Could it really be so bad a thing?

How can I judge? Am I a good or a bad thing, even? Yet now I must be a queen. Dear Ëvanya help me!

For though Luthiel was young, she was no fool. She knew that many would hate her as a queen, feared they'd blame her for a thousand things she didn't know or understand, felt in her deepest part that it must all make for a terrible end. The prophesy they sang as they deserted her formed half-images in her mind—like grotesque shadows on a jagged wall. These dark hints of what may come teased at the edge of her thoughts, refusing to become clear enough for her to know with certainty what lay ahead.

She shook her head to clear it. *Whatever happens will happen. I cannot change it. I can only change how I act in the face of it.*

"So I'm to be Queen of the Fae?" she said to Mithorden.

The sorcerer nodded. There was a sad look in his eyes. For some strange reason this made her smile.

"I'd rather be a Chosen for Vyrl. Doesn't seem so dangerous."

"But you are a Chosen of sorts," Leowin said sadly. "This time, the monsters are with us."

RIDDLES ON THE ROAD

Banners raised, they set out at first light. With no attempt to hide their movement, the army spread over the land. A show of power. A declaration of victory. She rode at its heart upon great Othalas. To her left, Leowin sat atop a white faenmare with Vanye on his dark charger beside. To her right, Queen Elayethel, in the form of a unicorn, glided along beside Mithorden. Ahead, the three Valkyrie took point with Galwin. His hand clutched the standard, its flag hanging in the still, hot, air. Vaelros kept just behind her. Aside from a few simple words, she resisted his attempts to talk.

Mithorden looked sidelong at her. Inclining his head, he edged away from the group. The dimness in the sky was growing. A strange mist gathering above the clouds. Suns still shone bright but the night before only the most brilliant stars were visible. Moons now wore red halos. It reminded her of winter. How a rising Gorothoth would pull up a darkness that consumed all but the greatest lights and even robbed the suns of heat.

She leaned a little, slowly guiding Othalas toward the sorcerer.

"They say Elwin is losing," she said softly to the sorcerer as she looked at the sky.

The sorcerer followed her gaze and slowly nodded.

"Who told you?"

"Valkyrie. But I don't understand. What is Elwin's battle? How does it change the sky?"

He glanced ahead, then gave Luthiel an appraising look. "To think only weeks ago I found you trying to trade your life for your sister's. Now look at you!" His eyes traced her foot to crown as he gave a small smile. "I will tell you what

I know soon. But you must promise to indulge me first," he said with a wink. "Important things are happening. Not the least is your forging *Weiryendel*."

Her hand crept to her sword hilt. "My sword? What about it?"

Mithorden raised a hand to her—palm open, fingers extended. "It is truly yours now. May I?"

Reluctant to let even the sorcerer hold it, she slowly drew the sword. As it cleared the scabbard, a pure and beautiful music filled the air. It seemed louder than usual and the tiny motes in the blade flared like a rain of stars. The light and music seemed to grow even brighter as she extended the sword to Mithorden. As his hand touched it, the song changed—becoming both subtle and powerful.

"Sounds like greeting," she said, captivated by the new music.

"It is," Mithorden said as he raised the blade. "It remembers."

"Is it alive?"

"Alive as a dream."

"You mean —?"

"Yes—*Weiryendel*, as you renamed her, is of the deep magic. She is a true dream."

Luthiel looked at her sword with new awe. "Something that crossed over?"

"As your father made her—the dream that cuts. A killing dream." Mithorden looked at her and there was respect in his eyes. "Do you realize what you're doing?"

Luthiel looked at the sword and felt a pang run through her. She thought of the past days of violence. Of all the things she'd killed and of those things that were somehow also spared. But she stayed silent—unable to give voice to her feelings.

Taking her silence as indecision, he continued.

"Out of all weapons ever crafted, Cutter's Shear was the most elegant, the most graceful, and also the most brutal. It was a masterwork. Among the greatest achievements of an age. And yet it was also a terror."

He handed the sword back to her. Its music changed again, becoming at once graceful and strong. It was a flowing thing—like water made music.

"You are doing an impossible thing. You are improving on your father's work."

"How?"

"Follow me."

They wound their way through the army, uncertain where the sorcerer was taking them. He led them away from the main force and then over a small rise. On the other side, the wood grew dense and shaded. Finally, when Luthiel was about to say something sharp he came to a stop. A pair of elves with bows drawn and arrows notched slipped from the underbrush to challenge them. But as they approached and noticed Mithorden they fell in beside them instead. Moving forward again, he pushed through a dense line of trees. Holding a last branch aside, he motioned ahead. A low place where the wood cleared a little opened up before them. Strung throughout the small clearing was a long line of giant walking sticks. They were like others scattered throughout the army bearing wounded. But these were also different. Instead of wounded, they bore great covered bundles. Among them moved elves. Each walked with a soft step and dressed in hooded woodland garb. They exchanged odd looks and strained expressions. Few spoke and when they did it was only in whispers.

Mithorden looked around, appraising them. "The others don't know about this yet. I had Khoraz find them. Blade Dancers carried them back." He guided Luthiel to one and uncovered it. As the cloth fell away it revealed the carcass of a Widdershae.

Luthiel pulled away in disgust. "But it's dead. Why —?"

"Look closer. Don't you recognize it?"

Luthiel turned back to the Widdershae. It was all curled up—legs drawn in tight. As she looked, Mithorden motioned to the elves and had them uncover the other bundles. Each one was a Widdershae. Some seemed to be crumbling away like brittle shell. Others seemed to still be alive—for they were faintly breathing. Then she saw it—tell-tale silver lines cutting across them. Every spider bore the marks.

"They're ones I fought."

"Not one is dead," Mithorden replied. "Come here. I want to show you something even more extraordinary." He moved to one of the crumbling bodies.

Reaching over, he broke a piece off its abdomen. The area beneath was hollow and light streamed in. There, curled in a ball, was a beautiful female elf. She had hair the color of hematite, skin as fair as white granite.

"It's an elf!" Luthiel said in shock.

"You did it—with *Weiryendel*. Somehow, the Widdershae has been cut away. Now only a Delvendrim remains." His voice lowered to a whisper. "The race the Widdershae extinguished is now returning."

Luthiel took a step back. After a moment, she held up *Weiryendel*—looking at the blade.

"Your father's sword is no longer just a weapon, Luthiel. It is also a healing thing."

She looked at the sleeping elf. "I did this?"

The sorcerer smiled and nodded. "It's important you know." He looked up, eyes catching some of the muddy daylight. "Now your question. So you want to find out what's happening?"

She nodded reluctantly. "Yes. Though I dread it."

The sorcerer's face seemed to fall, taking on a grim look, and he nodded. "You won't like it. Let's ride back. I'll tell you along the way."

As they turned to ride away, the elves recovered the Widdershae bodies.

"Before the fall of Gorthar Lord of Death," the sorcerer said after they'd ridden a little ways, "elves had never known winter. Some say Oerin's Eye heralded it. For the second sun opened just before the darkness came. Before that time, Oesha had only one sun. Not the two we know today.

"It started out as a black cloud among the stars rising just behind Gorothoth. With each passing year, it grew larger. In the times after the dark moon rose, suns began to grow dim and killing frosts fell over Oesha. The new season of cold and darkness brought with it hunger, death and terrors from the World of Dreams. Many kinds of plant and animal died off. Trees of Life became havens through the bitter winters. The cold did not hurt them. For they were sustained by great fires cupped in their roots. So despite the cold and dark each Tree of

Life flowered and bore fruit year 'round. Yewstaff fruit was the most famous. For it could heal. But the leaf-oats of Ithildar and a kind of meaty fruit from Woldspur made fine staples to fill winter stores. Some fae even took to caring for creatures of the wild in winter—scattering bundles of food throughout the lands. But with each passing year the darkness grew. The world watched on with growing dread —fearing that winter and darkness would soon cover all the world for all time.

"Then your father made the last two Wyrd Stones and sent them as gifts to his parents—the Lady Elwin and the terrible Lord of the Dark Forest. At the moment Elwin touched her Stone, she became aware of Gorthar and the awful spell he wove. For the darkness was his most terrible dreaming. An ancient weapon. One he had crafted in the depths of time to destroy worlds. Slowly, over the course of an age, he was bringing it back. With her Wyrd Stone, Elwin found a way to fight Gorthar in the dream world and to keep the darkness from growing. But at a terrible price. For she fell into a sleep of ages—and you know how the Dark Forest's Lord blamed your father for it.

"Unaware of your father's pain, Elwin did battle with Gorthar in dreams. For the span of this age, she held him in check. Life on Oesha began to adapt to a new, if harsher, rhythm. For nearly three months out of each year total darkness reigned. For two on either side of winter, the shadow impeded light but growing things could still manage. And for five months the darkness had no effect or was completely absent.

"Now in what should be the brightest part of the year, a dim veil descends over the luminaries. It seems Elwin is losing."

Othalas gave a low growl. Luthiel started, suddenly realizing they were back in the Vanguard. She looked up at him but there were no words she could make for a good reply.

"What will happen?"

"At best?"

"Start there."

"This age will end. With that ending will come a great time of trouble. The worst in twenty thousand years. Some races may never be seen on Oesha again."

"And at worst?" Her voice broke a little as she spoke. She clutched Othalas tight, for she was trembling.

"No life will remain on Oesha. This age will be the last."

She did her best to keep from shaking. Even Othalas seemed afraid.

"Zalos spoke of signs. What are they?" she finally mustered.

"Changes in the sky. First the moons and stars grew dimmer. It was gradual so most didn't notice. But Zalos keeps track—as do I. There are other signs too."

"Horns grow from the eighth moon's head?"

Mithorden looked Luthiel in the eye. "Yes," he said seriously. "Actually, horns will grow from every moon. But from the eighth moon first."

"How can a moon grow horns?"

"You may well see soon enough," Mithorden said grimly.

"Did you hear the song they sang?" she asked, irritated Mithorden hadn't answered her question. "The one about the Blood Witch. The one about me?"

Mithorden nodded.

"They mean to blame it on me. How long has that prophecy been around?"

"A thousand years at least."

Luthiel felt a sinking feeling in her gut. "A thousand years? You think Zalos could see so far?"

Mithorden grew quiet and very still. He drew a deep breath and then looked away. "This prophecy did not come from Zalos, though it has certainly informed him. It is a dream of Death. It came from Gorthar."

"Is it true?" there was a pleading sound in her voice she didn't like. But her fear had gotten the better of her.

"It is meant to become the truth as people see it. A weapon to make people fear you. To wish you harm. For if there is to be hope of survival for this world it is you and your family who will bear it."

"My family?" there was both hurt and hope mixed together in her voice.

"Yes! Your family! Your grandmother who is at this moment losing a centuries-long battle in the World of Dreams. Your mother, the very spirit of the blue moon, who is even now bound by Zalos in Arganoth. Your grandfather who is lord and master of the greatest Tree of Life and of the terrible yet vital forest that sprang up from its roots. Your father, who defeated the Vyrl and who yet lives in a horribly twisted shape. Your aunts—the Valkyrie who ride with us even now. You and your love for them all—even those you've never known.

"For only in mending old hurts can you overcome this terror. I know in your heart you wish to see them. To bring them together. It is your nature. This family's breaking has been the work of fear and death and of its master Gorthar for two ages. In that breaking lies the death of this world. And in its mending, hope of survival and the dawn of a new age.

"It falls to you to bring them back together."

"What do you mean bring them together? How?" In her own voice she heard the same hope and desperation she had heard in Melkion's plea for his father Faehorne. For the first time, she felt something in common with the little dragon. *We are both children of broken families trying to heal wounds that span generations.*

The sorcerer spread his hands. "You know well in your heart what can and must be done."

"Could I?" she looked at her hands. "I miss them and I don't even know them. It's mad to feel this way."

"A very normal sort of madness," the sorcerer said sadly.

"But why won't you tell me more? What should I do?"

Mithorden looked at her and shook his head. "I am bound by old laws from the making of this world—and the aftermath of an ancient war to break it. I can only shine a light on your path. But I cannot make or change it. You must decide."

"So you won't help me?!" she growled —wishing, for a moment, she had a voice like Othalas.

"I am doing my best to help. I understand how you must feel."

"What would you know about how it feels? My father's body broken and made into a weapon! My mother a captive! My grandfather wields his own son as a sword! A grandmother losing a war of dreams against the very lord of death! You tell me none on Oesha will live unless I bring them all together. But you will not tell me how?"

Mithorden shook his head. "I could no more tell you than I could reforge *Weiryendel* or save Vyrl. If I could do these things they would be done. I did not even know them possible. It is for you and you alone." He looked up at the sky once more. "One week. A day more. A day less, maybe. You'll see the signs well enough. Trust in yourself. You'll know what must be done when the hour comes."

"Come on, Othalas, I've heard about enough." Othalas turned and bore Luthiel away. They made for a small stand of trees and then disappeared from sight. A flight of Khoraz went to follow her. Vanye rode up to the sorcerer.

"You've upset her."

"I told her the truth. As is often the case, it became a riddle."

"What sort of riddle?"

"The kind where you have to choose what's right for you and hope it's the best thing for everyone."

Vanye nodded in understanding. "I'd be angry too. Should I send my brothers and sisters to watch after her."

Mithorden nodded. "Yes. But only those with discretion. I think she at least needs some small sense of privacy."

Vanye nodded and his Cat-o-Fae tilted toward Soelee—bending blades to send flashes of light to the group of Blade Dancers that rode behind them. Two broke off from the column and made quietly toward Luthiel and Othalas.

"A shame about Melkion," Vanye said.

"A shame? No. Not at all," the sorcerer replied.

"More riddles?"

The sorcerer stayed silent, his eyes searching the trees where Luthiel and Othalas rode alone.

THE ROAD TO YEWSTAFF

As they departed the Mounds of Losing, the lands grew less wild. Trees were more recognizable—untouched by the mad mists which would cause such oddities as pine and leaf, cone and flower, on the same branch. Here and there, villages began to spring up. Curious eyes watched them pass from the high branches of a Fae Holme on a distant hill. Belethial sent her runners and soon food, drink, and even fresh archers came from the nearby towns. Many wanted to see Luthiel, and she could read awe, fear, and even hate in their faces.

In just three days, they began to see the uppermost branches of Yewstaff, though they were still eight days from reaching it. He was a great tree—high arms sweeping green and gold against the sky. His shape—like a great cone—reminded her of an immense Fae Holme. For Yewstaff was tall as a minor mountain, his great trunk three hundred feet broad. But of all the remaining Trees of Life he was the smallest.

At night, she could see faerie lights, flir bug bulbs, and other bright enchantments sprinkled all across the great tree, making him look like a gleaming green cloud. From there, queen Belethial ruled. From there, Luthiel would call her first Faerie Court. She hoped they would make her a queen.

She turned her eyes northeast toward Ashiroth and wondered what her mother must be thinking even now. Had she heard news of her daughter's adventures? Did she know of Zalos' new betrayal? Of her coming coronation?

If they make me a queen, I know my first command.

She gripped *Weiryendel's* handle all the tighter and even its bright music seemed angry.

Though Mithorden would not speak to her freely of the trouble gathering above the world, there was still plenty to learn. Many things about the World of Dreams that she didn't yet understand, and even some more magic.

"We must be careful what we imagine, fear, or hope for," the Sorcerer said one day as they rode. "The echoes of our thoughts live on in eternity. If you convince enough people that something is going to happen on Oesha it eventually will. It can be an awful thing. It can also be a wonder. The Vyrl dominated the dreams of nations for an age. Through dreams they conquered Oesha. But your father learned to walk in dreams, to speak to people as they slept. It's how he overthrew the Vyrl."

Luthiel nodded. It was a difficult thing to grasp. All dreaming creatures helped shape the future. Her father had used this to overthrow the Vyrl.

"So how do you know when something is going to happen?"

"Signs start appearing in the real world. Things start changing."

Luthiel decided to hazard a question. "Like what's happening in the sky?"

Mithorden frowned and was silent for a while. Luthiel rode on beside him quietly thinking the lesson had ended. Finally, the sorcerer spoke up. "In part, I think what's happening in the sky would happen regardless of dreams. It was a weapon Gorthar made at the beginning. Something that's part of the way things work. But it would terrify many and so affect Oesha in dreams as well. I believe the appearance of Dimlock and Widdershae was made possible by this thing in the sky. People feared it and dreamed of terrible things. Eventually some of it happened. Elwin has managed to hold the darkness off all these years. Yet she is also fighting a deeper darkness. The arrival of more awful things than Dimlock and Widdershae."

At other times, Mithorden taught Luthiel Wyrd. This was frustrating, as she seemed inept at certain kinds of sorcery while excelling at others. FireWyrd, as Mithorden called it, was completely beyond her grasp and even the patient sorcerer threw his hands up in frustration after three days of botched lessons. She was equally useless at what Mithorden called battle magic. But magic involving life, defense, wind, water, transformations, and enchantment came with surprising ease. By the time they reached Yewstaff eight days later, she'd learned no less than seven words and songs of power. For shaping green and growing things—*Verde*. Enhancing physical strength—*Nos*. For protection from hurt—*Eshald*. Calling to wind and spirits—*Thymos*. She could use her name rune—*Liel*—to draw upon the luck and flexibility of water. Healing she already knew. But to aid her, Mithorden taught her a word—*Bellen*—which meant 'well-being.' Last of all came *Wolda* to summon creatures of the wild to aid her.

As she learned, she realized she'd unintentionally used some of this Wyrd before. It felt familiar. The names seemed like something she recalled from a dream. But putting the words and songs together allowed her to do more. When she sang the song for *Wolda Khoraz* a great flock of the crows blackened the horizon and came to her in no less than five minutes. *Wolda Firewing* took longer, as the birds had to cross the distance from their roosts in the Vale. But in less than an hour, the sky was ablaze with flame. She felt bad summoning them for no reason. But the birds did a wingover in salute before flying home again.

They also talked a little about her Wyrd Stone. Mithorden urged for more caution. To use the Stone only when absolutely necessary. Luthiel retorted by saying she'd be dead if she hadn't used it when she did. This seemed to quiet the sorcerer and they moved on to other lessons. *Bellen* song allowed her to heal faster and when she tapped her Wyrd Stone she didn't need to use her body to provide the energy for healing. If she could stay in dreams all day, she might heal a hundred or more. Someone smashed a flutterfler and without even thinking she touched her Stone and used Wyrd to piece its broken body back together. She filled its empty vessels with dreams and it became the stuff it used for blood. It brushed her cheek with its wings, then flew off—dancing in the hot air.

Of all things, *Bellen* and *Wolda* came with the most ease. Everything else required practice and she made mistakes. One day, practicing *Verda* she accidentally entangled an entire company of red cap when she was trying to part the trees before them. Instead, they wrapped around the little goblins—leaving them dangling by the feet or pinned beneath roots. It delayed them a full half hour as Mithorden worked to convince the trees to let the goblins go. Luthiel was busy trying to keep the goblins from taking matters into their own hands and biting their way out. Elves smirked and pixies laughed. Others, glancing at the changing sky gave scowls and the word 'bewitched' passed between them. It made Luthiel feel very young and foolish. Not at all like the queen she was supposed to become.

After Mithorden's lessons, Vanye came to instruct her in swordplay. If anything, he knocked her around worse than the first time. Leowin seemed to take a grim pleasure in watching and would sit by cheering for her, or laughing when Vanye tripped her up. Eventually, Vanye became irritated and told Leowin to keep quiet or to join in with Luthiel. In an instant, Leowin was standing beside her waving her practice sword carefully through the air.

In all it was a very bad idea. Both were left grumbling and covered in bruises. Watching the whole exchange, Luthiel realized the tension between Leowin and Vanye was almost at a breaking point. At one time, Luthiel managed to trip Vanye. But he caught Leowin by the arm and rolled her—using the momentum to spring back to his feet. For a brief instant, she was clasped tight in his arms. He came up flushed and red-cheeked. Leowin gasped as if winded.

From the look on her face, Luthiel realized it wasn't exhaustion. Afterward, she and Leowin were laying side by side staring up at a meteor shower. It lit up the sky in a brilliant rain beneath the fading stars.

"What do you think will happen with you and Vanye?" Luthiel asked without thinking. But her sister just lay there, eyes glowing with more than the light of shooting stars. Before she got up and walked away, she wiped her cheeks.

Luthiel had her own sorts of troubles. Galwin picked her flowers. Vaelros tried to write her a song. It all ended up badly. She did her best to graciously accept these offers but she was too mixed up to take them seriously. She sighed when she realized her worry for so many things would prevent any romantic feelings for a long time to come.

To throw them off, she would say things that confused them. But she was careful not to be cruel or to play them against each other. She needed their friendship and was wise enough to sense that spurned love can bring the worst kind of hate.

Stranger was Othalas' reaction. At first, he seemed to take their interest in her with a few rumbles and half-hearted growls. But as they became more persistent, he grew more protective. She found it both odd and strangely endearing. Perhaps the wolf could sense her distress better than the others. But the primal thing flashing in his eyes made her wonder.

As they traveled, the sky grew stranger. At night, meteor showers rained down with bright intensity. Dim stars winked out. Moons became redder and Cauthraus grew what looked like flaming hair. Worst of all were the two white points—like comet tails side-by-side—that rose up from the northern sky, growing longer night after night. During the day, the sky was milky white rather than the usual blue. People spoke of an early winter. But the days seemed hot as ever. A few, remembering the Blood Witch prophesy, spoke softly of the terrible ruler they were about to coronate and of the terror she was even now bringing to the land. Some of these deserted and were never seen again. Others argued with their fellows and too many heard them. Rumor of their passing spread throughout the Minonowe, and elves gathered at a safe distance to watch them. Curious children could be seen, peeking through the grass on hilltops, or clustering in the treetops—all daring to get a better look at the witch.

"If it gets any darker, I don't think I'll be the queen of much," she said to the werewolf as they rode late into one evening beneath the now nightly rain of stars. Cauthraus had risen. It wore a red mane, shining like a dim sun.

"Two fangs says Zalos left some here to spread nasty rumors about you. We should round them up and banish them. Better yet, let me bite them in half. That should make them quiet."

Luthiel trembled. "It's what they're looking for. Don't you realize?"

"If you're weak they'll come in quicker for the kill."

"I will not make myself a tyrant," she said severely.

"I would not see you become a martyr," the great wolf growled. "If you don't use your power others will take it from you."

To this Luthiel had no response. So she just sat quietly. They were only a day away from Yewstaff now. She was glad for it. The sooner the better. For it looked like at least part of Zalos' prophecy would come to pass. As she rode, she thought of Mithorden's words and wondered, even now, what might be happening in The World of Dreams.

IN DREAMING

That night, she went looking for Mithorden. The sorcerer disappeared at the oddest times! And often when she seemed to need him most. She finally found him talking quietly to the Valkyrie.

"I've not seen the Dark Forest in an age," the sorcerer was saying. "It's amazing to hear how large it has grown."

"The hunt masters ride almost with impunity," Elonwyn replied. "Hundreds of humans turn Changeling each year. It's only a matter of time before Romas comes to the Dark Forest in war."

"Maybe it's what the Forest Lord wants?" Mithorden said, stroking his chin. "Oh, hello Luthiel!"

They all stopped talking out of respect for the young queen. It made Luthiel a bit uncomfortable.

"I need your help with something."

The sorcerer nodded. "I'll do my best."

Luthiel glanced at the Valkyrie. For some reason, she felt uncomfortable talking about it in front of them. So she lowered her voice and leaned closer to the sorcerer.

"It's about Dreaming. Like what my father did. I think I need to learn how." She looked meaningfully at the army. "Zalos is poisoning them against me. It gets worse every day. Othalas says I should make examples. But I don't want to match cruelty with cruelty. The only way I can think of changing this is to go to them in dreams."

Mithorden shook his head. "I cannot tell you."

"How many times are you going to say that?" Luthiel replied.

Mithorden smiled. "I don't know how your father did it. I asked him once and you know what he said?"

"What?"

"He said 'I cannot tell you.'"

Luthiel sniffed in exasperation.

"But I do know he used *Methar Anduel*," Mithorden continued. "He would step into the World of Dreams while he slept. You did it with the owl, remember?"

Luthiel nodded fiercely. "I know! I just didn't mean to and I don't know how I did it."

"Maybe if you decided to go looking for the owl?"

Luthiel felt a chill run over her. "But the owl is dead."

"Yes. But if that's the last thing you remember of the dream world then it may be a good place to start. Try thinking about it before you go to sleep. Keep *Methar Anduel* close!"

She frowned. Thinking of the owl made her feel afraid and uncomfortable. It was a terrifying dream. One that almost got her killed. "Thank you, Mithorden," she said solemnly and then walked off to her bedroll. When she got to it, she found that Othalas was already asleep nearby.

Not fair, she thought. *He can just ball up and sleep anywhere.*

She plopped down and lay in her bedroll for a time watching as stars fell and the moons ghosted across the darkening heavens. When she thought of the owl, only violence came back to her. The flash of jaws. The fall of bloody feathers. She tried to turn back to the clearing. To think of the owl alive on the branch. But she kept returning to dragon jaws. *Methar Anduel* gave comforting light and she focused on the small spark inside, letting its warmth hold her eyes. She found herself drifting off into the light. It surrounded her. Finally she succumbed to sleep.

She felt as though she floated rather than stood. But the strangest part was she could look down and see herself sleeping beside Othalas. Everything seemed to come out sharper. Brighter. The World of Dreams swayed around her. She had this sense of Other. A threatening presence beyond her sight. A blackness in the sky near the northwestern horizon. She remembered Gorothoth, reminding herself his first rise was still a day away. Small comfort, for the sense of Other remained.

Like a spirit, she began to drift away. It was strange. She simply thought and she moved. If she looked at something, she could be there in an instant. She slipped through her army. Some, still walked awake. At first, she was worried they might see her and not understand or worse—be afraid. But no one seemed to notice as she passed among them.

I'm invisible.

Not knowing what else to do, she made her way to those who slept. She started with a group of Blade Dancers she'd seen glaring at her earlier. For a time, she stood there, watching them sleep. It was strange, for if she looked at their faces she could see flashes of their dreams. Now and then, something would rise up from them—a white spark or a shadow. It would hover above them for a time and then drift off—slowly taking shape. It made her feel uneasy and she wondered what lurked in this world she'd entered.

Almost completely by accident, she noticed the thread. It happened when she looked down. But there, like a thin strand of gossamer, was a silver thread touching her back and then running away to her body. If she concentrated on the thread she could still get a sense of her body—comfortably asleep many yards away. She turned her eyes back to the dreamers.

So how do I speak to them in dreams? How can I change their hearts as my father did?

Not knowing what else to do, she knelt beside one and touched him. He seemed to tremble and then pulled the covers closer despite the summer heat. Before her eyes a scene came together. It was as if she looked through a window and into his dreams. She saw him running through a forest—bow in hand. A brother ran beside him. They chased a deer through an early spring rain. She felt water on her face and realized she was there in his thought. She appeared before him bathed in a ray of moonlight but her face was warm as if with inner fire. Seeing her, he stopped, his eyes filled with awe and fear.

"I know what you thought of me," she said at a whim.

"Would you bewitch me even as I sleep?" He raised his bow and shot an arrow at her. She held out her hand and the arrow turned into a sparrow, flying away with a chirp.

"I am too late for that. You are already bewitched by a fear and a shadow on your heart." She stepped forward, lifted her hand and touched him on the chest. "I release you—fear no more."

He gasped and fell to his knees. Suddenly, the dream grew dark. A shadow seemed to be draining out of him and into the dream. For a light fell on him and, overhead, the stars and moons grew bright.

"I did not come to hurt you," she whispered. "Nor did I ask to be queen. You should not be wary of me but of those who lust for the power I would have gladly refused."

There was a flash and she was slipping away. She found herself in the camp again. The Blade Dancer was sitting up and, for a moment, it seemed he saw her. But he blinked his eyes and the recognition faded.

"Strange," he said. Then he shook one of his companions awake. "Arthes, I just had the oddest dream."

His companion wasn't happy about being awakened so abruptly. "A dream? Is that trouble worth waking me for?"

"It was about her." He nodded toward where Luthiel slept on the hill. "Our new queen. I think we might be wrong."

"Wrong? She's a friend to Vyrl, plain and simple."

"You've twice been sent by Vyrl to name Chosen. Are you a friend of Vyrl?"

"She let them get away with murder. Now look at the sky. See how its grown darker since her return? And still summer! You think it wise we let her rule?"

"But Zalos is hardly any better. He makes dark deals with dark things."

"Because he has to, I hear. You know politics. It's hardly ever a matter of choice between good and good, but the least of two evils."

"I just don't think she's evil, Arthes."

Arthes gripped him by the shoulder and smiled. "I understand why a young fae like you might have good dreams about her. She does seem fair. But seeming fair and fair are not the same. Sleep on it and if you feel the same way tomorrow we'll talk some more. For now I'm tired. Good night!"

So here are the limits of dreams, she thought. But it did seem to work for the young Blade Dancer. So she moved through the camp, entering the dreams of those she could. Some were closed to her. Over time, she realized she could only enter a dream. If a person slept without dreaming there was no place for her to go. One other thing she discovered—singing seemed to work on any dreamer within earshot. She wished she'd learned this at the night's start, for it would have saved her a lot of time.

As she walked, she made a song telling of her journey to the Vale of Mists. Telling how, if she didn't go, her sister would have been sent to be food for Vyrl. How the Vyrl made a bargain with her to save her sister's life. How her blood saved them from madness. Luthiel's song entered their dreams and they could see things as she had. Walk her paths. Share in her fears and triumphs. They trembled at the first sight of Othalas and struggled through the Cave of Painted Shadows. They listened to the Vyrl's plea and were forced to make the tough choices along with her. They saw the Vyrl's transformation and witnessed Ecthellien's sacrifice.

A number woke up shaking their heads. One shouted out "What else could be done!?" before sitting upright and awake.

It wasn't an easy story for her to tell. She still ached at the loss of Ecthellien. Still she felt as if she'd done wrong by freeing the Vyrl. But she sang on. And the song showed her heart and many understood, in dreaming, the troubles of Luthiel in life.

By the time Oerin's Eye brightened the eastern sky, she'd passed through about a quarter of the camp. She returned to her body and entered a deep, dreamless, sleep.

LINEAGE

She woke after only an hour, finding the Wyrd Stone cupped in both hands and feeling oddly refreshed. Camp broke and as they began the last day's march before reaching Yewstaff she thought she could sense a small change. Fewer people scowled at her and many returned her smiles openly. There was still a sense of anger and she realized there was a lot of work ahead.

She wondered if what she did was wrong. *Did I manipulate them? If they knew, would they feel betrayed?* She remembered the Vyrl's blood in the cup, the blood on her hands when healing. *Am I the witch after all?* As the doubt passed through her she rebelled against it. No. She would have sung the same song in the waking world if they would only have listened. She'd told no lies. Made no demand. She'd just found a way to share with them.

She realized then the power of this troubled time. To exploit dreams. To turn them into nightmares. And by doing so to gain great power. As surely as others were doing even as she tried to free them.

They continued along the path and the great tree grew ever larger.

"It really does look big as a mountain," she said to Othalas. "They've always seemed a mystery to me."

"Few know about the great trees."

"Do you?" she asked, feeling a sudden spark of interest.

The great wolf gave a gravelly laugh. "More than most."

"Tell me," she said, tugging on his fur for emphasis.

Othalas shook his head and gave a playful growl. "Well I will! If you just stop that!"

Luthiel let go with a laugh. "Go on then. I'm waiting for your words, oh wise wolf!"

Othalas snorted. "Some say they're World Trees. But that's only true about Anaturnar, the great tree of the Dark Forest. His roots stretch all the way to the heart of Oesha. These other trees came from different worlds."

"Different worlds?"

The werewolf gave a gravelly chuckle at her wild-eyed expression. "None of the great races arose here. They sailed across the sea of stars. And what do you think bore them?"

" 'The sailors on the starlight sea,' " Luthiel said thoughtfully. "I've always loved that story. I'd imagined they came on some kind of great sailing ship."

"Mmmmmrrrrrr Hhhhhurrrrrrr," the werewolf replied. "Half right. They did come on great ships of a sort. Living ships. Trees of Life."

Luthiel looked at Yewstaff with renewed interest. They were closer and she could see it much better now. Its branches grew out in great swoops and curls. They spiraled around making it look like a giant green tornado. "That's a ship?"

"It was. Once it set root to Oesha, it became a part of this world. Never to leave again."

"Amazing!" Luthiel said. "How could a thing like that be made?"

"The knowledge is lost. But it is said they grew with eternal fire cupped in their roots. Fires as hot as stars. Do you know the old myths, Luthiel? The ones that even most elves have forgotten?"

Luthiel laughed. "Which ones? I know a few."

The great wolf chuckled. "But there is one old myth you may not know of a world far away. A place that long ago was only inhabited by humans. Yet from them arose elves, goblins and all other dreaming creatures. Even angels."

Luthiel shook her head. "Now that's beyond believing. Everyone knows elves are the oldest race."

"Just because elves live longer now, doesn't mean they came before. But what would you know? You only grew up with elves. You're not one of them."

"What do you mean?"

"Your mother Merrin, is she an elf?"

"Well, I don't suppose. She's queen of the blue moon. Some say its living spirit."

"And that would make her?"

"Aedar—an angel." Luthiel's voice trailed off as she stared into the sky. "Now I suppose you're going to tell me angels are a younger race than elves or some other equal absurdity."

"They are," Othalas said with a gravelly laugh.

"Now you're really not making sense!"

"Remember, long ago, I was a human. So I had access to histories the elves have never seen."

"You said you were an elf!"

"I did not. You did and I just let you believe it. I said I was once a man. And that is the true part."

"But I saw you in dreams. An elf at the heart of you."

"Then you saw only what you wanted to."

Luthiel blinked at him, taking in what he was saying. "What I saw was true in dreams. Besides, a *human* would make his race the eldest."

"Truth, Luthiel. Believe it, deny it, or make your own. I don't care."

"Stubborn wolf-human."

Othalas ignored her, continuing to needle where he left off. "But what about your father? Do you think he's an elf? What's his lineage?"

Luthiel felt a lump gathering in her throat. "You're being cruel, Othalas."

"Don't you want to know about where you came from? Doesn't it mean something to you? For an immortal creature, I think it would. What are you anyway? It's something even I have wanted to puzzle out."

Luthiel was so overcome by emotion she didn't know what to say.

Othalas, seeming to not notice her distress, continued. "Let's think about it. Elwin is the spirit of Oesha and that makes her Aedar too—maybe one of the greatest. And then there's this mysterious Lord of the Dark Forest—her husband and your grandfather.

"What about him? He whose name must not be spoken? The tyrant of the dark wood. He looks like a Vyrl. But is he? He never joined them. He never devoured dreams—only the blood of his enemies. Some even say he's a demon. Did you know some people called your father half-demon?"

"I didn't know!" Luthiel almost shouted. All of Othalas' talk made her feel very freakish and out of place.

"Yes you did. You knew it. You just didn't want to put it all together. Like you didn't want to admit being a sorcerer—despite the obvious. Well this is also obvious. You're three parts Aedar and one part Vyrl or some other Demon. Close enough. Might as well get used to it Luthiel, you're not an elf. You're mostly an angel."

And there it was. Something she'd tried to keep from thinking about ever since this wild and ridiculous adventure began. For, more than anything else, Luthiel wanted to be normal. Wanted people to accept her. Wanted to be a part of something. But all these things—sorceress, angel, daughter of Vlad Valkire—kept her apart.

"And part a demon too," she said. "Maybe Zalos was right."

Othalas acted like he hadn't heard her. "You know what a demon is? It's something that was once an angel but was horribly twisted in some way. After all the good he did, do you think your father was a demon?"

Luthiel shook her head. It was all just too much. She couldn't help it. The grief and fear that had been filling her up ever since leaving Flir Light burst out. Tears rolled down her face, which she buried in Othalas' back.

"I just wanted to have a fun First Summer's Eve. To have as much of a normal birthday as is possible for me. Look what happened! I'm going to be queen. I don't even know my real parents. And my father only talks to me when someone near me dies. Most everyone wants me dead too. Now you're telling me I'm an angel, part demon? Why can't I just go back to being me?"

This silenced Othalas and he padded on as she quietly cried into his fur. "Luthiel?" he said finally.

"Please, just don't talk," she said between her tears.

"You could never be anyone but you," the great wolf said softly.

THE EIGHTH MOON'S HEAD

After a few minutes, Luthiel stopped crying. Her escort rode close, hiding her from the others. She realized she shouldn't show weakness—especially not now. But, oddly, she felt better as if her tears had washed something rotten away.

Othalas was right. I am what I am. Best get used to it.

She rode in silence for most of the day, Yewstaff grew larger and larger, standing like a green and brown mountain before her. Suns set and his lights joined the dimming stars. They kept marching. It was her order. She wanted to arrive as soon as possible. But even now, she wondered if it was too late.

For today was Summerdark. The first day the Black Moon showed his face. Just for about thirty minutes after midnight. Then not again for another two weeks. And once more a month later with the first of fall. But it heralded the coming autumn. What made her tremble were the white tails rising like fangs in the sky each midnight for a week. Growing longer with each passing day. No one would talk openly about it. Even Mithorden and Othalas clammed up when she asked them. And Leowin just gave her a sour look and walked off.

A few hours after sunset, she saw their tips. All through the evening they grew longer, seeming to rise off of something. She dared not think of what.

As they continued, silence fell over the army. There was a sense of expectation and of dread too. She couldn't keep her eyes off the tails. They were the largest and brightest things in the sky and even cast dim shadows. When it became apparent what was going to happen, Luthiel made a decision.

Yewstaff lay directly before her with the land rising gently to meet it. The hills meandered and swelled like a gentle sea before gathering into a massive rise made of earth and roots the size of small hills themselves. A trunk like a cliff-face capped with a cloud of brown and green lorded over it all—the great tree of life.

"Mithorden," she said to the sorcerer, "can you make them move faster?"

With a nod, Mithorden gave a signal.

"Forward!" the captains cried.

They broke into a trot and then into a jog. Making for the great tree. When they came upon the first great root, she nudged Othalas ahead and the wolf leapt up to the top. Raising her hand, she called the army to a halt. The army ground to a stop. All their faces turned toward her.

She'd feared the prophecy for two weeks now. The rising of Gorothoth. The darkness. The foretelling of the Blood Witch. She turned northwest, facing the great white horns. A few minutes before rising. She wanted to stare into its face. To stand and shout out her defiance of it. But first she had to make them understand.

"Fae of Oesha!" she cried out to them. "Do you see what is coming!?"

She threw her arm in the direction of black moonrise.

"It is the demon moon. And we can already see its horns."

The fae watched her and she could see dread in all their eyes. They'd all heard the prophecy by now.

"But I did not cause it as some have accused. What you see is a sign of coming war. Not a war against Vyrl. But a war against all this world."

The fae were listening now. Though it was clear they didn't like what she said.

"Have you noticed mists in the sky? Have you noticed how the suns dim and stars wink out? These are just the outriders of a greater darkness. For the War of Mists is coming. When this cloud in the sky will block out all lights and Gorthar will attempt to kill off every dreaming creature.

"Some have said this is my doing! Do not be fooled! For I intend to fight against it. To keep safe life."

She could see the first edge of Gorothoth rising.

"Mithorden!" she shouted down to the sorcerer. "Bring me one of the Widdershae!"

The sorcerer shouted orders and one of the giant walking sticks clambered up toward her. Upon its back it bore a bundled Widdershae. When it drew close enough, she pulled away some of the cloth.

"See this spider?"

There was a grumbling among the host.

"It is one I fought." She drew *Weiryendel*. "One I thought I slew."

Vaelros and Galwin removed the carcass from the giant walking stick and placed it beside her. She looked at the Widdershae. The shell had nearly crumbled to dust. She pushed through the shell and found an arm. It was the Delvendrim she'd seen a few days before. She breathed lighter now. Seeming closer to wakefulness.

She drew the lady elf up, sitting her upon Othalas in front of her.

A gasp ran through the army.

"No longer a spider! Welcome her back to Oesha!" she shouted. "My father's magic once broke the ancient curse. Endless nightmares the Vyrl set on all fae. My magic has now also broken a curse. The one that turned elves into spiders. I defy the dark moon! I defy even the God of Death who sleeps there!

"Zalos talks of survival. But he gives no importance to life itself. He would have us make choices hard enough to break us. He would make us killers. Yet I know a secret. Life supports life. If we become killers we turn upon the very thing that helps us survive—each other. But if we work together to preserve life then we all have a better chance. Not just a privileged few.

"I believe in the good in you. I believe in even the good in Widdershae and Vyrl. We can make our enemies into our allies! And we can face the coming darkness together!"

With that she set her Stone alight, placed it in the keyhole of *Weiryendel* and held the sword high in defiance to rising Gorothoth. With her other arm, she propped up the still sleeping Delvendrim.

"Black Moon!" She sang as it crested the horizon. "I defy you and the death you bring. A witch I am! For I am a woman of Wyrd. A blood witch I am indeed. For I have used my blood to heal both elf and Vyrl. A queen I will become. And in that charge I will defend with all I am the life of this land. I warn you! For I am fierce and would bear no threat, even from the great lord of death himself!"

Then there was a darkness upon her. It shot out of the black moon at her in a black ray. The air around her became very cold and she thought she heard a deep voice in a broken chant.

Skalos Ingurtharab!

Sound hissed about her like the flight of a thousand black arrows. There was a sucking sensation as the air rushed away from her. Then she felt a blow like a hammer over her whole body. The Wyrd Stone glimmered and went out. She went limp and fell from Othalas' back.

The Delvendrim awoke suddenly. Blinking her eyes, the first thing she saw was Luthiel.

"A terrible nightmare!" Her voice echoed out soft, but somehow carrying to every ear. "It seemed to last an age. Then I dreamed an angel came. She took my hand. Pulled me up and out. There was peace. Am I awake now? How then is the angel of my dreams fallen beneath me?"

The fae army let out a cry and, by the thousands, rushed up to help Luthiel.

To the northwest, a black and blood-red moon rose. It bore twin horns and behind it came a cloud of darkness that seemed to gape like a great mouth. But none deserted the army this night and some, thinking all should hear about what had happened, sent runners far and wide. Beasts and birds saw it too. Soon, all of the wild was amutter with what had happened.

Elf and goblin hands touched Luthiel and found her cold and barely breathing. Above, a flight of birds swooped up into the tree and came down bearing fruit. Scooping it into their beaks, they fed her the healing stuff. Her body warmed, her breathing strengthened. Then, elf and animal, goblin and pixie all gathered around her and carried her to the base of the great tree. There they made a bower of Yewstaff leaves for her and set a watch.

The Blood Witch had come to Yewstaff and many had come to love her.

THE BEST FISH

She would swim. Swim away from her prison.

Dive from the high wall—as she had a hundred times before.

Waters knew her. Could not hurt her. As she fell she could see the waves rising up to her like welcoming arms. One hundred feet, two hundred, five hundred. A whispered song and she returned to dreams.

Just above the water she changed.

Silver covered all her body. Her arms drew in and became rainbow fins. Her legs merged and became a great sweeping tail.

Splash! Her sleek body shot through the water faster than an arrow. So she left him. That mad lord to his darkening fortress and dimming thought.

He thinks I am bound here. But he broke the terms long ago. So I can leave. Does he suspect?

But she didn't care! Her daughter was alive! Little more than a month ago, she heard her song. And she went to her! Swam to Mithorden to have a good look. How that single look had filled her! Her breath caught at her likeness to Valkire, herself and even Elwin. Yes, some of Chromnos too in those strong eyes!

And now she was at work in the world. Already, Vyrl saved and the Faelands were coming together—much to Zalos' dismay.

Zalos. He was the reason she risked another journey. He'd heard Luthiel's defiant shout to the dark moon in dreams. Listened as his spies told him what happened. Reprimanded his captains for their failure to turn enough fae against her. Then word was sent. From the high walls of Arganoth flew six Graven. And on each griffon-raven's back—a deadly rider.

They were changing. Becoming darker. More like death. The Ming devoured flesh and spirit. Now they were sexless, gaunt. Continuing. But in an unnatural way. The fae they once were bound in a body with Gorthar's demon Ming. Luthiel had caught a glimpse at the rim. Mingolë.

Now complete in nightmares, they rode out to murder her daughter.

She would not allow it. For she deeply loved Luthiel. She would use all her power, all her cunning, to keep her from harm. She'd spent years playing a foul game with Zalos. Feigning interest to distract him, but keeping her heart secret and safe. Now Elwin was awakening. Now her daughter was at work in the world. It was time to break the bonds. Time to fight outright. Pay Zalos back for his betrayal.

For Merrin, wife of Vlad Valkire, was no fool. And she knew now, all too well, what Zalos had done.

Faster than a porpoise, she shot through the river. Swimming with the current, she made good time—even better than the flying Graven. She'd get there much sooner. For beneath the water lay a blue Lilani—one leading to a lake near Yewstaff. Over the past few years, she'd visited Yewstaff regularly. She knew him well, having years ago found a way to move about the great tree without being discovered.

As she shot through the water, a great Graven with white-tipped feathers flew out from Arganoth. It was the largest of all Arganoth's war birds and upon its back rode a fair figure in heavy armor. Zalos was going to war.

YEWSTAFF

Luthiel awoke the next morning with the taste of fresh Yewstaff fruit in her mouth. She still felt achy and tired. Her wounds had reopened again and oozed blood through the night. It took her a moment to recall what happened. When she finally did, she sat up blinking at Soelee light streaming onto her bed.

She lay in a fold of limbs and leaves shooting off of one of Yewstaff's main branches. Bright cloth and wind charms hung all around, giving her a feeling like home. Her bed was exquisite. It was a weave of tiny branches that came up out of the floor. On top were blankets and cushions of flir-silk. The branches swayed, giving her the sense that she floated.

Not wanting to get up, she stared through the branches and found small patches of sky. Above, she saw a tiny speck circling. For a moment, she thought it was Melkion, but her heart dropped when she realized it was a Khoraz.

I miss him, she thought sadly.

The Khoraz grew in size and she smiled when she saw Mindersnatch alight on a branch beside her.

"Maaarn—ning!" he squawked.

"Morning to you, Mindersnatch," she said blearily.

The Khoraz bowed. "Someone—coming!"

"Who?"

"Wisdom!" the great Khoraz squawked.

Luthiel sighed, irritated. "Can't they wait. I still feel tired. Last night was—tough."

Mindersnatch cawed and clicked sympathetically. "Risks! Reap strange reward!"

270

Luthiel laughed. The crow was right. Maybe she shouldn't have made such a show of her defiance.

But how else would I have won them?

She levered herself out of bed and began putting on the clothes that were left for her. They were nothing short of royal. A beautiful white dress with tiny moonstones woven into the fabric. There was also an elegant belt with a chain to hang *Weiryendel* from. It looped over the scabbard, catching it in two places.

When she was finished dressing, she looked around.

"Where's Othalas?"

"Below!" the Khoraz sniggered and clacked his beak.

"Doesn't like trees, then?"

The raven bobbed his head and laughed some more.

Luthiel had only sat down to some breakfast when there was a rustling at the curtains.

Vanye stuck his head in and, seeing her, gave a serious nod. "May I come in?"

Luthiel motioned him inside. The bed had unwoven and the little branches were now making a set of seats and what looked like a small table. A pair of pixies came in and swept up the blankets. They curtseyed to Luthiel as they passed.

Vanye gracefully slid into one of the new-made chairs. He also wore finery and looked far more princely than she'd ever seen. Even his Cat-o-Fae was adorned with flowers—tucked in among the blades. The polished metal and petals combined to make a stunning bouquet.

"We're to both see the Wisdom here. Since Elag left, things have changed. I think you'll be pleased."

"Why, who is he?"

"*She* was the only lady Wisdom to survive Elag's rule. She kept making herself too useful to send away. With Elag and his followers gone, the other Wisdom confided in her more and more. But after what happened last night, they made up their minds. The vote was just cast." Vanye gave Luthiel a meaningful look which she returned with a tired smile.

"I'm beginning to think Leowin is right. I take too many risks. I feel like Othalas sat on me."

Luthiel heard a laugh from beyond the curtain and Leowin walked in, curtsied with smile, and sat down beside her.

As Leowin entered, Vanye stood stiffly and inclined his head in greeting. Leowin smiled in return. Their eyes met briefly, then they both looked away. Leowin smoothed her robe and absently ran a hand through her hair.

"Glad to see you're starting to come to your senses," Leowin said pointedly. "I'd like you to stay here with us."

Luthiel raised an eyebrow at Vanye.

"We couldn't keep her away," the Blade Dancer said evenly. "She's even taken on a title. Queen's Secret-Keeper."

Leowin smiled slyly and she looked out of the corner of her eye at Vanye. The Blade Dancer gave a half-smile in return, then looked away.

"Yes. You need me around," Leowin said. "This way it sounds official. But it doesn't mean you're not my sister any more either. Next time you do something dangerous, like last night, I'll box your ears."

"Box my ears?" Luthiel smiled. Being a queen didn't change some things. Her eyes wandered over to Vanye who was still standing stiffly. Thinking of his discomfort, and looking sidelong at Leowin who'd gone back to smoothing her dress, Luthiel wondered at the tension between them. *How long has this been happening?* she thought. *How long could it continue? Will they wander forever at the borders of love?*

She turned her eyes back to the Blade Dancer who still stood straight as a bowstring. *There is deep danger too. He could fall into madness in an instant. Where would Ithilden be without a Faelord to lead her?* Taking one last look, an idea slowly formed in Luthiel's mind.

"I'm glad you both came to tell me about the Wisdom," she said. "But if you don't mind, I'd like to meet with her alone first."

Vanye's sharp eyes swung toward Luthiel even as Leowin stiffened.

"It'll just be for a moment, then I'll want you both to be here."

Vanye stood, gave a slight bow, and then was sweeping toward the entrance. Leowin seemed puzzled as she turned and walked blindly toward the opening. They both arrived at the same time. It was too narrow for them to pass together so they came to an awkward stop. Leowin looked up at Vanye who stepped back and lifted his hand, letting her pass.

As they exited, Luthiel stood and followed, poking her head through the opening and looking out after them. They'd only made their way a short distance along the branch when she caught them. It was narrow, with smaller arching branches forming rounded walls on either side. The tight confines pushed Leowin and Vanye closer together. Both walked stiffly down the hall. Leowin held her head tilted at a self-conscious angle. Vanye, uncharacteristically, didn't seem to know what to do with his hands.

"Vanye!" Luthiel called after them.

Together they turned to look at her. Turning around in such a tight passage brought them even closer together so that, though they didn't touch, only inches separated them.

"What is the extent of my power?" she continued in an official tone. "What can I command?"

"I am to be King of Ithilden alone, but you the Queen of all the Faelands. I am your man," Vanye replied.

Luthiel stepped forward into the cramped space and walked down the hall. She reached out, taking one of the Blade Dancer's hands in hers. It was large and rough. But there was also a gentleness to it. "Then I command you, Vanye. Tell me. Are you mad?"

Leowin's eyes flashed and her mouth narrowed in irritation.

Vanye's face grew stern and he took a step away from Luthiel, starting to withdraw his hand. But Luthiel tightened her grip, holding it fast.

"Mad? What do you mean?" Vanye replied.

Luthiel drew herself up. Her face became firm and she angled her head, staring Vanye directly in the eyes. "Have you fallen into madness?" She shifted her eyes to Leowin and then turned back to him. "Have you lost Li?"

Vanye stared back at Luthiel and his brows fell in anger. It was all Luthiel could do not to back away from his glare. But she held firm.

"Do you question me?" His Cat-o-Fae flicked in agitation. This motion sent petals flying. Some of them landed on Leowin who was squeezed in close beside him.

"You are in love with Leowin," Luthiel said.

Both Vanye and Leowin drew back from her.

"Luthiel!" Leowin exclaimed.

But Luthiel held firm. "You have broken your Blade Dancer's oath," she said to Vanye. "Many others would have fallen to madness by now."

Vanye's Cat-o-Fae twitched again, this time extending its blades like the flexing of great claws. Luthiel released the Blade Dancer's hand and stepped back, eyeing the weapon's threatening motions.

"I command a test," she said to Vanye and Leowin. "A test of Li."

Leowin turned to Vanye and then back to her. "Luthiel!" she said sharply.

Vanye bowed stiffly to Luthiel. "Very well. I will prove it to you this afternoon at sparring practice."

"That is not my test," Luthiel replied.

"Luthiel," Leowin said, this time with too much control.

There they stood, side by side, only inches from one another and still not touching. The narrow passage seemed to wrap around them like a cocoon pushing them still closer. Vanye who had seemed strong a moment before now looked uncertain. The warrior ever ready for decisive action, but suddenly without an aim or objective. Leowin stood straight as a board. Refusing to look at Vanye, she glared at Luthiel even as color slowly bloomed on her face. Luthiel saw her out of the corner of her eye but refused to acknowledge the demand in her eyes.

"What, then, would you have me do?" Vanye replied finally.

"I would have done with your pining looks," Luthiel said. "You are to kiss my sister."

Silence fell between them. All was still. Luthiel could see motes floating in the dim light streaming through the branches.

"This is beyond duty," Vanye snapped.

Leowin turned and began to storm off down the hall. But the violent motion brought her arm brushing against Vanye's and she paused. In that moment, before she surged away from them, Luthiel grabbed her sister by the hand.

"Leowin! Would you look at him? Should anyone else kiss him?"

Leowin lifted her head and stared proudly at Luthiel. Then she slowly turned her face to Vanye. Their shoulders squared, the passage so narrow the tips of their toes nearly touched.

"No. No one," she said softly.

Yet still they stood apart, close but with not an inch of them touching.

Luthiel took Leowin's hand and pressed it into Vanye's. It was as if a bow-string had snapped. At their hands coming together, Leowin leaned into Vanye and the Blade Dancer swung an arm around her to keep her standing.

"I am your Queen," Luthiel said with force. "I will brook no dissention. I command you both to kiss."

Then, leaning down, Vanye kissed her full on the lips. The kiss lingered and Luthiel could hear Leowin let out a little sigh.

Satisfied, Luthiel clapped her hands together. Startled, the two stepped away as though awoken from a dream.

"Blade Dancer, Vanye. You have demonstrated your ability to maintain sanity while being in love. It is no small feat for even a regular man," she said as a smile touched her lips. "But for a Blade Dancer it is truly exceptional."

Vanye seemed at a loss for words.

"You have my blessing," Luthiel said softly.

And at this moment, the Wisdom whispered around the corner at the hall's other end and slowly made her way toward them.

There was an awkward moment when they didn't see her and she stood there, conspicuously looking at a wind charm. But Luthiel's eyes found her. When they did, she felt a sense of calm interest come over her. The lady was of middle height and wore brightly colored robes. A pouch of luminous blue, green and aqua patches hung from one shoulder. In the pouch were books, what looked like a crystal wand with a loop at the end, and candies wrapped in leaves. Her hair was dark and pulled back and her kind eyes twinkled over spectacles. There was an air of comfort and fun about her. But beneath it all, Luthiel could sense a deep knowledge and understanding.

Leowin, who'd finally taken her eyes off Vanye, took the lady in. "Now there's a real Wisdom," she whispered in Luthiel's ear.

Luthiel nodded and took a step forward, extending her hand.

The lady looked a little fuddled but didn't hesitate to press her hand into Luthiel's.

"Hello Luthiel," she said with a warm smile. "My name is Margareth. I've come to help you. You and I are on the same side, I think."

Luthiel's sense of relief was overwhelming. She wondered how so few words could give such comfort. She stood for a moment looking at the lady and sensed in Margareth what she'd hoped to find in all Wisdom.

"Thank you, Margareth," she said after a little pause. "Please, come into my room and make yourself comfortable." She turned and led them back into the chamber. "I am very grateful," she said after they all were seated. "I didn't expect—"

"Help from a Wisdom?" Margareth finished for her. "We aren't all like Elag, if that's what you're thinking."

Luthiel let out a breath. "Where do we begin then?"

Margareth looked at her seriously. "I thought we would start with the Faerie Council and coronations." Her eyes fell on Vanye who nodded to her. "Lords and ladies of the fae are coming from all over the land to see you. As you probably know, many will not approve of you at all. Vyrl aren't well liked among the Fae. So we'll need to see to your safety. Zalos is still popular. His friends may attempt a coup."

"They still don't believe me?" Luthiel asked. "Even after last night?"

"What you did last night helped. But some will never hear or understand you."

"Well, I have the Blade Dancers," Luthiel said with a worried tone. "Then there's Mithorden, Othalas and the Valkyrie."

"Yes, swords and magic will help too. But I was thinking there should be a distraction. Something to keep your enemies guessing and off balance. Something to capture their attention while we lay a trap for them."

"What kind of distraction?" Luthiel was surprised at this lady's cunning talk. All the moreso as she seemed a very good person. Cunning wasn't something she often noticed in good people. It was an odd contradiction.

"I was thinking about a ball. Something just after the coronations. To celebrate. We'll announce it to all. Then we'll just have to keep tabs on who's plotting."

Luthiel smiled. A ball? It may do very well. Something to get everyone's mind off of all the trouble. "And how do you plan to find out who's plotting what?"

"Yewstaff has his secrets. One of the best kept are the Rumor Rats."

"Rumor Rats?" Leowin said with a laugh. But her eyes sparkled with interest. This was just the sort of thing she loved to find out about.

"Rictinno, are you here?" Margareth asked to no-one in particular.

Bemused, Luthiel looked around. Beside her a large rat nosed his way out of the leaves. He was spotted green and brown and blended perfectly with Yewstaff bark. About his waist was a black leather belt and at his side—a little needle rapier.

Rictinno padded silently in front of her, stood on his hind legs, curled his front paws before him and dipped his head. Aside from his color, Luthiel noticed other differences from a usual rat. He was larger and more lanky. About the size of a small cat, his hair was long and coarse, and an odd ridge with small black spines ran from the base of his neck to his dark tail. His eyes were different too—placed side by side in the front of his head and gleaming with an uncanny intelligence. "It is an honor to serve, Queen Luthiel," he said plainly. His voice was smooth, direct, and soft as a whisper. "I've heard a lot about you. My cousins have been chattering since First Summer. You know you've become a legend to the forest folk?"

Intrigued, Luthiel knelt in front of Rictinno. "It is an honor to meet you, little one. I think some of your cousins came to me before. They were very polite. And if it weren't for the forest folk, it's likely I wouldn't be here now."

"We love you as we love Elwin," Rictinno said. "You have her spirit. Animals know these things. Even if some elves do not." He set a hand to his tiny rapier.

"Not all elves are so bad," Margareth said to the rat. "Have you already forgotten who taught you to speak?"

"Elves, of course," Rictinno cocked his head and looked Margareth up and down. "They were the good ones. But elfish isn't the only language. I could talk well with my kind before the Vale and the elves' lessons."

"Vale?" Luthiel said. "You come from the Vale of Mists?"

"How else do you think my body became as it is?" He motioned to his tail, spots and spines. "Have you ever seen a normal animal use something like this?" He drew his rapier, handling it with as much skill as any elf—then, just as handily, put it back. "My whole family went in the time of Vlad Valkire. We wanted to see what had happened to the Vyrl for ourselves. But we came back to Yewstaff. My family's been living here since the great passage thousands of years ago. We even remember old Areth."

Now Leowin's brows lowered and she inspected the rat with a look of serious interest. "What did you say? I've never heard of Areth."

Rictinno looked ready to open his mouth to reply when Margareth interrupted. "There will be plenty of time for questions and answers later. Now we need to get down to business. Rictinno, can you tell Luthiel about your job?"

Rictinno looked annoyed. "Isn't it obvious?" he said. "I'm a spy. But I don't work for just anyone. You have to be friends of the forest folk. Margareth is the first we've had in a while."

"You're a Secret Finder?" Leowin asked. "Could you teach me what you know?"

"Secret Finding is a part of what we do. The other part is disinformation."

"Disinformation?" Luthiel asked. "What's that?"

"Spreading false rumors," Margareth said. "It works well if you want to confound people."

"But how?" Luthiel said.

"Oh, it's not too difficult," said Rictinno. "Especially since everyone relies on letters these days. A few strategically placed letters and you could change the course of a kingdom.

"And that's just what we plan to do. We'll steal our enemies' letters and spy on them to learn what they're up to. Then we'll change certain letters. Adding little inaccuracies to confuse them."

"You *forge* letters?" Luthiel asked. "Isn't that dishonest?"

"If you're dealing with liars," Rictinno said, "the best weapon is lies. Funny thing about liars. They're terrible at telling truth from fiction. And they never trust a soul. So it's harder to find out what's true and what's not."

"Rumor Rats," Luthiel said musingly, still uncertain if she liked the idea.

"Delightful!" Leowin said. "When do we start?"

THE FAE LORDS' COUNCIL

The Rumor Rats, lead by Rictinno, spread throughout the great tree readying for the coming fae lords. There was much to prepare. Ear horns needed to be ensorcelled. Paper readied. Rapiers dipped in sleep elixir. Luthiel watched it all with a sort of quiet curiosity. Even Mithorden didn't know what was happening and she took small comfort in knowing something the sorcerer didn't. But it was probably the only thing. The sorcerer had inserted himself into every part of the business of rulership. He was always there with papers for her to sign or asking for orders. He did his best to explain when she asked questions. It was so detailed she couldn't help but be mystified and there was always a nagging worry that she'd missed some key detail or that the sorcerer had overlooked telling her something crucial she'd need to know.

"Do all leaders have to deal with so much?" she asked him one day.

"Leadership," he said, giving her a serious look, "is about responsibility and responsibility is about hard work."

But the sorcerer had a knack for leadership and organization. He had a way of measuring people. Of finding out their strengths and weaknesses. Soon, he delegated many tasks to an ever-expanding staff. It made Luthiel think of Lenidras and how it was so well ordered.

Rictinno checked all newcomers to make sure they were loyal and wouldn't sabotage Luthiel or try to slip poison into her honey wine. So far, Mithorden had managed to keep out the rotten ones. She wondered how he did it.

"He's got some kind of second sight," Leowin said after she'd confided in her. "There was something in the myths about it. He was Valkire's Chief Advisor after all, and the general of his armies too."

It just puzzled Luthiel all the more. She already respected the sorcerer for his knowledge and magical power. But there was something more. Clearly some kind of innate knack for dealing with people, for weighing hearts and minds, for finding good people and for putting them in the proper places. Not only did they work well at their jobs, they also seemed extraordinarily satisfied with them. It was odd, considering the dangers. Despite his activity and many responsibilities, Mithorden seemed to appear just at the moment you needed him and was always ready to provide counsel or consolation.

"He really is a remarkable general," Luthiel said. "Little wonder the Vyrl had so much trouble with father. I'm glad he's *our* general."

Leowin nodded in agreement. "You should do something official for him. Give him some kind of honor or position."

Luthiel brightened at the thought. Many of the Council lords were still arriving. It would help set an example. Solidify her as a leader in their minds. "That's an excellent idea. Can you spread word?"

"I certainly can." Leowin said with a smile and then she was off.

Leowin was another wonder. Mithorden realized her talents for information gathering and communication immediately. So he put her in contact with all captains and told Luthiel to make announcements through Leowin.

Leowin didn't mind. It gave her a lot of time with Luthiel. It also presented her a good excuse to go digging for information. Luthiel had to know, after all.

Thinking about Leowin's idea gave her another.

I should officially recognize more than just Mithorden. I should give titles to everyone who's closest to me. Set my own High Council. The Faelords will each have a place. Vanye can be my Arms Master. Belethial could be my Treasurer—she has a knack for bargaining. Elayethel my High Healer. Mithorden my General and Chief Advisor. Othalas my Master of the Hunt. Margareth my Wisdom. And Leowin my Herald and Secret Finder.

She smiled. It felt right to recognize them. It was like giving gifts. And giving gifts was something she particularly enjoyed. She pulled out a reed-quill, dipped it in some berry ink, and began writing a brief note to Leowin on a piece of leaf-paper. Halfway through the first line, she paused, wondering—*how does a ruler officially appoint titled lords?*

One by one, the lords and ladies of the Council made their way to Yewstaff. These were the minor nobles. Ones who either by election or accumulated power had secured a place on the Council. They were mostly a widely varied mish-mash of elves—Tyndomiel, Valemar, and Ithildar. A few Gruagach and Goblin also came. But regardless of what they were they all had to officially refuse loyalty to Thrar Taurmori and Zalos. In an ominous, but not unexpected sign, very few Lords came from either Ashiroth or Rimwold. Only fifteen out of the one hundred who entered were from these lands. The rest either refused to denounce their Lords or never came to Yewstaff at all.

One irate Gruagach lord, angered when told he would have to denounce Zalos to attend, caused a row at Yewstaff's roots.

"You call this just!?" he shouted. "How can it be a real vote if not everyone's allowed? There are many who have views—legitimate views—that Tuorlin was bewitched into naming Luthiel. Zalos has as much right as she—if not more!"

The clerk, a harried Gabouter—a kind of tree gnome that inhabited Yewstaff—snatched his papers and scampered away from the angry lord. His fists were clenched and he looked like he was ready to hit him.

"She's a witch!" the Lord shouted. "A witch!"

Looking around to make certain a Blade Dancer was nearby, the clerk spoke up.

"This *witch*, as you call her, is the direct descendant of Vlad Valkire. He was our *first* and *greatest* King. Or have you forgotten? Tuorlin was wise to recognize her. You would be wise to do the same if you wish to sit on *her* Council."

"What proof does she have? How do you know she's not a fake? She has no written record of lineage. No legitimate claim!"

The clerk straightened his uniform and adjusted his glasses. Normally, he didn't get involved in arguments. But he was tired of hearing such narrow remarks. This Lord was the final straw. He *liked* Luthiel. Liked better the kinds of changes she was making. Why, just the other day, she'd ordered shipments of food to his mountain kin who'd experienced crop failures this summer. They blamed the dimming light and unusual heat. She'd also ordered the bee keepers to bring every hive they could find back to Yewstaff. More bees meant a wider variety produced by Yewstaff. For sweet fruits weren't his only crop. Some of his flowers were edible and when baked became a fine bread. More bees meant higher yields. The extra honey was an added benefit. Vlad Valkire once said Yewstaff alone could feed all the Faelands and more—if put to good use. Now his daughter was doing it!

"Records?" the clerk said angrily. His aunt happened to still live in those mountains. "What better record than history? She has her father's old sword and his Stone too! Both only Vlad Valkire himself could use! Who but his daughter could hold and keep them?"

"Tricks! Counterfeit!"

"So it's counterfeit she healed Vyrl? Counterfeit she broke the Widdershae's curse? I've heard quite enough."

The Blade Dancer had also heard enough. With a nod, three guards moved to escort the lord away. A few of the lord's own guards moved to block them. This lord had twenty or so armed elves with him.

"Down! Down! The Witch!" they chanted. The chanting kept on for about an hour before they moved off and then it was only under the watchful eyes of Ithilden's archers.

Luthiel heard it all from her perch high up in Yewstaff. It wasn't the first conflict she'd seen over her coronation.

"Won't be the last," she muttered.

Nearly all one hundred lords had arrived and though many of them signed the papers claiming they respected Tuorlin's decrees, it was clear that at least some had lied. Rictinno had given her an ensorcelled ear horn so she could listen in on the Council's preliminary sessions. A particularly vocal Ithildar named Cambian was just now making a case for a delayed coronation and a period of transition. At least that's what he called it. From what she could translate, it basically amounted to putting her under holme arrest for an indefinite period while those in the Council against her figured out how to otherwise undermine her.

It was reassuring that at least half the Council seemed to disagree with Cambian and those like him. These were the ones, Rictinno said, who'd been bullied by Zalos and who sympathized with Tuorlin. They amounted to an old guard who still viewed Vlad Valkire as a hero and who were doing their best to stop the religious reformers.

Luthiel had heard her fill about reformers from Mithorden and she understood better why the sorcerer had wanted her to wear a disguise when she first came from the Vale. Seeing how hard they'd worked to change the myths and to assert their beliefs filled her with outrage and apprehension. They'd written a book of their new myths claiming it was 'divine truth.' It contained all the changed beliefs and provided a way for those spreading the myths to instruct and enforce obedience. In order to quiet dissent, they claimed the text was literally handed down to elfin scribes from Ëvanyar. As in their past stories, the new book erased all significant mention of Ëvanya. It referred to her instead as creation itself—or worse, a temptress— but failed to mention her as a force in the world. Not a word was left for the song of songs—the Ebel Kaleth—that showed love as the source of creation. The book entirely focused on the force of Lumen—light, but never that of Lumiel—music.

"It is a religion wholly out of balance," Mithorden had said. "One meant to dominate rather than to give hope and inform. If it is a spirituality it is a very dark and dim brand of it. Standing between elves and enlightenment rather than leading them on the path to it."

Luthiel did her best to keep out of religious matters. But if there was any part of religion she felt a connection to, it was the song of songs—the Ebel Kaleth. The love it symbolized was a beautiful thing. To her heart it seemed only right that creation should come from that love. And to know there were those who sought to stamp it out made her sad and angry.

"It has to do with women," Othalas growled one afternoon as she confided in him. She'd taken to visiting him in Yewstaff's lower chambers at least once a day. The great wolf was too large and not enough of a climber to make it onto his higher branches. Luthiel missed him. So she made a point to come down and spend time alone with her wolf. "They want power over women. To gain it means erasing what came before. Mithorden says it's dark. I think it's the religion of war. There are even words in that wretched book saying war can be good. Holy. There is no such thing as a holy war."

"But you're a werewolf, Othalas," she said, looking sidelong at him. "A hunter. A great fighter."

"A Hunter? Yes. But I have no love for war," he rumbled. "The hunter serves nature's order. We kill the weak to survive and life benefits. Have you ever seen a forest without wolves? Trees become stunted as deer and boar grow too numerous—tearing them apart with antlers or gnawing at the roots. Unlike hunting, war serves no natural purpose. The killing of hundreds or thousands with no aim other than the taking of power. Sometimes wars must be fought. But they should never be celebrated or considered holy."

"Zalos says you must fight to survive."

"He's right to a point. Sometimes you must fight to survive. But it's better if you don't end up having to. You said it yourself. Life supports life. Life cooperates to survive. Like the wolf pack."

"You served abominations—Vyrl. Why?"

"The Vyrl were hunters driven mad by hunger. I understood them. They may have fallen to the level of a beast—killing to survive and feed an endless hunger. But after Valkire they never fell to the level of an abomination—wrecking life's order by wanton slaughter." Othalas paused for a moment before continuing. "You changed the Vyrl, and they weren't the only ones you changed."

Othalas and Luthiel shared a quiet moment. She sensed Othalas had brought her into his confidence and it was better she keep silent for a while.

"Mithorden said it well," she said finally. "It's worshipping death. They say they follow light. But, in the end, they're really following desolation, division, the end of things. You should hear their prophecies—war, destruction, only special chosen people are spared." She felt sad and angry. Worse, she wondered to what ends people who believed these things would go to assert their views.

Othalas sniffed the air around her, sensing her fear. "Don't worry, my little queen. If they come for you, they will have to first deal with the Hunter." He flashed his teeth and she leaned into him, hugging his great neck.

Some weeks passed before the ball. During this time, Luthiel put the Rumor Rats to good use and at night did her best to visit as many dreamers as possible. It had a noticeable affect. But she was hobbled by the Black Moon for she dare not enter dreams when its face was visible. There lurked hundreds of Dimlock and other nightmares under his black face; and the power that had nearly killed her seemed to radiate off it like cold from an anti-sun. So she had about two weeks, and then was forced to wait for a week when the second dark of summer came. After that there was another month, and then the Black Moon rose with the first day of fall.

Still she was able to reach many of the Council and there were a number who had a change of heart. The Rumor Rats kept track. A large, but slowly diminishing, minority remained—working hard to undermine her or to water down the coming coronation vote. They were led by one Tannias Rauth.

Little surprise. Luthiel had thought to herself. But despite the obvious and somewhat loud presence of his father, Tannias, Luthiel couldn't find trace of Vane. For all she knew he left with Zalos or even Widdershae.

I saw him with Saurloth. He even seemed to help me. How strange.

Despite all the attempts at political sabotage, the Rumor Rats found no plots against her. No letters of intrigue. No plans of overthrow. Nothing outside of Council and the regular political workings of the Faelands.

It made Margareth happy, but she seemed a little concerned too. "It's going well. Somewhat better than I expected. Is it possible we're missing something?" The last question was more to herself than anyone else. But it made Luthiel wonder too.

Toward the end of this time, preparations for the ball became frantic and complex. Vaelros and Galwin were both persistent in their attempts to invite her to appear with them. Many times she'd slip away from one or the other if she saw him coming around the corner. It always made her feel a bit embarrassed. It was really a silly circumstance; why didn't she just command them to let off and have done with it? But she didn't have enough heart to tell them. Deeper down, there was a strange feeling of being wanted that she did not wholly dislike. She chided herself for it. It wasn't fair to them. Both Vaelros and Galwin felt for her. If she ever did give in to one, the other would be crest-fallen. In a way, she thought it better to disappoint them both. In any case, she was uncertain if either was really right for her. Vaelros, whom she'd felt a strong first attraction to was, after all, many years older. And though age didn't matter so much to elves, she felt some hesitation. There were also his episodes of dark-ness. Times when he fell into a depression she felt powerless to pierce.

Galwin was another extreme. Awkward but cheerful, he often fumbled then laughed at himself when around her. She appreciated his humor but she felt him a friend and little more.

"I just don't think either is right for me," she said to Leowin one day. So if she did something with the one, she made a point the other was there as well.

Most times, she brought Leowin along and they rode out over the lands surrounding Yewstaff. Riding was safe because Othalas was the perfect chap-erone and both Galwin and Vaelros behaved better around him. They sparred too, swam in the many crystal lakes surrounding Yewstaff, played at games of archery, tap and turn, runestones, or three corners. Despite the romantic ten-sion, it was a wonderful time for Luthiel. A rare span where she felt unburdened by the world and all her troubles.

But there were always reminders.

Most terrifying were the changes in the sky. All blue was swept away from the daytime and the sky took on a white-brown color. Soelee turned red then grew larger. Oerin's Eye became pale as a ghost. At night, only moons were visible. The only stars that could be seen were shooting ones. But these fell in prodigious showers setting all the sky atwinkle with a rain of sparks.

Worst of all was the black mass of cloud that followed. At first it looked like a great shadow coming only with sunset. Then it stretched out, widening into a shape like a vast set of jaws with long teeth of black mists.

"A warg in the sky?" she asked Mithorden pointedly one day as they stood on a high branch at the top of Yewstaff. She'd been trying to corner the sorcerer.

To get him to talk. She needed to know what was going on. Why it was both so dark and so hot at the same time. Why the light was failing and with it all the crops of her people.

Mithorden looked at her and nodded. "It has been called that. But not by me. You shouldn't quote the prophesy of your enemies."

Luthiel turned back. "It does look like the jaws of a great wolf—stretching out to devour heaven."

Mithorden grabbed her hand—looking at her with eyes so ageless and full of depth it stole her breath. They were calm and controlled at the surface but underneath there were flashes and hints of a terrible knowledge. Worst of all, she realized, even the sorcerer was afraid.

"It has always been thought of as the wolf," he said. "Some called it the 'big bad wolf.' Others the warg, Fenrir, Maugris. Ten ages, each with the span of about twenty thousand years, have passed since the time humankin beheld the first wolf. We were younger then. We didn't understand what was happening. We thought the gods were angry with us. That we were punished for our sins. We have since learned differently. Ten ages. Each with its wolf. The world was made this way, Luthiel—with great death in it. As each age dies there too comes with it a great dying off. The warg is, indeed, one of Gorthar's pack. Yet it is both a thing of destruction and of creation. For at the end of each age, after all the dying, there comes new life in forms as varied and wondrous as the stars themselves. Their dust from which we are all made. This is the laughter of Ëvanya and Ëvanyar. For though Gorthar has afflicted the world with this destruction. They have ever made mockery of it."

When he said the last part, he smiled and some of the fear seemed to clear from his eyes.

"But that's just what happens after a great hurt," Luthiel said, thinking of her wounds and how some still ached. "Sometimes healing comes. But things are never as they were."

"You can turn your face and run from the wolf," Mithorden said. "But it is in the instant you give in to fear and think there's no hope, that there won't be."

"Then we must face the wolf?"

"Yes," Mithorden said. "And Gorthar too. But first Zalos. For though all seems quiet and you have everything well in hand. I doubt he has played his last card."

"Margareth thinks so too," Luthiel said.

"Does she? Well she's always been a wise one, Margareth," he said with a smile.

Luthiel gave a sigh of exasperation. "Don't do that!"

"Do what?" Mithorden said.

"Smile like you know something I don't!"

Mithorden laughed, then he sputtered. "Dear me! You are Valkire's daughter through and through! I can't even smile about something without you thinking I keep secrets."

"What is it you smiled about?" Luthiel said in a lower voice. Her heart was pounding now, but she didn't know quite why. There was something extraordinary about Margareth. Luthiel had really grown to like her and she didn't want anything bad to happen to their budding friendship.

"You are a good heart Luthiel and so is Margareth. I smiled because your alliance is one of those things that gives comfort. You are right to treasure it," Mithorden said, looking out over the branches.

Realizing she should be happy Mithorden had even talked about the sky, she returned to it. "Would you tell me what we can expect?" she said, looking at the growing shadow.

"A long time of hardship. Flood. Darkness. Freezing. Fire. Flood."

"In that order?"

"Usually. But not always."

"I'd expect you could tell me more about this sky wolf and how to manage the trouble it brings."

"I'm already helping you as best I can, Luthiel. Count yourself lucky for knowing what you do. Before humankind, before elves, there was no legend or language to give it name or shape. But the wolf was there. It always returns at the end of an age. And no world is safe from it."

CORONATION

So the day finally came when the Council of the Faelands met to decide whether or not to support and grant patronage to Luthiel—Queen of the Faelands. The fae lords gathered. Some final points were made. Cambian and Tannias tried to delay the vote as long as possible. They were eventually hushed by a slim majority. Finally, the votes came. Of those assembled, forty-two decided not to grant support to Luthiel. They would remain lawful citizens of the Faelands and obey her law but they would not give patronage to the new Queen. The other fifty eight pledged her their full support and patronage. Fully thirty more fae lords never appeared. These did not recognize Luthiel or any claim she made to the Starlight Throne.

It was an important vote for two reasons. First, Luthiel became the first true Queen of the Faelands. Second, Luthiel was the first ruler of the Faelands ever to have so few endorsements by the Fae Council.

Confronted with such conflict, Luthiel became the fourth ruler of the Faelands since the Vyrl's downfall. Never would a ruler, before or since, be faced with so much trouble in the first days of reign.

For Luthiel was to be coronated into a catastrophe. Even now, it was all Mithorden could do to help Luthiel keep the Faelands working together. Rimwold and Ashiroth, except for small enclaves, were not responding to communication. So Luthiel ascended into a state of ongoing war. The long summer heat and new encroaching darkness resulted in food shortages all across the Faelands. So the two Trees of Life remaining under Luthiel's control—Ithildar and Yewstaff—were being aggressively harvested to make up any shortfall. All about the Faelands there was a deep-seated fear for the wolf in the sky. Conflict broke out in otherwise peaceful communities. Banditry, unheard of among the western fae, appeared and then became more widespread.

Even more disconcerting were the reports of nightmares. Dimlock and other dark creatures appeared in their usual haunts but well before late fall, when such things normally happened. Garrisons were raised. Moonsteel weapons were distributed and the Faelands began to prepare for an indefinite time of trouble.

Given the terrible happenings and rumor of more terrible things on the way, it might be thought that the mood of Luthiel's coronation would have been subdued. Quite to the contrary, it was raucous. Those who supported Luthiel prepared for an even larger party than First Summer's Eve. In fact, to many, her coronation marked the greatest celebration in living memory—and an elf lives a long, long, time.

To those who feared Luthiel, who thought of her as the Witch, it was the perfect opportunity to give voice to fears.

Fae came from every corner of the Faelands to witness and to show their support or antipathy. Long trains of them could be seen for miles around. Women came, children came, beasts and birds. Before she entered there were shouts, roars, chirps and cheers. Some chanted her name. Others tossed straw dolls dressed like Luthiel into the multi-colored bonfires. Some even sang the Blood Witch prophecy and afterward talked loudly of the sky and of the doom Luthiel was bringing to them all. There was food. There was wine. The fae sang and danced. Some of them even dueled and a few were taken away to be buried.

Through the revelers skipped a little elfin girl. She was dressed in a black skirt and wore high black boots. In the crook of her arm she carried a little straw Luthiel doll. It was one she'd rescued from the bonfires. Now and then as she skipped through the partiers, she'd raise the doll up with both hands and twirl around. She hummed a tune and then broke out into a little song.

When winds blow hard and darkness falls
Who's afraid of the big bad wolf?
Fa la la la la

When stars aren't seen and demons come
Who's afraid of the big bad wolf?
Fa la la la la

Whose house is strong
When the big wolf comes
Fa la la la la

Twig or wood or stone or life
Fa la la la la
Where will the four little goblins fly?
Fa la la la la

Now that we see him one and all --
Who's afraid of the big bad wolf?
Fa la la la la

With the last, she pulled the straw Luthiel doll close to her chest, swinging it beneath her breast as if it were her own baby and then shouted—"Ashes! Ashes! We all fall down!"

Other fae watched her sidelong for she had a Sith look about her. Some even whispered wondering if she was a changeling. For such songs weren't sung in the Faelands. They had a distinctly humanish quality.

At the last light of day, Vanye appeared on a high branch of Yewstaff. He lifted a horn to his lips and let out a loud peal. He was dressed in kingly robes of navy blue with silver patterns. His horn was white and golden and his highly polished Cat-o-Fae glittered on his shoulder like a starburst. Then he descended the long and winding ridge in Yewstaff that served the elves as a stair. When he reached the bottom he stopped and looked up. An expectant silence fell upon them. There was a pause, then Luthiel appeared at the top of the stair. A hushed whisper rustled through the crowd. Dressed in the finest robes the Faelands could weave her, she smiled down to a hundred thousand faces.

It was just nightfall and all the flir bug bulbs were atwinkle. The nightly star showers seemed even more intense. But the moons were quite dim and ghostly. Few, even those who feared her, could dispute her beauty that night. Never was a bride more beautiful on her wedding day. A crown of light blazed at her brow and it seemed to draw out her eyes—each like a window into an ocean. Some whispered that she shouldn't have a crown yet. But others hushed them. For she was already a queen of the Vale of Mists.

The dress she wore was of white with patterns of flowers and of stars set with clear gems. Through her star crown, were placed flower petals of peach, light blue, yellow, and pink. And the smile she gave them was enough to soften even the stoniest of hearts—if only for an instant.

She descended slowly, giving them the chance to watch her. Some looked up with anger in their eyes. She did her best to smile at them as well. Of all times, now was when she needed friends the most.

I've gained quite a few. But it never seems enough.

Finally, she was standing beside Vanye and they walked together through the crowd. A long aisle was made for them and this was carpeted in flower petals. Posts of Yew wood were strung with borders of flir-silk and bright bulbs hung from them like lanterns. They walked along this aisle of lights, making their way to where Belethial, Margareth, Elayethel, and Mithorden stood. Margareth and Elayethel held the crowns. Elayethel held Ithilden's. It was of blue and silver metal made in a shape like waves that flowed over glittering sapphires. Floating in Margareth's hand was the Starlight crown. It was a small thing and seemed to be made of mist and globes of light. She held her palm up, fingers outstretched, and the crown made a perfect circle seeming to spin above her hand.

Vanye and Luthiel drew up to the front. Together, they knelt before the Faelords, Mithorden, and the Wisdom.

Mithorden raised his voice to those assembled.

"We are gathered here today to witness an event of historic consequence. For today we crown the new King of Ithilden. We will also crown a lady of great importance. The very daughter of Vlad Valkire, who was the first to rule these lands—Luthiel Valkire."

A whisper made its way through the crowd at mention of her name.

"Before we begin. I would like to say a few words. I have had the rare pleasure and privilege to serve both Valkires as teacher, general and advisor. Luthiel is her father's daughter. In every way and more. She has proven herself in valor and compassion many times. Her first adventure, to the Vale of Mists, resulted in the restoration of Vyrl. Her second, in the defeat of a terrible enemy—Widdershae and, again a restoration. For now we have living among us Delvendrim who were once thought lost forever."

He nodded to a gathering of Delvendrim near the front of the assembly and they gave a cheer and made the sign of Oerin's Eye to Luthiel who looked over her shoulder and nodded at them, smiling.

Those who love me, love me well at least, she thought. *But those who hate me hate me just as deeply.*

"Finally, before our new Fae Queen and Lord of Ithilden are crowned, I would like to put to rest a dreadful rumor. For some have made mention of the Blood Witch prophecy in an attempt to sow doubt about our new queen. But she is not responsible for the fading light nor this darkness that seems to hunt our suns. That darkness is an ancient terror. Something that has been with all living things since the beginning. Something that returns at the end of each age. Long before Luthiel was born, this terror set out across the heavens and began its hunt for Oesha and her suns. It is not her doing. Instead, it is used by Gorthar as a weapon. Luthiel may well be our best hope against it."

Utter silence fell over the gathering. Mithorden seemed pleased. For he smiled and nodded to Elayethel. She stepped forward and raised Ithilden's crown high.

"For the lands of Ithilden," she chanted. "For their magic and their secret mazes. For the great tree Ithildar and for her navies of Aerinwe. For her people, fair and wise. I give you Vanye, grandson of Tuorlin, King of Ithilden and former High Lord of the Faelands."

She lowered the crown, placing it lightly on Vanye's head.

"May you rule well, Vanye. May you serve your people with love, honor, and compassion. And may they return it."

There was a pause after which Elayethel said "Rise Vanye, King of Ithilden!"

There was a cheer among the elves and a formation of Blade Dancers drew their swords in simultaneous salute. Then they pivoted and together, their Cat-o-Fae flew out. Making a formation like a great V they shot out over the crowd, swooped up through Yewstaff's higher branches, made a great arching loop, and then returned to land on the Blade-Dancers' shoulders.

"Hail Vanye! King of Ithilden!" They shouted. The cry was answered by the crowd. Vanye drew his own sword in salute.

"People of Ithilden!" he cried. "I promise to serve you well and with heart. As I promise to serve the great lady who will be my Queen!" At this, he bowed once to Luthiel and then, sheathing his sword, stepped to the side so that she was alone.

Now Margareth came forward. There was a warm look in her eye. Again, Luthiel wondered at the sense of comfort about her. At the strange familiarity. Then, Luthiel was startled as Margareth knelt so that she was eye to eye with Luthiel. She leaned close and then in a quiet voice, sang softly to Luthiel.

Born of the blue abyss
As my moon I stand alone
My beauty is with loss entangled
Forged a soul of sea and stone

My lover was the great Valkire
My enemy the ancient Vyrl
Yet Vlad was broken by his sire
Left me alone to bear his daughter

Luthiel felt a chill come over her and it had nothing to do with this lady's breath whispering past her ear. As she pulled back, she looked deep into her eyes and there found great love.

"Mother?" Luthiel whispered, afraid that if she spoke too loud the spell would break and her hope would be ruined.

With a smile, Merrin nodded. "I wanted you to know who it was that crowned you. Long have I watched you from afar. Always wishing to be closer. But terrible danger kept me away. I am sorry, Luthiel. But you must know this—I am very proud of my daughter. Ever have I loved your father. I love him still and you are the miracle that came out of my love for him."

Out in the gathering, fae were whispering. Jostling to get a better view as Luthiel and Merrin spoke. But all they saw was the Wisdom speaking privately with Luthiel. It seemed to add tension to the assembly and a great air of expectation. The mood touched all but Leowin whose brows lowered as she strained to hear. Her face puzzled as Merrin spoke. Then her mouth fell and there was wonder in her eyes.

Finally, Merrin kissed Luthiel on the cheek, and then rose. Looking down at her, she said—"Are you ready?"

Luthiel nodded. There were tears of joy in her eyes. Despite all the troubles, despite all those who still hated her, this moment was one of the happiest in her life. Merrin had come to her! Merrin was free of Zalos! Her own mother would crown her Queen of the Faelands! The tears spilled out and ran down into her ears. She almost laughed. At her hip, *Weiryendel* seemed to hum merrily.

Yes. My father's sword would know her well.

"Fae of Oesha!" Merrin cried out with both joy and spirit. "On this day we are most blessed! For I am here to crown not one who came to power out of desire. But one who came to it out of love.

"Love you ask? How so?

"Well it was love that made Luthiel venture alone to the Vale of Mists to save her sister." She nodded toward Leowin who stared at them both in amazement.

"Love it was also that brought her here to you. For by her mercy, by her grace, she came to ask you to forgive. To forgive even Vyrl—in the name of love.

"What is so great about love? Why is it so celebrated?

"True love is the very sign of divinity. If you are filled with love then you are filled with the most essential thing in all creation.

"Fae of Oesha. You are blessed. For the queen of love has come to be your queen. The queen of mercy. The daughter of Aëdar and Elohwë. Who has proven herself to be an angel.

"Rise, Luthiel, in the name of love you came and in the name of love I crown you!" Then she placed the Starlight Crown above Luthiel's head and it hovered there like a halo. Slowly, it dropped down until it touched her Netherduel. Then, picking it up, it lifted back above her head and was filled with light. Slowly, it began to spin. Winds moved with it, rustling her dress making her hair blow. Then it stopped and she was there before them all, crowned in brilliance.

"Hail Luthiel! Queen of the Faelands!" Merrin cried out. "Hail Luthiel! Queen of Love!"

The calls were echoed by the assembly and then, as one, they knelt before her.

Queen of Love? she thought. *Do I deserve such a title? What of the vengeance I would wreck on Zalos!*

But the thought felt hollow now. For Merrin was with her and she wanted nothing more than to spend time with her. To know her. Luthiel's heart was singing. But a small voice deep inside called out. *Never forget! He betrayed your father!*

The Dance

Immediately following the coronation, came the dance. The dance they'd been planning for weeks now. It had seemed a useful tool for drawing out her enemies in the Council. Rictinno had, just before the coronation, exposed three plots—one assassination attempt, and two abductions. Not all too surprised, she learned Cambian was behind the assassination and Tannias the abductions. Both were being held, awaiting trial. She felt a twinge as she thought of Tannias. Father of Vane and lord of Rimwold. She wondered if his father was behind his son's actions. Perhaps now she'd have the chance to find out.

People gathered for the dance. A place had been made between two vast roots. It was sprinkled with flower petals and great vines of flir bug bulbs cast dancing light all about. From one of the roots, a flat shelf projected and on this were a group of minstrels with lulutes, kal sticks and thom thoms. These were four of the best known in the lands—Viel for her voice, Keth for his skill with the lulute, Sonde for the thom thoms, and Sosh, his wife, for the kal sticks. They'd practiced for the better part of a week and Luthiel smiled at the beautiful music. Many flir bugs, free of their bulbs and seeking mates for the summer, drifted through the air, making it seem filled with sparks. Already fae were dancing—elves on the ground and pixies in the air.

Luthiel found herself surrounded by a throng of lords and ladies, all wanting a chance to speak with their new queen. Luthiel did her best to be polite and greet them all. But she found herself anxiously searching through the crowd for Merrin. Time dragged on, but the press of people showed no sign of thinning. At last she saw her drifting gracefully through the crowd surrounding Luthiel. Relieved, she turned to the lord speaking to her and politely but firmly begged her leave. Weaving through the crowd, she made her way toward Merrin.

Luthiel smiled. "It's beautiful," she motioned to the dance as she came up beside Merrin. Standing so near, Luthiel had to resist the urge to reach out and embrace her. Instead, she stood and looked at her, drinking her in.

"Mother." Luthiel tested the word and liked the way it felt on her tongue.

Merrin put an arm around her shoulder and pulled her close. "Shhh. Keep quiet about that," she whispered. "I must still be a secret."

Luthiel nodded. "Promise me, then, you'll spend time with me. There's so much I want to ask!"

Merrin's eyes glistened with moisture. "There's so much I want to tell, Luthiel. I intend to spend as much time as possible."

Luthiel drew in a deep breath and smiled. Despite the beauty of the music, all she wanted to do was find some private place where she and Merrin could go and talk. Without saying another word, she leaned forward and embraced her mother. "I love you," she whispered.

"And I you," Merrin replied, holding her tight.

Then she forced herself to let go and Leowin was there, grabbing her hands and pulling her off into the crowd. "Be careful," Leowin said in a low voice.

"You knew?" Luthiel said, feeling a pang ripple through her.

"Not before you!" Leowin hissed.

"When? How?" Luthiel asked, this time confused.

"When you did. How? Well, I am a Secret Finder after all," Leowin said slyly. Then Leowin was pulling her again, skipping merrily as she went. "A dance! A dance! And much better than the last one! This time, there's no need to be afraid of Vanye!" She hopped and swung Luthiel around her. "My sister! Queen of the Faelands! We must celebrate!"

Then she took her hands and made her do a spin. By this time, Luthiel had lost sight of Merrin. *I can't run off just yet. People will expect to see me.*

"Ah! But first some drinks!" she cried as a fae with a silver tray stacked with crystal glasses walked toward them. She scooped two up and handed one to Luthiel. "To you Luthiel!" she said, raising the glass. Some of the Fae who'd been watching Luthiel and Leowin, laughter in their eyes, raised their glasses as well. "Who saved my life and this land too! May your reign last from now 'til the end of time!" She tipped the glass and drank down some of the bubbly blue liquid. It ended up being blueberry wine. The finest of which came from Yewstaff itself—whose limbs supported a number of blueberry orchards.

Luthiel drank as well and couldn't help but press her lips together as the stuff tingled on her tongue. "This is superb!" she said to Leowin.

"Haven't had any yet?" her sister chided.

"Well, no."

"Then drink up! You've earned yourself a little fun!" And with a laugh, she hooked Luthiel by the arm and ran her back into the crowd so they were much closer to the players.

The music was thick with energy and passion. Luthiel felt a big smile bloom on her face. She couldn't ever remember being so happy. She was here with Leowin and her real mother had returned to her. All seemed right. For a moment, her thoughts returned to the owl, Ecthellien, Tuorlin, and the thousands lost. Her mood slowly sobered. Taken by an inspiration, she lifted her glass and cried to those around her in a clear voice.

"To those who sacrificed to make this day possible! May their memory never fade!"

Those around her lifted their glasses and before they brought them back down for a drink, Vanye appeared with his own cup raised.

"To the noble dead!" he cried.

"To the noble dead!" they echoed and drank.

The word 'dead' gave Luthiel a little chill. But then she was drinking and the bubbly stuff seemed to warm her again. Leowin gave her a little wink and then skipped over to Vanye. He put his drink on a table, grabbed her with both hands about the waist and held her high while spinning. Her hair flowed like a golden flame as it swept out from her head. Her laughter sounded like bells. Then they were off dancing like the two most graceful things she had ever seen. The way they complemented made her chest twinge with just a little jealousy. But that was immediately replaced by embarrassment as she saw Vaelros walk toward her.

"I was hoping we'd have some time," he said. "Lately, things have been so hectic—" he trailed off. She realized he was making excuses for her. But seeing

Leowin made her feel a little reckless. So, without a word, she grabbed Vaelros by the arm and pulled him out to dance.

He laughed. "Not much for words tonight?"

"I have words. But for now I prefer action," she said with a laugh. She laughed even more when she saw him flush. But he swept gracefully into the dance with her and his face shone with a brilliant smile.

"My lady, how you shine this evening," he said easily.

And Luthiel was indeed radiant. Her dress illumined by the lights at her brow, her eyes casting out like the stars themselves.

She nodded at the compliment and smiled all the brighter. "I am merry, Vaelros. For the first time in a long time." Without realizing what she was doing, and more on an impulse than anything else, she leaned forward and kissed him. It as a simple, yet firm kiss and she pulled back after only a moment. But it sent a thrill through her.

He leaned down for another. But she put her finger on his lips to stop him.

"That was my reward to you," she said as they danced. "Don't squander it."

"Reward?" he asked still seeming both surprised and delighted at this unexpected attention. "What for?"

"Why for living, Vaelros. And for doing so much else to help me. I will have you rewarded in state as well. But that was just from me."

She saw Vaelros flush and she gave a brilliant smile.

"You don't like my reward?" she asked.

"I do!" he replied. "I want only to learn how to earn more."

The music was fading. The song was ending. Luthiel stepped back and let her hands drop.

"It is a mysterious thing, my heart," she said. "For it will not tell even me."

And with that she was dancing away. "Fear not, Vaelros! You will learn one day!"

He stood still for a moment—a grin exploding on his face despite himself.

She laughed as she danced deeper into the crowd.

"May I?" said Mithorden, who had appeared suddenly before her.

She mock bowed to him and took his hands.

"I saw your dance with Vaelros. Do you think it was wise?"

Luthiel held back a scoff. "It did him good. You should have seen his face. Why? Are you worried?"

"A little. But he does seem to be doing better lately. I've had the Valkyrie keep an eye on him. I was encouraged when a friendship budded between him and Elonwyn."

Luthiel laughed. "So you're trying to keep Vaelros away from me, Mithorden? Well you should have little to worry about. My young heart is hardly ready for full blown love. What harm is a little kiss?"

"Be careful whom you kiss, Luthiel, and how you do it. A little kiss from the right lady is enough to make or break the heart of a man."

"Always gloomy aren't you, Mithorden? Come! Cheer up! This is our victory dance! Yours and mine and all who came with us! It's what you wanted isn't it?"

"It is something worth celebrating," Mithorden said, finally smiling, and his step seemed to lighten a little. "As was Merrin's song and her love for you. A mother and daughter reunited. Now that is something truly worth celebrating."

"I'm exuberant!" Luthiel said, wondering if the sorcerer knew all along. "And yet I'm afraid too. What if I don't have enough time with her. There are things that must be done. Zalos. Thrar Taurmori. War." She said the last word with dread.

"You're a wise one, Luthiel. I expect Zalos will bring War to us ere long."

"If not, then I would bring it to him." Her voice suddenly became fierce. "I know all too well what he's done. What he's become. It's worse than Vyrl. Worse than Widdershae."

"Do not be so swift to cast out judgment or to seek a fight, Luthiel. Remember the lessons you've learned. Of love. Of forgiveness. Keep them close. They are your most precious allies. They will lead you through this trouble."

"Forgive Zalos? After he has done so much? How?"

"I did not say not to be wary of him. Nor even to expect good from him. But is it the right thing to attack him unprovoked? We should give him every opportunity to back down. To change."

"While he masses armies against us? Mithorden! You are the general."

"I am. That is why I say—better to allow him to amass armies than to assail him in his place of power and walk directly into a trap. If I know anything. I know that Zalos is cunning and will seek to draw you out. Put you in a weak place while he holds the strong one. Be careful, Luthiel."

Luthiel nodded somberly and pulled back from Mithorden. "Thank you—" she said and looked away. "I'll be going now. Enjoy the dance, Mithorden. It may be the last one we have for a long time."

She walked away from the sorcerer, took another drink, and found her wolf. He stood at the edge of the festivities watching it all with bored interest. When she approached him he let out a frustrated snort. "Been a while since I could take part in this sort of fun."

She threaded her fingers through is fur, feeling a little surge of pity for the great wolf. "Each time we ride, I am dancing with you," she said. "Each draft of air in my face is better than any draught of wine and far more heady."

"You're just saying it to make me feel better," the great wolf growled. "I know you well enough, Luthiel." And then he let out another snort—this one laughter. "Just do one thing for me tonight."

"Anything for my wolf," she said languidly.

"Don't give out too many kisses."

"You and Mithorden both!"

"For once I agree with that sorcerer about something." Then he sat down and let her scratch his ears.

A Mysterious Stranger

She stayed with Othalas for a few minutes more enjoying the quiet and her time with him. Then she stood.

"I should go back."

The great wolf nodded. "Then I shall see you soon. I wish that ratty dragon were here. There's no one around as fun to bully."

Luthiel looked off. "I understand. I miss him too."

With a wave of her hand, she walked back down the slope to rejoin the party. She did so just in time to see a curious group enter the crowd. They were all dressed out in fine black robes and had intricate masks over their faces. They looked like walking pieces of artwork. Something from a beautiful mummer's play. Each mask was different. She saw an eagle, a great horned beast, a lion, a bear, a vulture. Somewhere near the back she saw a dragon. She was about to turn away when the man with the lion mask stopped in front of her.

He bowed gracefully and she was taken in by the care and precision of his movements. "Queen Luthiel," he said softly. "As lovely as ever. May I have this dance?"

When he spoke the words there was a chill that ran through her. "Do I know you?"

"You do. I am known by those you love."

"But do I know you?" she persisted. "What's your name?"

"Now what sort of fun is that?" he said smoothly. "The mask is there for a reason. This is a dance after all. Can we forgo the dance of words and continue on with the dance of bodies?"

Something about this man intrigued her. The way he moved so proudly. It couldn't be Vaelros. His form was a little shorter and a little stronger. It couldn't be Galwin. This man was far too sure of himself. But if not those two then who? Some other lord, perhaps?

How could I know him? But the mask revealed nothing and she stood there for a moment, wavering on the verge of indecision.

"If I dance with you, promise me you'll take off the mask when we're done and show me who you are."

"You have my word."

He stretched out a hand, and hesitating one more moment, she took it. Then they were dancing across the soft grass. She felt as though she were flying. The music swelled and her feet responded. He was an amazing dancer, the best she'd seen since Vanye, and it was all she could do to match him—form for form, move for move. He was refined to the point of perfection, as though his body had been trained to respond to each thought flawlessly.

"How did you learn to dance so well?" she asked at a slower part in the music.

"You could say I'm a dancer."

"A Blade Dancer?"

"Yes. I was called that at one time." His intricate mask left just enough of an opening for her to see him smile and she could tell he was enjoying the game.

The music swelled again and she was lost to the dance once more. The other masked figures stood a little away from them, watching or seeming to chat among themselves. Luthiel noticed they stood apart from the crowd, who seemed to avoid them.

Must be the masks, she thought. *It does make them look a little odd.*

Luthiel hardly had a moment to think throughout the dance. It was such an amazing thing. Like her partner knew how to make art with their bodies. She found herself dreading the end. *What if it's someone I don't like?* she thought. For she'd come to deeply admire this dancer and as she did she began to fear what knowing his identity might bring.

The song slowed. It dropped off. Then, altogether ended.

For a brief moment they stood together. Looking at each other. Luthiel was at a loss.

"It was lovely," she said finally.

Her mysterious partner bowed and offered his hand.

"Come then and I will reveal myself."

"You need not. We could simply part ways here and then—" she trailed off unable to articulate her feelings.

"And then what?" the dancer said. "You would never know who danced with you this night."

"I think I prefer that," she whispered.

"Come, Luthiel, where is your courage? The courage that brought you to the Vale of Mists. The courage you showed when you charged to save the Lord Tuorlin. The courage I have heard you showed against Thrar Taurmori. It does not fit the spirit of a warrior to back down so easily. And I well know you are a warrior. One of great talent, for you have surprised even me many times."

"Fair enough," she said, her voice dropping. "But I am also a lover of mysteries. So let me savor it a moment more."

"Very well. Come and walk with me for a minute."

He offered his arm which she took and they were walking away from the dance and toward the great tree.

"How do you know so much about me?" she asked finally after they'd come very close to the tree. In this place the land dropped and some of the roots were exposed creating a sort of cave of earth and wood. From beneath the tree a light shone. Only bits of the light came through. But she could tell it was a bright light like the sun. Seeing it shining from between roots like hills, her pulse quickened.

"Well there are many ways to know someone," he said. Then, noticing the look on her face, he pointed to the light. "Do you know what that is?"

Luthiel could well have guessed. But she'd never yet seen it. "Is it the fire eternal?"

"Yes. See, you surprise me again. This is the flame eternal which is cupped in the great roots of Yewstaff. It is the great light that keeps this tree alive and all the things that depend upon it. Want to have a closer look?"

Luthiel was captured by the beauty and by some compelling quality in his voice. The way he said the words made them seem more appealing.

"Yes, I'd like that," she said. "But you didn't answer my question. Funny, you reminded me of Mithorden just then. Answering around the question. But never getting to it."

"Ah, he does do that. Doesn't he? Maybe I learned it from him."

Her father? Her heart thrummed at the thought. *It couldn't be. He's been broken all these years.* Or perhaps it was Chromnos? If his very name were forbidden, certainly he would hide his face. Though the earth beneath her feet was warming with each step, the thought made her arms prickle with gooseflesh.

They walked beneath the great roots of Yewstaff. The land continued to drop and as they walked the light grew brighter. It shone up through the roots in the same way sunlight might shine down through branches. After about five hundred feet, the bottom dropped out and she gazed down into a great hollow beneath Yewstaff. Above she could see the base of the massive tree, its roots fanning out around the chamber in broad crescents. The earth here was blasted by heat. So much so that it had turned to glass. Some places gleamed with yellow or orange where the heat had recently remelted it. The undersides of the roots were covered in stony green splotches that seemed to draw in the light.

At the chamber's center was a great round light. It was large—about four hundred feet across. And it looked like a sun. But this sun was no more than three hundred feet from where she stood. They'd made their way to a natural shelf of root and rock and gazed down at it. It gleamed, brighter than the day star and she couldn't look at it for long or she began to see spots. After a few moments, they had to stand back from the shelf. For the heat was unbearable.

"So this is it?" she asked. "The reason the great trees bear fruit all year 'round?"

"Yes. It is the source of their power. The reason they endure for all time."

Luthiel found she was sweating. The temperature was searing where she stood and a great column of heat rose up from the fire beneath her making little sparks as something ignited. She could see distortions in the air before her and she wondered what would happen if she held her hand out over the ledge and above the fire.

"Now, in answer to your question," the mysterious man continued. "There are many ways to know someone. To be a friend is a good way. To love. That does well too. But the best way to learn about a person is to fight against them. And that, Luthiel, is the reason why I know so much about you."

With a single, fluid, motion he lifted his hand to the mask and removed it. Luthiel found she was staring into the handsome face of Zalos, Lord of Ashiroth.

A Dark Proposal

Luthiel felt her hand inching toward the hilt of *Weiryendel*. "You!" she shouted in fury.

"Wait!" he said lifting an empty hand. "Would you strike me now? As helpless as I am?"

Luthiel looked him over. Helpless? He was apparently unarmed. Yet probably still very dangerous. Remembering what Mithorden said, she hesitated. "Why did you come here!??" she shouted. "What is it you want!?"

Zalos smiled. "I've made you angry, haven't I? Good then. Anger is the other side of fear. Fear comes in the face of death. A temporary gift to help you survive. To use anger in Wyrd is to use the magic of death."

Luthiel felt a chill come over her. But her hand was wrapped around the hilt of *Weiryendel*. She could feel its angry hum through her hand. "What do you want, Zalos?" she repeated. "You're an outlaw here. This time I am Queen."

"Really? If that spectacle you put on means anything, then yes it seems you're a queen now. But for how much longer without my help?" He motioned with his hands—taking in the chamber. "Why can't we speak? You didn't seem to mind dancing. Won't you just talk to me?"

"Speak then," she growled. But she was inching away from him as a person might move away from a dangerous viper. At his words about her rule, the heat seemed to press in on her and she blinked against the sweat. Had something happened?

It couldn't. Rictinno. His rats would have alerted me. But a worry and a doubt had come over her. *What if they missed something? Zalos and Elag know Yewstaff far better than I. And Zalos' knowledge spans centuries.* In that moment, Luthiel felt very unsure. For nothing other than comfort, she gripped more tightly the hilt of *Weiryendel*.

He turned to her and looked directly at her with those dangerous eyes. "I have come to make you an offer."

"What would you offer? To kidnap my mother again? Betray my father again? Order my death again?" Her voice was hollow. Full of fear and wariness.

Zalos gave an easy laugh. "If necessary." It was confident. Unsettling. "But before any of that, I wanted to try offering myself."

"What do you mean?!"

"Marriage, Luthiel. After war, the oldest way of gaining power."

Luthiel stood stunned. "Why would I ever marry *you?*"

"To save lives. To prevent rebellion. To make the Faelands whole again. You see, in the face of catastrophe—a catastrophe you're causing, I might add—you have also managed to divide the Faelands. I am only trying to save them, Luthiel. And I'm giving you a chance to amend your misdeeds against them."

Luthiel felt as if a strangling hand had clamped down on her throat. The audacity of Zalos' proposal, lies and accusations was almost too much to grasp, let alone respond to. What angered her more than anything was the tone of clarity that rang through his words. "My *misdeeds?!* You serve Death! And you would blame *me* for the catastrophe Gorthar Lord of Death made as a weapon against all!"

"Death is author as well as ender. With each death new life springs up," he said with a tone of benevolence. "Ages must end, Luthiel. But you know this, being the harbinger of *this* age's ending. The very lord you mock already uses you for a scapegoat. In my generosity, I am giving you this last choice. Marry me and I will make you a goddess! Fail to make this choice and you will become a martyr."

"A goddess of death!? Some dark and terrible queen? I have seen what you did to Wyrd Stones, Zalos. I will not let you do that to me. And what of my mother? Didn't you desire her? Didn't you want her for your wife?"

Zalos looked down at his hand which he was clenching and unclenching. She didn't like it. Looked like some kind of threat. "I have many wives Luthiel.

Your mother is but one. If she'd only recognize me I would make her first among them and give her all of my greatest affection. Unfortunately, she does not share my sentiments."

"I shouldn't think so. *Many wives?* What reason have you given her or me to ever love you! Leave now—before I set the wrath of the Faelands on you!"

"Is the Faelands' wrath even yours to set?" Zalos snapped. "And what is love?" he spat the word as if he didn't like how it tasted. "A heart's delusion? I never said anything about love, Luthiel. I'm offering you power and a chance to survive. Think what good you could do with that power. Think of how many you could save as this age came to its end."

"Don't you realize, Zalos, it's the magic of love that brought me here? Ruined all of your carefully laid plans? But for love I never would have left the Faelands. And you would have probably murdered the Vyrl by now. Finishing what your master started."

"Master? I am my own. As for Gorthar we all end up serving him—whether we want to or not."

"No. To willingly serve and to fight—even without hope—are two different things. If you wish to surrender, then by all means do so. But I will take no condition. Least of all, marriage." She was so angry she felt as if her body had caught fire.

"Of course, you must realize, I expected this answer. This is the last chance. Have me for your husband or—"

"What?"

"Or become an example." He said the words softly, slowly, drawing them out. They hung in the hot air.

There was a ringing sound as Luthiel drew *Weiryendel.* "You would murder me then? The lady you just proposed to?" She pointed the sword at his heart.

"Execution is entirely lawful. Even you must realize—sometimes, killing is necessary. If you love life, accept my offer. If not, by all means—die."

Luthiel paused for a moment and looked at his dangerous eyes. Then her body grew still and she felt calm flow over her. Lowering her sword, she took a step forward.

"So it comes down to another death threat, Zalos? That's the worst thing for you, isn't it? I think I understand. You love life more than anything else. And so to live as an evil thing is better than to die a hero."

For the first time, Zalos turned his eyes and looked away.

"Weren't you friends with my father once? And my mother too? Didn't you fight together to overthrow the Vyrl? Yet now you would put yourself and the Dark God in their place. What happened? Why did you change?"

Zalos' eyes slowly came back. "You're just barely a woman, Luthiel. How could you begin to understand my mind?"

"Understand? That's too much. But I could guess. Something made you jealous or afraid a long time ago. Enough to break something in you. Now you seek power out of fear. Power to cover up for something you could never have. But I guess it was never really love that drove you to my mother but want of possession. You lacked the depth to feel love so you sought power instead."

"There is nothing, Luthiel. Nothing but power. Elves did not spring up from the earth. Death shaped us out of lesser creatures. We were strong and survived. Love and other such nonsense is sentiment of the weak."

"Elves are immortal. The oldest race." Even as Luthiel said it she thought of Othalas. "And love is, among other things, the sharing of power. If we care for one another we can help each other. Can you tell me a deeper and more subtle power?"

"Elves are not immortal. Elves just don't die of disease or old age. What do they live? Five hundred? A thousand? Three thousand years? But eventually by accident, catastrophe, or foolish sacrifice even elves die. The world is full of massive things in motion. Little creatures get hurt. As for love—It is little more than a morality for slaves."

"It is the morality of wholeness."

"A delusion of comfort."

"You have lost your heart, Zalos. A hollow man. Dead on the inside. And yet you ask me to marry you? But not out of sentiment. Not out of any sense of mystery or value of something in me. Other than what power you could gain through me. And I, I am supposed to be tempted by blackmail. To have my life spared. To become powerful. And to save other's lives by subjecting myself to you.

"But listening to what you say, I don't see where anything would be saved. You would make as many become like you as you could and then prey on the rest."

"So your answer is no?" Zalos said quietly. He seemed to tense. His body lowered into a slight crouch.

"As life sprang up in defiance of death eons ago. No! As worlds call for peace and love of the life they bear. No! And as a woman given a false proposal to marry from a hollow heart. No! A thousand times no!"

"*Wellenwythe*," Zalos hissed.

A thin stream of shimmering air formed the shape of a sword in his right hand. Through the air, a coil of fire burned, sending off a wisp of smoke. "I didn't expect you to say yes. I always knew you for one who lacked sense," he snapped. "I Zalos, lord of Ashiroth and heir to the Faelands place you under arrest for High Treason! Lay down your sword! Submit to judgment! Confess your wrongs and you will be spared!"

Luthiel held *Weiryendel* before her in defense. Over the past weeks she'd learned much in her sparring with Vanye. Yet she was certain it could never be a match to the mastery of Lord Zalos. She knew it was hopeless to fight him. But as the blood pounded in her ears and the rage rose within her, she knew she must.

"Never Zalos. Not till my body is dead and broken. Not till I have breathed my last."

"Yield Luthiel. You don't want me to take you by force."

"Come and try it. I'll give you the justice you earned."

His first strike came on vicious and direct. She lifted *Weiryendel* to block and on contact Zalos' Wyrd-formed blade exploded into a burst of hot air. It hit her like a hammer and sent her flying back. She rolled and when she stood little bits of her clothing smoldered. She felt dizzy. But the moment passed and she steadied herself. In the brief moment she had away from him, she cut her lower dress away. Legs freed, it was easier to crouch, move, jump.

Zalos clenched his fist and the blade of air and fire reformed. "Something I made with you in mind," Zalos said with a vicious smile. Hopping on the balls of his feet, he shook the Wyrd-formed blade at her. Then, he lifted his left hand.

"*Cauth!*" he said. A ball of black and orange fire formed. The firelight flick-ered in his face a moment giving his handsome features a demonic cast. Then he tossed it at her. Luthiel leapt up and back and then landed on a root some fifteen feet away. The fire struck where she stood only a moment before and exploded. The blast cast flame beneath her feet.

"First you demand to marry me? Now you want to burn me?"

"There are two ways to tame a witch. One is by marriage. The other is by burning." With the last words, he threw another ball of fire.

"*Eshald!*" she sang out. A white glow appeared in front of her and the fire exploded around it, leaving her untouched.

Zalos smiled. "Mithorden's teaching you then?"

"Yes," she growled.

"Good. Did he show you this —"

He lifted his hand and made a snapping gesture.

"Narbarak!" he cried.

Her light shield filled with black cracks and shattered. One of the pieces cut her as it shot by leaving a little streak of blood on her temple.

In that instant she was jumping up and over Zalos flipping in the air then coming down behind him. The sweep of her sword aimed directly at his head. He was there one instant and not the next. With a casual sidestep, he avoided her blow and then struck at her with his Wyrd-sword. She saw the flame blade slicing toward her and dropped beneath it, cutting at Zalos' legs. Now Zalos sprang away and her blade met only air. But as he did he dropped another black and orange ball of flame. She saw it fall and sprang up an instant before it hit ground.

The fire licked at her legs—blistering them or leaving them covered in little red burns. Worse, the black stuff gummed her shoes and when she landed she found herself stuck.

"*Ethelos!*" she sang and then with two swift cuts of *Weiryendel* ran free. She drew her *Cauthrim* knife and, barefoot, charged Zalos. So great was Luthiel's talent for hiding that even Zalos was fooled. His face became a mask of doubt as he strained to see her.

"Betrayer! Betrayer!" she shouted as she leapt at him. Yet Ethelos even masked her cry so that to Zalos it seemed an eerie whisper.

There was fury in her such as she'd never imagined. Tears fell from her eyes. She knew this was it. The only chance she'd ever have against this dread lord who'd done so much hurt to her family. Not since coming to the Vale of Mists had she felt so wild. So full of rage and fear. *Weiryendel* made a ringing cry and seemed to leap out toward him. Despite her yelling, a quietness seemed to come over her as instant followed instant.

She struck low.

Though Zalos still couldn't see her, somehow he sensed the attack. He dropped his Wyrd blade to block even as she circled, spinning away. She caught his sword on her *Cauthrim* knife then she struck high with *Weiryendel*.

"For Father!" she cried.

In an instant she would cut through his neck and all would be finished.

But Zalos' mind and senses were far beyond the ken of even Fae. For he'd mastered black arts taught by Gorthar himself. His magic touched even the strange dreams of time and chance. So Zalos moved at the last moment and *Weiryendel* only cut him on the jaw. Yet it shaved deep. Blood flowed, spilling on the ground.

The blow was enough to make him stagger away. The Wyrd sword dispersed and he swiftly drew a Narmiel sword. It was purer than even Vyrl's blades. Its black and blood red steel seemed to drink up the light and a rime of ice glittered over its jagged length. A chill mist fell from it, spilling onto the ground.

He seemed to slump with weariness and she made for him. She struck out. The cold blade snaked through the air, slapping *Weiryendel* on its flat. At contact, *Weiryendel* gave off a sound like a bell's toll and her hand become numb with cold.

Zalos' eyes focused and fell upon her. "I see you!" he growled and then swung at her viciously. Now she was forced to spring away. She tried to cut the sword, but he was too swift and each ringing contact stung her hand with both its force and its cold. There was an opening and Zalos punched her on the chest.

The air was crushed from her and she rolled to the ground, spinning away, barely keeping hold of *Weiryendel*. He walked toward her. His steps were lazy now. When she stood, she found herself perilously close to the great tree's fire.

"You fought well. But it's over."

He lifted his left hand and at the entrance she saw five figures approaching her.

"Mingolë," she whispered, and she could see their maskless faces. She gasped—any sign of their humanity was gone beyond recall. Where eyes once were, only sunken pits remained. Their noses seemed to have blended into their faces and their mouths were sewn shut. Around each neck was a black and blood-red box. Their movements were impossibly smooth as though some will beyond fae imposed utter and perfect control over their bodies.

Behind them came six massive creatures. Their heads and wings black like those of great ravens. But their bodies were in the shape of a massive black cat. They were large—larger than Urkharim—and she could hear their claws clicking along the pebbled floor as they approached her.

"What did you call them?" Zalos asked as he walked toward her.

"Mingolë!" she growled.

"Servants of nightmare?" he said the words as if he savored them. "A fine name! And what better captains to have in battle? What better to serve you in time of war than a horror?"

He looked at her and there was naked admiration in his eyes and sadness too. Luthiel felt her breath catch in her throat. *How could he possibly pity me?*

"You're naive, Luthiel. But there is more than a touch of your father in you. You have his flair for naming things. I think I'll keep Mingolë, if you don't mind?" He gave a slight nod of his head in acknowledgement to her then waved a hand at the great raven-panther creatures. "And these already have a name. They are graven. Some of the most vicious beasts in all the Faelands. These ones came from Arganoth and are, of course, quite tame."

Now Luthiel hovered on the edge of a second rage as Zalos gloated over her. But she knew he'd bested her. In a moment she might have won. But that moment had passed. She couldn't beat him alone now, much less with five of his Mingolë and six graven. So she moved away slowly.

Think! she chided herself, eyes looking around, rapidly taking in the chamber. She circled away from the fire blazing beneath her and Zalos gave a nod, eyes glittering. *I need to know what's really going on!*

"So you'll burn me then? Cast me into the fires now and have an end of me?"

"Not now. No. There must be a trial first. Without law there would be chaos. Even I cannot act without its precedent." He touched at the blood on his face. His fingers came away wet with it.

"A trial? How would you try me when I am queen?"

At this question, Zalos grinned broadly. "Oh things have changed quite a bit in the few minutes since we entered this chamber. I trust the Fae Council will be reassembled now with all its proper members. The rest, well, the force I brought was overwhelming and few of yours were ready to fight. Some even helped me. But less than I expected." He said the last with a nod to her. "You are a worthy foe, Luthiel. Only hopelessly outmatched. Even Merrin unwittingly worked against you. Her party was the perfect diversion. I would have never been able to plan this otherwise."

Luthiel fell to her knees.

Zalos' smile broadened.

"I had help. Armies. Mithorden. Secret Finders."

"You mean the rats? Well, unfortunate for you, I already knew about them. And once you know the presence of spies, it's easy enough to feed them false information."

He took another step forward and he was nearly within reach of her. He lifted his empty hand showing her his blood. "You're a better fighter than I thought. Both on the battlefield and off. More people believed you than I considered possible. And news of you spread far. I'm afraid there will be rebellion if I execute you. But the only way for you to live is by marriage and submission. You see that now, don't you?"

Tears streamed freely down her cheeks. She felt as if a part of her had been hollowed out. With a shudder, she looked at the Mingolë.

Marry?

Now she had her information. It was not what she wanted to hear. But it was enough. Luthiel didn't know how much was truth and how much was a lie. What she did know was she had to escape. To get as far away from Zalos and his servants as possible. First that meant getting out from beneath Yewstaff. And, if necessary, away from Yewstaff itself.

She looked around at the roots poking out into the chamber. They re-minded her of branches. The branches she and Leowin had hopped to and from a thousand times in their tap and turn games.

Zalos took another step forward and she sprang up and back, tearing the Wyrd Stone from where it hung around her neck. She landed on the first branch and Zalos eyed her curiously.

"Luthiel!" she sang and the World of Dreams swirled around her. No soon-er did that wavering light pass over the chamber than she was launching into another song. A spell of Wyrd. One she hoped would help her escape.

Lunen Estel Celesti!
Lunen Solari Elenti!
Nani a mi Lunen!
Lunen Eni Methar Anduel!
Lunen Eni Luthiel!

Which means—Light of stars in heaven! Light of suns eternal! Here be my light! The light of *Methar Anduel!* The light of Luthiel!

And with those words a light so brilliant it blinded all those around her erupted from the Stone. Never had she seen such a light. Not even at the Stone's first awakening. Nor when *Weiryendel* reformed. And not when Tuorlin cast his spell to stop the elves. Yet somehow she was able to keep her eyes open and to see about her. As even Zalos held his hand up against the light and the Mingolë used their cloaks to blot it out, she sprang from root to root. A graven snapped blindly as she passed. Its beak caught in the roots and then she was away beyond it. Her only loss was a bit of sleeve which the graven had snipped off. Then she was out from beneath the tree, racing for the open hillside. What she saw made her heart quail. All around, the hilltops burned. In the sky, she saw a fire like a bloody comet and knew in a moment it was Narhoth.

Before her were the guests—sitting under the guard of Gruagach, troll, and goblin. A quick glance was all she managed. She could not see her mother, sister, or any of her friends. *Oh please let them have escaped!*

Those seated below saw her light and many had to turn from it. Others sang out with joy for the sight of her gave them hope. But their cries turned to anguish as behind her rose up a great shadow. She glimpsed it out of the corner of her eye and sprang away.

There was a shout among a group of nearby Gruagach. They pointed, holding hands up to block the light. Their captains barked orders, and a score of soldiers charged her. Blade Dancers and Cat-o-Fae rushed toward her from the opposite side. She lifted *Weiryendel* high in challenge even as she sprinted for freedom. Yet the darkness grew large behind her and, with a roaring battle cry, a group of trolls pounded over the rise before her. She turned left, running for a small cut in the land that led out to open woods. Darkness pushed in from every corner, blocking out her vision, until all she could see were the ten feet around her. She rushed on blindly—making for what she guessed was woodline.

Then trolls surrounded her. With a cry of "Merrin!" She struck out with *Weiryendel*. One, then another of the great giants fell. But there were too many. She was lifted roughly. Her sword was knocked out of her hand. A foul cloth was stuffed into her mouth. Before it gagged her she managed to shout—"Nin Alhandra!"

The Stone closed and its light winked out. She choked around the cloth as she was held down and bound hand and foot. Tears streamed from her eyes. How could this have happened!?

She could see fine boots walking toward her. Zalos stooped and, with a gloved hand, picked up *Weiryendel*. There was a flash of light and a smell like burning. The sword fell point down, its blade sinking into the ground. Zalos knelt beside it holding his hand. He ripped the glove off. His hand was covered in red burns with gray splotches of charred flesh. The glove smoldered then ignited into flame.

Luthiel felt the ground tremble beneath her. From the earth, tiny Yewstaff roots sprang up, wrapping around the sword until only the hilt was visible. A healer approached Zalos to tend his hand.

"It is of little consequence," he said to Luthiel. "Valkire's sword will never trouble me again."

She was heaved roughly to her feet—forced to walk back toward the great tree and in front of those gathered beneath it. There she saw Elag gloating down at her. To her horror, she was forced to walk up to the long-faced elf.

"Luthiel Valshae," the Wisdom said slowly and with relish. "You are hereby arrested on grounds of high treason. Your charges—conspiring to assassinate High Lord Tuorlin, conspiring to replace him as ruler, impersonating the daughter of Vlad Valkire, and practicing unholy Witchcraft causing this current darkness. How do you plead?"

Rough hands removed the gag from her mouth and she coughed. For a moment, she could not speak. In one deep breath, she gathered her voice with all the strength she could muster.

"I am innocent!" she shouted. "Your charges are as false as your court! Thief and liar to call himself Wisdom!"

The hands pushed her to the ground and Elag looked her over with a menacing eye.

"You are hereby held awaiting judgment. Your trial is set for Cauthsday one month hence. Until that time you will be prisoner of the Faelands."

As Elag spoke, Luthiel had a chance to get a better look around her. It appeared a good number had escaped—including the Faelords and many Blade Dancers she knew were loyal to her. She felt her stomach drop when she noticed dead bodies being piled up by a small band of goblins. She wondered how many were hers. Yet the bodies could not account for all those missing.

Count your gifts, Luthiel, what few you still have.

Her heart sang to think that many may have slipped away. Maybe there was still some reason to hope? Glancing up at the long face of Elag, she dreaded to think what would happen after Cauthsday a month from now. She was made to stand and then marched off toward Yewstaff. There was still some noise coming from high places in the tree. She could hear battle cries along with calls of "surrender and you will be spared!" Then she heard a cry of "For Luthiel! For the queen!"

So there's still some hold-outs fighting for me. She felt new tears glistening in her eyes at the thought of more death on her behalf. *I have failed! Oh, how I have failed! Even mother may have died for me. They all might have died for me!*

As they dragged her away, she saw far off, beneath the dragon's firelight, a lone figure on the back of a unicorn. It may have been some trick of the light or phantom of the mind, but she thought it was Leowin, holding up her bow to the sky. She turned, seemed to see Luthiel, then fled to the forest. It gave her faint hope as they dragged her up and into the great tree.

APPENDICES

APPENDIX I:
THE ELFIN RUNES

The elfin runes were characters drawn to represent shapes in nature—the curl of a wave, the silhouette of a fish in deep water, the body of a serpent threading between two stones. To the elves these characters have special significance, for they understand them—their shapes and sounds—to be the very language of creation. In them, there is the most basic magic of forms and definitions. But also in them is the deeper understanding of spirit. For while the runes describe shapes and sounds, they also hold deeper meaning and are the key to understanding both the mysteries of the self and of the boundless universe. So here, in these motes and marks, in these slashes on the page, in rock, or earth, is the language of stars and moons, of wind and water, of wyrd and dreams.

	ELFIN	ENGLISH
LEOWE		A
RAE		B
BELIR		C
VALA		D
NIN		E
FEHRIS		F
WINAE		G
SHAELYN		H
MELLWYTHE		I

	ELFIN	ENGLISH
LILANI		J
NOS		K
LIEL		L
TIRNA		M
FAE		N
OMAH		O
TOSH		P
ZAE		Q
RILNO		R
AELAS		S
ELOH		T
ENRIS		U
VALKIRE		V
WELOWEE		W
DIRNA		X
ERNON		Y
KIRNA		Z

APPENDIX II:
THE SUNS AND MOONS
OF OESHA

Soelee: First sun of Oesha. Soelee is slightly smaller and dimmer than the day-star of Earth but is by far the brightest object in the skies of Oesha. A white-yellow star, Soelee rules the skies of day.

Oerin's Eye: Second sun of Oesha. Bright enough to dim most stars, Oerin's eye rises first and sets last extending the time of gloaming both morning and evening. Oerin's eye is an almond shaped white-blue star.

Lunen: The first moon of Oesha is the color of pearl. Associated with peace and wisdom, Lumen's glow softens the skies of Oesha at night and in the hours of gloaming.

Merrin: The second moon of Oesha is the color of ocean waves. A wild and mysterious moon, Merrin is the patron moon of sailors and of storms.

Silva: This moon shines like a bright silver penny in the sky. The third moon of Oesha is associated with grace and goodness.

Sothos: Somber grey, Sothos is associated with dreams and sleep. The fourth moon of Oesha is sometimes difficult to find in the sky as its dim disk often blends well with the background. Also called the sleepy eye, Sothos is sometimes associated with the magic and mystery of dreams.

Tiolas: The fifth moon of Oesha is banded yellow and green. A wild place, Tiolas is associated with the primal spirit of nature. The Tyndomiel claim Tiolas as their patron moon.

Veolin: Wrapped in rainbow hues, Oesha's sixth moon is the one most often associated with the mysteries of wyrd and magic.

Cauthraus: The color of blood, Oesha' seventh moon is considered the patron of warfare and bloody conflict. The harsh moon seems to burn with deep red fire as it shines down upon Oesha. It is the brightest of the eight moons and is easy to see during daytime.

Gorothoth: The eighth moon of Oesha lurks like a shadow in the sky. Veins the color of old blood cross its face and cold seems to radiate down from it. Gorothoth is visible in the sky only for half of the year—from late fall until First Summer's Eve. The black moon is associated with all things ill upon the world of Oesha.

GLOSSARY

Aelin—(the elves) Aelin represent the first born of the thinking races and make up all the elves that dwell upon Oesha or elsewhere. They include Ithildar, Sith, Valemar, Tyndomiel, and Gruagach.

Aëdar—also called angels, the Aëdar were among those spirits to aid the Elohwë in the great works that shaped the world. Of the Aëdar there were the Ahrda—the spirits of the elements that make up the worlds which are earth, air, water, fire and spirit; the Melear—the spirits of life; the Maehros—spirits of the void; and the Minowe—spirits of light and music. Dragons were among the Ahrda and Narcor (Malcor when corrupted) who are spirits of fire and Keirin who are spirits of storm and many more who are not named here. Vyrl, who were the masters of life and blood and of the dreams of living things, were among the Melear as were the Elvanna who were the spirits of all things good and growing, as were the Mordrim who were the spirits of new life and of changes in form and function. Of the Maehros little is known except that they were dark and strange and that they hungered to devour all things and ever they held the expansion of the world in check for their gluttony was boundless. Keirin were also counted among the Minowe for though they were spirits of air and storm granted to them too were the lights of rainbows and of stars. The Elkala were also among the Minowe and these were spirits of song and of inspiration and of good dreams—both waking and sleeping. So too were the Anari who were the great spirits of stars and the Elune who were spirits of moonlight, gossamer, and sleep.

Aeowinar—also called Cutter's Shear, this mighty blade was the masterwork of Vlad Valkire. It was said that *Aeowinar's* sharpness was unmatched and that there was not a thing which it could not cut.

Ahmberen—one of the three Vyrl in the Vale of Mists. The name Ahmberen means memory in the elder tongue.

Almorah—cakes of dense bread filled with oats and honey. Almorah are often used as a staple by Valemar, Ithildar, and Gruagach.

Arganoth—the fortress of Zalos that lies at the head of the falls that form the river Gwithemlo.

Ashiroth—the Land of the Gruagach that lies to the north of Minonowe.

Black (references to and meaning of)—the evil associated with shadow. For example: the black moon Gorothoth.

Blixx—a race of goblins and the cousins of the Red Caps. Blixx hold a hatred and resentment for all things elfin. They have a long-standing alliance with the Trolls and often fall under the Dominion of Thrar Taurmori. But their chief lord is Korde Morgurlag. Blixx live in tribes in the badlands of the Rimwold.

Bwandirin—the giants. These include the tree folk and the blue giants of Maltarmireth who were servants to the Vyrl.

Chosen—children sent to feed the Vyrl in the Vale of Mists.

Dark (ith. Neth) (references to and meaning of)—"dark" in elfin has a dual meaning. In its first reference, it can be associated with blackness or evil. But in its second it is associated with those things hidden or concealed. Dark, this sense, is the beauty of mystery and of all things wild or unknown. It is the dark of twilight which is filled with stars. Ironically, the dark is full of lights yet to be revealed.

Dark Lady—*see* Elwin.

Detheldris—the Paths of Terror. A region of the Drakken Spur Mountains that are now inhabited by Widdershae.

Dimlock—during the Age of Dreams, Vyrl ruled over all of Oesha feeding on the dreams of men and elves. The dreams were drawn through their eyes which fell away like brittle ash. Those devoured in this way became wights, serving only the will of the Vyrl, lusting after eyes which were their only food. Deprived of this food, the wights would become shrunken and twisted, eventually fading into shadow until they were never seen again. It was not known what became of these creatures until the dark moon rose and beneath its orb black goblins slinked from the shadows. These are the Dimlock, natives of the moon Gorothoth and who have life only beneath its darkness, upon its face, or with the other nightmares in the world of dreams. For in the sunlight they are only shadows but in the darkness of deep winter they appear, ambushing the unwary, carrying them off to the black moon where their flesh is subjected to unspeakable tortures or they are tossed into the great fires.

Drakken Spur Mountains—the mountains beyond the Gates of the East. Long ago, elves would travel through the Drakken Spur and into the lands of Sith and Humans beyond. Now the Mountains are inhabited by Widdershae and passage to the lands beyond is only possible by sea or through the scorched lands to the south of Felduwaith. Few other than Sith and sailors have made this journey.

Ecthellien—one of the three Vyrl in the Vale of Mists. The name—Ecthellien—means chance in the elder tongue.

Elohwë—mighty beings who were the first offspring of the creators Ëavanya and Ëavanar. Each represented a spirit essential to the forming of the world. Aehmiel Eversong, Lumen of Light, Gorthar of Death, Chromnos of Will, and Eldacar of Sight are but a few Elohwë. Also called archangels, the Elohwë have ever had a hand in the shaping of the world and in the commitment of great deeds within it. Both the Aëdar and Elohwë live with one foot in the waking world and the other in the world of dreams.

Elshael—one of the three Vyrl in the Vale of Mists. The name, Elshael, means "sorrow" in the elder tongue.

Elwin—also called the Dark Lady, she is the spirit of Oesha given flesh and form. Perhaps the greatest of the Ahrda, she is also the wife of the Lord of the Dark Forest. For thousands of years now, she has slept—much to the grief of her lord.

Fae— (also known as Elder, and Valas) A family of magical creatures including, elves, trolls, goblins and faeries.

First Summer's Eve—the first day that Gorothoth is not present in the sky. It also represents the beginning of summer. Among the elves, First Summer's Eve is the most holy day of the year.

Glendoras—Luthiel's foster father.

Gorothoth—the terrible moon that rides in the skies of Oesha from late Fall to early Summer. Gorothoth is the source of terrors that walk the face of Oesha including the Widdershae, Dimlock and many more. Also called Lunmir or Shadowmoon.

Grendilo—strange one-armed, one-legged creatures who possess a grace and agility greater than any creature that walked on two legs. Natives to the Vale of Mists, the Grendilo serve the Vyrl who live there.

Gruagach—the physically powerful and wilder cousins of the Ithildar. They were the third-born of the Aelin. Blood of sap, flesh of wood, the Gruagach are a hardy breed who have formed a pact with a tribe of dire wolves, the Urkharim, who live among them as equals.

Himlolth—the land of the Tyndomiel that lies to the north and west of Minonowe.

Ithildar—first born of the Aelin—High Elves. Fair of face and form the Ithildar are the most beautiful and magnetic of the Fae. The glory of their presence is such that men and goblins have worshipped them as lesser gods and of all the elves they are the most advanced in art and knowledge. Ithildar learned the elder language from Aëdar—dragons and spirits of light and song—they have since been its keepers among the elves, teaching it to their kin and children alike. For that reason, the elder speech bears their name—Ithildar (ith). Ithildar is also the name of the great tree of life at Ithilden's heart. The tree is often referred to as Great Ithildar in speech.

Ithilden—the land of the Ithildar that lies to the west of Minonowe.

Leowin—Luthiel's foster sister. Daughter of Glendoras and Winowe.

Lilani—magical gateways that allow passage between Oesha and its moons. Lilani form where wyrd, the magic of dreams, concentrates into vast streams flowing over far greater distances than any of the rivers on Oesha.

Lorethain—Luthiel's foster brother. Firstborn of Glendoras and Winowe.

Melkion—the Vyrl's dragon messenger.

Merrin—queen and spirit of the ocean moon that bears her name. Merrin was also one of the companions of Vlad Valkire and, later, his wife.

Mithorden—(Spiritwatcher) he was summoned by Elroth long ago on an errand of which he will not speak. He is a mysterious sorcerer wandering the lands, consorting with both the strange and powerful. He has been known to appear during the direst of times and some have said that his appearance is a sign of ill things to come.

Moons of Oesha—silver Silva, pearl Lunen, blue Merrin, green and gold Tiolas, smokey Sothos, rainbow Veolin, red Cauthraus, and black Gorothoth.

Moonsteel—metals from moons of Oesha, often thought to have magical properties. Silva—*Silen*, Lunen—*Lumiel*, Merrin—*Marim*, Tiolas—*Tiloril*, Sothos—*Sorim*, Veolin—*Viel*, Cauthraus—*Cauthrim*, and Gorothoth—*Narmiel*.

Neltherduel—the crowns of light. Shaped by Aëdar, these crowns were light as gossamer upon the brows that bore them and woven into their silvery metal were lights like stars.

Netharduin—the four crowns of shadow. Forged of old by Gorthar from *Narmiel* (shadow-steel), these fell crowns are invisible except when touched by the shadow of Gorothoth or of the void itself. Then, it is visible as a dark metal of shifting hues like smoke cast off by a smoldering fire. Each crown houses a spirit of want, rage and bitterness bent to the will of Gorthar, which soon corrupts any who wear it, twisting their lives until all their works result in death and ruin. The ruling *Netharduin* was worn, for a time, by Chromnos until he broke it. The shards of this crown were later reforged by Zalos who used it to corrupt the Wyrd Stones which were, in turn, used to ensnare the Mirghast.

Nethril—the blood silver of the dark forest. This metal grows out in spiral veins from beneath the great tree of life Anaturnar. Sometimes the Dark Fae forge Nethril into terrible weapons. But the metal is difficult to work.

Oesha—the world. According to ancient myth, Oesha was the first living world conceived among the stars. The same myth states that Oesha was the proto world after which all other living worlds were crafted. But only on Oesha, it is said, can dreams be brought to life through the magic of wyrd.

Othalas—eldest of werewolves, Othalas serves the Vyrl in the Vale of Mists.

Ottomnos—the Vyrl's Castle in the Vale of Mists. First ruled by Vyrl and later by Vlad Valkire, Ottomnos was returned to the Vyrl three thousand years ago. There they reign over that misty land and all creatures that dwell within it.

Red-Caps—a kind of goblin friendly to the elves and living among them. Red-Caps are known for their fiery red hair, strong jaws and pointed teeth. Though friendly to elves in general, they harbor a great hatred for humankind and have been known to attack them whenever they perceive advantage.

Rendillo—a grendilo who serves the Vyrl in the Vale of Mists.

Rimwold—a land of elves and goblins to the south of the Minonowe.

Shadow (ith. Nar) (references to and meaning of)—an aspect of evil. Shadow is associated with the drawing of precious warmth away from life. It is the cold of death and of unnatural life beyond death. It is also associated with lies, deceit and treachery. Shadow is the black of evil.

Shadow Webs—these are the dreaded webs of the Widdershae. They are spun of the black that lies in the wells of night. An ancient darkness that, but for these webs, is known only in what can be seen between the stars after both suns fall.

Sith—second born of the Aelin. Elves of the Dark Forest who serve the lord there whose name must not be spoken and who also serve the Dark Lady who sleeps there.

Teluri—small Lilani that were fashioned into mirrors. It is said that a great sorcerer could use them to watch things from afar or to transport themselves to any active Lilani. It is said that those possessing the Teluri may use it to communicate with one another over great distances. The lords of the elves are in possession of four of the original seven Teluri; the other three were lost.

Tuorlin—Lord of Ithilden and High Lord of all the Elflands. Tuorlin is one of the few surviving Chosen who went to the Vale of Mists.

Tyndomiel—of all the elves, Tyndomiel are the strangest as they each possess the ability to shape-change. Tyndomiel group themselves into clans of like kind. All varieties may be found—bears, wolves, dogs, cats, lions, birds, dolphins, sharks, and many others—throughout the lands of Himlolth and the water surrounding it.

Trees of Life—great and ancient trees that have been growing on the face of Oesha since her birth. Many of these trees have died off or been killed over time. But three are still known to remain—Anaturnar in the Dark Forest, Ithildar in Ithilden, and Yewstaff in the Minonowe. Others may grow in hidden places, for some were uprooted by the dragon Faehorne during the strife of the treekillers.

Valemar—an offshoot of the Ithildar, the Valemar are the youngest of the elves. Feet as nimble as the breezes, forms as flowing as water, the Valemar are the most graceful of the Aelin. The Valemar have taken Minonowe for their home.

Vanye—A Blade Dancer of Ithilden, Vanye has been sent on an unhappy mission to name a Chosen. Renown among the Blade Dancers for defeating the leaders of Nine Trolls Army, and the grandson of High Lord Tuorlin, Vanye would rank higher among the Blade Dancers were it not for his sometimes failing to follow the rules.

Veil—the border that separates the world of dreams from the physical world.

Vlad Valkire—the great lord who broke the Vyrl's Tyranny over elves. The name Vlad Valkire, in the elder tongue, means "a lad Valkyrie." For he was the first male born of the Dark Lady Elwin, who was the mother to all Valkyrie. Vlad is also the son of the Lord of the Dark Forest, who killed him.

Vyrl—of old, they were Aëdar, before they were corrupted by the dark will of Gorthar. Once angels, they are now demons of hunger and malice. It is rumored that only three Vyrl remain alive on all of Oesha. Three rule in the Vale of Mists. Each year, according to an ancient promise, a child must be sent to feed the Vyrl. These Chosen seldom ever return.

Werewolves—elves who were transformed into wolves by the changing influence of the Vale of Mists. Werewolves possess incredible vitality and are nearly impossible to kill, recovering from all hurts unless their bodies are entirely destroyed.

Widdershae (Widd-ur-shee)—spider-elves. A branch of elves of the middle house called the Delvendrim (deep-elves), who were wiped out by a terrible plague that turned them all into giant spiders. The Widdershae succumbed to the poison of Saurloth, queen of the Ingolith and so they were twisted in form to resemble those spiders of the great void. The wise count them among the Ingolith. For their forms have been twisted by spirits of the void which possess them. Great magic may still drive these spirits out and restore the Delvendrim who were thus twisted. Delvendrim returning to the world in this way can recall their lives as Widdershae only through nightmares.

Winowe—Luthiel's foster mother.

World of Dreams—a place parallel to the real word and overlapping it. This place responds to all desires, fears and dreams of humankind and the greater spirits. Only sorcerers can sense the existence of the world of dreams and the only physical beings who can look into it are those who possess a Wyrd Stone. Of late, the world of dreams has become a dangerous place, populated with Dimlock and other nightmares.

Wyrd—a word that stands for both dreams and magic. It represents the deep connection between dreams and the mystical arts.

Wyrd-Stones—thirteen Stones fashioned by Vlad Valkire while under the instruction of Mithorden at Lenidras. They are crystals that have within them each a bit of the song of Aehmiel and the light of Lumen. Powerful aids to sorcerery, the Wyrd Stones transport their users into the world of dreams which is the world from which all things spiritual and magical come. Wyrd Stones wholly reveal what sorcerers must sense in order to practice their art—the raw stuff of creation—true dreams, making it readily available for use in magic. When activated, the Wyrd Stone causes its user to become ghost-like and semi-solid. Things of the physical world other than moonsteel or nethril affect them less, passing through them with only slight resistance. Great wounds become minor. Hunger, fatigue, pain, all become insubstantial while in the world of dreams. On the other hand, creatures of nightmare and dream may directly affect a sorcerer traveling through the world of dreams, making use of a Wyrd Stone very dangerous in the current day.

Zalos (or Zaelos)—The Lord of Ashiroth. Also former companion of Vlad Valkire.

ABOUT THE AUTHOR

Robert Fannéy's abiding love of fantasy began as a nine year old boy when he was first introduced, by happy chance, to *The Hobbit*. He has been hopelessly lost in the World of Dreams ever since. He began writing *Luthiel's Song* at the age of 22, while at Flagler College in St. Augustine, Florida. After numerous careers and many stolen hours on nights and weekends, the first part of the tale—*Dreams of the Ringed Vale*—published in 2005, followed by *The War of Mists* in 2009. Robert is currently working on the third book in the *Luthiel's Song* series—*The Empire of Winter*.

Robert lives in Virginia with his wife, Catherine, and three talkative cats.

You can find out more about Robert, *Luthiel's Song* and the World of Dreams at **www.luthielssong.com** and **myspace.com/luthielssong**.

CPSIA information can be obtained at www.ICGtesting.com
Printed in the USA
LVOW081905090413

328363LV00006B/755/P